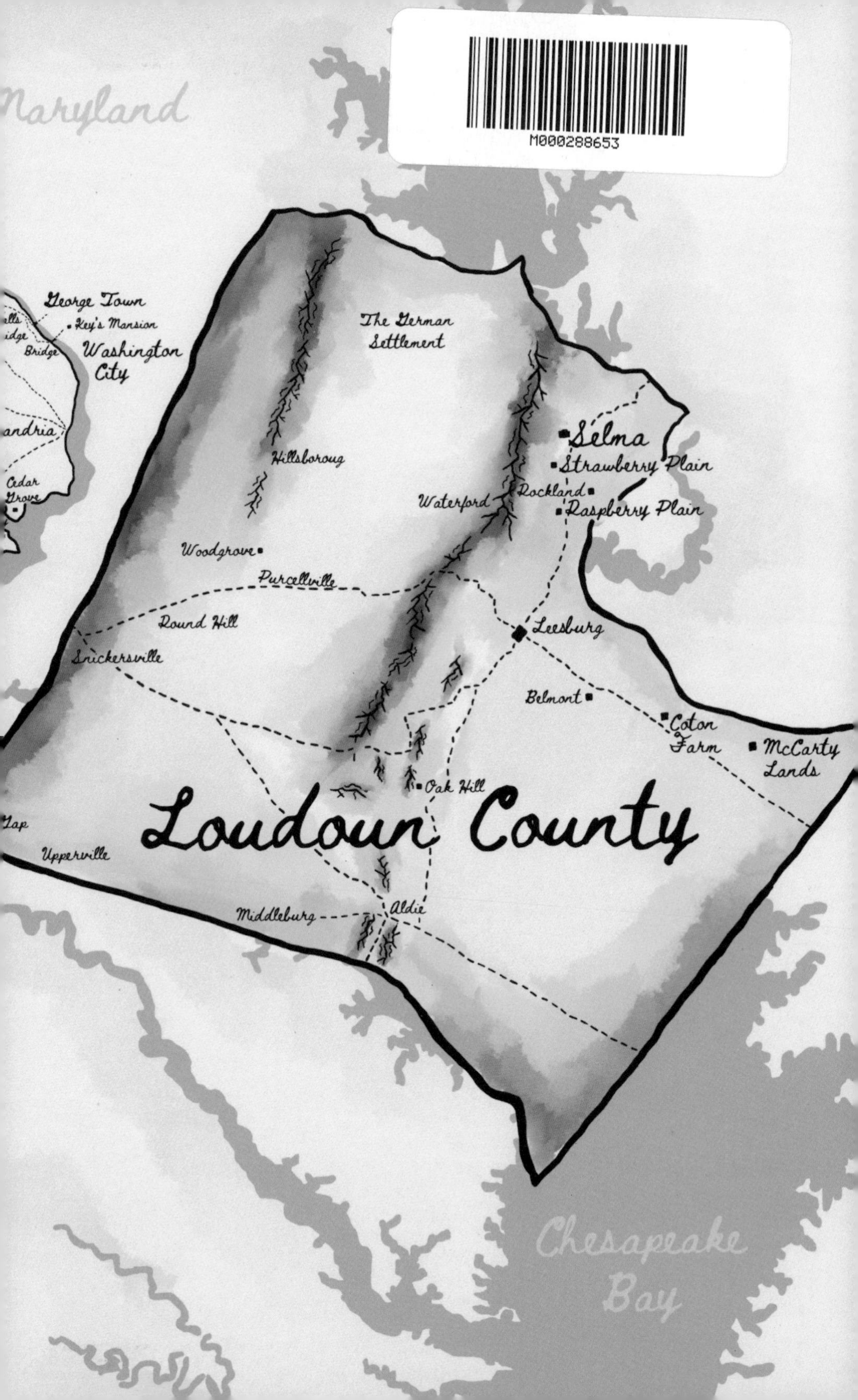

Maryland
George Town
Key's Mansion
Bridge
Washington City
andria
Cedar Grove
The German Settlement
Hillsboroug
Selma
Strawberry Plain
Rockland
Waterford
Raspberry Plain
Woodgrove
Purcellville
Round Hill
Leesburg
Snickersville
Belmont
Coton Farm
McCarty Lands
Oak Hill
Loudoun County
Gap
Upperville
Middleburg
Aldie
Chesapeake Bay

MASQUE
of HONOR

SHARON VIRTS

RosettaBooks®

NEW YORK, 2021

Masque of Honor
Copyright © 2021 by Sharon Virts

First edition published 2021 by RosettaBooks

Cover and interior design by Alexia Garaventa
Cover art by Maria Morga–@Morgastudio
Cover portrait by Ron Rundo
Interior art by Lucas Mason
Map by Hannah Blankenship

ISBN-13 (print): 978-1-9481-2270-2
ISBN-13 (ebook): 978-1-9481-2271-9

Library of Congress Cataloging-in-Publication Data:

Names: Virts, Sharon, author.

Title: Masque of honor : a historical novel of the American South / Sharon Virts. New York : RosettaBooks, 2021.

Identifiers: LCCN 2020044998 (print) | LCCN 2020044999 (ebook) ISBN 9781948122702 (hardcover) | ISBN 9781948122719 (ebook)

Subjects: LCSH: Mason, Armistead Thomson, 1787-1819—Fiction. M'Carty, John M. (John Mason), 1795-1852—Fiction. | Virginia—Politics and government—1775-1865—Fiction. | GSAFD: Historical fiction.

Classification: LCC PS3622.I784 M37 2021 (print) | LCC PS3622.I784 (ebook) | DDC 813/.6--dc23

www.RosettaBooks.com

Printed in Canada

RosettaBooks®

For my sons: James, Lucas, Zachary, and Nicholas

FIRST FAMILIES OF VIRGINIA

SELECT MCCARTY AND MASON FAMILY TREES

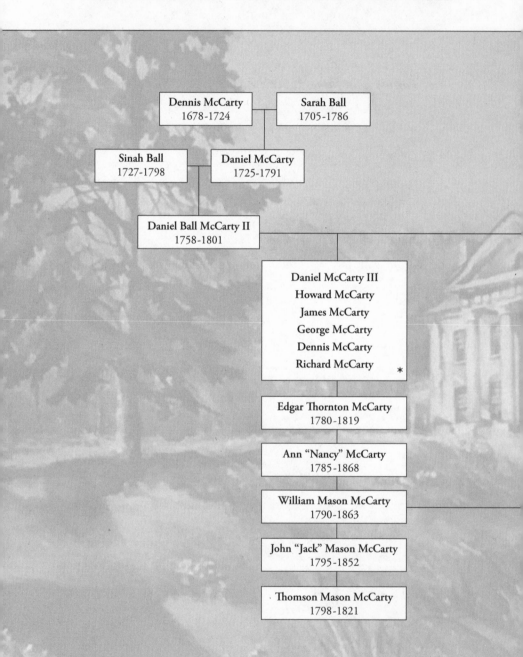

Dennis McCarty
1678-1724

Sarah Ball
1705-1786

Sinah Ball
1727-1798

Daniel McCarty
1725-1791

Daniel Ball McCarty II
1758-1801

Daniel McCarty III
Howard McCarty
James McCarty
George McCarty
Dennis McCarty
Richard McCarty   *

Edgar Thornton McCarty
1780-1819

Ann "Nancy" McCarty
1785-1868

William Mason McCarty
1790-1863

John "Jack" Mason McCarty
1795-1852

Thomson Mason McCarty
1798-1821

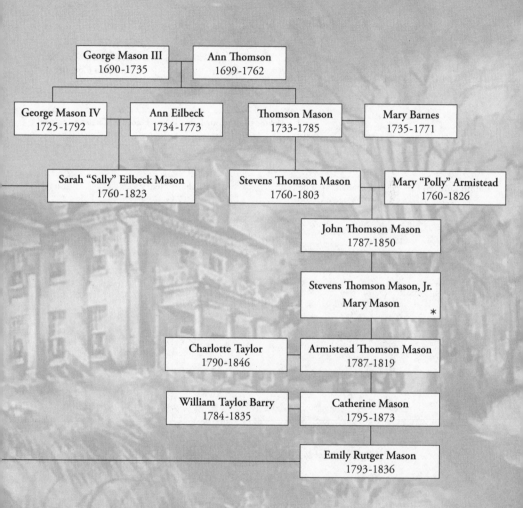

George Mason III
1690-1735

Ann Thomson
1699-1762

George Mason IV
1725-1792

Ann Eilbeck
1734-1773

Thomson Mason
1733-1785

Mary Barnes
1735-1771

Sarah "Sally" Eilbeck Mason
1760-1823

Stevens Thomson Mason
1760-1803

Mary "Polly" Armistead
1760-1826

John Thomson Mason
1787-1850

Stevens Thomson Mason, Jr.
Mary Mason   *

Charlotte Taylor
1790-1846

Armistead Thomson Mason
1787-1819

William Taylor Barry
1784-1835

Catherine Mason
1795-1873

Emily Rutger Mason
1793-1836

*Deceased before 1816

FIRST FAMILIES OF VIRGINIA

SELECT LEE FAMILY TREES

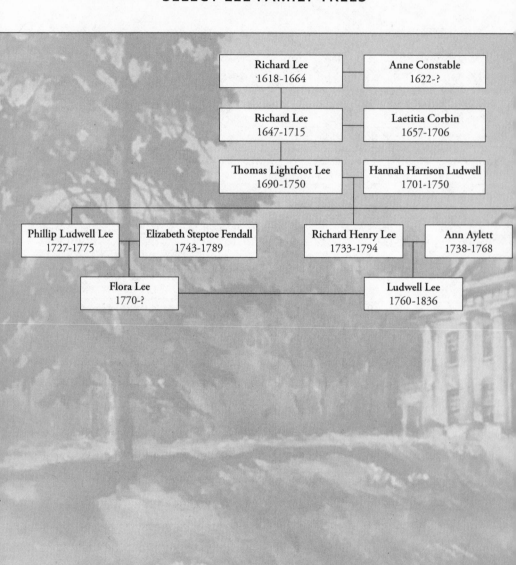

Richard Lee
1618-1664 — Anne Constable
1622-?

Richard Lee
1647-1715 — Laetitia Corbin
1657-1706

Thomas Lightfoot Lee
1690-1750 — Hannah Harrison Ludwell
1701-1750

Phillip Ludwell Lee
1727-1775 — Elizabeth Steptoe Fendall
1743-1789

Richard Henry Lee
1733-1794 — Ann Aylett
1738-1768

Flora Lee
1770-?

Ludwell Lee
1760-1836

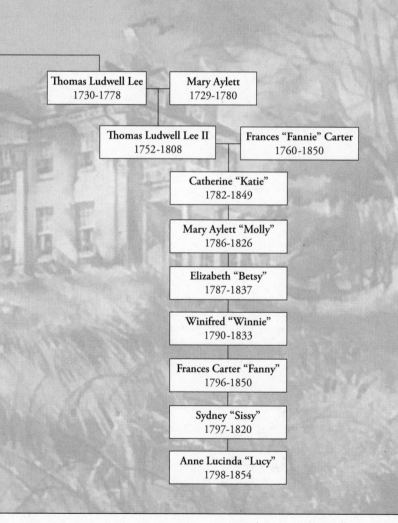

Thomas Ludwell Lee
1730-1778

Mary Aylett
1729-1780

Thomas Ludwell Lee II
1752-1808

Frances "Fannie" Carter
1760-1850

Catherine "Katie"
1782-1849

Mary Aylett "Molly"
1786-1826

Elizabeth "Betsy"
1787-1837

Winifred "Winnie"
1790-1833

Frances Carter "Fanny"
1796-1850

Sydney "Sissy"
1797-1820

Anne Lucinda "Lucy"
1798-1854

"WHOM THE GODS WOULD DESTROY

THEY FIRST MAKE MAD."

—*Henry Wadsworth Longfellow, "The Masque of Pandora"*

PROLOGUE

FEBRUARY 6, 1819,
BLADENSBURG, MARYLAND

A crowd of onlookers had gathered in the half-light of dawn as wind whipped through the bare branches of alders along the banks of the Blood Run. Despite the unrelenting storm, both the bloodthirsty and the curious had traversed nearly a mile from the edge of town through blowing snow to the grove along this stony tributary to bear witness to this morning's affair of honor. The townspeople gathered in silence, huddled against the tempest and bitter cold, as they waited for the formalities to conclude and the signal to be given.

On the south bank, where the stream ran east through a gauntlet of ice and stone, two men stood out from the rest. Facing each other, they braced against the storm, not four paces apart. Each held a long-barreled musket at his side. One, wearing a rounded cap, heavily skirted overcoat, and calfskin gloves, stood tall and proud with a nobleness of demeanor and a fiery determination in his eyes. The other was coatless, gloveless, and hatless, with raven locks blowing in the violent wind. He, too, was tall, with piercing eyes and an unyielding grittiness about him. The tension between them lay heavily in the air, yet not a word had been uttered. The only sounds were the howling wind and the low gurgle of the icy creek beyond the reeds.

The field marshal muttered something to the contestants, awakening excitement in the crowd, whose size had slowly grown in numbers. As the marshal finished his mumbling, each of the men nodded in response, the one adjusting his shoulders to stand even taller, while the other tightened his grip on the musket, throwing his head back to toss unkempt hair from his brow.

At the marshal's next word—the signal to fire—both men rushed to raise their muskets. They were positioned so close that the ends of the barrels nearly touched. Within a split second, the silence on the field shattered as the guns' hammers sparked the flints, igniting the black powder so loudly that the echo between the hills seemed to rip open the sky. In a fiery burst, cold lead propelled hotly down the muskets' barrels, exploding for but a fragment of a moment into the snowy air before entering each man. The crowd cried out in unison, first startled by the crack of gunfire and then horrified by the gore that immediately ensued. Through the blur of smoke and the acrid smell of burning powder, they gasped as they watched each man fall. Black blood quickly engulfed the whiteness of the snow as the bodies lay motionless on the frozen field. Here, on this remote field in the court of last resort, what lay behind the mask of honor finally was revealed.

PART ONE

"PREMONITIONS, FORESHADOWINGS

OF SOME TERRIBLE DISASTER

OPPRESS MY HEART."

—*Henry Wadsworth Longfellow, "The Masque of Pandora"*

CHAPTER 1

AUGUST 15, 1813, PEACH ORCHARD CAMP, FORT NORFOLK, VIRGINIA

Lieutenant John "Jack" Mason McCarty woke with a pounding in his head and a stinging on his neck. Swatting at the biting black fly, he shifted on the cot to find a more comfortable position in the sweltering heat. The movement caused the throbbing in his head to worsen. He rolled onto his back and gulped at the hot, muggy air. The hammering in his head pounded even louder. Bringing a hand to his forehead, Jack grasped his temples. Amid the pulsing pain, a voice boomed somewhere above him. He opened an eye. Blinding rays of filtered light cut through the storm thundering inside his skull. He squinted. A shadowy figure stood over him.

"Get up, Jack!"

The shrillness of the voice compounded the intensity of the throbbing. Jack moaned unintelligibly and squeezed his eyes shut.

"Christ Almighty, Jack, you need to get up!"

Jack rolled away toward the tent wall. "Go away!"

"Come on, Jack! Colonel Mason called the officers, and you already missed this morning's roll. Now, get up!" Lieutenant James Dulaney kicked the leg of the cot where Jack lay.

The thud of James's boot on the cot's wood reverberated through Jack's body like a mallet on a drum. "Stop that!"

"I'll stop when you get up!" James kicked the cot harder.

Jack rolled toward James, his head on fire and his temper beginning to flare. "For chrissake, you are worse than my mother!"

James laughed. "Your mother would have thrown a basin of water on you by now!" Jack grunted. "Come on, Jack. Up, or I'll be forced to turn you out of that cot!"

Jack groaned. With a defeated huff, he sat up and steadied himself on the cot's edge. The pulsing in his head made him woozy.

"God, you look awful!"

"And good morning to you, too, Sally." Jack spit a putrid taste from his mouth onto the floor.

James shook his head. "In the lowers again?" Jack nodded as he rubbed the back of his neck. "You know how Colonel Mason feels about his officers gambling with enlisted men."

Jack scoffed and spit on the floor again. "Colonel Mason!"

Lifting his head, he glared with bloodshot eyes at his friend. Growing up on neighboring plantations in the Northern Neck, the two had known each other since they were children. Both were members of Virginia's landed gentry, with James's home located along the Potomac River adjacent to General Washington's Mount Vernon, and Jack's family seat situated across the Pohick Bay from his grandfather's plantation of Gunston Hall. Having just reached their eighteenth years and following in the footsteps of their fathers who had fought in the Revolution, both were serving as staff officers in this latest war against the British. Like Jack, James was tall, standing just over six feet, with broad shoulders that narrowed to a trim waist. His hazel eyes were shaped like almonds and set wide on either side of a long, aquiline nose. Normally, James's sable-brown hair was brushed neatly from his face, but this morning his locks were as black as Jack's and glued to his forehead in a sweaty paste. Dressed in full uniform, James was glistening with perspiration.

Jack nodded in the direction of James's jacket. "It must be a hundred degrees. Why are you in that?"

"As I said, Colonel Mason's called for us."

"Why?"

James exhaled an exasperated sigh. "That's what colonels do, Jack. Call their officers … issue orders."

Jack threw James a look. "But it's Sunday. Even God gave it a rest on Sunday."

"Tell that to the British."

A sudden seriousness darkened Jack's face. "Are they coming up the river again?"

"Not today. At least not yet." James glanced at the floor before bringing his eyes back to Jack's. "Captain Alexander's patrol captured McNally this morning."

"Shane?" James nodded. "Jesus." Shane McNally had grown up on the McCarty family estate, and Jack and James had known him all their lives. "Where?"

"Dunno. But you need to get cleaned up. The colonel called us at ten." James pulled a timepiece from his waistcoat. "Which by my watch is in twelve minutes."

Jack lifted his head and drew in a long breath, gathering the wherewithal to stand.

James shook his head. "That's what happens when you imbibe that coffin varnish the enlisted men drink." Jack shot James another dirty look as he stood from the cot. He noticed his boots were still on from the night before. With his first step, Jack stumbled over his hat and nearly fell into the washstand. James reached for Jack's arm to steady him. "Careful there." James scanned the floor and spotted the coat of Jack's uniform lying half under the cot. He picked it up from the floor and brushed dirt from the sleeve with his hand. "Your quarters are a mess."

"Yeah, well." At the washstand, Jack skimmed dead insects from the basin before pouring more stagnant water from the pitcher. He cupped his hands and splashed his face.

"It's not helping, my friend. You still look like hell."

Jack took a handful of water in his mouth and rinsed before spitting it on the floor. "Tastes like something died."

"Probably a drowned rat at the bottom of one of those crocks you were drinking from last night."

Jack threw another look in James's direction. "And when did you become a saint?"

James laughed. "I'm no saint. I'm just of no mind to punish myself so."

Jack wiped a hand over the stubble on his chin before pushing water from his fingers through his hair. He tucked the shirt into his trousers and straightened his collar. "Do you see my waistcoat?"

Glancing around the canvas walls, James spotted the vest on the back of a chair. He grabbed it and tossed it to Jack and watched as Jack struggled to put it on. "I'm worried about you, my friend. Since William left, you've been—"

Jack stopped buttoning the waistcoat and glared at James. "Since my brother left, I've been what? Being who I am?"

"You're not one of the enlisted, Jack."

"How do you know what I am?"

James lowered his eyes, kicking the toe of his boot into the floor before looking back at Jack, who was still staring at him. "We need to make haste. We don't want to keep Colonel Mason waiting."

Jack scoffed. "That man has little patience for anything." James remained silent while Jack finished dressing and the two exited the stifling heat of the tent.

What once had been rows of fruited trees surrounded by mounds of grass and golden mustard were now axed stumps engulfed in powdered dirt that turned to thick black mud when it rained. Built to protect Fort Norfolk's flank, Peach Orchard Camp was a mix of tents and log cabins aligned in a grid, with officers' quarters near the gate and enlisted men's at the rear. Far from the eyes of the officers were shelters along the camp's rear earthen wall. Jack was all too familiar with "the lowers," where jugs of grog were plentiful, and games of hazard could be found on any given night.

With little breeze stirring and the August sun baking overhead, the temperature outside was oppressive, the air pungent with fetid odors of men and death. The suffocating misery of heat and sickness was routine in the lowlands along the Elizabeth River. During the day, biting flies and swarming gnats tortured the encamped soldiers. At night it was mosquitos that plagued them. But their greatest source of suffering came from boredom and a longing for home.

As Jack and James made their way across camp, a wagon carrying the bodies of two men kicked up a cloud of dust as it rolled by on its way to the grave-pit. Jack pulled a handkerchief from his pocket and covered his nose and mouth, fighting to keep from losing his stomach. He had been told that he would get used to the smell, but he had not.

The officers of the Fifty-Sixth Regiment of Virginia's militia had gathered outside their commanding officer's quarters. As Jack and James approached, Major George Rust, with dark, deep-set eyes, gave Jack a once-over and a disapproving look. Jack lowered his gaze and fell in with the others waiting in the hot summer sun for the colonel to emerge. When the last officer had joined the group, Captain Gerard Alexander leaned through the doorway of the log cabin and called inside. Within moments, Colonel Armistead Mason stepped from the shadows, the epaulets on his shoulders and the buttons on his dark-blue coat glimmering in the hazy sunshine. His trousers were white and crisply pressed, and his black boots polished to a high gloss. A round hat, tilted to the left with a black cockade, covered most of his auburn hair. Despite the sweltering heat, there was not a visible drop of sweat on the colonel. He gleamed in the morning light, every part of his appearance in perfect order. At his emergence, the officers saluted. Jack, too, straightened his shoulders and raised his right hand to his temple.

"At ease, gentlemen. At ease." The men relaxed their salute, but the tension was as thick as the sweltering air. Colonel Mason cleared his throat and scanned their weathered faces. "Upon my arrival here two weeks ago, this regiment was in complete disarray. My first priority has been to establish order and instill discipline among the men. As you would expect, not all are happy with the rigor of military doctrine. Last week, three of these dissenters abandoned their posts and absconded from camp. Desertion, gentlemen, next to insubordination, is the greatest enemy of an army. And I will tolerate neither." Colonel Mason removed his hat from his head and tucked it under his arm. Pulling a handkerchief from his pocket, he dabbed his hairline.

He sweats after all, Jack thought as the colonel pushed the handkerchief across his forehead and back into his pocket.

"Captain Alexander's patrol apprehended one of the deserters this morning and has returned the man to camp." Colonel Mason turned to Gerard Alexander. "Well done, Captain. Well done, indeed." The colonel outstretched his hand to shake the captain's as officers nodded. Gerard Alexander, who was sporting an ear-to-ear grin, reminded Jack of an obedient puppy waiting for a bone and a pat on the head.

"Gentlemen," Colonel Mason said, his brown eyes nearly black with intensity, "we must set an example among the men that desertion will not be tolerated." Jack's stomach tightened into knots. "The federal army has experienced these same issues and has implemented policy to execute absconders. Since then, desertion has largely ceased in the federal ranks. Now their regiments in the northern campaign are stronger than ever against the enemy. I have studied these methods and discussed it with General Taylor and the governor. We all agree on the need for a firm hand."

The knot in Jack's gut began to twist. Officers shifted their stances and exchanged glances.

Major Rust cleared his throat and broke the silence. "Are you suggesting, sir, that we execute McNally?"

"I'm not making a suggestion, Major. I'm issuing an order. Once Captain Alexander convenes a firing squad, we shall muster the men onto the quad and execute the private as an example to the others."

"You can't be serious!" The words flew from Jack's mouth before his lips had time to stop them.

Colonel Mason tilted his head in Jack's direction. "Excuse me, Lieutenant?"

"McNally is sixteen years old, Colonel. He's not a soldier, but a boy!" James moved behind Jack and squeezed Jack's elbow in warning.

Colonel Mason's dark eyes narrowed. "Who asked you to speak? Are you questioning my authority, Lieutenant?" Colonel Mason scanned Jack from head to toe. "Look at yourself. You're completely out of order."

"Colonel Mercer would never have issued such a command," Jack said, feeling blood rush up his neck, desperate to do something—anything—to intervene.

"Colonel Mercer isn't in charge here anymore, now, is he?" Colonel Mason snapped. "Might I remind you that Colonel Mercer was too sick to command. Not that he was effective in leading his regiment in good health either!"

Captain Alexander snickered under his breath at Colonel Mason's insult as the other officers exchanged cautionary glances. An angry flush spread from Jack's neck to his face. Colonel Charles Fenton Mercer, a mentor and friend, had recruited Jack into the regiment, and Jack had served as both Mercer's aide-de-camp and his personal secretary. By all accounts Fenton Mercer was brilliant and had taught Jack more than any teacher he'd ever known. James increased his grip on Jack's elbow. Jack shrugged free as Major Rust interceded.

"Colonel, I believe Lieutenant McCarty's reaction is representative of the response we may receive from the entire regiment should we execute McNally as you suggest. It's not that I nor any one of the officers question your orders, sir, but such punishment will most certainly erode morale and could possibly incite desertion *en masse* or, worse, mutiny. With all due respect, Colonel, I believe we should be measured in this instance. Punish the soldier, yes. But having him face a firing squad without knowing the consequence of his actions beforehand may be considered extreme."

Colonel Mason fixed his pensive eyes on the major. The major stared back, unwavering. Not a word was uttered, and the silence between the two men grew awkward.

Another long minute passed before Colonel Mason shifted his eyes away from Major Rust to a point beyond the camp. Then Colonel Mason nodded, seemingly to himself, before looking back at the major.

"Very well, then," Colonel Mason said. He pinched his shoulders and straightened his posture before looking back at his officers.

"Colonel Mercer's lack of leadership is at fault here. Had he provided proper training and adequate discipline, we would not have such insubordinate behavior and the ensuing morale issue." Colonel Mason paused his lecture and raised his voice to declare his verdict. "McNally shall be lashed. Going forward, should he or any man abscond from their post, they shall be executed. Let this be the first and final warning. Deserters will be hunted down and dragged back to camp to stand before a firing squad. Might I remind each and every one of you that my father, like your fathers, sacrificed greatly to free this country from the tyranny of the British. And we, gentlemen, have been called once again to face the enemy. It is kill or be killed, and we shall not relinquish our responsibility—the responsibility to defend Virginia and to preserve our nation's freedom!"

With sweat now glowing on his brow, Colonel Mason again removed the handkerchief from his pocket and wiped his forehead before returning the hat to his head. "Captain Alexander, order every man to the quad to witness the lashing of Private McNally."

———————◆———————

Jack squinted, shading his eyes from the blistering sun with a hand while he watched them drag Shane McNally to the quad. Shane seemed small as he stumbled through the dust, his face smudged and scratched, his ginger hair dirty and matted. There was fear in his eyes, but he shed not a tear as his hands were tied to the post. *Stay strong, Shane*, Jack thought as the boy's soiled shirt was pulled from his shoulders and left hanging from the waist of his trousers.

As Captain Alexander raised the whip, Jack turned his head. At the first whistle and crack of the lash, Jack closed his eyes. When the whip cracked on the boy's back a second time, Jack flinched.

The whip whistled and cracked again. Shane McNally screamed. Jack clenched a fist and held it close at his side. *Stay strong.*

WHACK! Shane McNally began to cry, pleading for forgiveness. With his eyes still closed, Jack shook his head and clutched his fist tighter. *Don't beg, Shane. They won't forgive you.*

WHACK! Shane screamed again. Jack dug his thumb into the side of his leg as he clenched his fingers tighter and tighter, remembering the feel of the leather strap and his own warm blood running down his side before the world had gone white.

CHAPTER 2

APRIL 6, 1816, LEESBURG, VIRGINIA

WHACK! Jack flinched when a low branch smacked the window as the carriage jerked to and fro through the mud and ruts of the Carolina Road. Pulling a heavy gold watch from his vest, he checked the time. Nearly half past five. Snapping its lid closed, his eyes caught the portrait of the smiling maiden enameled on its casing. *Grandma Sinah.*

Jack moved his gaze from his grandmother's image to the bleakness of the early-spring roadside beyond the window. *Of all the families William could have married into!* He rubbed a thumb over the face on the watch's casing as his apprehension churned.

"Now, now, Jack. Don't you fret about the time. All those pretty girls will still be waiting for you and Tommy when we get there."

Jack turned his attention to his mother sitting across from him. Her visage was lively and animated under a bundle of winter trappings. With all the fur around her face, she looked as if she were embarking on a northern expedition into Indian territory rather than traveling in the family's coach to an engagement party. A chinchilla stole was wrapped so high on her neck that it blended into the matching cap on her head. Her heavy cape was pulled up to her chin, and the rest of her was hidden under a woolen blanket draped over her lap. Her eyes twinkled with delight at toying with him as she waited impatiently for him to take the bait. Jack released a long sigh before obliging.

"You know that you've made us late, Sally."

His mother insisted that her children call her by her first name, since mothers, in the world of Sally McCarty, were "old, matronly, and boring."

"Of course we're late! By design, my dear Jackie. By my own design," Sally said.

Jack glanced at his younger brother Thomson sitting next to him. Sally tossed her head with a laugh. "Better to give Cousin Polly something of my choosing to gossip about than to have her invent something to suit her fancy." She laughed again with a sparkle of mischief in her eyes.

Jack grunted. She had a point. The Masons of Raspberry Plain had a knack for drama. And for the life of him, Jack could not understand why his mother still considered Polly Mason family when it was Polly's late husband, Senator Stevens Mason, who was her first cousin.

Sally pulled a mittened hand from under the blanket and patted her son's knee. "It's quite all right, Jackie, my boy. You let me handle ol' Polly Mason. You just focus your attention on those Lee sisters. Or on that Taylor girl that Armistead is so sweet on. Now, if you could turn her attention, that would surely get ol' Polly's tongue wagging."

"I have no interest in turning the head of any woman attracted to the likes of Armistead Mason."

Sally raised an eyebrow. "Now, John McCarty!" she said. "That is not the attitude to take into Raspberry Plain tonight! Whatever bone you have with Armistead, I will not have you pick it this evening."

"I find him more of a tool than a bone," Jack said, leaning back on the bench. Thomson chuckled.

Sally raised her right brow higher as her left eye narrowed. "And you, my clever monkey, will not be making a cat's paw of him this evening either. Are we clear, Jack?"

Jack glanced out the carriage window at the row of oaks standing tall and bare above the roadside brambles before bringing his eyes back to hers. This was not the first time she had invoked the fable of the monkey who convinced a gullible cat to pull chestnuts from a hot fire with its paw. And not the first time she had called him her clever monkey.

"Of course, Sally. I have no chestnuts to roast tonight, but roast him I might with the toast I have planned for William."

Sally gave him another sharp look. "A toast? Considering how moody you've been over this engagement, I question your motives."

"Since Armistead is about to become my brother-in-law, I will simply offer him the same congratulations I offer to William. There's no harm in that now, is there?"

Sally narrowed her eyes as she studied his face. "I don't know what you are up to, John McCarty. But there's enough trouble lurking outside a door without having to invite it in."

Jack turned his attention back to the window. The sun was hovering just above the ridgeline to the west. *Perhaps you should have this conversation with William. He's the one who invited trouble by proposing to Armistead's sister!*

The coach rattled and jolted as it lurched through another muddy rut.

"So, Jack," Sally said, breaking the quiet and the seriousness that had settled among them. "You boys were up with Fenton half the night last evening. Anything exciting happening in the Statehouse that would interest your dear old mother?"

Here we go, Jack thought, welcoming the change in subject. While he appreciated his mother's interest in politics and shared many of her viewpoints, her often quirky and outrageous observations could, at times, drive him to madness. And she was anything but old. For a widow who had raised nearly a dozen children on her own, she was amazingly youthful. Hardly a gray hair on her head, and the only wrinkles on her face were laugh lines around her eyes and her smile. Her heart was huge with generosity and kindness. Her mind was as sharp as a tack, and her wit equally as keen. Sally McCarty was an amazing woman, and Jack knew it.

"We spent most of the evening playing cards—"

"And drinking whiskey," Sally interrupted.

"And, yes," Jack said, "there was a little whiskey to accompany the card game." Indeed, there had been more than a little whiskey poured at Fenton Mercer's house at Aldie where they had overnighted, but Jack wasn't admitting that to his mother. "We talked more about what was going on in Washington City," Jack said. If Jack knew his mother, Sally would want to know all the latest gossip.

"Washington City?" said Sally. "Any news on Mr. Madison's plans to campaign for a third term?"

"With the president leaving Washington defenseless during the last war, I cannot imagine a scenario in which Mr. Madison wins reelection. But let's pray that he does run again. I believe it's our best chance of taking back the presidency."

"In addition to the presidency, our Federalist Party could gain more seats in the House of Representatives this election cycle," Thomson said. "Men across the country are in an uproar over Congress giving themselves a pay increase."

"And that gives our man Fenton an opportunity," Jack said. A puzzled look fell over Sally's face. "Our congressman, Joe Lewis, voted for the pay increase. If old Joe can be convinced not to campaign for re-election, it would clear the way for Fenton to become the Federalist candidate for the House of Representatives."

"I know who Joe Lewis is, Jack!" Sally snapped. "And for the life of me, I do not understand why you boys are so enamored of Fenton Mercer. He was overindulged as a child, coddled as an adolescent, and now he's, well, besides all his 'woe-is-me' nonsense, he's just too opinionated and pompous for my liking!"

"He's brilliant, Sally," Jack replied. "He can argue the law better than anyone I know. And his ideas on industrialization will revolutionize our economy and our country."

"Industrialization? Rubbish! That's the last thing we need in the South. Fenton's ideas are too liberal for Virginians. Your brother William would be better suited for Congress to represent us."

"William?" Jack said in disbelief.

"And why not?" Sally asked. "He's got a good head on his shoulders. He's conservative. And certainly better-looking and has a much better disposition than Mr. Melancholy!"

"That's not nice, Sally," Jack said. Beneath her cape, Sally folded her arms across her chest.

"But William has never held office," said Thomson.

"Doesn't matter," Sally retorted. "William's the only one with any hope to win against Armistead."

"Armistead?!" Jack and Thomson said in unison.

"Yes. Armistead. He ran for the Republicans last time. I would imagine Armistead will run again," Sally said with a confident nod.

"Armistead was just appointed to the United States Senate," Jack said. "Why would he campaign for a seat in the House of Representatives?"

"Don't you boys underestimate what Thomas Jefferson and his Jacobins will do for total power and the destruction of General Washington's legacy!" Sally exclaimed.

"Agreed, but what has that got to do with Armistead?" Jack asked.

"If someone of your brother's stature steps forward for the Federalists, Mr. Jefferson's Republicans will be forced to field their best candidate. As I see it, Armistead is the best they've got. And since they control the Virginia legislature, they can easily elect another Republican to the Senate in Armistead's place. I'm betting they force him to run for the House, whether he wants to or not," she said with a twinkle in her eyes, the one that glimmered when she knew she was right.

"No way Armistead will resign from the Senate, Sally. No way," said Jack.

Sally leaned forward, putting a hand on Jack's knee. "Mark my words, boys. Mark ol' Sally's words. Mr. Madison will announce his retirement. It'll be Mr. Monroe running for president. And it'll be Armistead Mason who campaigns for the House."

Jack was about to challenge her further when the coach abruptly stopped. From the window he could see the white columns of the portico that fronted the manor house of Raspberry Plain. With all the discussion, he hadn't noticed their turn off the Carolina Road and the drive up to the Mason estate.

"Well, my heavens," Sally said, leaning back and looking out the window to gather her bearings. "We've made it here already? I haven't had time to prepare myself."

Jack watched his mother's sudden shift from speculating about the next election to unbundling from her winter garb. All worries about Fenton Mercer and Jefferson's Jacobins were gone from her mind as she physically transformed from "Sally, Northern Explorer" to "Sally, Party Queen." She flung off the blanket and kicked it under her feet. She pulled off her mittens and tossed them on the seat beside her, released the collar of her cloak from her chin, and pulled the chinchilla stole from her neck to a much lower spot on her shoulders. She wiggled about inside her cloak, adjusting God knows what, patted her cheeks several times to make them flushed, and rubbed her lips together to redistribute the waxy paint she had applied before leaving Aldie.

She caught Jack chortling at her fidgeting and snapped at him. "Now, don't you start, young man! And put your cap on that wild head of yours. You boys need to look like proper gentlemen and not like sons of an overseer pretending to be genteel."

Jack gave his mother a wistful smile. "Now, Mother, that would mean that you'd have had to marry an overseer, and I just can't fathom you doing the likes of that."

Sally humphed back at him. "Well, right about that you are. And don't 'Mother' me, please!"

With both hands she removed her chinchilla cap and let her hair, which had been set in one long curl, fall to her left shoulder. She smoothed the strands that had been displaced by the hat and reformed the soft curls around her face with her fingers.

"How do I look?" she asked.

They nodded approval.

"Come on now," she announced, "let me show off my handsome boys to the ol' Polly-girl."

Jack laughed under his breath and pulled a rounded black hat over the thick waves of his ebony hair, which refused to stay out of his eyes. Glancing at Thomson, he nodded in silent acknowledgment. It was going to be one hell of a party with Sally McCarty tonight.

CHAPTER 3

APRIL 6, 1816, RASPBERRY PLAIN PLANTATION, LEESBURG, VIRGINIA

The Great Hall of Raspberry Plain, with its high, white, plastered walls and walnut trim, was alive tonight with the laughter of guests enjoying whiskey and wine. The gaiety of the gathering offset the somber portraits of dead Masons that hung high on the walls, their watchful eyes downcast on the living souls below. The chandelier glowed brightly, its tallow candles casting prismed light on the faces of revelers as they talked and laughed and drank. There were even more guests in the parlor, where a giant Madeira-filled punch bowl sat in the middle of the room. Somewhere a harp was entertaining the crowd with a melody almost indiscernible over the noise of the party.

As they worked their way through the crowded hall, Jack and Thomson conspicuously drew the attention of unmarried ladies in the room. The McCarty men, known for their striking good looks and charismatic charm, were the wealthiest bachelors of neighboring Fairfax County. They were of Irish descent, athletically built, with thick black hair and piercing blue eyes. Jack, the second youngest of the clan, was the tallest, with broad shoulders and a form that looked to have been chiseled by Michelangelo himself. Thomson, a few years his junior, possessed the same good looks on a slightly smaller and thinner frame. The bachelors' arrival had turned a number of heads in their direction, and Jack enjoyed the attention.

A raven-haired beauty with dark eyes caught Thomson by the elbow. "Why, Thomson McCarty! Were you about to walk right past me without so much as saying hello?" She batted her eyelashes at Thomson as she smiled.

A black widow luring prey into her web, Jack thought, for the beautiful Fanny Lee had been torturing Thomson for years.

"Why no, Miss Fanny! I was headed this way just now to find you, as I had been looking forward to seeing you all day," said Thomson. Young Thomson was smoother than Jack had thought.

Where there was one Lee girl, the others weren't far behind. There were seven altogether, each one more beautiful than the next. Fanny, with her high cheekbones, arched brows, and flirty eyes, was third youngest and hadn't changed a bit since the last time Jack had seen her. She had a figure like Venus, voluptuous curves in a tight-fitting dress that accentuated her slender waist and firm breasts. It would be a challenge to keep Thomson from being distracted by her this evening.

Jack looked around for the other Lee sisters who were usually surrounded by a gaggle of doting admirers. He didn't have to look far. Winnie Lee, the fiery, red-haired, hazel-eyed beauty, was directly behind Fanny, sitting in an oversized chair between the fair-haired Sissy and the dark-haired Molly. There were nearly a half dozen men at their feet. Just as Jack was about to interrupt their soiree, a young woman touched his sleeve. She was a pretty girl with a heart-shaped face and pouty lips the color of the flush on her cheeks. Her long blond hair was swept off her face and styled in loose curls that fell about her slight shoulders. But it was her eyes that captivated Jack. They sparkled with mischief and mystery and were the blue of cornflowers blooming in early summer. Miss Blue Eyes was draped in a soft pink gown with balloon-cap sleeves and a neckline cut low enough to reveal most of her shapely breasts. Between the low neckline and her eyes, Jack had a difficult time maintaining his focus.

"John McCarty? Is that you?!" Miss Blue Eyes asked with the gentle drawl of a proper Southern lady. *Do I know her?* Certainly had he met her before, he would have remembered.

"Yes," Jack said. "I am John McCarty, miss, but my friends call me Jack." He bowed to her politely as Miss Blue Eyes placed both hands on her hips.

"You don't recognize me, do you?" Searching her face, he glimpsed familiarity, but for the life of him he couldn't place her. She stood without a word, waiting for him to remember. Desperate for a clue, he noticed the mischievous glint in those pools of blue. It took a moment for the memory to come. It was after the Battle of Bladensburg two years before, when his regiment had taken respite at the Lee family plantation on their return to Leesburg, battered, beaten.

Lucy Lee! She was younger then, still a child in face and form. She and her sisters had been helping to serve the soldiers with biscuits and gravy that awful morning. And those eyes, so blue and filled with mystery. He remembered how they had intrigued him as he watched her through steam while she poured him coffee. "Lucy Lee! I hardly recognized you. You've grown up so."

Lucy extended her hand. "Lucinda Lee, if you please. Only my friends call me Lucy."

Jack took her extended hand and held her gaze with his own. Surprisingly, she didn't glance away, her spirited eyes daring him further. He gently drew her gloved hand toward his lips, not once moving his eyes from hers, pressed his lips against her hand, and allowed the warmth of his breath to penetrate the glove's weave. Only when blush ran hot through her cheeks did he move her hand from his mouth to touch it to his own cheek. Lucy narrowed her eyes.

"Are you always so fresh, Mr. McCarty?"

He moved her hand from his face without releasing it. "As fresh as is the month of May, Miss."

"I see that you are a scholar of Chaucer." Of the numerous occasions on which Jack had been accused of being fresh, Lucinda Lee was the first woman he'd met who called him out on quoting Chaucer.

"Ah, but the greatest scholars are not usually the wisest people."

Lucinda recited in kind. "Full wise is he, Mr. McCarty, that can himself know."

Now Jack was impressed. "And if he is indeed full wise, he himself must know that she, Miss Lee, is as fair as is the rose of May."

Lucinda smiled again. "A rose I may be, but it's a thorn I might give you, Mr. McCarty."

"But if you prick me, Miss Lucinda, I may bleed."

"There will be no blood tonight, Mr. McCarty." She laughed out loud and pulled her hand away. "So, Mr. McCarty, where have you been keeping yourself? It has been forever since I've seen you."

Jack moved closer, engrossed by her beauty and demonstrated intelligence. "In Williamsburg, finishing my law degree."

"Impressive. And now? Will you become a planter-politician like the rest of them?"

"Like the rest of whom?"

"Isn't that what you gentlemen do once you come of age? Receive your birthright, inherit your lands, build your plantations, and launch your political careers? I mean, just take a look around, Mr. McCarty." Lucinda gave an exaggerated look about the room. "All I see are planters and politicians."

"I have no interest in becoming a farmer, Miss Lucinda."

"My apologies if I offended you. But if not a farmer, then what?"

"No offense taken, but farming requires growing roots. Something that I have no interest in doing. And you, Miss Lucinda? I assume that you, like the rest of the ladies in this room, are looking for a planter-politician husband?"

"To the contrary, Mr. McCarty. I can assure you that what I am looking for is not in this room."

Jack moved his hands to his lapels, straightening his coat, and lifted his chin. "Well, Miss Lee, since I have only just arrived, I am not sure you can make such a statement."

"Let me assure you otherwise, Mr. McCarty."

Jack placed a hand on his chest, feigning injury. "You cut me to the quick! If not me, then who is the lucky gentleman who holds your heart?"

"Not who, sir, but what."

Jack tilted his head, intrigued. "And what might that be?"

Mischief sparkled in her eyes. "Now, Mr. McCarty, why on earth would I share my heart with a near stranger?"

"Well, in that case, my lady, I shan't be a stranger should I get to know you better."

Thomson emerged from the crowd. "Pardon my interruption, Miss Lucinda, but I must borrow my brother." Jack could tell by the look on Thomson's face that he had had enough of Fanny Lee's tormenting for now.

"If you borrow him, you'd have to return him. Perhaps you could keep him for the evening," Lucinda said with a clever smile.

"You did not answer my question, Miss Lucinda. Perhaps I might call upon you sometime?"

"Only if you should bring your handsome brother Thomson along to save me from Chaucer and Shakespeare," Lucinda said with an eyebrow raised at Thomson.

"I can't fathom the need for rescue from dead poets, but I am happy to oblige and bring Thomson along for entertainment," said Jack.

"Very well then, if you will excuse me." Lucinda curtsied and turned her attention to another gentleman she recognized in the hall.

"Be careful with that one, Jack," Thomson said under his breath as Jack watched her walk away. "She uses her heart like a weapon." Jack shot his brother a quizzical glance as the two made their way down the corridor to find their brothers, stiff whiskey, and spirited conversation.

CHAPTER 4

The study of the late General Stevens Thomson Mason was situated in the far northeast corner of the manor, isolated from the rest of the house. Tonight the room was filled with the restless energy of young men and impassioned discussion on the latest political quandaries of the fledgling nation. From the corridor, Jack could hear the buzz of conversation reverberating down the hallway.

As the pair reached the room, Jack grabbed Thomson's sleeve. "Hold up a second," Jack said, stopping at the study's doorway. Jack scanned the room through a haze of heavy smoke and spotted his brother William in the far corner. Swirling a glass filled with whiskey, William was hard to miss. Taller than most men, he was impeccably dressed, wearing red tartan knickers and a deep-blue jacket embroidered with the McCarty family crest—a mailed fist holding a lizard with words in the Celtic language declaring bravery and honor.

Loud laughter erupted on the other side of the room, diverting Jack's attention. Dressed in a general's uniform with black leather boots buffed to a high polish, Armistead Mason reclined against the edge of a desk. More than a dozen uniformed officers surrounded him. Armistead lifted his chin and said something that caused the men to laugh heartily again. The sight of the newly promoted General Mason holding court with his retinue made Jack's stomach churn.

Jack's attention was diverted again as their brother Edgar emerged from the haze and walked toward them. Edgar, William, and Thomson were all that were left of Jack's nine brothers. At the death of his twin, Edgar became the eldest of the remaining McCarty clan. He was also the shortest and the stoutest. With a mass of hair on his head and much the same on his arms and the back of his hands, he reminded Jack of a big black bear. Edgar was always happy and smiling, ready with a joke or a hug depending on the need. Without exception, Jack couldn't name a soul on earth who didn't love Edgar McCarty.

"Edgar!" Thomson said as Edgar approached.

"Greetings, brother!" Edgar said, opening his big, burly arms and embracing Thomson.

"You're leaving already?" Jack asked.

"Only momentarily to relieve myself of some of the drink!" Edgar said, as he adjusted the waistband of his trousers under his round belly.

Jack glanced over Edgar's shoulder at Armistead, who was laughing again. "Sounds like a hornet's nest in there."

"Hornets indeed," Edgar said. "Now you mind yourself, brother. You don't need to poke at a hornet to get yourself stung." Grasping Jack's forearm, he leaned close and lowered his voice. "They sting just because they can."

From concerns over planting in this year's colder-than-normal weather to the establishment of an American colony in Africa for manumitted and freed people of color, the study was electric with words of clashing opinions and clinking glasses of whiskey and rye. Jack had slipped into the room behind Thomson and had found his way to a wall of oak shelving lined with leather and clothbound books as conversations whirred around him. At one corner of the room, a group of physicians was discussing recent correspondence with the Necker Institute in Paris regarding a listening device to diagnose disorders of the heart and lungs. The topic monopolizing the throng around General Armistead Mason was a highly controversial bill recently passed by the Fourteenth

Congress to impose a duty on goods imported from the territories and provinces of His Majesty of Britannica.

"You see, gentlemen, this is not simply a matter of protecting northern industries, but of protecting the nation as a whole," Armistead said, leaning against the front of his father's desk with a glass of rye whiskey in hand. "We must never surrender to the British, militarily or economically."

"If the tariff will pay our war debt and what is still owed to our militiamen, then you have my support, Armistead," said the recently promoted Colonel George Rust.

"I'm in agreement with you, Armistead," Captain William McCarty said, having joined the group. "The British cannot be trusted to uphold any accord they make. Treaty after treaty, they interfere with our commerce and threaten our independence."

Despite Edgar's warning, Jack was unable to hold his tongue. "While I certainly agree that the British cannot be trusted, I cannot agree with the general's position on the tariff."

"Come again?" Armistead asked, frowning as he shifted on the desk to see who was behind him. "Lieutenant Jack McCarty! How did you manage to slip in without my notice? Now, why is it that you disagree with my position?"

"It's Captain McCarty now. And it's a reckless policy and one that threatens the stability of Virginia's economy."

"My apologies, *Captain.*" Jack felt Armistead's sarcasm. "But the British are undermining the ability of our industries to manufacture goods at profitable prices."

"Virginia doesn't rely on the selling of manufactured goods," Jack said as he stepped closer to the desk. "Our economy relies on exporting tobacco and grain to England and Europe. Have you considered the impact on your farm's profits if the British retaliate with a tariff of their own?"

Armistead appeared amused, as the epaulets on his shoulders caught the reflection of the lanterns overhead. "I will agree that there is a risk, but it is high time to stop Britain's interference once and for all." Armistead rocked his glass, the ice clinking repetitively against the crystal. "Without a duty to normalize pricing, they will continue to buy our economic future with our own dollars. And we will be made their slaves once more and fools all the while!"

"Hear, hear!" George said, lifting his glass with a pipe clenched between his teeth, its smoke rippling in the air.

"Hear, hear!" the men chanted with glasses raised.

"As long as it doesn't lead to war again," Jack said. Armistead's friends were unaccustomed to the general being challenged by anyone, especially in his own house. They bristled, shifting shoulders uncomfortably as they muttered among themselves.

"And what would you know about war, son?" asked Armistead, his patience clearly growing thin.

"You are familiar with my service, General, and I am familiar with your proposed changes to the militia bill. If enacted, your amendments will completely undermine our ability to defend ourselves against the British or any other aggressors who wish us harm." A number of the uniformed officers mumbled their disagreement with Jack's view while others nodded in concurrence.

"Am I to assume that in addition to my vote on the tariff, you disagree with my proposed amendments to the militia bill?" Armistead's face reddened and his agitation showed.

"I am completely opposed to such amendments," said Jack.

"I must agree with my brother on this one, Armistead," said William. "We cannot allow the government to buy substitutions for those unwilling to serve their country."

"Not those unwilling to serve, William, but those who are morally opposed to war due to their religious convictions," Armistead clarified.

"And what about boys too young to serve?" Jack asked.

Armistead stood from the desk and turned toward Jack. "Tell me you aren't still smarting over that."

"Jack's simply pointing out an oversight of the amendment," George said, interrupting the escalation of the exchange.

"And what might that be, George?" Armistead asked, the annoyance in his voice continuing to grow.

"That every coward will claim a religious exemption," said Jack.

"The Quakers are not cowards," Armistead said. "While the ones under my command may not have held a gun, they were never afraid to be on the battlefield, unlike those who served as secretaries and aides."

"What are you implying, General? That because I served as aide-de-camp, I was afraid to fight?" An uneasiness crawled over the men surrounding the desk.

"I am aware of your service and that you were behind the lines."

Glances were exchanged as Jack stepped toward the desk. William placed a hand on Jack's shoulder. "He followed his orders, Armistead," William said.

"And a fine aide-de-camp you were, Jack," George said, throwing a glance at Armistead. "We all served as we were ordered. And I think we can all agree that there is not a coward among us." The officers nodded in agreement.

"Agreed, Colonel. Not a coward in the room," Edgar McCarty said as he reentered the study holding a glass of whiskey high in the air. The men around the desk nodded with raised glasses and pipes.

The chimes for supper sounded with a loud clanging that momentarily muted their voices. Armistead cleared his throat and straightened his jacket. "Gentlemen, I believe it is time to retire to the dining room. We certainly do not wish to keep Mrs. Mason waiting." Armistead pushed his chin forward and started for the doorway. The officers fell in behind him, and he led them from the room.

William grabbed Jack's arm and held him back from following the others. "You ought not goad him like that, Jack. It only inflames him," William said in a low voice, his brow heavy with concern.

Jack shrugged away from his brother's grip. "Inflame him? He inflamed me! How dare he question my service, especially after Bladensburg and what I endured at Peach Orchard Camp."

"I understand, Jack. I do."

"You couldn't possibly understand, because you left."

"My tour had ended! What would you have me do? Just stick around because Mercer went home sick?"

"And now you are bringing this bully into our family!"

William blanched. "What are you talking about, Jack? The Masons are already family. Not close relations, but still family. And I'm bringing his sister into our fold, not Armistead."

Jack shook his head. "You don't know what he's capable of."

"Whatever it is, Jack, you need to let it go."

Jack drew in a long breath and shook his head again. "You forgive what you want, Will."

William dropped his gaze to the floor. After a long moment, he lifted his head and looked at Jack. "For one night, can you put whatever it is aside for me, Jack? I have found the love of a lifetime and all I want is to share my happiness with you and our family. Just get to know Emily. I promise that she is nothing like the rest of the Masons."

Moving his gaze to the window, Jack pushed his hair from his forehead and sighed before looking back at his brother. "All right, Will. I will remain impartial regarding your fiancée. I promise to do nothing further to interrupt the harmony of the evening."

"It means a lot to me, Jack."

Jack nodded. "It's your night, after all."

"It is, isn't it!" William slapped Jack on the back and put an arm around his shoulder. "Come now. Let's find Sally and hope that she has left some Madeira for the other guests!"

CHAPTER 5

The mood of the dining room was warmed by the flicker of burning candles and the glow of oil lamps, while the cool air of the evening sky pushed against the windows' panes. Two long tables set side by side were covered in fine embroidered linens and adorned with bouquets of ground cedar, pussy willow, and cherry blossoms. The fireplace at the end of the room was burning brightly as aromas of stewed meats and baking breads and cakes wafted through the air. Armistead's mother, Polly, was seated at the head of the first table with his fiancée, Charlotte Taylor, with her back to him. Her chestnut locks, cascading in long ringlets from under a green velvet turban, fell almost perfectly between the narrow shoulders of her matching velvet dress. Armistead paused momentarily at the doorway to admire his fiancée's beauty.

"Armistead?"

At the sound of his name, Armistead turned to find his sister Emily behind him. The cut of her yellow silk gown exposed too much of her bosom for Armistead's liking. He frowned in disapproval until he noticed her eyes. Usually cheerful and sparkling like the ocean, they were stormy and clouded with concern. "What's wrong, sparrow?"

"There's something important I have to speak with you about." Emily placed her hand on his arm and leaned toward him, whispering. "Before the evening grows old, please give me a moment? Just you and me alone. Please, Armie?" Emily's eyes cast nervously about the room.

"Of course, Em. Let's slip out to the west pantry after supper." The west pantry had been a favorite spot for sharing secrets when they were children. Emily nodded and walked into the dining room. Armistead made his way down the other side of the table, seating himself between Polly and Charlotte.

"Armistead!" Charlotte said, a happy clamor in her voice. Tall and thin, Charlotte Taylor was a beautiful girl with stunning looks and a milk-white complexion. Her face was long with fine features and a delicate nose set between the most emerald-green eyes.

"Where have you kept yourself? With your mates, I hope, and saving the nation, I pray!"

"As I should be! A gentleman's work requires great sacrifices, and being apart from you is the greatest sacrifice of all." Armistead gently squeezed her hand.

"As long as that sacrifice is not forever, I shall remain a contented woman."

"I always find my way back to you, my Charlotte." Armistead glanced over at his mother. Polly, with an all-too-familiar scowl on her face, seemed distracted. Armistead moved a reassuring hand to his mother's forearm.

"Armistead," Polly said, her pinched expression relaxing. A hysteria of laughter erupted from the other side of the table. A matron with painted lips was gabbing in a most exaggerated manner. The scowl returned to his mother's face as the painted woman threw back her head and laughed again. The woman was Sally McCarty.

Charlotte leaned toward Armistead and whispered, "Your mother seems to find Mrs. McCarty quite, hmmm, what's the right word?" She thought for a second. "Off-putting."

Sally's animations were interrupted by William and Jack's entrance.

"Mrs. Mason," William said, acknowledging Polly at the end of the table.

"William, it is good to see you have joined us," Polly said.

William nodded, taking his seat next to Emily. "Pleasure as always, ma'am."

From the look on William's face, it was clear to Armistead that there was little pleasure for William in his relationship with Mrs. Mason.

Armistead's eyes caught Jack's as he neared the table. "General," Jack said, respectfully. Whatever tension had existed between them in the study seemed to have dissipated. Armistead nodded a silent reply.

Standing behind his mother, Jack bent and kissed her on the cheek before taking the chair next to her. "Oh, Jackie, you devil, you, sneaking up on your poor old mother like that! Why, if it hadn't been you, I'd like to have fainted, thinking some strange fellow was going about kissing old ladies," Sally said, loud enough that most of the table could hear.

"Heaven help the strange fellow who has the nerve to kiss you without an invitation," Jack said.

Thomson, who was already seated, laughed. "He'd have either the fists of four sons or the slap of Sally McCarty's four fingers to contend with!" Sally McCarty threw her head back, cackling with laughter.

Polly drew a sharp breath, her jaw tightening around her clenched teeth. Armistead patted his mother's arm lightly and leaned close. "You must learn to suffer her."

"If only it were as easy said as done," she whispered as the vein on her temple pulsed blue.

As the McCartys settled into their chairs, servants brought out the supper. Trays of shucked oysters along with loaves of hot bread and preserves of last summer's fruits were placed next to roasted turkeys that had been sliced beforehand. With the last tray served, Polly rose from her seat. As the gentlemen pushed their chairs back to stand with her, she waved a hand at them to sit and tapped a crystal glass, bringing silence to the room.

"Good evening, friends. I am so pleased that you all have joined us this evening for supper here at Raspberry Plain. For many tonight, the recent past has been a time of much hardship and sorrow. We have all been touched by the horrors of war and the pain of death. The Masons have not been immune, as we lost my beloved son Stevens just last autumn to the fever that consumed so many of our neighbors and our friends.

"But the war is won, and the fever gone. And we live on to celebrate a new year and the renewal of life that comes with spring. We are here tonight to celebrate new beginnings and new bonds between us. This evening we honor the impending marriage of my beautiful daughter, Emily Rutger Mason, to Captain William Mason McCarty. May I present my daughter, Emily, and her fiancé, William, to you all."

Polly paused and, with a gesture of her hand, invited Emily and William to be received. William stood and assisted Emily with her chair. Gazing admiringly at her fiancé, Emily looked happy. The clouds in her eyes that Armistead had noticed just moments ago were gone. Armistead smiled at them as William took Emily's hand while she curtsied to the guests' applause. As the couple sank back into their chairs, Polly continued.

"There is one other announcement I'd like to make this evening. In addition to the engagement of Emily and William, there will soon be another marriage in the Mason family. My dear son, General Armistead Thomson Mason, has proposed to the lovely Miss Charlotte Taylor, and she has accepted!" There were many "ohhhs" and "ahhhs" and light applause throughout the room. Armistead rose and pulled out the chair for Charlotte. Taking her hand in his as Charlotte stood, he smiled at the guests. He bowed graciously, and Charlotte curtsied before they returned to their chairs.

"It brings me such great joy to host you all here this evening. May God bless each and every one of you, and may we relish the many gifts and favors granted to us by His grace. Please enjoy the food, the company, and the evening. Reverend Littlejohn? The blessing?" She waved her hand to the minister as Armistead pulled out Polly's chair to seat her. Before the Reverend could stand, Jack McCarty, with a glass of wine in hand, rose from his chair.

"Before the benediction, Reverend, might I propose a toast?" Jack asked with a bow and the utmost Southern polish. "Mrs. Mason?" Polly shot a nervous glance at Armistead for guidance. "General?"

Armistead, uneasy, nodded. "All right then."

Jack smiled as he addressed the guests in the room. "As many of you know, the McCartys are of Irish blood. And I thought it appropriate to propose a toast in our native tongue to my brother and, with tonight's news, also to General Mason."

Jack raised his glass as he spoke in perfect Irish. "*Seo a leanas le caimiléireacht, goid, troid agus ól! Má cheat tú, cheat tú bás. Má ghoideann tú, ghoid tú croí mná. Má tá tú ag troid, tá tú ag troid ar son do dheartháir, agus má ólann tú, ólann tú le cairde.*"

Sally McCarty chuckled and raised her half-empty glass. "Here's to the drinking! And to the happy couples!"

Edgar and Thomson joined her in lifting their glasses. "And to cheating, stealing, and fighting!" they cheered in unison.

The guests looked confused as the McCartys toasted and laughed.

"I see that many here are unfamiliar with our native tongue. Allow me to translate," Jack said. "Here's to cheating, stealing, fighting, and drinking!"

An uncomfortable hush fell over the room. Armistead pushed away from the table. Before he could get out of his chair, Jack raised his glass to Armistead and William.

"But, if you cheat, gentlemen, may you cheat death," Jack said with a broad smile.

Charlotte moved a hand to Armistead's sleeve to discourage his interruption. Jack raised his glass to Emily and Charlotte. "And if you steal, may you steal the heart of a beautiful woman."

Turning toward his brothers, Jack continued. "If you fight, may you fight for your brother."

With a wide grin and his glass raised high in the air, Jack addressed the guests in the room. "And when you drink, may you always drink with friends! To the happy couples!"

The guests raised their glasses and joined in. "To the happy couples."

Jack took a hearty drink from his glass and returned to his chair. Charlotte turned her head toward Armistead and smiled at him. Armistead faintly smiled back, drawing comfort from her gaze, calming his outrage.

The Reverend Littlejohn looked around the room to ensure there were no further toasts and gave his blessing. With the toasts and the benediction finished, the guests moved their attention to Polly Mason for permission to begin the feast. Smiling graciously, Polly looked out over the trays of food to the faces of her guests. With pride in her voice, she said, "Well, please, please, let us dine."

CHAPTER 6

The west pantry was a narrow, windowless room lined with shelves and bins that stored wheat, grains, and other staples. Two lanterns hung on each side of the door, casting flickering shadows over the plastered walls. The wooden planks of the floor creaked eerily as Emily paced, waiting for her brother.

"Where is he?" she asked under her breath. *Surely he saw me leave the table. It has been at least ten minutes now. Where in the devil is he?*

Emily's thoughts darted erratically as she smoothed the folds of her dress to calm her nerves. *Maybe I shouldn't tell him.* Picking up her skirts, she hurried to the door and put her hand on the knob. There it was again—that voice in her head. *"It's all about family honor, Em. Family honor. What makes us who we are."* Isn't that what Papa always said?

Emily imagined herself walking into her father's study, seeing him in his chair with books stacked on his desk, a quill in hand, drafting a correspondence. She imagined him looking at her over his spectacles with his dark, piercing eyes. *"Yes, my little sparrow?"* he would say, smiling at her interruption. She imagined telling him everything. And what would he say?

What, Papa? What would you say? She closed her eyes, concentrating to block the muffled noise of the party so that his words might come.

"Such matters are not for a lady to carry, Emily. Confide the truth to your brother and trust him to do what's right."

She drew in a deep breath and let it out slowly.

"Em?"

She opened her eyes at the sound of Armistead's voice outside the door.

"Yes," she said in a loud whisper. "I'm here." Armistead turned the knob and entered the pantry. "Where have you been?"

"I know I'm late and I'm sorry," he said, closing the door behind him. "Now, what is it? What's troubling you?"

All week long she had rehearsed her words, but her doubts moments ago had erased them from memory. "I don't know where to start."

"The beginning is usually the best place."

She smiled at his teasing and drew a long breath. "All right, then. Last week Aunt Mary and I had gone to Alexandria for sundries and stopped at Cedar Grove to overnight. I was tired when we arrived and decided to nap. I hadn't slept for very long before I awoke. As I came downstairs for some water, I heard men in William's study talking in loud voices. It's not unusual to hear loud voices because William often argues with other attorneys in his meetings, but I heard one of them say your name." Emily paused with a nervous sigh.

"My name?"

"Yes, your name. That's why I was eavesdropping—because I heard your name. And, oh, what awful things they said! They were very animated in their talk with William, they were. And William was quite disagreeable with them."

"What did they say exactly?"

"Before I tell you, you must promise never to utter a word of this to William. He would be unhappy with me if he knew that I was listening to his private meetings. Please, Armistead. Please promise."

"Look at me, sister," Armistead said, lifting her chin. "You have my word as a gentleman. I promise."

"All right, Armie. Just know that I am telling you this so that you can understand more about your enemies and for no other purpose." Armistead nodded. His eyes, dark and intense, studied hers. And in that moment, Emily saw in Armistead's eyes her father's and heard his words ringing again in her head.

"The conversation went something like this: The one gentleman said Armistead Mason is a bully, arrogant, and thinks he is better than everybody else. That the legislature should have never elected you as Virginia's senator. That you somehow soiled Father's good name by using it to pressure the legislature to appoint you. And that you cheated in the election for the House of Representatives against Mr. Lewis last year."

"You said 'the one gentleman.' Do you know who he was?"

"I don't know the one gentleman who said these things." The words now fell from Emily's lips without thought or hesitation. "But the other gentleman said that he was in violent opposition to your election to the Senate, that he didn't know about the cheating and all, but agreed that you have never earned any of the positions that you hold. That the only reason you were promoted to general was because of favoritism, and it had nothing to do with your heroism in the war. He also said that you were elected to the Senate because President Jefferson owed our father many favors. He said that you have a hot temper and are prone to childish tantrums when you don't get your way. And that he had voiced these to the legislature and, when the vote came, he was overruled by the Republicans."

After she had repeated all that she remembered, she searched Armistead's face. Despite his outward calm, Emily saw hurt in her brother's eyes.

"I am so sorry, Armie. It was awful that anyone would utter such untruths. It was all I could do to keep quiet and not scream out!" Emily felt her emotions rising again.

Armistead wrapped an arm around her shoulder. "I know it is upsetting, Em. You did the right thing by telling me. You should never have had to bear witness to such blasphemy." He turned her toward him and looked into her face. "But I need you to think for a moment longer about that dreadful afternoon. You said that the second gentleman had voiced his concerns before the legislature, implying he might be a member of that body. Think, Emily. Did you recognize the second gentleman's voice?"

"Not at first. Then I saw them walk to their carriage. The one gentleman wasn't familiar at all. I had never seen him before. But the other gentleman, he was familiar." Emily bit her lip. "It was Charles Fenton Mercer, Armistead. Fenton Mercer of Aldie."

———

As Emily closed the pantry door behind her, Armistead slammed his boot into a wooden bin, kicking it as hard as he could. The wall of the bin collapsed, and its grain spilled onto the floor. In a fury he kicked at the grain, sending it flying at the wall.

"God damn him!" he said aloud, kicking the grain a second time and causing it to scatter across the room. *How dare they? And Mercer, of all people!*

Armistead paced furiously across the grain-strewn floor, his mind rifling through all the reasons he loathed Fenton Mercer. *How dare he question my achievements?* He curled his fingers into fists to control the shaking of his hands. *It was Mercer who cowered in the face of the enemy. Mercer whose promotion was a favor.* Hurt and insult and anger coalesced into a tumultuous rage that roared so loudly he could barely hear his own thoughts. *That imperious son of a bitch!* Bringing his hands to his temples as if to hold his head together, he paced between the bins and shelves of the pantry walls like a caged animal. *How dare he!*

Only once could Armistead remember having been this insulted. He drew a deep breath as the words of the officers of Maryland's Fifth and the sounds of war echoed in his mind. He squeezed his eyes to block out the memory of Baltimore and Hampstead Hill. *Not tonight. Not here.* He needed to think clearly. He made an effort to calm himself. Rolling his head from one side to the other, he opened his eyes and looked again at his hands. *A bit steadier.* Opening and closing them, Armistead forced his breathing to slow. Pushing the anxiety deep within him, his composure returned. *I am a senator of the United States Congress—a decorated war hero. I am General Armistead T. Mason.*

He pushed his shoulders back and lifted his chin. *I will deal with you, Fenton Mercer, soon enough.*

Armistead unlatched the pantry door and hurried down the back corridor toward the study, nodding at the gentlemen milling about in the antechamber. As he turned the corner, he saw Jack McCarty approaching. *Mercer's secretary! He's even staying with him at Aldie!* As Jack neared, Armistead lowered his shoulder and, as hard as he could, he knocked into Jack as he passed.

"Watch yourself!" Armistead snapped.

"Watch myself?" Jack said with a combination of outrage and surprise in his voice. "You ran straight into me!"

"I did no such thing." Armistead placed his hand on Jack's forearm and leaned toward him. "But you, Captain McCarty, you need to mind yourself and who you associate with," Armistead said in a low voice. "And you can tell your friend, Mr. Mercer, that he'll be hearing from me soon."

Releasing Jack's arm, Armistead turned his back and walked into the study, leaving Jack standing with his mouth agape in the middle of the hall.

On the credenza Armistead found what he had been looking for: the rye whiskey that had been made at Raspberry Plain for as long as he could remember. From a crystal decanter that his father had bought in London years before, Armistead filled a snifter nearly to the rim and drank it down. The whiskey's fire burned his throat. It took a second, long drink to extinguish the fire raging inside him. He topped the glass off again.

With drink in hand and his temperament improved, Armistead left the study to find Charlotte. Rounding the corner to the corridor that led to the Great Hall, he nearly collided with a voluptuous brunette in a blue silk gown.

"General Mason!" said Molly Lee as the wine in her glass splashed over the rim. "You will have me wearing red tonight! Where are you going in such a hurry?"

"I am terribly sorry, Molly." Armistead took her elbow to steady the glass. "Did any of it spill on you?"

"Why, I don't quite know. Is there?" Stepping closer to him, Molly brought her hand up to the dress's neckline and pushed her bosom toward him.

Armistead stepped back. "Not that I can see."

"Don't mislead me, General. How can you know for certain unless you have a closer look?" Molly lifted her chin and came near him again, providing yet another invitation to examine her bosom.

"I would never mislead you, Molly." Armistead was having difficulty ignoring her cleavage and her breasts protruding from the low, taut neckline. On any other occasion, he might have suggested a private rendezvous later in the evening. But he had business to attend. And things were different now.

"Armie, that is simply not true," Molly said. "You have indeed misled me now that you've proposed to someone else. You leave me no choice other than to marry one of those old widowers that my mother has arranged and live the rest of my life in misery!"

Armistead, quite accustomed to the drama of Molly Lee, offered a sympathetic smile.

"Now, now, Molly. My engagement is no reason for you to marry someone that won't make you happy."

"I can't have what makes me happy!" Tears were welling in her eyes.

Lifting her chin with a forefinger, Armistead indulged her with a smile. "Why are we going back through all of this again? You know that I have enjoyed your company. Let's just leave it there."

With a quivering lip, Molly made a weak effort to smile. "You enjoy my company, Armie?"

Armistead drew a weary sigh and removed his hand from her face. "As I've said, yes."

"Perhaps you might grant me one little favor then, to help heal my heart?"

"What might that be?" Armistead was not certain that he wanted the answer.

Stepping toward him again, Molly placed her hand on his forearm. She leaned toward his ear, whispering in her breathy Virginia drawl,

"Meet me one last time in your mother's pantry. Just one last time, Armie, for old times' sake?"

The sweet smell of her body so near to him filled his senses, tempting his every resolve. He drew a long breath, resisting the urge to consent. "Molly, as much as I do enjoy your company and could easily submit to your request, I cannot. I have promised my heart to Charlotte. Certainly you can understand."

"Please, Armie?" Molly leaned in closer. "Just one last tip of the velvet?" Armistead could feel her breath on his neck.

Armistead grasped her forearms and held her at arm's length. "I cannot, Molly." He narrowed his eyes and looked into hers. "It is time that we both moved on. Now, if you'll excuse me, I must rejoin Charlotte in the hall."

Before he allowed her to say another word, he released her, turning his back and continuing down the corridor.

Maneuvering her way through the mass of people, Charlotte searched for Armistead. Men were laughing heartily, enjoying the grog and whiskey, while the women were gossiping in loud whispers in order to be heard above the noise. When she reached the rear of the hall, she spotted Armistead engaged in conversation. She was only a few yards from him, when she saw her.

Molly Lee!

Charlotte had known about Armistead's courtship with Molly Lee before his marriage to his first wife. Charlotte had also heard rumors that their relationship had continued after his wife's death despite Armistead's vehement denials. As Molly leaned close to Armistead, Charlotte froze. Her heart pounded into somersaults, her tongue tingling with a numbness that quickly spread throughout her body as she watched Armistead grasp both of Molly's arms as if to embrace her. In that instant, Armistead pushed Molly from him and moved in her direction. Somehow, Charlotte managed to lift her arm to catch his attention.

"There you are, my handsome," Charlotte said, finding her voice and forcing a smile as he approached her. She noticed an uneasiness in his eyes. "Armistead, is everything all right?"

"Everything is fine, my love. I was detained in the study by a mob of young Republicans inquiring about the defense of Baltimore." The lightness of his mood earlier in the day had turned dark.

"I know that you would never deny an admirer a request; however, I also know you. Something is troubling you, darling. I can see the worry on your brow."

Armistead released a heavy sigh. "There is something. I can't discuss it here with you now but will share all later." He leaned close and whispered, "I must get away from all this noise to gather my thoughts and determine my recourse. I'm sorry, but I need to return home now. Would you like to come with me or stay here and return to Selma later with your sister and her husband?"

Between the strain on his face and the distress in his voice, Charlotte knew something was terribly wrong and that it had nothing to do with Molly Lee. And she knew him well enough to know that whatever had happened had created bile within him that could erupt at the slightest provocation. The specifics of the injustice were irrelevant. Its mitigation was what mattered, however disappointed she'd be that he was leaving the party early.

"I understand completely, my love, and I'm coming with you. But we can't simply leave; we must craft a reason." She thought for a moment. "I'll tell the others that I have a headache."

"That is a perfect excuse!" She saw the relief on his face.

"We'll have to make sure that my sister thinks it's just a headache so that she doesn't feel compelled to leave with us. Otherwise, we'll have company."

"Please, no!" Armistead said with a roll of his eyes. "You'll have to be very convincing, my love."

Charlotte smiled. "That I can be!"

CHAPTER 7

APRIL 6, 1816, SELMA PLANTATION, LEESBURG, VIRGINIA

A fire burned gently in the drawing room's fireplace, its dancing flames casting shadows on Armistead's face as he warmed himself. Visions of Mercer's corpulent figure in the Statehouse spewing insults filled his head until his thoughts were interrupted by the rustle of Charlotte's skirts behind him.

"Come and warm yourself by the fire with me," Armistead said, cradling a snifter of brandy in his hand. Charlotte had changed into a simple cotton dress nearly as white as her skin. She tucked her arm through his and nestled close to him. "I had the servants bring you some tea."

"Not now, thank you. How about we sit by the fire and talk for a bit," she suggested.

Armistead closed his eyes momentarily to organize his words, not anticipating how difficult telling Charlotte would be. He put the snifter down and turned to face her. As his eyes met hers, he found himself wanting to take her into his arms, yearning for the comfort of her embrace. He drew a long breath to gather his composure before taking both of her hands in his.

"This evening a friend informed me of slanderous comments made against my character to the Virginia legislature during my election to the Senate. Subsequently, one of these gentlemen and another man made the most vulgar statements impugning my character further, claiming that my promotion in the militia was due to favoritism, that I had cheated in the election for the House of Representatives last year, that I was condescending, and numerous other falsehoods questioning my honor. One of the individuals who said these things was Charles Fenton Mercer, the legislator from Aldie who represents our district here."

Charlotte's eyes widened as he spoke. "Oh my God, Armistead! Such conduct is unfathomable. Why would someone of Mr. Mercer's position say such things?" Charlotte sank onto the settee.

"I have no earthly idea." Armistead's eyes darted across the fire, seemingly searching for the answer in the flames.

"Do you think that perhaps he said these things out of greed?" Charlotte asked. "Because it was your name offered as senator and not his own?" Armistead turned to look at her. "There are many who look at you with envy, my love."

"The vice of greed does not excuse him to impugn my character!"

"Of course not, darling."

"How could Mercer, who pretends to be so honorable, make such declarations that, frankly, reflect his own character more than mine?"

"He cannot legitimately, Armistead."

"Of course he cannot! He, who is so covetous, is the one who used his family connections to get a military commission from the president, yet when granted the favor, refused it." Armistead paced between Charlotte and the fire. "Then he realizes that he cannot win the Federalist party's attention without serving his country, so he begs Governor Barbour for a commission in the militia. And the governor, owing favors to Mercer's uncle, makes him inspector general." He stopped in mid-pace, looking at Charlotte incredulously.

"Inspector general, Charlotte! And even after this appointment, Mercer goes so far as to speak out against war with the British. For heaven knows Fenton Mercer and his monarchist friends do love the British! Or perhaps the appointment was a cover, for certainly an inspector general would never be required to step foot on a battlefield. But worse happens! The coward is asked to command a regiment. And when faced with the prospect of combat, he professes illness to shirk his duty. Charlotte, you should have seen the state of that regiment when I relieved him of his command. Ill-equipped and ill-prepared, and not an ounce of discipline in the camp." Armistead resumed his pacing.

"I remember from your letters, but I didn't realize it was Mr. Mercer," Charlotte said quietly.

"Cockburn and the British Navy were wreaking havoc on the Chesapeake. Then, after we beat them back at Craney Island, I had to use all my resources and all my efforts not only to resupply my own regiment but to restore order to his."

"I remember, darling," Charlotte said, her fingers mindlessly touching the lace at the neckline of her dress.

"For weeks I had to command both regiments while Mercer was home with malaria. Malaria!" Armistead nearly shouted the word as he threw a hand into the air. "We all had malaria! I, too, was sick from it. But I fought through it, as we all did. If it didn't kill you, you stayed with your men. But not Fenton Mercer. He went home. And do you know what, Charlotte?"

"No, what, darling?"

"They rewarded Charles Fenton Mercer for his cowardice. The governor promoted him because he felt sorry for him. And afterward, Mercer had the audacity to complain that it should have been he, not I, who was awarded major general. Can you believe it, Charlotte? Can you believe it?!" Armistead's eyes were bulging from their sockets, and the pulse on his temple was visibly throbbing.

Charlotte, too, appeared aggravated, color rising on her pale face.

"It was my regiment, under my command, that stopped the British at Craney Island and saved Norfolk from certain annihilation. My regiment that defended Baltimore at Hampstead Hill the following year. My men who chased the British through Godley Wood on their retreat to the sea. And now his jealousy has given him the nerve to insult my honor." Armistead stopped in front of Charlotte, his anger in full flow.

"I realize that you are upset, darling, and *rightly so*." There was outrage in Charlotte's voice. "No man has the right to question your honor or slander your character or the character of your family." Charlotte stood from the settee with crossed arms, pacing a few steps before turning. "I have a thought, Armistead. A way to prove his cowardice. Only an honorable man has the character to either stand behind his words or apologize for them. But a coward—a coward will deny them. A coward has not the courage to account for his words or take action." Charlotte bit her lip. "Provide Mr. Mercer the opportunity to either deny or admit his actions."

"And what if he does have the courage to admit his slander, but provides neither adequate explanation for his words nor an apology?"

"If he is of weak character, as you suspect, he will not admit to the blasphemous language." Charlotte drew a long, hesitant breath. "While I have no desire to suffer any further loss in my life, I cannot stand silent while this coward insults you and jeopardizes our family's future with his slander. You must demand an explanation or an apology."

Armistead listened intently as she spoke. "You understand, Charlotte, that such a demand might require that I call Mercer out."

Charlotte understood his meaning, for to call out another gentleman was to challenge him to a duel. "I have no cause for concern, darling." Her gaze filled with intensity as she fixed her eyes on his. "A coward, given a choice between his hide and his pride, will choose his hide every time."

CHAPTER 8

APRIL 7, 1816, MERCER HOUSE, ALDIE, VIRGINIA

Jack woke up with the sun on his face and a hot fire in his head. *How many whiskeys did I drink last night?* By the pounding in his head, he had clearly had too many. He rolled over to escape the burning rays streaming through the window. Deciding to stay in bed, he pulled the quilt to his chin and closed his eyes. *No! Sally is here.* In his mind, he could hear Sally's scolding: *"There's enough time to sleep in your grave, John McCarty!"* He opened his eyes. *Fine then, I'll get up.*

Tossing the bed linens aside, Jack lifted his throbbing head from the pillow and pulled himself onto the edge of the mattress. Still wearing his jacket and trousers from the night before, he looked down at his feet. *At least I didn't sleep in my boots.* With what strength he could manage, Jack drew a deep breath and stood. Walking presented a greater challenge as he moved his leaden feet to the washbasin. Scooping the water from the bowl with cupped hands, he splashed the coldness onto his face. He found his face in the mirror. Although he didn't look hungover, his head was telling a different story. He rubbed the icy water on the back of his neck, hoping to ease the pain. It didn't.

As he washed up and changed his clothes, his mind wandered through the foggy events of the night before. His mother had been in rare form, and his brother William looked happier than he had ever seen him. William's happiness, however, hadn't made Jack any happier about the engagement. And there had been his encounter with Miss Lucinda Lee. His mind was racing with lustful thoughts of the lovely Lucy, when he remembered Armistead nearly knocking him over outside the study. The aroma of frying ham wafted up from the kitchen. He checked his watch; it was already half past ten.

In the dining room, Jack found his brothers Edgar and Thomson at the table with Fenton Mercer and a fourth guest, John Randolph, who, from the looks of it, had also spent the night.

Pulling up a chair to the table, Jack noticed a tension in the room. He had no sooner poured himself a cup of coffee than Edgar handed him a letter.

"What's this?" Jack asked.

"I received it this morning from George Rust," said Fenton. "It's from Armistead Mason. We've been discussing what to make of it—and of him."

The men resumed their discussion, while Jack scanned the correspondence.

"What did you supposedly say before the legislature, Fenton?" Jack asked.

"That's the issue," Edgar said with a mouth full of ham, eggs, and biscuit. "Fenton couldn't have participated in Mason's election to the Senate. You weren't in Richmond that day, were you, Fenton?"

"I had better things to do that day than listen to accolades for General Armistead Mason," Fenton said, spitting a tobacco leaf from his tongue onto the floor.

"You see? Fenton wasn't even there," Edgar said again, waving his fork in Jack's direction.

Jack continued reading: "*... compel you to promptly repair the injury you have inflicted on my character and the feelings you have exposed as a result of your inflammatory language and insulting conduct.*" Jack whistled under his breath, reading the words again: "*promptly repair ...*" *Those are fighting words.*

SHARON VIRTS

A woman with a calico turban wrapped around her head, one of the several people enslaved at Aldie, entered from the kitchen carrying a steaming pot of coffee. Jack thanked her as she topped off his cup.

"To be fair," said Fenton, nodding at the woman as she refilled his mug. "It is no secret that I opposed Mason's election to the Senate. But none of the arguments I made privately to my colleagues thwarted the legislature's view of his qualifications. They were hell-bent on electing him, no matter what I or anyone else said."

"I can't fathom how they came to the decision to elect him," Randolph said, picking at a biscuit. "Even by Republican standards, he is radical and reckless."

"My objection," said Fenton, "had nothing to do with the fact that he's a Republican, nor did it have anything to do with his sympathies for the Quakers. In my opinion, the man is unstable. We've all heard what happened at Norfolk during the last war. And we've all experienced his temper."

"What happened in Norfolk?" Thomson asked as he stopped playing with the eggs on his plate.

"He used some exceedingly harsh punishments at Fort Norfolk, and he ...," Edgar said, looking down at the crumbs he had made on the table. He pushed them over the table's edge, watching them fall onto the floor and shuffling them with his boots. "Armistead ordered the execution of any man who abandoned his post." Edgar lifted his eyes from the floor to Jack and then to the others in the room.

Jack avoided Edgar's glance and pushed the memories from Peach Orchard Camp to the far corner of his mind. He turned to Fenton. "I suggest that you call his bluff. Demand to know what specifically he heard and from whom he heard it."

"That's what we were discussing before you came down, Jack," said Edgar, as the woman in the calico turban reappeared with a platter of fried ham.

Randolph lifted his head and stopped picking at the biscuit. "Exactly how old is Mason? Jack, do you know his age?"

"Armistead is twenty-eight. Why do you ask, sir?"

"No reason in particular," said Randolph, lightly rubbing his fore-finger around the rim of the plate. "I simply find it interesting that one who is so young can be so highly acclaimed."

"Due to his late father's memory, Armistead has been offered many opportunities that others must earn on their own merit," said Jack, taking a bite of the ham. "That's how many of us see it, sir."

"That's how I see it, too, Jack," Fenton said as he pushed away from the table and stood. "I'd like to think about my reply further before responding. John and I are traveling to George Town tomorrow, where we plan to stay for a few weeks. John, would you be so kind as to assist me in drafting my response?"

John Randolph moved his attention from the rim of the plate to Fenton and smiled. "I would be more than happy to oblige, my friend, more than happy."

CHAPTER 9

APRIL 10, 1816, COTON FARM, LEESBURG, VIRGINIA

"Miss Lucinda," said a voice from the hallway. Lucinda glanced up from her reading. Mr. Deese, a middle-aged Scotsman hired by her mother to assist in managing the estate, was standing just outside the door. "You have a caller."

Lucinda beckoned him to enter and took the ivory card from his hand. *John Mason McCarty, Esquire.* She dropped her hand into her lap, still holding the card, and turned to the window. *Why, Lucinda? Why did you approach him?* She exhaled a frustrated sigh and stared over the river to the fields in the distance. *The morning after the British burned Washington City, that's why!*

Two summers before, Lucinda had heard the pounding of cannons and the scream of rockets in the distance. That night, fires glowed red beyond her window as Washington City burned. The next morning, Lucinda had been watching the black smoke billow on the horizon when she spotted an army fast approaching from across the river. Having heard the horrors of what British soldiers and their mercenaries had done to the women of Hampton, Lucinda had been terrified. She and her sisters huddled in her bedroom behind a locked and barricaded door, peeking through the shutters, watching the army advance. Her mother had ordered every one of Coton's enslaved into the manor house and armed each with whatever tool might serve as a weapon to defend against what Fannie Carter Lee was certain was a British invasion. Fannie, too, had taken up arms to defend her home and her daughters. Holding a loaded musket, she had positioned herself in a chair by the front door, ready to shoot any redcoat who dared to enter.

Lucinda had seen it first. It started as a golden flicker above the river. The pole grew taller and taller, but its drapery lay still as its bearer struggled up the embankment. Then a breeze stirred, rustling its folds open. As the breeze picked up, a starry field of blue cloth rippled in the wind above stripes of red and white. Lucinda screamed at the top of her lungs, "It's the militia, Mother! It's our militia!" The events of the remainder of that morning were a blur. That is, until Lieutenant John Mason McCarty walked through the doors of Coton's manor house.

Her mother welcomed the Fifty-Sixth Regiment to Coton Farm with the utmost Southern hospitality. She ordered the enslaved to prepare a feast of fried chicken, biscuits, and gravy to feed the weary and battered men. Hosting the officers in the dining room, Fannie brought out her finest Canton china on which her daughters served ham and biscuits. Lucinda had already known Jack McCarty for a number of years, but it was that day she could not get out of her head. His face was tanned by the sun and smudged with marks of battle. He had blood on his shirt that he said wasn't his own. When she poured him coffee, he touched her arm, stirring something within her. He lifted his face, smiling as his gaze met hers. And his eyes—they were haunting and kind and the palest blue she had ever seen.

Lucinda shook her head again, interrupting the warm feelings creeping into her chest. She knew all about men like Jack McCarty, she told herself, and her exchange with him at the party at Raspberry Plain had confirmed it. She'd witnessed her sisters' hearts being torn apart by too many of them. Men like Jack McCarty cared more about the thrill of the chase than the prize itself. Once he caught his quarry, the appeal would be gone, his interest lost, and his attention would move elsewhere. But Lucinda Lee was not any woman. She was too clever to let a man like Jack McCarty distract her from her dreams.

"Thank you, Mr. Deese. I will take it from here."

With the card in hand, Lucinda rose from the chair and headed to the sitting room where her mother was arranged on a floral settee with a skein of fabric on her lap. Fannie looked up from her needlework, peering at her daughter above a pair of wire-framed spectacles.

"There's a gentleman here to see me, Mother. Would you receive him and turn him away?"

Her mother furrowed her brow. "Why is it that you refuse to allow gentlemen to call on you?"

"I allow Hank Carter to call on me."

"Yet you have professed no interest in courtship with Hank Carter."

Lucinda released an exasperated sigh. "Would you just tell the gentleman at the door that I am not at home?"

"Lucinda, I simply don't understand what harm there is—"

"I just don't want to give him the wrong impression," Lucinda said, interrupting the lecture.

Her mother narrowed her eyes and put the fabric aside. "How is allowing a gentleman to call on you giving him the wrong impression?" Her mother was scolding her now. "You need to find yourself a husband, Lucinda."

Lucinda rolled her eyes. "Please, Mother, just ask him to leave, would you?" Lucinda pushed the calling card into her mother's hand.

Her mother sighed. With a shake of her head, she moved her eyes to the card. As she read the name, her face tensed and the muscles at her jawline twitched.

"I will take care of it, darling."

Lucinda was confused. Where were her mother's usual protracted defenses of the caller, pointing out the good family the gentleman came from, how well his farm was faring, what fine children he might give her, or some other attribute worthy of Lucinda's consideration?

"Seriously, Mother? You will turn him away?"

"Of course, darling. Now get back to your reading or whatever it was you were doing. I'll take care of it momentarily."

Lucinda lifted her skirts and walked across the room to leave. She stopped in the doorway and turned to face her mother, who was still staring at the card in her hand. "Do you know something about him, Mother?"

Her mother lifted her eyes. "I know the family, as do you. But I can't say I know this boy."

Lucinda nodded, not certain she believed her. "All right then. Thank you, Mother."

Fannie offered her daughter a weak smile. "You are welcome, my child."

As Lucinda disappeared into the hall, Fannie abstractedly rubbed her finger across the engraved lettering of the card in her hand. *John Mason McCarty.* She thought a minute to recall what Polly Mason had said about him. *Barmaids, brothels, and brawls.*

Lucinda certainly didn't need such a reputation, no matter how much wealth Sally McCarty's son had. Her daughter had enough challenges with her headstrong ideas and spirited notions.

Fannie reached for the lace cap with its obscuring veil to conceal the smallpox scars that had disfigured her face more than thirty years before. With the calling card in hand, she rose from the chair and headed toward the stairs.

Standing near the door of the foyer was a young man with dark, windblown hair in a tanned leather overcoat that hung below the tops of his brown suede boots. He wore a deep-blue coat with an ivory linen shirt and waistcoat over chestnut-brown trousers. Fannie was taken aback when she saw the angular lines of his face—the aquiline nose, high cheekbones, dimpled chin, and his pale-blue eyes. He was more handsome than she had expected.

"My apologies, Mr. McCarty, but Miss Lucinda is not at home," Fannie said through thin lips that disappeared with her smile.

"Not at home?" Jack asked with a puzzled look.

Fannie walked toward him with her arm extended and forced the card into his hand.

"Not at home. Surely you understand." The boy would understand all too well that a returned calling card meant that Lucinda did not want him to call on her again.

Fannie saw the disappointment on Jack's face as he took the card and put it back into his pocket. She smiled again as she politely showed him the door.

"If Miss Lucinda should change her mind—" he started.

"I can assure you that she won't."

CHAPTER 10

With the wind in his hair and reins firmly in his grip, Jack spurred his Appaloosa, Dove, to a canter. *Lucinda Lee!* The chill of the spring air seemed to cut to his bones as the mare sped across the floodplain along the Potomac River.

How could she refuse me? James Dulaney had shared salacious details of a stroll he'd had a few weeks earlier with the brunette sister Fanny. James's boasting had further fueled Jack's fantasies of Lucinda, and all week Jack had been looking forward to seeing her.

From Coton Farm, Jack headed south along the river to his newly inherited lands. The property was not at all how he remembered it from when the lands were first promised to him. They had seemed to be vast open spaces with streams and tributary access to a great wide river. While the acreage was just as large and impressive as ever, the opportunities he had dreamt of as a boy were limited when viewed through the eyes of a man.

His plan had been to build a mill—like Fenton had at Aldie, a mill that would be a center of commerce—and possibly even a village or a town. His village. His town. But he knew now that the river's tributaries, prone to uncontrolled runoff, were unable to support a mill's paddle wheel. And the river, situated as it was above the great falls, was unnavigable, eliminating all opportunities for shipping or barging. And though the islands in the river belonged to the estate, flooding prevented them from serving any useful purpose. His dreams seemed impossible.

Jack's thoughts returned to Lucinda. The more he thought about her, the more he fumed. *Not only did she refuse to receive me, she returned my card!*

Jack halted the mare and dismounted, his boots sinking into the river delta. He reached down and picked up a clod of earth. It was black and rich and ideal for farming. "Farming!" he said aloud with an exasperated sigh. Farming would mean transferring enslaved field hands from Cedar Grove, hiring overseers and managers—all things that meant being anchored by responsibility. It meant his dependency on the land and the dependency of people who worked the land upon him. Jack threw the clod across the field. *How can I be the best at something that I know nothing about?*

Jack pushed the fingers of both hands through his hair and interlocked them on the top of his head. Turning in a full circle, he scanned the floodplain as his frustration mounted. Perhaps he could divide the land for rent, but more outbuildings would need to be built, more barns, more dwellings. *More dependency.* Industry, trade, land prospecting, and the building of towns interested Jack—anything but planting. Yet planting seemed his only option. He threw his hands up into the air before kicking at the ground. His thoughts wandered back to Lucinda.

What had she said? "Are you going to be a planter-politician like the rest of them?" He had followed her eyes across the room as she scanned the gentlemen wearing their finest coats and cravats. *I am not like them, Lucinda! And why in the world do I care what you think?* He kicked the ground again and sent a small stone flying.

Jack pulled himself back into the saddle and spurred the mare to start. *By God, I am a McCarty! Daniel McCarty's son. The grandson of George Mason IV. Isn't that enough?* He turned the mare toward the road to Alexandria.

At a modest clapboard ordinary where the road to George Town intersected with the road to Alexandria, Jack changed his plans. Instead of a quiet supper at Cedar Grove with his mother, he needed a night of drinking and fornication. He turned the mare due east toward the falls and the bridge below that led to the comfort of the bars and brothels of George Town's waterfront.

CHAPTER 11

APRIL 20, 1816, GEORGE TOWN, DISTRICT OF COLUMBIA

"Sir, there's a gentleman for you at the door," said the butler, handing Armistead a calling card. Armistead, recognizing the name, glanced through the window for confirmation. Standing in the doorway of his uncle's George Town home was a diminutive gentleman with spindly legs and a long, beaky nose.

Good God! What does he want?

"Don't invite him in just yet. I'll receive him as I leave for the Capitol," said Armistead.

He grabbed his cloak and satchel and prepared himself to deal with the impertinence on the front porch. When he opened the door, John Randolph of Roanoke was standing on the stoop holding a sealed communication.

"Good morning, Congressman," Armistead said as he closed the door behind him. "What brings you to my doorstep on such a fine spring day?"

"I have a communication from Mr. Charles Fenton Mercer that requires your immediate attention." Randolph's voice was high-pitched, his coat bright purple and ill-fitting.

"Thank you, Mr. Randolph," said Armistead as he plucked the letter from Randolph's crooked fingers. "Tell Mr. Mercer that I shall give it my attention this evening after today's Senate meeting is adjourned."

"Mr. Mercer had expected that you would attend to his correspondence immediately."

"I am not responsible for managing Mr. Mercer's expectations. Am I, sir? You can inform Mr. Mercer that I will respond to his correspondence with the same courtesy he paid mine. Now, if you will excuse me."

Armistead could see color rising in Randolph's face as he stuffed the letter into his pocket. Pushing past him, Armistead quickly made his way to his coach waiting on the street. Mercer had taken weeks to respond to Armistead and now had the audacity to send Randolph to bully him into an instant reply. The thought of being intimidated by the likes of Randolph, a man half his size, was laughable. Armistead scoffed under his breath as he climbed into the coach and shut the door behind him.

Armistead's carriage lurched and started down High Street. He waited until they had turned onto Bridge Street toward Rock Creek before he pulled the letter from his pocket. Breaking the wax seal from the wrapping, Armistead unfolded the parchment to read Mercer's long-awaited response.

Sir,

I can only assume that your accusation that I insulted your character—without the slightest indication of what I supposedly said—is a deliberate attempt to provoke me. As a result of the aggression displayed in your correspondence, I refuse to reestablish any friendly relations with you until you provide the specific slanderous language that I purportedly said.

Armistead looked out the coach's window. *Friendly relations? As if I care! He doesn't have the courage to admit his blasphemy.* Turning his attention back to the correspondence, he continued reading.

I demand that you make known the name of the individual who has spread such falsehoods and malignity. Notwithstanding the above, I can assure you that I made no injurious comments regarding your character to the General Assembly, as I did not participate

*in your election to the Senate, nor was I present in the General
Assembly of the Virginia legislature on the day of your election.
C. F. Mercer*

He read the last line a second time. *"Nor was I present on the day of
your election."*

"You know full well you said what Em overheard!" Armistead
fumed aloud as the coach passed the blackened shell of marble and
stucco remains of the Capitol that the British had burned two years
before. *She has no motive to lie!* he reasoned. But did Mercer say those
things openly in the General Assembly before the election or in private?
There was no way to know for certain. And he couldn't disclose his
source: his sister, and a woman to boot. And there was also his promise
not to involve William. Mercer had boxed him in.

Armistead crumpled the correspondence in his fist, closed his
eyes, and exhaled a long, defeated sigh. As difficult as it would be to
draft, Armistead had no option but to write a letter taking Mercer at
his word. He would offer no apology but let the matter go for now.
And never again would he underestimate the perfidiousness of Charles
Fenton Mercer.

CHAPTER 12

OCTOBER 26, 1816, ST. JAMES EPISCOPAL
CHURCH, LEESBURG, VIRGINIA

"And you are certain that you want to go through with this?" said Jack, without moving his eyes from the gallery of guests that had filled the church.

"I've never been so sure of anything in my life," said William, as the two stood at the altar in matching red tailcoats, ivory shirts and ivory breeches, and black, pin-striped waistcoats with black cravats tied around their necks. William scanned his brother, from his neatly combed hair to his polished black boots. "You clean up well, Jack. You should try it more often."

"It's my gift to you on your wedding day."

The guests, too, were dressed in their finest as they packed the church's pews, awaiting the start of the ceremony. Their mother sat in the front row on the left, Thomson on one side and Edgar and his wife Peggy on the other. Sally looked like sunshine, lovely as always, in yellow silk and wearing a large hat that radiated like sunbeams in a cloudless sky. Behind them sat his sister Nancy and her family. Polly Mason was across the aisle, sitting with her daughter Catherine and son-in-law from Kentucky and Armistead's fiancée.

As the organist played "The Prince of Denmark's March," friends and family quieted in eager anticipation of the procession. Jack adjusted his cravat and glanced over at William.

"Last chance to make your escape," Jack said under his breath.

"She is my escape."

Jack followed his gaze to the back of the church. Dressed in a silver lama gown trimmed with glistening lace, the maid of honor appeared in the doorway. Blonde and petite with plump lips, she was holding a nosegay of white chrysanthemums as she walked down the aisle. Jack had difficulty finding his breath. The maid of honor was Lucinda Lee.

When the bride appeared on the arm of her brother, all eyes in the church turned to the back of the room. All eyes but Jack's. His were focused on Lucinda as she took her place on the other side of the altar. When her eyes caught his, he smiled at her and winked. A blush rose to Lucinda's cheeks and she shifted her gaze to Emily and Armistead advancing down the aisle.

The bride, her hair swept back from her face in long ringlets under a silver lace cap and netted veil adorned with pearls, was radiant. Her gown was also silver lama over a tissue slip and cut low on the bosom, its bodice and skirt embroidered with ivory shells, pearls, and silk flowers of silver, gray, and white. The sleeves were embroidered and trimmed in finepoint Brussels lace. Unlike Lucinda, Emily wore a manteau of glimmering silk lined in white satin over the ensemble, fastened at the neck with a diamond pin that glittered like moonlight on the evening tide. Watching the exchange of glances between the bride and his brother, Jack felt an awkward warmth. For the first time he understood what William meant when he said that he had never been so sure of anything. His brother genuinely loved her.

When Armistead and Emily reached the altar, Armistead extended his hand to William. "Take good care of her, Captain. That's all I ask."

William nodded and shook Armistead's hand. "You have my word, General."

Moving Emily's hand to William's, Armistead kissed his sister's cheek. "Be happy always, Em."

Emily's eyes were glistening with joyful tears. "Oh, Armie, I am!"

As Armistead retired to sit with his mother and fiancée, the bride and groom turned to face the rector. He explained God's purpose for matrimony, charged the bride and groom to confess any impediment that might prevent them from being married, and asked the witnesses to speak now or forever hold their tongues should they know of any reason why the two should not wed. As they exchanged vows—to have and to hold from this day forward ... thereto I plight thee my troth—it was William's promise when he placed the gold-and-diamond ring on Emily's finger that stirred Jack's emotion. It started as a tingling in his toes that moved like birds in flight through his legs, gut, and chest.

"... and with my body I thee worship, and with all my worldly goods I thee endow." Water welled in William's eyes as he spoke. Watching his brother make the solemn vow, Jack's eyes caught Lucinda's once more. The birds in his chest soared higher as warmth rushed over him again. As much as he wanted to turn his gaze from her, he could not. There was something more to her than her beauty—something behind her eyes.

CHAPTER 13

OCTOBER 26, 1816, RASPBERRY PLAIN

The Great Hall, parlor, and drawing and dining rooms of Raspberry Plain were overflowing with flowers, fruits, and the scents of autumn: chrysanthemums and cattails, goldenrod and bittersweet, branches of birch and fronds of pine, sunflowers and Spanish nettle, asters and apples, and the spices of mulled cider. Yet all Lucinda Lee could smell was Jack McCarty, a combination of horse and handsome that was intoxicating—the worn leather of a saddle, the earthiness of the forest floor, the wildness of a young colt. The scent of him was unforgettable.

During the dance of the wedding party, Lucinda was able to avoid Jack's eyes, but she was completely unable to avoid the smell of him as they waltzed together across the floor of the parlor. After completing the first figure of duple minor steps, Jack pulled Lucinda close and whispered in her ear. "I do believe that I am the luckiest man in all of Virginia, Miss Lucinda."

"And how is that, Mr. McCarty?"

"Because I have the most beautiful angel in my arms."

"I do believe your brother would disagree with you."

Jack placed his strong hand at the small of Lucinda's back and turned her. As they began to move through the second set of figures in the dance with William and Emily, Jack pulled her close again. His exhilarating presence filled her senses.

"Beauty is in the eye of the beholder, and I behold you as the most beautiful." Jack attempted to catch her gaze, but she refused to submit.

In the third procession of the dance, however, he caught her glance. The sincerity in his eyes—those muted tarns of blue—was magnetic. An excitement erupted within her as their gazes met.

"Allow me to call on you, Lucy. Allow me to show you what you are searching for."

"And what might that be, Mr. McCarty?" Lucinda asked, unable to remove her focus from him.

"My utmost admiration." He gave her a smile that dimpled his cheeks and took her breath away.

As the final exchange of the dance began, he held her close, twirling her through the last of the steps. His magnetism pulled her. When the dance ended, the couples bowed to each other and then to the applauding guests. Jack smiled at Lucinda appreciatively. She forced her breathing to steady and smiled back.

"Would you join me in the next dance, Miss Lucinda?" Jack asked with a gracious bow, her hand still in his.

"I would be most delighted. Perhaps later?" she said, turning her attention to the blond gentleman in a blue tailcoat and mustard-colored breeches who was approaching. She pulled her hand from Jack's and offered it to the newcomer. "Mr. McCarty, you and Mr. Carter are acquainted, I'm sure," she said, introducing the two.

"Indeed, we are," Jack said with a gracious bow. "Mr. Carter, I must admit that I am finding it difficult to give her up."

Jack leaned toward Lucinda's ear. "I shall claim that dance later." He pulled away with a flirty wink before excusing himself. She struggled to keep a smile from her face.

The swagger in his stride and the strength of his shoulders under his crimson-tailed coat caught Lucinda's attention as he left the room. She shook her head to rid her mind of the visual, but the smell of him lingered. Not only was he handsome and charming, he was smart and quick-witted. But it was his authenticity that captivated her. And that's what made him so incredibly interesting and so terribly dangerous.

CHAPTER 14

What could Lucinda Lee possibly see in a prat like Hank Carter? Jack thought as he left the parlor. Despite his resolve not to pursue her, he felt more captivated by her than ever.

Jack sauntered down the corridor for a glass of the rye whiskey that the Masons kept in the study. At the sound of Armistead's voice booming from inside, he halted just outside the door.

"Picking off Lewis will be like shooting a duck on a still pond. A religious man like Jonathan Heaton will defeat him decidedly. Why, there's not a merchant in Prince William or Loudoun who won't vote for Jon once they learn of his moral principles. And once we get a Quaker in the House of Representatives, he and I can build a coalition of support in both chambers of Congress and get the votes needed for my amendments to the militia bill to become law."

"But a Quaker, General?" said a gentleman with a deep, rugged voice who sounded to Jack like Colonel George Rust. "How can a Quaker win the trust of the freeholders to represent them in Congress?"

"We'll present to the public that he's a God-fearing man, which is more than can be said for Joe Lewis." Laughter erupted in the room. "I'm telling you, gentlemen, this Compensation Act is the end of Federalist rule in this district. Joe Lewis giving himself a raise has put the last nail in their coffin, and Dr. Jonathan Heaton is just the man to swing the hammer!"

Although Jack knew that Joe Lewis had agreed to retire his seat, he saw no reason to alert the Republicans that the intellectually unmatched Fenton Mercer would be the candidate campaigning against Dr. Heaton. Jack drew a long breath. Straightening his shoulders, he gathered his composure and entered the room.

"Good afternoon, gentlemen," Jack said, striding into the study with his head held high.

"Captain McCarty!" said Armistead, leaning against his father's desk. "Or perhaps I should now call you brother-in-law."

"Brothers-in-law, indeed!" said Jack with an extended hand. "Congratulations, sir, on the marriage of your sister."

"And to you and the good fortune of your brother," said Armistead as the two shook hands. "Would you like to join us, Captain? We were just discussing politics, a subject I know that you enjoy."

"While I appreciate the offer, General, I must decline. You see, there is a lovely lady in the parlor to whom I promised a dance before dining. I just came for a little of that rye whiskey you keep in here."

"I see. Well, one must never keep a lovely lady waiting long," Armistead said with a grin. "The rye is right over there." He gestured behind him toward the credenza. "Help yourself!"

"Thank you, General."

"You are welcome, lad," Armistead said and turned his attention back to his friends.

"Lad?" Jack turned toward the credenza, his mouth tightening over clenched teeth. *Mind yourself,* he cautioned himself as he struggled to push his annoyance aside. He drew a silent breath and poured himself a drink.

"Good day, gentlemen," Jack said as he made his way toward the door and left the room. As he turned the corner into the hallway, William's new bride was walking toward him.

"Mr. McCarty," Emily said. "I thought I might find you here."

"It sounds like you were looking for me."

"In fact, I was. I would like to speak with you."

"Perhaps we could step out onto the veranda?"

"There's no need for privacy. What I have to say, I can say openly."

"What is it, Miss Emily?"

"Emily will do. Or just Em."

Jack nodded. "All right, then. Emily."

Emily drew a quick breath. "I sense that you do not approve of this union between me and William, but I want you to know how much I love your brother. And how much he loves me—"

"It's not that I don't approve—"

"Now, now, Mr. McCarty," she said with frowning brows. "You must pause to allow me to say what it is I sought you out to say. And when I am finished, you will have your turn."

Jack was taken aback, unaccustomed to such abruptness from a woman. "I apologize for my interruption. And, please, call me Jack."

"All right, Jack. What I am trying to say is that William and I are now a family. And I know how important family is to him—and he cares about you very much. That means that I care about you, too." She lowered her eyes before bringing them back to him. "A year ago, my brother Stevens died. With his passing I lost a part of my heart. My hope is that I can fill that hole with love for you and your family. I know that you and William have lost parts of your hearts with the passing of so many of your brothers. And I cannot expect in any way to fill that void for you. But I can hope that you will accept me into your family with open arms."

Having lost six of his brothers, Jack, too, knew the void that she had spoken of. "Of course I will. You are the woman who brings a shine to my brother's eyes. Please know that I have no quarrel with you, Emily."

"But you do with my brother, Armistead." Jack's eyes darted away from her for a moment. He said nothing. "It's all right, Jack. I know how Armie can seem. But most men hide behind a facade of some sort. While on the outside Armistead can be"—she paused as she searched for the right word—"rigid, on the inside, I can assure you, he is a caring, sweet man."

Jack all but scoffed aloud. "I'm not sure 'sweet' is a term I would use to describe your brother."

Emily drew a long breath. "My desire is for you to see him through my eyes. I know that if you give him a chance, you will come to love him, too."

"I think 'love' is a far reach, Emily."

She gave a frustrated sigh. "All right, then. Maybe you'll come to like him?" Emily's eyes pleaded with his.

"I will do my best to maintain friendly relations with him. How's that?" Jack offered a thin smile.

"Wonderful!" she said, her eyes wide and her voice excited. "That's all I can ask—your willingness to give it your best effort." Emily leaned forward and kissed him on the cheek. "Thank you, my brother! Oh, how nice it is to call you that!"

CHAPTER 15

DECEMBER 2, 1816, MCLEOD'S TAVERN, WASHINGTON CITY, DISTRICT OF COLUMBIA

At a table in the far corner of the room with his back against the wall, James Barbour, the former governor and now the senior senator from Virginia, sat across from Armistead. With a heavy brow over deep-set eyes and a hawk-like nose, James's powerful features more closely resembled those of an ancient Roman gladiator than a member of Virginia's gentry.

"How is the construction on the new dwelling coming along?" Armistead asked, as the tavern's owner delivered plates heaped with roasted meat and root vegetables to the table.

"The architecture has proven difficult," James said as he drove his fork into the pile of potatoes on his plate, "and with the erratic weather this past year, it's been slow."

"I feel your frustration, friend. In my experience, construction is never-ending." Armistead lifted his glass and washed a mouthful of supper down with wine.

The two Virginia senators shared their vexation at building and managing their estates while the conversation at other tables whirred around them. As the last of the wine was poured, James surveyed the surrounding tables with his dark eyes.

"Armistead, I need to talk with you about two very important matters." James leaned forward and lowered his voice. "We have it on good authority that Joe Lewis is not seeking reelection to represent your district in the House of Representatives."

"I am not surprised at all." Armistead flashed a confident smile before taking another drink from his glass. "Lewis must have realized that his vote for the Compensation Act was a death knell for his reelection. We certainly knew such a self-serving law would inflame the voters, especially after the devastating weather this year."

"Rumors are that the Federalists are presenting Fenton Mercer as their candidate for Lewis's seat in the eighth district." James shifted in his chair and leaned farther on the table. "This presents us with an interesting dilemma and the second issue I need to speak with you about."

Armistead narrowed his eyes. "Concerning Mercer?"

"No. Concerning you."

"Me?"

James nodded and sat back in his chair. All day James had dreaded this conversation. But the Democratic Republican Party leadership—Mr. Jefferson, the former president, and Andrew Stephenson, the Speaker of Virginia's House of Delegates—had insisted that he be the one to tell Armistead of their decision. James drew a long breath. "The party wants you to run against Mercer."

"Me? Jonathan Heaton is campaigning as the Republican candidate for the eighth district."

"Against Lewis."

"Against whomever the Federalists offer."

James narrowed his eyes. "Do you honestly think a Quaker is electable against Fenton Mercer?"

"Do you honestly think I would give up my seat in the Senate for one in the House?"

"No." James inhaled sharply. "That is exactly what I told Stephenson. Then he reminded me that you are filling the remainder of Senator Giles's term, a term that expires in April. And since the constitutional requirement for the election of a senator is thirty years of age, you do not qualify. According to Stephenson, the legislature simply cannot reappoint you to a second term."

"That's preposterous! Stephenson knew my age when I was elected last year. Why is this an issue now?" Color was rising on Armistead's face.

"I know this is not what you expected. And I've gone so far as to talk with Mr. Jefferson on your behalf. But he agrees with Stephenson. They want you in the House. And if you take a moment and think about it, you will agree that you are the ideal candidate to run against Mercer. Mercer has no federal legislative experience. You do."

"And if I refuse?" Armistead's mouth was tight, his jaw twitching.

James let out a long sigh. "Look, Armistead. The party expects you to run against Mercer and claim that seat for the Republicans. That is the priority. And I have assurances that you will be rewarded for your efforts."

"Rewarded how?" Armistead's voice was devoid of emotion.

"Campaign against Mercer and win that seat, and we will do all we can to assure that the legislature elects you as the next governor of Virginia."

A long minute passed. "It's not as if I have a choice, now, is it?"

"It's your path to the governor's office, Armistead. And frankly, I hope it's one you will take."

"I'll take it under advisement." Armistead pushed back his plate.

Satisfied that Armistead understood what was expected, James picked up his fork to finish off the last of the roasted meat. He raised his eyes from his supper to find Armistead's gaze fixed upon him.

James shuddered. The cold look in Armistead's eyes brought memories of Hampton and the summer of 1813 flooding forward. *What atrocities!* James could see the singed eyes of those officers who had witnessed the civilian carnage in Hampton. *Major Rust, Captain Osbourne, Captain Mains.* Yet they had kept silent about Armistead's role. James lowered his gaze to his plate at the thought of the British soldiers shot with their hands in the air at Armistead's order. And it was the innocents of Hampton who had paid the steep price. James glanced back at Armistead, whose icy eyes were still fixed upon him. Having lost his appetite, James rearranged the remaining vegetables with his fork, unable to forget that summer and Armistead's dark, chilling stare.

CHAPTER 16

MARCH 20, 1817, LEESBURG, VIRGINIA

The town was still brown with winter, but the sky was warm with spring as the March sun cast its rays through the bare branches of the oaks overhead. The streets were teeming with townspeople from across the county who were browsing wares on display outside merchant shops. Across the way in the courtyard, dozens of men were milling about as they talked and laughed and ignored the gentleman on the top step of the courthouse professing the accolades of General Armistead Mason, the Democratic Republican candidate vying for the eighth district's seat in the House of Representatives.

Jack, too, was only half listening to Dr. Jonathan Heaton's sermon when his eyes fixed on a pretty blonde standing alone under the colonnade of the inn on the north side of the courthouse. Her fair hair, most of which was tucked under a white bonnet, caught the sunlight and illuminated her head like the halo of a celestial being. She wore a yellow pelisse trimmed in gold cording, which added to her overall divine impression. As he squinted in the morning light to see more clearly, Jack's stomach stirred with excitement. Picking his way through the thawing mud of the street, he settled against a wall just behind her and watched her while she listened to the speech. When Dr. Heaton finished his lesson on the merits of military substitutions for conscientious objectors, Jack caught her attention.

"Good morning, Miss Lucinda."

"Why, Jack McCarty!" Lucinda said, turning toward him. "It seems you have finally found me!"

Jack was surprised she was so forthcoming about having avoided him for months now.

"So, you admit that you have been deliberately hiding from me!"

"Well now, sir, had I been deliberately hiding from you, you would still be looking for me." Lucinda laughed, extending a hand. He took it and kissed it lightly. She held fast to his fingers. "No fresh-Jack-McCarty today? Or is a leather glove too much of an encumbrance?"

"No encumbrance at all, Miss Lucinda." Jack took her hand again to kiss it more slowly before moving it to his cheek.

Lucinda smiled at him appreciatively. "Now, that's the Jack McCarty I remember!"

"So, what brings you here? A pretty girl like you should not be out here all alone."

Lucinda gave an exaggerated look around the courtyard. "I am hardly alone here, Mr. McCarty. Half the county folk are here, at least the liberal-minded ones."

"Excuse me, but I meant that you should have an escort among all these menfolk, and I am more than happy to oblige." Jack bowed and tipped his hat.

Lucinda laughed again. "Oh, what a character you are!" Her face grew more serious, and she touched his arm. "Do you happen to know where it is on the hour? General Mason is supposed to speak at eleven."

Jack pulled his watch from his waistcoat. "It's eleven o'clock now."

"May I?"

Surprised by her interest, he unlinked the watch from his waistcoat and handed it to her. The casing was gold and decorated with jewels surrounding the enameled portrait of a lady in its center.

"It's so heavy." Lucinda turned the watch over in her hand. "And so old."

"It was my father's."

Lucinda brought the watch closer to examine the painting on the case. "Who is this?"

"My grandmother, Sinah Ball. She and General Washington's mother were cousins."

Lucinda ran her finger over the image, studying the face. "She has such forgiving eyes."

Jack, too, had been fascinated by the portrait's eyes. "To me, they've always felt kind."

She nodded as her focus on the portrait intensified. "An heirloom?"

"Of sorts, I suppose. My father gave it to me before he died. To remember him by. Frankly, I don't remember much of him, as I was not yet six years old when he passed."

There was a sudden sadness on her face. "I, too, was a young child when my father died and abandoned me." Her eyes met his as she handed the watch to him.

As he reattached the watch to the chain on his waistcoat, he felt a sympathy for her that was surprisingly personal and frighteningly warm.

"So, Miss Lucinda, what is your interest in a speech on the conscription of soldiers in the militia?"

"I'm not necessarily interested in the conscription of men in the militia." Jack raised his brow in question. "While I might not have the right of suffrage, I certainly have the right to influence the thinking of those who do."

He was surprised and now intrigued. "And what might that thinking be, Miss Lucinda?"

"I am of a conservative mind, Mr. McCarty. Apparently, just like my father and, although I do not remember his politics, my mother tells me that I share his same passions."

"So how is it that your conservative mind brought you to bear witness to a liberal rally of the Republicans?"

"How else might I learn to distinguish the palate of men of liberal persuasion if I have not tasted for myself the poison they enjoy?"

"An interesting perspective. I, too, am a conservative."

"Well, it looks as if we're about to get an earful of liberalism." Lucinda moved her attention from Jack to the courthouse.

Jack followed her gaze. From the southern edge of the courtyard, General Armistead Mason emerged tall above the crowd. He was in full uniform with shiny buttons and golden epaulets glistening in the morning sunshine as he climbed the stairs to stand between the two center columns. Uncharacteristically, he was hatless, and his auburn hair was cut short and brushed forward.

A hush settled over the townspeople as the statesman smiled broadly at the crowd. A number of townspeople applauded as he flashed his famous, heart-melting grin. The soft applause grew to cheers and shouts in support of the man who many referred to as Leesburg's favorite son.

When the praise of the crowd subsided, Armistead began. "My fellow Loudouners. It was once a high crime in this county for a Republican to ask publicly for your vote, and anyone who was brave enough to do so was met with the foulest abuse. I had hoped that those times were gone. Imagine my disappointment when I returned home from Congress and had barely crossed the threshold of my door to find the most sordid and base misrepresentations of my public conduct, as well as the most unjust and contemptible insinuations regarding my private character."

The crowd erupted in many "ohs" and "nos," along with shuffling and the shaking of heads in opposition to the conduct of those who had attacked their beloved General Mason.

Armistead, in full form, continued. "It is not my intent to respond to that farrago of nonsense and falsehood. And if any man who has the reputation of a gentleman puts his name to an attack upon my character, then I promise to call him out for it."

Although Jack found Armistead's rhetoric irritating, he stood stoic and expressionless as the crowd nodded in agreement and Armistead droned on.

Lucinda leaned close and whispered in a low voice, just loud enough for Jack to hear, "The general is quite charming, isn't he? And so handsome, as well." The corners of her mouth lifted in a slight smile, inciting Jack's annoyance, but he remained silent. "It certainly seems that he has most people convinced."

Jack turned to look at her. "Am I to assume that you are not one of those ladies who bathe in his trail of glory?"

Lucinda scoffed. "Armistead is not all that he seems, Jack. Surely you know that."

"I have my opinions, of course. I'm just surprised at yours."

"I may be alone in my opinions. Every woman I know is enthralled by him. My sister Molly, for one, has been smitten with him for as long as I can remember. Yes, he is the richest man in all of Loudoun County. Yes, he is handsome, charming, and has an impeccable reputation. A general *and* a senator, at that. On the surface, he is kind and beautiful. But that's not what I see." Lucinda looked Jack straight in the eye. "There is something sinister inside that man, Jack. I see it in his eyes every time he looks at me. I realize that you and he are blood relatives, and I pray that you do not harbor the same unwanted guest within you that lives in the soul of Armistead Mason."

Jack returned the intensity of her stare.

"You may be right. There may be something dark within the general that he wishes us not to see. We all have our secrets, Lucy."

"And you, Jack? What secrets might you have?"

"My penchant for pretty girls would be my downfall." Jack gave her a flirty wink, not wanting to discuss Armistead any further.

"And the brothels of George Town, I hear."

Jack placed his opened hand on his chest, feigning injury. "Miss Lucinda, what kind of gentleman do you take me for?"

"I only know what I have heard, Mr. McCarty."

"I can assure you that my reputation is as pure as virgin snow."

"After a few days of melt and mud perhaps." Before Jack could respond, she turned her attention back to Armistead, who seemed to be wrapping up.

"... with this explanation, I leave it to each of you to decide whether the militia bill is better with or without my amendments, and whether I deserve the abuse and denunciations that I have suffered as a result of it. As your humble and obedient servant, may God bless you all."

The crowd erupted in applause, while Armistead smiled broadly and began to shake the hands of the men surrounding him. Jack scoffed to himself and redirected his attention to Lucinda.

"Are you heading back to Coton Farm this afternoon or are you staying here at the inn for the day?"

"I'm meeting my sister in a moment for tea before returning home." Lucinda tilted her head. "The property that you inherited is not far from Coton, is it?"

"Yes, my property is quite near your farm."

"Where exactly is the estate?"

"Coincidentally, the north end of it abuts your south end." Jack managed to keep his amusement from his face.

Lucinda didn't blink. "You don't say, Mr. McCarty. I had no idea that your north end was so close."

"Indeed, it is! Though not as fine as your south end, my north end is quite handsome, if I say so myself." Jack maintained his straight face.

She smiled matter-of-factly. "If it's as handsome as you imply, I'm sure that you must show it off all the time."

"Oh no, Miss. I am too modest to show it to just anyone. But it would be my pleasure to show it to you, if you so desire."

Lucinda struggled to maintain her composure. "I am most certain that the pleasure would only be yours, Mr. McCarty!"

"Now, now, Lucy, you underestimate me! Let me assure you, the pleasure would certainly be yours as well."

Lucinda broke her stoicism with a laugh. "Jack McCarty, you are shameless! You know that, of course. You have absolutely no honor at all!"

"Should I have no honor, as you say, then I am surely cursed to a life of shame."

"Well, shame on me for allowing you to coerce me into such ridiculous discussions." Lucinda laughed again and turned to leave.

Suddenly serious, Jack grasped her arm, his eyes catching hers. "Allow me to call on you, Lucy." In the shade of the bonnet, her eyes looked even bluer, like a mountain lake under a summer sky. "Each time I try, the beautiful Lucinda Lee escapes me. Please, Lucy?"

"You will find me if you try hard enough, Jack."

At her words, the sparkle of her eyes ignited like a blue flame, warming him at once with a heat that rushed through him. "Tell me where to look, Lucy."

Lucinda bit her lip. "There's a dining at my Uncle Ludwell's Saturday after next. Perhaps you'll find me there."

Jack, who foxhunted with his friends at Belmont Plantation on Saturdays, had been invited to the dining but hadn't planned to stay.

"It would be my pleasure to join you at Belmont."

"Of course, I will have to disinvite one of my other suitors to make room for you," she teased, breaking the intensity of his gaze.

"Disinvite them all, as I am more than enough to keep you entertained." A smile that dimpled his cheeks broke over his face.

"We shall see if you live up to your reputation, Mr. McCarty."

"I'll be counting the days until Saturday, Lucy."

Lucinda nodded and picked up her skirts to return to the inn. As she reached the door, she stopped and looked back at him. "I'll be counting them, too."

CHAPTER 17

MARCH 29, 1817, BELMONT PLANTATION, LEESBURG, VIRGINIA

After a morning of hard riding on the hunt with the hounds, Jack and his friend Dr. Cary Selden were sipping on cool juleps as if it were May instead of March. And, as usual, the politics of the impending elections monopolized conversation.

"Armistead's notice in the *Genius of Liberty* newspaper was a blatant attack against Fenton's position on suffrage," Jack said, reclining in the cane rocker on the back porch of the manor house. "And his proposed amendment to the militia bill ..." Jack rolled his eyes. "Preposterous!"

"We both know his true intention," said Cary before taking another drink from the sterling cup holding the whiskey and mint. "To win, he needs to appeal to the Quakers and Dunkards in Loudoun, and the young aristocracy in Fairfax. That is the only reason he is suggesting that those who have not yet inherited their property be afforded the right of suffrage."

"If Armistead and the Republicans have their way, the overseers and the indentured whites will soon be lining up at the hustings to cast their votes!"

"True enough, although Armistead did state that their fathers must hold clear title to 'immovable property' to vote. That's a condition that would certainly disqualify them."

"Does he define immovable property? For all I know it could be a fence post!" Jack added with a chuckle.

"He claims to trust the intelligence of these commoners and says that he is willing to acquiesce to their decisions."

"The day that Armistead Mason acquiesces to a commoner is the day that I eat my hat!"

Cary raised his mug to Jack. "To the consumption of your hat."

"To the hat I will never have to eat!" Jack, raising his cup, clinked it against Cary's.

Both men laughed as servants brought platters of food to tables that had been moved outside for the guests to enjoy the unseasonably warm day. Jack glanced around the yard to see if Lucinda had arrived. There was no sight of her.

"I think it is time, my friend, to dine." Cary pushed himself from the chair and stood.

"I'll catch up with you in a few. I've got to check on something."

"It wouldn't be Lucinda Lee, would it?"

"Perhaps." Jack grinned as he stood from the rocker and headed toward the house.

Jack entered the back hall to make his way to the parlor where guests were congregating. He passed Colonel Ludwell Lee's wife, Flora, in the corridor.

"Pardon me, Miss Flora. Would you know if your niece, Miss Lucinda, has arrived?"

"Why, yes. Miss Lucinda and her sister Miss Fanny arrived a bit ago."

"Do you happen to know where the ladies might be?"

"Last I saw them, they were with the Carter twins out on the north porch. Perhaps you will find them there."

The Carter twins! Jack was more than annoyed. His feelings were injured, and it was all over his face.

Flora smiled sympathetically. "I'm sorry, Jack."

"Nothing you need to apologize for, ma'am. Thank you for letting me know where to find them." Jack turned back down the corridor and went out on the south lawn to join Cary.

The warm weather had caused gentlemen to shed their coats and ladies to open their parasols to shade their heads. Canopies of sailcloth hung above the tables, protecting guests from the midday sun. Helping himself to another julep, Jack scanned the lawn. Squinting through the brightness, he found his friend waving from a table on the west side of the garden.

Much to Jack's surprise, Lucinda was also sitting at the table. With filtered sunlight illuminating her hair and face, she looked stunning in an especially low-cut dress. She was sandwiched between the Carter twins, with her sister Fanny sitting across from her. Jack was hesitant to join them. When she smiled warmly at him, his resolve to snub her was futile.

"We held a seat for you, my friend," Cary said as Jack greeted the group.

"Mr. McCarty, I see you have left that handsome brother of yours at home," Fanny said, offering her hand.

"He is in George Town today. But his loss is surely my gain," Jack said.

"Good day, Mr. McCarty," Lucinda said, smiling as Jack leaned across the table to take her hand. "That's quite all right, Mr. McCarty. There is no need to reach so far."

"There is no distance I would not travel to reach you, Miss Lucinda." Jack took her hand and kissed her in his usual brash fashion.

"Fortunately, you only have a wooden table to traverse this afternoon," she said, the color rising on her face.

"A few planks of wood cannot keep me from you," Jack said, caressing the back of her fingers with his thumb. Mischief returned to her eyes as she pulled her hand from his and tucked it back under the table.

"Did you find what you were looking for, Jack?" asked Cary with a smirk.

"I did indeed, and with a slight surprise," Jack said as a servant placed a plate of hot barbeque in front of him.

"You seem to me to be the type of gentleman who enjoys the suspense of the unknown and the thrill of the unexpected, Mr. McCarty," Lucinda said.

"And she who is so wise, Miss Lee, is full of surprise," Jack said, picking up his fork to dig into the pork on his plate.

Lucinda responded with a glimmer of naughtiness flashing in her eyes. "Agreed, Mr. McCarty. For she is certainly wise who knows it is not the prize but the thrill of the chase that wins the race."

Jack smiled, impressed by her repartee. "Ah, yes, but it is patience that is the conquering virtue."

"Amor vincit omnia," Lucinda recited.

The agility of her mind only further enticed Jack's warm feelings for her. "Alas, love may indeed conquer all, but as I recall, Chaucer compared a woman's love to hell. His words, I believe, were 'to barren land where water will not dwell.'"

Lucinda wasted no time. "As I recall, he also compared a woman's love to a quenchless fire, the more it burns, the more its desire."

Jack grinned from across the table. "And love will find a way, through paths where wolves fear to prey."

"And you know what Lord Byron says about a pathless woods?" Lucinda asked with a knowing smile.

"Indeed, I do! And the pleasure, Miss Lucinda, would be all mine."

The Carter brothers chuckled nervously at each other, confused by the banter between the two.

"Speaking of woods and prey, I hear there was a hunt this morning, Mr. McCarty. Were the hounds lucky?" Fanny asked, shifting attention from her sister.

"Not today," Jack said. "Seems the foxes were too clever."

"Well, good!" said Fanny. "I think the entire sport is just mean and cruel."

She turned her attention to Richard, batting her thick, dark lashes in his direction. "Richard, you don't hunt now, do you?"

"Only when I need to," Richard sputtered.

"And he needs to every Saturday morning!" Hank said with a laugh.

"I'm surprised you gentlemen didn't join us this morning then, it being Saturday and all," said Jack as he took another drink of the julep.

"Well, we would have, but when Miss Lucinda accepted Hank's offer to drive the ladies over in our coach, we decided to pass on the hunt," Richard said, smiling proudly.

Jack glanced across the table at Lucinda with hurt in his eyes, but just as quickly moved his gaze away. "Well, aren't you two the lucky boys, then!"

"Hank and Richard were just being kind. Isn't that right, Hank?" Lucinda said, moving her hand to Hank's sleeve. "As Fanny and I are staying the night here at Uncle Ludwell's, and with Mother having the coach in Richmond, it only made sense that we ride to Belmont with another guest."

Unable to ignore Lucinda's hand resting on Hank's arm, Jack struggled to keep his emotion from his face.

"Just because these nice fellas offered to bring us here in their coach doesn't entitle them to all of our attention," Fanny added, turning to Jack. "And since your brother is not here, I might be persuaded to give you a dance tonight, Mr. McCarty."

Jack directed his attention to Fanny. "I could certainly be persuaded to ask, Miss Fanny."

"And what might persuade you?" she said playfully, batting her eyes all the while.

"I find that nothing arouses my persuasion more than a nice long *stroll*, especially on a lovely day like today," Jack said, using all his charm. "Perhaps Miss Fanny might stroll with me later this afternoon, when the sun is not so high in the sky."

"Why, that is a grand idea!" Fanny smiled contentedly. "And you realize, Mr. McCarty, that there is little I enjoy more than *strolling* on the arm of a dapper gentleman such as yourself."

"You know, it has become quite warm out here with all this hot air blowing about. I think it is time for us ladies to go inside where it's cooler," Lucinda said, rising from the table. "Come, Fanny. Gentlemen, if you'll excuse us."

"It's not that uncomfortable, sister," Fanny said.

"Indeed it is. Come, Fanny, we'll catch up with the gentlemen later, after our rest."

Fanny gave a defeated sigh and stood from her seat. "Fine, then!" She turned to Jack, batting her lashes again. "And I will be expecting that stroll later, Mr. McCarty."

"It will be my pleasure," Jack said. He glanced at Lucinda, catching her eyes just long enough to see the hurt. Turning her back to him, she started for the house with her sister. Jack had expected to feel vindicated by her injury. Instead, as he watched her walk away, he felt a gnawing ache in the pit of his stomach.

"I think she likes you," Cary said in a low voice that only Jack could hear. Jack furrowed his brow and turned to look at him. "You got to her, Jack. And no one gets to Lucinda Lee."

———

As the afternoon wore on, Jack grew increasingly tired of the party at Belmont, and the idea of George Town became more appealing with every sip of his whiskey. Deciding to leave the party early, he sought out the party's host to say his good-byes. Jack found Colonel Ludwell Lee in the library.

"Colonel," Jack said, as the colonel poured himself a drink from a decanter on the credenza, "please extend my appreciation to Miss Flora for her hospitality. I have another engagement this evening that I must attend."

"Leaving already? You know that the best part of the day happens at night!" said the colonel with a playful glimmer in his eyes.

"Indeed it does, sir, but I must be on my way."

"Well, we appreciate that you could join us for the day. And I will see you next Saturday on the hunt." Colonel Lee nodded and returned the stopper to the crystal vessel before leaving the room.

Noticing that there were new books on the shelves since his last visit to Belmont's library, Jack took a quick minute to peruse the titles. On the center shelf he spotted a recently published journal on Lewis and Clark's travels to the source of the Missouri River. Though he was in a hurry to reach George Town before losing the light, the book proved too tempting. Jack opened the cabinet's door and removed it from the shelf. He had dreams of exploring the western territories. In just a few weeks he would be on his way to Kentucky and down the Ohio and Mississippi Rivers to explore new opportunities. *Ah, but to one day go north instead of south.* His excitement grew as he opened the book and skimmed the book's preface.

A small voice from behind interrupted. "Jack."

Startled, he turned to find Lucinda in the doorway, her form glowing in the backlighting of the sun. He once again found himself catching his breath at the sight of her. *Steady, Jack. Remember Thomson's warning! Don't let her beauty overwhelm you.*

"Uncle Ludwell says you are leaving." Jack was unsure if it was a statement or a question.

"I am, Lucinda. I have an engagement in George Town this evening," he said, closing the book and summoning his defenses.

Lucinda brought her eyes to his. "I'm disappointed, as I was hopeful that you might stay for the dance."

So pretty she was, standing in front of him, and so tempting it was to say yes. *"Yes, I'll stay and dance the night away with you, Lucinda."* But she had jilted him for Hank Carter. *Show no forgiveness, Jack. None.* Jack offered her a small smile.

"Not tonight, Lucinda. I really must keep my appointment." Making a mental note to ask Colonel Lee next week to borrow the book, he put it back on the shelf and turned to leave. Lucinda had moved between him and the doorway blocking his path. He stepped toward her, expecting her to move aside, but she held her stance.

"Jack, I am sorry," Lucinda said, her eyes teeming with sincerity. "I am truly sorry. Please forgive me."

"There is nothing to be sorry about, Lucinda."

"You and I both know different. In the future, I shall not attempt to injure your feelings as I have done today. I simply wanted you to know that."

Her admission stripped his defenses.

As she picked up her skirts to leave him, a wave of warmth rushed over him. On impulse, Jack grasped her arm and pulled her toward him. She lifted her face, her eyes searching his. The feeling of her so close to him filled his every sense and the warmth in his chest ignited. As he bent to kiss her, his heart leapt from behind its shield. In that instant, he felt suddenly terrified, his heart exposed and vulnerable. Before his lips touched hers, he eased his grasp on her arm, and stepped back.

"I really must go," Jack said, clearing his throat.

"Well then, I suppose you should be on your way," Lucinda said with formality, the uneasiness thick between them.

With her head bent and her eyes cast to the floor, she stepped aside and allowed him to pass.

Through the wavy glass of the library's window, Lucinda watched as Jack's horse was brought from the stable to the front of the house. Her stomach was in knots as she watched him pull himself into the saddle and start down the long drive. With dust flying into the air behind the mare's hooves, he rounded the bend behind the cattails along the pond's shore and disappeared from her sight.

Lucinda stared into the dusky sky, torn between wanting to rid him from her mind and wondering how long it would be before she would see him again.

A burst of loud laughter from the hallway interrupted the tug-of-war between her head and her heart. Drawing a deep breath, she prepared herself for a night of dancing with the witless Carter brothers. A night that would leave her restless and bored. And later, long after the dancing was done and guests were gone and sleep finally came, she would find Jack McCarty where she found him most nights since the party at Raspberry Plain, haunting her dreams.

CHAPTER 18

MARCH 29, 1817, NEAR MIDNIGHT, GEORGE TOWN

The House of Rose on George Town's Water Street was a brick-and-clapboard two-story building that faced the Potomac River. While the establishment was not impressive on the outside, the inside was another matter. With its red carpeting, gilded mirrors, opulent furnishings, and crystal chandeliers, its interior design rivaled some of the District's finest hotels.

"Looks like you've had a long night, mate," said the bartender as Jack walked in.

"Long enough, Paddy. Long enough."

Paddy pulled a bottle of Irish whiskey from under the counter. "This ought to take the edge off," he said with a bit of brogue as he filled a glass.

Jack raised the glass to Paddy before drinking it down. As he put the glass on the counter for a refill, a plump, pasty-faced woman with rouged lips nearly as red as her hair rounded the corner from the back hall.

"Mr. McCarty!" the woman exclaimed in a voice tinted by too much whiskey and tobacco. She, too, had a bit of the old Irish brogue.

"*Tá sé le fada ó do chuairt dheireanach,*" she said in her native tongue, teasing Jack that it had been too long since his last visit.

"I was just here last week, Rose! And that cost me plenty!"

"Aye," she admitted, "'tis true. However, I cannot reserve Lillie the night before the Sabbath if you are no longer her regular customer."

Lillie had been with another customer last Saturday when Jack arrived, causing him to pay double for the evening with her. Tonight would be another expensive night.

"How much, Rose? How much this time?"

She thought for a moment before answering. "*Trí huaire an gnáthráta.*"

"Three times! Three times the usual fee! The night is half gone already, Rose."

"Aye, but she waited for you and not five minutes ago took a fella upstairs. This time I will have to return his money and give him another girl as well. That's three, Jack. One fer you with Lillie, one back fer him, and one fer the other girl."

Jack could hardly understand her logic, but that wasn't unusual when negotiating with Rose. Jack groaned and considered his predicament as he threw back another shot of whiskey.

"*Ceart go leor,* Rosaleen! All right, I shall pay three times, on the condition that she is clean. If her customer has spoiled her, then you've made your money and I owe you nothing more than the usual fee and the inconvenience of requiring him to leave early."

Rose thought for a moment before hurrying down the hall. Jack heard her feet on the back stairs, keys clanging, and the rumble of muffled commotion. Rose was, first and foremost, a businesswoman.

Jack liked Rose. Perhaps it was her stories of Ireland before the revolution, stories of romance, chivalry, honor, and the days of the old country. Or perhaps it was her fearless independence and determination. Like his mother, she was strong-willed, free-spirited, and not afraid to speak her mind. And next to his mother, Rose was probably the wealthiest woman he knew, having earned a small fortune from the profits of her numerous business ventures. She was a native-born Irish lass named after an Irish love song often used to describe Ireland itself. Jack thought it ironic that Ireland's most iconic nickname was shared with one of the most notorious madams in the District of Columbia. With a wry smile, Paddy pulled the Bushmills bottle out from under the counter once more to refill Jack's glass. The patron upstairs could be heard complaining at the interruption as he was ushered into another room. It wasn't long before Madame Rose re-emerged from the back hallway.

"Jack, I think we are both in luck this evening," Rose said happily as she approached. "Your flower is as pure as a lily on Passover!"

"The luck of the Irish, Madame," Jack said and thanked her. "*Go raibh maith agat.*"

"*Tá fáilte romhat!*" Madame Rose said. "You are welcome indeed! Now go and enjoy your fresh flower!"

Jack bade Paddy good night, took his glass of whiskey, and made his way to Lillie's room. At his knock, a strawberry blonde with dancing eyes peeked from behind the heavy oak door.

"My, my! Had you forgotten all about your Lillie, Mr. McCarty? Come in and let me restore your memory," she said in the thick accent of the Emerald Isle.

"Now, Lillie, it is not my memory that needs restoration."

"I can solve that problem, too, my love."

With a seductive smile, Lillie pulled the door open for Jack to enter and latched it behind him as it shut. She turned to face him, wearing nothing but a corset and boots.

"Hello, my Lillie." Jack grabbed her by the waist and pulled her toward him. "Undress me and restore the part of me that missed you most."

Lillie moved her fingers to the waistline of his breeches and unbuttoned them. As she worked her way into his trousers, he moved his mouth to her neck, kissing her as she aroused him with her hands. When he moaned aloud at her touch, she dug her nails into him until he cried out.

"Ouch, Lillie! That hurts." He winced, trying to pull away. She kept him in her grasp.

"Aye, as it should, Mr. McCarty." She dug her nails in harder. "Have you forgotten? How can you feel the heights of pleasure without first experiencing the depths of pain? And now for the bliss, my love." Lillie fell to her knees in front of him.

"No, Lillie. Not yet." Jack pulled her from the floor. "Lash me first." She offered him a crooked smile and walked to the dresser in the corner.

"Well, a lashing it will be. Where do you prefer it?"

"The back. And make it hurt. Really hurt."

"As you wish." Lillie opened the drawer and pulled out a leather strap as Jack unbuttoned his shirt.

And so it went, with Lillie inflicting torture upon him before bringing him to elation, her punishing pleasures distracting him from his troubled mind. It wasn't until the break of dawn that Jack finally dozed off, exhausted yet restored.

He had managed to sleep for an hour or so when Rose rapped on the door. It was her first call for the patrons to leave; if they weren't gone by the third knock, she would add another night's stay to the tab. Although the knock seemed early, Lillie was already up and dressed, having added pantaloons to the corset. Jack lifted his head from the pillow. She had a pot of tea and a tray of biscuits waiting for him.

"Good day, sunshine," Lillie said as she poured him a cup. She held up a decanter of whiskey. "Toddy?"

"No, thanks," Jack said. He sat up on the edge of the bed, rubbing the back of his neck. Lillie brought the tea to him and sat beside him. She handed him the cup and reached under the sheet. Jack quickly moved to stop her advance.

"Let's not, Lillie. I've got to get up and moving today."

"Aye, I'll have you up in no time, Jack, and I will do all the moving, if you like." Lillie reached under the sheet and made a second attempt to arouse him.

"Not this morning, Lillie. You'll cost me another night! And all of my day! I promised to visit my mother today. And breaking a promise to my mother would cost me in ways that neither of us would want me to suffer."

"*Ceart go leor, mo ghrá.* I understand, my darling. But only out of respect for your mother." She tilted her head and smiled. "Might I ask, who is Lucy?"

Jack shifted his shoulders. "Lucy? Why do you ask?"

"Because, my love, you called me 'Lucy' numerous times during our fornication last evening, and this morning you were talking about 'Lucinda' in your sleep." She leaned toward him and tapped her index finger on his chest. "Makes me think that someone may have finally pierced the shield over that heart of yours."

Jack thought he saw genuine caring in her eyes as she waited for his answer. For reasons that he could not rationalize, he trusted her. "There is someone named Lucy. Lucinda, actually. Lucinda Lee."

Lillie pulled her legs up onto the bed, crossing them under her, and turned to face him. She reminded Jack of a young child sitting at a mother's feet during bedtime reading. "Tell me about her."

"There's not much to tell, Lillie."

"Blarney! I know you're a-fibbin', Jack. A bad liar you are!"

"All right, Lillie. I submit. Lucinda is a lovely girl. I suppose she's about seventeen or so, though I don't exactly know her age. She's fair of face with hair the color of straw and eyes as blue as the sky. She has a bright mind and an indelible memory for poetry and repartee. To add to my temptation and my torment, God has blessed her with a well-proportioned frame and an abundance of bosom. A Venus, she is—a goddess. And although she may be delicately formed, she has a sharp tongue that will cut you apart like the sword of Bellona! She is strong-willed and unpredictable. And I'll be damned, she is fickle. Frankly, I don't know why I have wasted my time attempting to court her, as the more attention I give her, the less affection she gives me in return!"

"She sounds like someone I know."

"You mean there are two of the vixens out there?!"

"She's you, Jack." Jack furrowed his brow. "You just described yourself in the likeness of a woman." Lillie smiled at him as she repositioned herself on the bed. "Most men, they want a woman who is the opposite of them to feed their ego. If a man is strongminded and outspoken, he will choose a wife who is soft-spoken and weak. It makes the man feel important because his wife needs him to be strong for her and to speak for her. But you are not like most men, Jack McCarty. You do not need a woman to make you feel important. What you need, Jack, is a woman who is strong. One who challenges you."

"And how do you know all of this, Lillie?"

"Because I know men. I make it my business to know exactly what they want."

"Perhaps, but a soft-spoken, weak-minded woman would be less frustrating."

"And such a woman would not haunt your dreams. Iron sharpens iron, Jack. Iron sharpens iron."

CHAPTER 19

APRIL 15, 1817,
LEESBURG COURTHOUSE

Jack looked up at the bright blue Virginia sky. The leaves on the trees above his head were glittering in the morning sunshine like tiny emeralds perched along the limbs. He moved his gaze out across the courtyard to the more than one hundred men gathered in the square, drinking coffee, smoking pipes, and socializing with their neighbors, waiting for polling to begin. Drawing a long breath to quell his anxiety, Jack worked his way through the throng of gentlemen toward the courthouse.

The clerk of the court, Charles Binns, stood from his seat behind a long table that stretched in front of the white stone pillars of the courthouse entrance. At the table were the county sheriff and his deputy. Armistead, wearing his officer's uniform and a black hat cocked on the left side, was seated at a table to the left, and Charles Fenton Mercer, in a black coat and white waistcoat with a black cravat tied at his neck, sat at the table to the right. With Fenton having lost the majority of the vote in Prince William County the week before, Jack knew that without a win today at the Loudoun hustings, Fenton's chances of victory would be over. Jack also knew that General Armistead Mason's brother-in-law putting his name on a rival's poll would surely encourage others in the line behind him to do the same. Butterflies took flight in Jack's stomach as he reached the front of the line.

Clerk Binns cleared his throat and announced the opening of the polls. Jack stepped forward. "Your name, sir?" Clerk Binns asked. The crowd of men quieted.

Jack caught Armistead's gaze. Jack nodded and swallowed hard as he attempted to calm the flutter in his stomach. "John Mason McCarty," Jack said, bringing his eyes back to the clerk.

"On whose poll do you cast your first vote, sir?"

Jack glanced at Fenton. At Fenton's smile, the nervousness in Jack's gut settled. He lifted his chin and adjusted his waistcoat. "I cast my vote for Charles Fenton Mercer."

Armistead threw his head back with disbelief and insult on his face. "I challenge this man's eligibility to vote!" The crowd startled as his voice boomed over the courtyard.

"What?" Jack looked at Armistead and saw fire in his eyes.

"On what grounds, sir?" Clerk Binns sputtered with confusion.

"He is not qualified. This man is not of age."

A surge of adrenaline rushed through Jack's veins and the taste of lightning was on his tongue. "I am indeed of age, as I am twenty-two years old."

"Then with God as your witness and on your honor," Armistead said, his voice rising even louder, "swear an oath here and now attesting to your age and qualifications."

"No gentleman would require such an oath!"

"A gentleman would not bear false testimony regarding his right of suffrage!"

Jack threw his shoulders back. "False testimony? A gentleman would respect the honor of another gentleman."

"How dare you challenge me, boy?"

"Boy? I am no boy!" The exchange between the two had grown so loud that it silenced nearly all the chatter in the courtyard.

Armistead settled back in his chair. A smug smile spread across his face. "Clerk Binns," Armistead said with a dismissive wave of his hand.

"Would you please take an oath from this impertinent scoundrel, as certainly he will not perjure himself before God Almighty?"

Jack clenched his fist. It took every ounce of restraint to keep from charging Armistead where he sat and pummeling him. "Fine, then! I will take an oath to humor this rascal!" The smugness on Armistead's face was replaced by a glowering scowl. Jack glared back.

A murmur rumbled over the courtyard as a Bible was brought from the courthouse. Clerk Binns asked Jack to place his left hand on the Bible and to raise his right. With God and more than one hundred men as witness, John Mason McCarty offered his testimony confirming his date of birth and his qualifications for the right of suffrage.

Armistead's face turned beet-red as he roared at Jack's testament. "A damned perjured villain!"

"Step out from the safety of your chair and accuse me of perjury again, and I'll damn you to hell!"

Armistead was barely on his feet before Jack lunged at him, swinging a clenched fist at Armistead's head. Armistead ducked just in time, his hat falling to the ground. The sheriff leapt from his chair and stepped between the two men as Armistead's friends, George Rust and Gerard Alexander, hurried from the crowd to Armistead's side.

"A damned blackguard and bully, you are, Armistead Mason!" Jack shouted as Gerard put his body between the sheriff and Jack.

"And John Mason McCarty is a perjured liar! A liar!" Armistead seethed as George held on to his arm.

Jack shoved Gerard out of his way to lunge at Armistead a second time. This time it was the sheriff who kept Jack at bay. Jack shouted over the sheriff's shoulder as James Dulaney rushed forward and grabbed his arm. "Let the word 'liar' come out of your mouth once more, and I'll fill it with the knuckles of my fist!"

"Enough of this, or I will have to charge you both with disrupting the peace!" the sheriff said as he pushed Jack back.

Shock engulfed the faces of the voters standing in line. Picking up his hat from the ground, Armistead straightened his uniform and regained his composure. "There will be no need for arrests today, Sheriff.

We have an election to attend." He smoothed his hair, returned the hat to his head, and sat down.

Jack shrugged free of James's grip. Pushing the hair from his forehead, he continued his rant. "As a gentleman, I gave my word under oath regarding my right to suffrage. You saw me approach the bench and offered no challenge to my eligibility until you learned that I would not cast my name on your poll." Jack raised his voice so loud that the entire crowd of men could hear. "At which point, you then challenged my eligibility. Had I supported you, would you have made the challenge? I think not!" Jack straightened his shoulders and turned to face the gentlemen in line behind him. "General Armistead Mason showed his true colors here this morning, my friends. Only if it does not serve him does General Mason object. He manipulates the truth to suit his purpose and his purpose only. Is this the kind of man you want to represent you? Is this your voice? The voice of Loudoun?"

Armistead glared across the table, his eyes like daggers. "You have insulted me, and I responded in kind. In time I will call you out appropriately for it, but not here today." Armistead turned to the clerk, his voice calm and steady. "I remain steadfast in my challenge of John Mason McCarty's vote."

Jack turned back toward him and scoffed. "Challenge away, General."

Armistead could not maintain his composure. "And a vote for Charles Fenton Mercer only endorses the violent conduct of such rogues as his protégé John Mason McCarty."

"Take a look at your own conduct, General, before you label others with such blasphemy." Jack glared at Armistead with his pale eyes piercing. "The truth will prevail and prove you to be the bully you are." Jack turned again to the men waiting their turn in line. "Gentlemen, do not fear General Mason's verbal abuse when you cast your vote against him. Do not allow him to intimidate you when you vote for the only honorable candidate to represent you—the only candidate who does not manipulate the facts to suit his purpose. That candidate, gentlemen, is Charles Fenton Mercer. He has my vote, and I am proud to call him my friend."

Straightening his coat, Jack put his cap back over his unruly locks and moved his eyes to the table where Fenton Mercer was seated. Fenton, looking rather pale, offered a weak smile through thin, pursed lips. Jack nodded and turned to leave. As Jack was walking away, the next gentleman in line stepped to the center table and announced himself to the clerk. In a bold voice that could be heard across the square, the freeholder declared his vote for the candidate to represent the eighth district of Virginia in the U.S. Congress—Charles Fenton Mercer.

CHAPTER 20

APRIL 16, 1817,
ALDIE

Coatless with sleeves rolled to their elbows, Jack and Cary riffled through papers strewn over an oak table, while a half dozen men stood over them with their coffees in hand. The mood was cautiously joyful in the smoke-filled room, except for the moroseness emanating from the far corner where Fenton Mercer sat removed from the others.

"Despite winning in Loudoun yesterday, we captured very little of the merchant and innkeeper suffrage. This may be a problem for us in the final polling in Fairfax next week," Cary said, handing a paper to Jack.

"Hmmm," Jack said as he reviewed the tally and scratched some figures onto a sheet of paper. "By my calculations, we'll need those votes."

William turned to Fenton. "You should focus on canvassing the taverns and the towns. The merchants in Fairfax are more conservative than those in Loudoun, which bodes well for us."

"I will not disgrace myself by mixing with the common stock of the county in their taverns," Fenton said from his broody perch. The gentlemen fell quiet with astonishment on their faces.

These "common stock," Jack thought, *are the people you profess to care so much about in all your speeches.*

"Without the freeholders in the towns, you'll lose the Fairfax poll," Cary said.

"By my calculation," said Fenton, "Mason will need over two hundred votes in Fairfax to win the overall election, a number he surely cannot achieve."

"General Mason may need significantly less than that number when he contests the polling in Loudoun," Jack said.

"What are you suggesting, Jack?"

"I am merely suggesting what's obvious. There were dozens of fraudulent votes cast on your poll yesterday."

"Fraudulent votes?" said Frank Lee, Colonel Lee's brother, who was leaning against the doorway that led to the hall.

Jack moved his gaze to Frank. "When William Handy, a good friend of the general's, cast his vote for Armistead and then, not two hours later, another gentleman, who clearly was not William Handy but who presented himself as such, proceeded to cast his vote for Fenton, it's more than obvious. It's fraud."

Frank scoffed. "For all we know there are two gentlemen in the county with that name. And let's not forget that when the second Mr. Handy announced himself, he went so far as to offer his middle initial, which the first Mr. Handy did not do."

Jack was incredulous. "While Armistead may not possess the highest degree of intelligence, he's not stupid. And what he lacks in brains, he offsets in bravado, as he so brashly indicated at the very start of the polling. Look how he came at me when I cast my vote."

"Armistead objected to your vote because you blindsided him," William said. "And the fact that you let your temper get the better of you didn't help the situation."

Jack shot his brother a testy look. "Blindsided him? What did he expect me to do? Ride out to Selma and tell him that I wasn't planning to vote for him?"

"That's exactly what I did, Jack. And although he was disappointed, he was gracious in accepting my decision."

"Since when am I required to consult Armistead Mason on my right of suffrage?"

"It's not a requirement, Jack," William snapped back. "But a courtesy considering his position. Every now and then you might give the man the benefit of the doubt. He is not always as obstinate as you assume."

"It is not his obstinacy that I deplore, William. It is his self-righteousness," Jack said, his temper flaring. "And what courtesy do I owe to his position?"

"He was your commanding officer."

"For five entire weeks. And that was five weeks too long."

"Let's not go there again, Jack. While there are those who believe he's not entitled to the honors he holds, there are those of us who do." William shot an accusing glance toward the corner where Fenton sat. Jack followed his brother's eyes to find Fenton looking uncomfortably at his boots.

"I'm certain that there is just as much irregularity on Mason's side as on ours," Colonel Lee said, interrupting the quarrel between the brothers. "Let's not dwell on this too much, as yesterday was a good day for the Federalist Party. As I see it, Loudoun belongs to Fenton, and damn the man to say otherwise."

Jack glanced at his portly mentor in the corner, who said not a word.

With Fenton unwilling to campaign further, the conversation shifted from politics to planting, leaving Jack little to add. Throwing on his coat, he stepped out onto the front porch, into the crisp morning air for relief from both the tobacco smoke and the exchange with his brother. Colonel Lee followed behind him with a pipe in one hand and a mug of hot coffee in the other.

"No reason to get yourself tied in knots over a few irregularities at the hustings, Jack," Colonel Lee said as he puffed on his pipe. "You'll find these indiscretions happen from time to time. Both sides are guilty. Can't find too much fault in some overenthusiastic supporters trying to ensure their candidate gets the upper hand. Of course, the candidates themselves are ignorant of the schemes these zealots concoct. Like I said, it happens on both sides and, at the end of the day, it all works out evenly."

"It's wrong, sir. And I'm not convinced that it's simply overenthusiastic zealots. To my eyes it appears organized and one-sided."

"With age and experience, your vision will become more clear, my boy." The colonel laughed and drew on his pipe, puffing smoke. "Miss Flora tells me that you were looking for my niece Lucinda at the barbeque a few weeks back. And spent some time with her in the library after our meeting."

Jack's adrenaline surged with this new subject, and he felt uneasy. "Yes, I did."

"She's asked about you, Jack."

"*She* being Miss Lucinda?"

The colonel laughed again. "Well, of course Miss Lucinda! I certainly hope it wasn't Miss Flora inquiring about you, or you and I would be having quite a different conversation."

Jack laughed nervously along with the colonel. "What did Miss Lucinda ask exactly?"

"Oh, just when you might be to Belmont next and if there was any particular lady you might have interest in." Colonel Lee winked as he brought the pipe to his mouth again.

"I assume Miss Flora informed her that my interest extends only to politics and foxhunting."

"You know that women do not share with us menfolk the details of their nattering, but as I recall, son, you were inquiring about her— meaning Lucinda, and not my wife—a few weeks back." The colonel gave another wink and chortled at his obvious clarification. "And now that you have caught her attention, you might want to set about calling upon her before the lass loses interest and those ambitions of hers confuse her head again." Colonel Lee smiled broadly with his pipe clenched in his teeth as Jack shifted his stance.

"It sounds to me that these ambitions you refer to are her principal interest."

"She's just confused, Jack. Confused, is all. God gave her too much up here, you know," he said, tapping his temple with his index finger. "Lucinda is a lovely girl and has caught the eye of many young men. Of all her sisters, I believe she is the loveliest. Like her father, she is. Just like him, indeed. And it's all that intelligence that gets in the way of finding herself a husband."

"I am in no market for a wife, sir. I, too, have ambitions, and they do not include taking on the responsibility of setting up household and managing a dowry."

Colonel Lee cleared his throat uncomfortably. "I don't want to be talking out of turn, but I thought your mother would have told you, considering your interest in Lucinda."

"Told me what?"

The colonel cast a nervous glance around the porch, his eyes darting to the door. "Lucinda has no dowry. None of the sisters do." The colonel paused to let his words sink in. "In spite of the seeming wealth of the family, the old widow is broke. Poor thing, such a difficult life she has had. Afflicted with the pox that scarred her beautiful face, losing my dear brother Thomas, with all those daughters to raise alone, and all the debt that was left for her to bear." Colonel Lee shook his head and drew a long sigh. He brought his eyes to Jack's. "And I'll have you know, Jack, that my brother had indeed satisfied all his debts before his death, but the attorney misplaced the documents. Then the executor, before I became involved, mishandled the creditors. I was able to get the courts to grant the old woman a reprieve to keep Coton Farm, but the estate will be sold at her death with little going to the girls." He drew on his pipe, but its cherry had gone cold. Taking it from his mouth, he examined its contents. He scoffed at the bowl before tapping it against the porch railing to dislodge the tobacco and ash.

Jack was having difficulty comprehending what Colonel Lee was telling him. "I don't understand how they—"

"The farm pays their expenses and supports their opulent life, and therefore no one is the wiser regarding their situation. But the girls have no inheritance other than their beauty, God-given talents, and good family name. That's why the ones who are married have the husbands they do. Either first cousins or widowers nearly twice their age." The colonel paused, shaking his head again, and looked at Jack. "Jack, my boy, you are wealthy enough that you don't need a dowry, and Lucinda would make a fine catch. A woman like that will bear you sturdy, intelligent sons. You've turned her head, which is damned difficult to do, I might add. For the life of me I can't understand how a girl without a dowry can be so damned capricious! But I want what's best for her and what's best for you, as I love you and your brothers like you were of my own flesh and blood. You and Lucinda would make a fine pair, a mighty fine pair indeed."

Jack was struggling to wrap his mind around the colonel's words. Courtship was one thing. Courtship with a woman without an inheritance was something different.

"While I have inherited a great deal from my father's estate, I have no interest in taking on a wife at present, dowry or no dowry. Lucinda is indeed a beautiful woman, and while I enjoy her wit and her company, my ambitions, as I said, lie elsewhere."

"You young folks and your ambitions! I wish I could say I understand, but that would be a falsehood. As you wish, Jack. I shall let it rest." Colonel Lee exhaled in exasperation. "How about we go inside and see about breakfast. And while we're at it, maybe we can persuade Fenton to actually campaign over the next week."

"If you don't mind, Colonel, I'll just linger out here a little longer."

"Suit yourself. We'll call you when the food comes." Colonel Lee turned and went back into the house, letting the screen door snap closed behind him.

Jack gazed across the road to the wheel of the mill slowly turning into the current of the Little River. As water fell from the paddles, Jack thought about his struggles with his own heritage. Forever being compared to a man he could barely remember. So many expectations he could never fulfill. He'd grown up watching his brothers in their efforts to live up to the legend of their father. He had watched them fall short. And watched as they died trying. Jack's ambitions were different. He wanted a different life. He wanted to create his own legend.

As he watched the water fall, he couldn't keep his thoughts from Lucinda. He understood her pain of growing up without a father. What was the word she had used at the courthouse? *"...when he died and abandoned me."* Jack had thought her word choice odd at the time, yet it fit his own feelings. But to grow up without an inheritance? He closed his eyes and tried to imagine life without the security of his wealth. He drew a deep breath and imagined himself in Lucinda's position. As the crisp morning air bit into his lungs, fear washed over him— overwhelming, all-consuming. He saw the judging eyes and knew the feeling of being less than. The more he felt it, the more he understood her. And more than anything, he wanted to see her.

CHAPTER 21

APRIL 16, 1817, AFTERNOON,
COTON FARM

"Jack McCarty! What brings you to Coton today?" Lucinda asked as she greeted him in the parlor. His hair was windblown as he stood by the fireplace in tan breeches and a hunter-green coat. "Mr. Deese informs me that you were quite resolute."

"You, Lucy. I came to see you." Jack grinned as he played with the hat in his hand.

"And to what do I owe the pleasure?" Lucinda said, offering her hand as she approached.

Jack's eyes twinkled. "I was told that you had asked about me."

Men are worse than old maids with their gossip! She had known that she would come to regret asking her uncle about him. Jack took her hand in his brazen manner. As his breath warmed the skin of her ungloved hand, an excitement stirred in her bosom. When he brought her hand to his cheek, all her resolve to toy with him dissolved.

"I was curious, I suppose. As I told you after the barbeque, I felt horrible that I had been so insensitive toward your feelings. It was unfair of me to invite you to a party and then arrive in the company of someone else. I would have been insulted and, well, hurt had you done that to me, and I just wanted you to know that." She could see from Jack's expression that he had not anticipated her candor.

"And I owe you an apology as well. For blatantly flirting with your sister and for not calling on you sooner to relieve your anxiety." With his sincerity, the warmth in her chest grew.

"Well, you are here now, and I have received you. Would you join me for tea?"

"Do you ride?"

"Pardon?"

"Do you ride? It's a remarkably warm day, and I thought I might show you my property. If you recall, it abuts the south end of your estate." Jack winked and sported a grin that dimpled his lean face.

She resisted the impulse to smile back. *You are shameless!* The proper thing to do was refuse such an invitation without a chaperone. But Lucinda was accustomed to doing things her own way. The words fell from her lips before she could stop them. "Of course I ride, sir. And … I would be delighted to survey your north end." *Lucinda Lee, what are you doing? Mother will have your head!*

Jack's face lit up like a child's at Christmas. "Wonderful! Shall I wait for you at the stables?"

"That would be fine. I must first change into my riding habit. Ask the boys to ready my mount, if you please." Her heart leapt as she headed for the stairs.

"Very well, then." Jack bent an arm across his waist to bow. "I shall see you shortly."

Jack and Lucinda spent the afternoon on horseback, riding through the freshly plowed fields of Coton, along the flood plain of the Potomac, and into the wooded knolls along the bluffs above the river. When they reached Jack's estate, he showed her the outbuildings, explained his plans for monetizing the property, and shared his ideas for industrialization projects. "Can you imagine," he had said, "a mill powered by the great current of the Broad Run with stones large enough to grind the cob with the corn. And a town built high above the river. Maybe a canal with locks traversing the falls to make navigation possible to markets in George Town, Alexandria, and all the way to the Chesapeake." His eyes were wide and gleaming as he spoke of seemingly endless possibilities. He also shared his frustrations concerning the property's limitations. "Runoff and disastrous flooding unless I can construct some sort of dam …" His mind raced as he mulled solutions. He told her about his loathing of planting crops and his interest in starting a business, sharing his misgivings and fears just as easily as he was sharing his passions. His enthusiasm was infectious, drawing her to him and his ideas.

As the day wound down, Lucinda learned that Jack McCarty was not at all what he seemed on the exterior—a wealthy, brash rake who most certainly was shamelessly shallow and self-absorbed. In fact, the Jack McCarty with whom she had spent this afternoon was quite different from what she had told herself about him and what had been affirmed by her sisters. Yes, he was wealthy and a consummate flirt, but she found him also to be thoughtful, considerate, and completely self-aware. There was an authenticity about him that she found difficult to describe, but it was patently there amid his humility and his humor. Above all, she was surprised that he was such a gentleman.

On their return to the manor house, they came upon an old trail that cut through a tangle of thicket toward the river.

"Whoa, whoa," she said, pulling back on the reins. "Jack, come this way." She turned her horse toward the right. "There's something I'd like to show you."

Jack and his mare followed behind her down the trail. After a few hundred yards, they came upon a clearing at the top of a high bluff that overlooked the river. Lucinda dismounted and tethered her horse to an old post. Jack followed her lead, leaving his mare with hers as he walked with Lucinda toward the river.

Lucinda stopped near the bluff's edge and stared out over the calm of the river toward the shores of Maryland on the other side. "This is my favorite place. We would picnic here when I was little. My father would put me onto his shoulders and let me throw pebbles into the water from right over there." She pointed at a spot to the left of where they stood. "When the weather is warm like it is today, I ride down here to watch the moon rise above the water. When it is full and low in the sky, it is as if I can touch its face—its kind eyes smiling as it listens to my dreams. Do you ever do that, Jack? Sit in the quiet of twilight and share your dreams with the moon?"

Jack stepped close beside her, their long shadows falling over the cliff and down to the water's edge as the sun sank low in the sky behind them. They stood silently together with only the flutter of nesting birds in the brush and the stir of the new spring leaves in the breeze. "I'm leaving, Lucy. The day after tomorrow."

"Where are you going?"

"Natchez. To explore opportunities." Lucinda nodded her head, saying nothing and keeping her eyes focused on the opposite shore. And then it came. He took her arm, turning her to face him. She thought for certain he would attempt to kiss her, but instead he brought his hand to her brow to push a strand of hair from her forehead. Moving his hand to her cheek, he smiled at her. "Will you wait for me, Lucinda? Until I return?"

"Wait for you?" She raised an eyebrow. "Whatever do you mean?"

"I don't know." His eyes darted away before returning to hers. "I was just hoping that when I return, you would still be here ... That you would be here for me."

There it was again, that something in his eyes—an honesty, a rawness. This time she didn't look away.

A voice in her head screamed *No, Lucinda!* as her mind fought the warmth radiating from her heart.

"I'm flattered. Truly I am, Jack. But to wait for you is tantamount to being in courtship, something I don't think either one of us is ready for." Her heart cried at her words, pleading with her to throw caution aside.

"But I thought—" Jack began.

She interrupted him before her emotions defeated her resolve.

"Go find what you are looking for, Jack. If you return and I am still here, we shall see what happens then. But dreams wait for no one. Go find yours."

He pulled her closer. The intensity in his cool eyes burned with passion. "All right then, but please, Lucy, let me taste you once before I go."

She lifted her chin, wanting to fall into his arms and so desperately to say yes. *You can't allow it, Lucy!*

Lucinda brought a hand to his face and held his gaze. "No, Jack. This is not what I am looking for. Not now. And it's not what you need either." Sensing his desire and fighting her own, she stepped away from him and took his hand to lead him back to the horses. "I must get home before it gets too late. Otherwise, Mother will send Mr. Deese out with instructions to shoot you."

"Just what I need—to be shot down twice in the same day."

Lucinda gave him a sympathetic look but said nothing. Jack didn't want to leave. With her hand in his, she urged him forward. "Come, Jack, help me onto my mount."

Hand in hand, they walked in silence back to their horses. As Jack helped her onto her horse, her heart begged her to change her mind. *Dreams wait for no one, Lucy,* she reminded herself as she waited for Jack to pull himself onto the gray mare. When they started on the trail, Jack halted his horse and turned toward her. His eyes met hers once again.

"Thank you, Lucy."

"Thank me for what?"

Jack smiled a dimpled smile that pulled at her heartstrings. "For keeping us honest."

CHAPTER 22

APRIL 24, 1817, ESMONT, ALBEMARLE COUNTY, VIRGINIA

In a storm-blue jacket, Armistead cast his gaze across the field toward the Southwest Mountains, searching for their summits through the obscurity of the clouds. The sky was dreary, and the air damp and still. In the valley below, fog hovered over the Rivanna River, protecting the waters from the fire of the rising sun that struggled to melt the mist away. Armistead, too, was struggling through an unyielding cloud of disappointment and embitterment that was as persistent as the haze that hovered over the countryside. Weighted by the burden of his loss, he had traveled through the night to Charlotte's home in Albemarle, desperate to reach her.

Charlotte! How do I tell you? Hearing the sound of Charlotte's slippers crossing the porch behind him, he turned to face her. She wore a simple white blouse tucked into a blue skirt with a dark woolen shawl wrapped tightly around her shoulders. The mere sight of her brought him comfort. He closed his eyes and took her into his embrace, smelling the gentle perfume of her hair as it fell about his face.

"I have missed you, my darling. It has been dreadful these last nine days." Armistead's voice cracked as his emotions broke free from the dike that had contained them.

"It's all right, darling." Her voice comforted him like the warmth of a blanket. "There will be other elections."

Armistead looked at her and forced a smile to mask the injury he'd endured. "How did you know?"

She answered his smile with her own. "I would have to be dead not to have felt it."

Armistead moved his eyes to the fog lingering over the valley floor. "I did everything right, Charlotte. I ran an honest campaign on principles that are true to my beliefs and are good for our citizens. I visited them in their taverns and ordinaries, their churches and social halls. I gave speeches, discussed with them their concerns, and assured them I would be their voice in determining how they are governed. And I was defeated." He closed his eyes again to force away images of the faceless men in the shadows waiting for the vote tally, the flames of their torches flickering erratically in the cool night air.

"It's God's will, my darling."

Armistead turned his eyes to her as his anger rose to shield the wound. "It was not the hand of God but the hand of man!"

"We may not understand His purpose, but it is best to accept His will and move forward—"

"Are you not paying attention, Charlotte? Mercer stole the election from me, not God! The deciding votes cast were as fraudulent as that impertinent scoundrel himself! He robbed me of what is rightfully mine."

"What?" Charlotte sank into one of the wicker chairs as his meaning registered. "How could he steal the election?"

"He cheated, Charlotte! He and his Federalist friends defrauded the election!" Armistead threw his hands into the air and began to pace in front of her. "Men were casting their name on Mercer's poll who had no right of suffrage. Imposters posing as legitimate gentlemen, fraudsters who were voting at all three hustings, men who had yet to receive their inheritance. Yet each was convincing enough for the clerk of the court to record their vote on Mercer's poll."

Charlotte brought her fingers to her lips, her brow knitted in confusion. "How can they do that, Armistead? Can't you contest their votes?"

Armistead stopped his pacing and turned to face her, pointing his index finger at her as he spoke. "That is exactly what I intend to do. After our wedding next week, I plan to gather the evidence to prove their trickery. I shall not rest until I have proven his fraud and revealed his perversion for all the country to see." He leaned forward, his eyes piercing and black with conviction. "And I swear to God, Charlotte, I will never let Mercer and his Federalist bloc beat me again."

CHAPTER 23

MAY 1, 1817, ESMONT

Charlotte pushed the curtain back once more, hoping against hope that there might be a hint of sunshine somewhere in the tumultuous sky. Her disappointment remained as steadfast as the rain.

"Don't fret," said her sister Sarah. "The day will be beautiful no matter what the weather."

"First the election and now this! It has been sunny and bright all spring. Why must it rain on my wedding day?" Charlotte startled as lightning flashed in a forked rage outside the window. Both sisters jumped at the crack of thunder that followed.

"You know what you always say, my dear. It's God's will."

Charlotte turned her attention to the window once more. *God's will!* That's what she had told Armistead after he lost the election. *"We may not understand His purpose, but it is best to accept His will."* Hadn't those been her words? *What is Your purpose in bringing storms on my wedding day? Why are You punishing us?*

"Staring at it won't make it stop," Sarah said. "Let's get you dressed before Mrs. Mason finds us and attempts to decorate you as she has the house!"

Charlotte turned her attention to her sister. "Now, Sarah. I know she can be demanding, but she means well." Since her arrival a few days earlier, Polly had taken over Sarah's home, barking orders and rearranging every detail of the ceremony and celebration.

"You do realize that she is impossible," Sarah said, while adjusting the hem of the wedding gown that hung from the dress form. "She forced the slaves to decimate my garden, taking every bloom. And, still not satisfied, she sent them out a second time to cut the remaining buds and forced even them into blossom!"

"It isn't that she's impossible, Sarah. She just becomes a bit impatient when her expectations aren't met."

"And what have those expectations and impatience gotten her? Half her children moved to Kentucky to escape her control, and the ones that stayed, well ..." Sarah's voice trailed off suggestively as she continued to stitch the hem.

Charlotte crossed her arms over her chest. "What are you implying, sister?"

"Charles told me how hard she pushed poor Armistead when he was young," Sarah said as she glanced up from the hemline with one eyebrow raised.

"And just look at how accomplished he is! There is nothing wrong with a mother's encouragement."

"There is a difference between encouragement and being completely incorrigible!"

"She is to be my mother-in-law in a matter of hours, Sarah. Exodus 20:12? 'Honor thy mother'? Sound familiar?"

"Well, thank God she's your mother-in-law and not mine!" Sarah tied off the stitch and cut the thread. "There!" Sarah stood back from the dress to inspect her work. She had sewn the dress from an ivory brocade and had embellished it with lace and pearls. As the ceremony was initially planned to be held outdoors, she had embroidered flowers on the sleeves in purple and pink silk thread to mimic the blooms in the garden—lavender lilac, soft-blushing spring roses, and the creamy petals of dogwood. Now that most of the garden was indoors, the embroidery accentuated the dress even more.

"It's beautiful, Sarah." Charlotte lifted the sleeve, running her fingers over the delicate stitching. It was beautiful indeed.

"Anything for my dear sister. Come on, darling. Let's get it on you and see how it looks!"

———————

Wearing the beautifully embroidered gown, Charlotte reached the bottom of the stairs having seen none of the guests in the hall. Her focus was on her handsome Armistead standing by the fireplace waiting for her. He was shining from head to toe in his uniform, its gilded braids and buttons catching glimmers of the candles' dancing flames. When her eyes caught his, he smiled at her with that grin that melted her heart every time. They held each other's gaze as she joined him at the makeshift altar. Charlotte had never been happier than she was now, standing in front of the small gathering of family and friends as she committed her life to him. In the exchange of their promises to remain faithful and steadfast through good times and bad, in the worst and best of health, regardless of prosperity or poverty, neither moved their eyes from the other.

"With this ring I wed thee, Charlotte Taylor, and with my body I promise to worship thee, and with all my worldly goods I thee endow for now and all eternity. In the name of the Father, and of the Son, and of the Holy Ghost. Amen."

As Armistead slipped the gold band on her finger, she cried tears of joy. The moment she had waited for had finally arrived. General Armistead T. Mason, the man whom she had fallen in love with on a hot June day so many summers before, was at long last her husband.

CHAPTER 24

Amid congratulations, Emily cornered her brother in the hallway just outside the dining room doors. "Armie!" she said as she slung her arms about his neck. "I could not be happier to have Charlotte as my new sister!"

"I am happy that you are happy, Em. And I can assure you that I am even happier!" Armistead said, smiling as his younger sister held on to his neck.

"Might I have a quick word?" A feeling of dread rushed over Armistead as he removed her arms from him.

"What is it, Emily? Will it ruin my mood?"

"It's just a simple request. Nothing that will upset you." Armistead raised his eyebrows. "It's just that I heard there was trouble between you and William's brother at the hustings."

"Sister, what is wrong with your head? I am just married, and you bring this to my attention? Here?! Now?!"

"Yes, yes, I know. And I'm sorry, but I must beg you, Armie, please let it go. Please do not challenge him, even though you would be right to do so. He's William's brother. The two of them are close, and the family doesn't need any fighting like this. Jack was wrong, yes! And I'm certain that he knows it. Can you find it in your heart to let it go—for me? For my marriage to William? Please, Armie?"

Holding her at arm's length, he looked into her pleading eyes. He had not planned to challenge Jack McCarty, however incensed he had been at the hustings. It was Mercer who had aggrieved him. Mercer who had cheated at the polls. Mercer whom he hated almost as much as he hated the British. Almost.

"Emily Mason McCarty. What to do with you?" Armistead shook his head at her and yielded a surrendering sigh. "Fine. I will agree not to challenge the younger McCarty as long as he does nothing further to provoke me. For you and your marriage. Happy?" Armistead saw the instant relief in her face.

"Oh, yes, Armie! Thank you!" Emily threw her arms around his neck and hugged him again.

"All right now, sparrow. Enough of all this. It's my wedding day, and you are keeping me from my bride!" Armistead chided her as he took her elbow and moved her toward the door. "Let us join the others. I cannot keep my wife waiting."

"How wonderful it is to hear you say those words again!"

PART TWO

"O MY BROTHER! THOU DRIVEST ME

TO MADNESS WITH THY TAUNTS."

—*Henry Wadsworth Longfellow, "The Masque of Pandora"*

CHAPTER 25

MAY 15, 1817, BARRY HOUSE, LEXINGTON, KENTUCKY

"Ladies, allow me to introduce Mr. Townsend Dade of Culpeper and Mr. John McCarty of Cedar Grove," said Catherine Mason Barry as Jack and his friend Townsend entered the drawing room of the Barry home. "Gentlemen, may I present to you Miss Virginia Henderson and her sister, Miss Caroline Henderson of Abington."

"I've heard about Abington," Jack said, his attention focused on Virginia, a striking woman with fair hair and wide-set blue-green eyes. "Your father's horses have quite the reputation. Some say that the farms on the long island of New York cannot produce such quality of breed."

"New York?" Virginia said in a low-country drawl. "I can assure you that my father's are the finest in the country!"

"His horses or his lovely daughters?" Jack asked with a wink.

"Such flattery, Mr. McCarty!" Virginia offered Jack her hand. Jack took it in his customary style—bringing his eyes to hers, leaving his lips on her hand long enough for her cheeks to run hot, then touching the side of his face with her fingers.

"I am pleased to meet your acquaintance," Jack said as he kept his eyes focused on hers.

"Well, aren't you just as fresh as a peach on the first day of summer!"

"And just as sweet to the taste, I can assure you."

"My, my, Catherine, wherever did you find him?" A blush erupted on Virginia's cheeks as she moved her gaze from Jack's.

"At my sister's wedding last fall. Mr. McCarty had said he was planning a trip to Natchez, and since Lexington was on his way, I invited him to stay with us. Coincidentally, when Mr. Barry and I were returning from my brother's wedding in Albemarle just last week, he and Mr. Dade were on the very same stage."

"You don't say! And how was it that Mr. McCarty was in attendance at your sister's wedding?"

"Mr. McCarty's brother William is married to my sister Emily."

"Is that so! I had heard that your sister married herself quite the dandy."

"According to my sister, Mr. McCarty here is even more incorrigible than his brother!" Catherine said with a laugh.

Jack shot a bemused glance at Townsend. "I am hardly incorrigible," Jack said, having had enough of the two talking about him as if he weren't in the room. "I'm just determined when it comes to getting what I want."

"And what is it you might want, Mr. McCarty?" Virginia said with a tilt of her head and a hand on her hip.

"Jack. My friends call me Jack. And it all depends, Miss Virginia. It all depends on what interests me."

"My friends call me Ginny. And it is my pleasure to meet your peachy acquaintance," she said with a nod of her handsome head and a twinkle of mischief in her eyes. Jack nodded back with intrigue and every intention of getting to know the striking Miss Virginia Henderson better.

"Why don't we retire to the veranda, as I do believe it is cooler out there," Catherine suggested.

"Mr. McCarty, would you be so kind as to show me the way?" Virginia asked, offering Jack her arm.

"The pleasure would be mine." Jack took her hand in the crook of his elbow and escorted her to the veranda. It would be the first of many occasions over the coming weeks when Virginia Henderson would offer Jack her arm, and the beginning of an unexpected relationship between the two.

CHAPTER 26

JUNE 12, 1817, BARRY HOUSE

"I say we forgo the rest of the trip and stay the summer in Lexington," Townsend proposed. He and Jack were on the veranda of the Barry house, playing cards and sipping juleps to the singing of cicadas in the trees above. "If we get ourselves into courtship with the Henderson girls, we can secure those dowries by Christmas and be headed back to Virginia having doubled our wealth."

Over the previous month, Jack and Townsend had integrated into the social circles of Lexington, attending picnics and parties, races and receptions, barbeques and balls. Along with a throng of admirers, the Henderson sisters, too, had attended every function. But the men the sisters admired most were the newcomers from Virginia, with Caroline on Townsend's arm at nearly every function, and Ginny hanging on to Jack's.

"Have you gone mad, Towns? That would mean taking on a bride and all that comes with it." Jack shot a piercing glance at Townsend over a fan of cards.

"Well, isn't that ultimately the plan, Jack? Find a woman to share it all with?"

"I thought the plan was to go to Natchez and establish our trading business. To seek out land speculation opportunities in new territories.

To make our mark on the world by our own efforts. I don't recall the plan including finding wives in Lexington."

"You do realize that in addition to their dowries, they are the only heirs to General Henderson's estate? And the man is as old as Methuselah!" Jack ignored his friend and kept his focus on the cards in his hand. "We have to take wives at some point." Jack shot Townsend a disapproving look. "Come on, Jack. You must admit, you're sweet on Ginny. And for certain, she is sweet on you."

"Towns, if you think that enjoying the company of a pretty lady constitutes 'being sweet on her,' I'd hate to know your idea of what constitutes being in love!"

"Being in love? And what would Jack McCarty know about that?" Jack moved his eyes back to the cards in his hand without responding. Townsend raised an eyebrow. "… Or has someone perhaps at last impaled his heart?"

"I told you, Towns, she's a nice girl, but I have no intention of courting her."

"It's her, isn't it?"

"Virginia Henderson has not impaled my heart—no matter how big her dowry might be. Besides, I don't need it. The dowry or the aggravation of a wife."

"I'm not talking about Virginia Henderson."

Jack shot him another look. "I am not discussing this any further. If you want to stay in Lexington on our return from Natchez, that is perfectly fine with me. But you'll stay on your own, for I have no business here other than to enjoy the remaining week before we leave."

"I never thought I'd see the day."

"I don't know what you are talking about. What day?"

"The day a woman got under your skin."

Jack rolled his eyes. "For God's sake, man. Ginny has hardly gotten under my skin! I barely know her, and frankly, she's too, I don't know, too bossy for my blood."

"I'm not talking about Ginny. It's Lucinda Lee that you're avoiding."

The mention of Lucinda's name caused Jack's heart to palpitate. "Lucinda Lee is not under my skin."

"Oh, I think she's more than under your skin. And she's quite the prize, should you catch her. She's prettier than Ginny, that's for sure. And all that Lee land and wealth …"

"Towns, you are too concerned about wealth and dowries. And should you find it in your heart to court Caroline, then you have my condolences. Meanwhile, I am pouring myself another drink while you show me your hand. I call."

CHAPTER 27

JUNE 19, 1817, ABINGTON FARM, LEXINGTON, KENTUCKY

Jack whistled. "He's a beauty." A black stallion with a shimmery coat neighed and pranced in the stall.

"He's my father's favorite and the envy of all of Lexington," said Ginny, squaring her shoulders proudly while Jack leaned over the stall door, admiring the lines of the animal.

"I can see why. He's quite impressive."

"He's just now back from the Ward farm. Father is hopeful he'll sire some beautiful colts next spring."

"Now that's something I can see myself doing, breeding horses. I've never been too keen on planting, but horses—"

"You know, Jack, I could arrange for you to take him out tomorrow, if you'd like."

Jack raised a brow and turned from the stall to face her. "Is there a condition attached?"

"Now why on earth would you think my offer was conditional?"

"Oh, I don't know, Ginny. Perhaps because everything you offer seems to come at a price," Jack teased.

"You are exaggerating, Mr. McCarty. I am simply direct in communicating my expectations. If you'd like to ride the stallion, I shall ask my father. Of course, you certainly don't need me to arrange it. You could ask him yourself."

"I will speak to him tomorrow about it." Jack turned his attention back to the horse.

"Jack." He looked at her again. "I don't know how to tell you this." Ginny stepped toward him and roped her arms around his neck, lacing her fingers behind his head. "I am in love with you."

Her declaration and affection stunned him. "Surely your heart has confused fondness for love." Using both hands, Jack removed her arms from him. "For I am very fond of you, Ginny. But love—"

"No. My heart is not confused." Ginny reached for his hands. "And neither is yours, for I know your heart. It wants to love me."

"Ginny, you are a beautiful woman, and my heart is indeed fond of you, but I can assure you it is not love."

"But you do have tender feelings for me." Ginny looked up at him and stepped closer. "As our courtship progresses, love will come."

Jack stared in disbelief. "I'm not sure where you got the notion that we are in courtship."

"What do you think we have been doing this last month? We have spent nearly every day together. Here in Kentucky, that's what we call courtship."

"Where I come from, courtship is not a presumption."

Ginny's eyes narrowed. "I haven't presumed anything. I have given you all my company at the expense of other suitors. For you to deny our courtship is disingenuous, Mr. McCarty."

"I haven't been disingenuous. I have been completely honest with you. You knew that I was only in Lexington for a few weeks. And yes, I have enjoyed your company, but my desires lie elsewhere."

"Your desires lie elsewhere?"

Jack chose his words carefully. "I'm sorry, Ginny, but it was not my intent to mislead you. I thought it was clear that I have other interests."

An angry flush rose on her face. "Other interests?"

"Yes, other interests beyond courtship."

"What kinds of interests have you that could possibly compete with me?" Ginny crossed her arms and glared at him. "There is someone else, isn't there?"

Jack shook his head. "As I've told you all along, I have business interests in Natchez."

"Sure you do." There was sarcasm on her face and in her tone. "I've spoken with Catherine. She warned me about you—to be careful with my heart."

"Catherine knows little about my life, Ginny. Until William and Emily's wedding, I hadn't seen her since we were children."

"She knows all about you! And all about *her*! I told her you would never have interest in someone like that, but now we know, don't we!"

Jack's brow wrinkled with confusion. "Who are you talking about?"

"You know exactly who, Jack McCarty!" A fly buzzed around the hat on her head, irritating her more. She swatted at it angrily. "Catherine knows her. They went to academy together."

"Virginia, I have no idea what you are talking about."

"That Lee girl!" Ginny stammered, spitting the words at him.

"Lucinda?"

"See? I knew it! How can you stand here in courtship with me and profess your desire for another woman?" She waved her hand wildly as the fly continued to pester her.

"I'm not professing my desire for Lucinda any more than I am in courtship with you!"

"Unlike me, she has nothing to offer you." Virginia pointed her index finger at him, her voice filling with anger. "Nothing!"

"What?"

"Don't tell me you don't know."

"What are you talking about?"

"The woman has no inheritance. She offers you nothing more than an overseer's daughter could!"

A fuse ignited within him. "I don't think you understand, Virginia. I don't need a dowry. What I need is far more than a dowry can buy!"

"Oh really, Mr. McCarty! Like what? Like a horse farm? Can Lucinda Lee give you that? Marriage to Virginia Henderson can! You have an affinity for politics. How would you like a seat in Congress? Marry me, and my father will arrange that for you, too! You see, not only does my father have wealth and resources, Jack, but he has influence and power. There is nothing he won't do for me. Just look at me. By your own admission, I am beautiful and witty and charming and all that a man like you desires. And, unlike that Lee girl, I enjoy the utmost impeccable reputation in society."

The fuse on Jack's temper was burning hot and fast. "What are you insinuating? That because she lost her father and the estate was mishandled, her reputation is less than yours? That her misfortune somehow soils her character? You have no right to judge her like that!"

Virginia looked at Jack with daggers in her eyes. "How can you defend that harlot?"

"Harlot? How dare you!"

"Well, you know what they say about those Lee girls." A smirk curled on Virginia's angry face. "Their legs spread just as easy as butter."

You mongrel bitch! Jack all but yelled the words as his wrath detonated. He thought he might strike her. "You know nothing about my Lucinda!"

"Your Lucinda? *Your* Lucinda?!" Ginny was now shouting. "Is that the kind of woman you want?"

"What I want is a woman with *ambition*. A woman with a *soul*, Ginny. Something your father can never buy for you." Jack turned his back to leave.

"Are you walking away? Just like that? After I shared my feelings, you are walking away?"

Jack paused momentarily and turned to face her. "As a matter of fact, I am, Virginia."

Ginny put her hands on her hips and glared at him. "There is not a gentleman in the state of Kentucky who walks away from Virginia Henderson!"

"Well, Miss Henderson, there's a first time for everything."

———————◆———————

Long after the sun had set, Jack sat on the front porch of the Barry house with only the moon to keep him company. He was lost in thought watching lightning bugs drift carelessly through the warm night air, their green-gold lights marking where they were with no indication of where they might go next.

And what about you, Jack? Is that what you are? An insect that drifts through life, flashing your insignificance without direction, without purpose?

Jack closed his eyes. So much was riding on this trip. *A chance to prove myself!* He and Townsend had planned this trip to Natchez for months. Natchez was the region's slavery hub, where people were traded from Virginia to cotton plantations in the deep Southern states, and Jack was convinced there was room in the market and money to be made. They would buy a small tract of land to the east of the larger markets at Forks of the Road and establish their own market. Townsend would run the sales operation in Natchez, while Jack managed the supply side in Alexandria. But that was before Townsend decided to stay in Lexington. That was before the Henderson sisters.

Sally has said it a hundred times: "Your penchant for pretty girls will be your downfall, John McCarty!"

Jack shook his head as he recited aloud his mother's words, "Judge not a man by his clothing, or oft you'll admire a heart that needs loathing."

Sally! He drew a sigh at the thought of his mother—the mischief in her eyes, the rasp of her voice, her silly antics and cheerful laughter. He longed to see her, to breathe the air of the Pohick, to foxhunt at Belmont, to see his friends and his family. How he missed home!

And then there was Lucinda.

For weeks now, he had tried to push her from his mind. How alive he'd felt that afternoon standing with her on the bluff. His heart had soared, and he'd felt as if he could have leapt from the edge and flown with the birds had she only said yes.

"Yes, I will wait for you." "Yes, I will care for you." "Yes, I will love you." Is that what you want, Jack? Love?

Jack looked up at the star-studded sky and the moon, round and bright with its cratered smile. He wondered if Lucinda was sharing her dreams tonight with its smiling face rising over the Potomac. *Are you there, Lucy? Out on the bluff dreaming?* Staring at the sky, he envisioned Lucinda's moon-bleached face high above the silver water of the river, her sapphire eyes smiling back at him. He closed his eyes and lifted his face toward the heavens as he drew dusk's air into his lungs. *What are your dreams, Lucy?* Although she was hundreds of miles away, he was certain that he felt her presence and sensed her thoughts—thoughts of the two of them together. A warmth rushed through him in torrents. His chest ached, yearning, longing to be near her.

"Good night, Lucy," he whispered as he opened his eyes and fixed his gaze on the moon. "Sweet dreams, my love. Sweet dreams."

CHAPTER 28

OCTOBER 28, 1817, SELMA

Armistead knew that there was something dreadfully wrong the moment he saw his butler's face.

"Praise the Lord, you are home, Marster!" Joe said, rushing the coach as it halted in front of the columned porch. He unlatched the door and swung it open. "Marster, hurry!"

"What is it?" Armistead asked, lifting from the seat his satchel overstuffed with notes from the day's testimonies against Mercer's election.

"It's Miss Charlotte, sir! Nelly and I sent for your mother and the doctor, but only Missus Polly is here with Hester."

Armistead shoved the satchel into Joe's hands as he jumped from the coach and pushed past him. Leaping up the marble steps to the house, Armistead raced inside and upstairs to Charlotte's chamber. He flung the door open. Charlotte was lying in bed with Polly and Polly's maid Hester at her side. Armistead's maid Nelly was at the footboard, bent over and attending to something. Blood-soaked linen and rags were in a basket on the floor. Polly stood abruptly and rushed across the room, grim-faced with creases of worry etched on her forehead.

"Out of here, Armistead!" she said, pushing him through the door.

"Mother, what is it? What has happened to Charlotte?" Armistead's heart was pounding so hard he could hear it in his ears.

"Armistead! In the hall! Please! Now!" Polly pushed his chest with her palms and forced him out of the room. "She's miscarried, Armistead, and we can't stop the bleeding."

Armistead's tongue was thick and his mouth dry. "The child? Are you saying she has lost the child?" He had been elated by Charlotte's news at the end of the summer that at long last he was to be a father. Next to winning the governorship, there was nothing more important to him than an heir to ensure his legacy.

"I'm afraid so, although one could hardly call it a child. But Charlotte—we … we can't stop the letting."

"What do you mean?"

"Charlotte, son. We can't stop her letting."

Her letting … letting … bleeding. Oh, God! Armistead's knees gave way. *Not again! Not Charlotte!* With his fear, adrenaline rushed forward, fueling his instincts, and spurring him to take control. He shouted for Joe at the top of his lungs.

"Yes, Marster!" Joe raced up the stairs.

"Ride as fast as you can to Rockland. Tell Colonel Rust to get Mrs. Rust here in short order. Hurry, Joe!"

"Joe, you are to do no such thing!" Polly said before turning to Armistead. "Armistead, I have already sent for the doctor." Ignoring his mother, Armistead reiterated his instructions.

"I am your master, Joe, and you take your orders from me!"

"We do not need that ill-tempered woman in Hester's way. Hester is an experienced midwife. Have you forgotten that it was Hester who brought you into the world?"

"My entry into the world is irrelevant, and I don't rightly care how ill-tempered Maria might be. I have already lost one wife to miscarriage on your insistence that we wait for the doctor. I will not lose another!" He turned to Joe. "Now go, Joe! Go get Mrs. Rust!" Joe, wide-eyed at the exchange between Armistead and his mother, raced down the stairs and out the front door.

"Eliza's death was God's punishment for her adultery! I had nothing to do with it!"

"I will not stand here waiting for a doctor, relying on Hester to save her."

"Maria Rust will get in the way."

"Then you'll have to put up with her in your way, because I cannot bear to lose Charlotte! I can't, Mother. Now let me see her!"

"You mustn't see her in this condition, Armistead."

"Nonsense. I've seen more on the battlefield than what awaits me in that room." Armistead pushed his way past Polly and through the bedroom door.

Hester, sitting in a chair at Charlotte's bedside, was holding her hand. Try as he might, his eyes could not avoid the soiled linens at the foot of the bed. Following his gaze, Nelly picked up the basket and removed it from his sight.

"Marster Armie, you shouldn't be in here," Hester said.

"My place is here beside her. Now go, Hester. I'll take care of her until Mrs. Rust arrives."

Hester shook her head as she rose from the chair. "I ain't never … ," she said, shuffling across the rug to the door.

Taking Charlotte's hand in his, Armistead pulled the chair close. Charlotte looked ashen, her eyes sunken, her face anemic and gray. He interlaced the fingers of one hand with hers and brushed the hair from her forehead with the fingertips of the other. She was cool to the touch, and he thought momentarily that she might be dead. A gut-wrenching despair churned in his core.

"Please, my darling, do not leave me." At the sound of his voice, Charlotte slowly opened her eyes. "I am here, darling," Armistead said, forcing a reassuring smile. It was all he could do to hold back his tears as her pale lips attempted a weak smile.

"I will not allow your God to take you from me, Charlotte. I will not."

Charlotte opened her mouth to speak.

"Shhh, my darling." Armistead moved a forefinger to her lips. "No need for words. Rest. You are safe now." Her lips thinned to a faint smile, and she closed her eyes.

Clasping both hands around hers, Armistead waited, gently stroking her skin and whispering reassurances as much for himself as for her. "Maria is coming. She will know exactly what to do." And, indeed, it wasn't long before Maria Rust burst through the door, followed by Polly, Hester, and Nelly.

"General Mason, you must leave here at once!" Maria commanded, her wild hair flying like a warning flag. "You'll give her an infection just as sure as you're sitting there! Out! Out!" She pushed her way past Armistead and placed her hands on Charlotte's forehead and face.

"No fever, praise the Lord, but by God, from the coldness of her, she has lost a lot of blood!"

Maria Rust, though younger than nearly everyone in the room, was not shy when it came to giving orders in matters such as these. The child of a physician, Maria had learned as much from her father as any son. She was an experienced midwife with a temperament as fiery as her hair. Even Polly Mason, now standing behind her, was afraid to get in her way.

"Nelly, start a fire on the stove and warm me some blankets to put over her before she goes into further distress. We need to get her warm and keep her warm. And, Hester, nothing comes into this room unless it's been boiled!"

She moved her eyes to Polly. "Mrs. Mason, we'll need clean cloth. Muslin or linen will do. Certainly there are sheets we can cut into strips. Oh and, I'll need salts for the water, and witch hazel and nettle, which surely you have growing here somewhere. If not, George will ride to Rockland and bring some from home." Maria turned to Armistead, who, still reeling from her abruptness, had not moved.

"General, please remove yourself and tell that butler of yours to round up a wooden crate or a box or even an empty lard can. We need to raise her legs up as high as we can. And pillows. I'll need pillows. Quickly, now, hop to it!" After delivering her orders, Maria turned her attention to the patient in the bed.

"Poor Charlotte, what have we done?" Maria pulled the blankets back to begin her examination. Armistead was still standing at the bedside. "General Mason, please! I need you to leave now so that I can help your wife. Now go! Find me that box and those salts at once."

Armistead withdrew. Hester and Nelly hurried out of the room in front of him, heeding Maria's instructions. Joe, who had been standing outside the doorway with George, was already headed down the stairs to retrieve the salts, witch hazel, and anything that could be used to raise his mistress's feet. Armistead did what he normally did when he lost control—he fumed and he paced. He paced on the landing outside Charlotte's chamber for what seemed like hours before exhaustion overtook him. When he finally sank into the chair that Joe had brought for him, he hung his head, unable to rid his mind of images of his first wife in the same bed.

Eliza.

It seemed so long ago that she had died. He couldn't remember if he had loved her, although he knew for certain that she hadn't loved him. If only Eliza's father had allowed her to marry the man who had truly claimed her heart. But Armistead had been happy with the arrangement—marry a superior officer's daughter in exchange for rank and title. Until her betrayal, that is. And the lies. And then a child conceived while Armistead was entrenched on Craney Island and sorting through the aftermath of the annihilation of Hampton. He had swallowed his anguish and the shame she had brought on him—and his guilt and grief and regret that God had answered his prayers for retribution.

Armistead rubbed his face and pushed his fingers into his temples to force the past away. *Not my Charlotte! Not this time!* Armistead turned his head to the chair where George sat waiting with him. George had been with him at Norfolk. George had been with him when Eliza died.

As though reading his mind, George looked at Armistead and said, "She'll pull through, Arm. God won't forsake you again."

Armistead dropped his gaze to the floor and held his head in his hands. The two waited for hours in silence, watching Polly, Hester, and Nelly going in and out of the room with basins of water, clean and soiled linen, warm blankets, and whatever else was needed. It would be well after midnight when Maria, her flying hair now under a kerchief and pulled tightly away from her face, emerged from the chamber. "The letting has been contained, praise be to the Lord! She's weak from the loss and is distraught with pain. She needs much rest."

"I need to see her."

"Not for several days, General. I'm afraid the risk of fever is too great. Your mother, Hester, and I will stay with her until she is well enough to receive you."

George put a hand on Armistead's shoulder. "Maria knows these things, Arm. We have to trust her."

"She is weak but determined. Give her time," Maria said with a tired smile. "I'll be back in the morning to check on her and will stay as long as she needs."

"How much time? Before I can see her?"

"Get some rest, General. Please." Armistead brought his eyes to hers, pleading. "Get some rest," she said gently, putting her hand on his sleeve.

Armistead drew a long sigh, torn between wanting to see his wife and heeding Maria's better judgment. At last, he relented. "As you wish," he said, covering her hand with his own. "Thank you, Maria."

"You are welcome, General. And I will see you in the morning." Maria squeezed his forearm before pulling her hand away. She turned to her husband. "Come, George, let's get us home. Mrs. Colonel Rust, too, needs her rest." Taking her husband's arm, she and George headed downstairs to their coach waiting outside. Their carriage had just pulled away when Polly emerged from Charlotte's room. She looked exhausted.

"She's like you, Armistead. She's a fighter." Polly wiped the stray hair from her brow that had fallen from underneath her cap.

"I can't lose her. I couldn't bear it." Armistead's voice was breaking with emotion.

"I know, my son. I know." Polly stroked his cheek with her hand. "You're exhausted, darling. I'll stay with her the rest of the night."

"But if something should happen—"

"I promise to wake you. Now go. She needs your strength. Get some rest." Armistead took Polly's hand and glanced at the chamber door. He drew a long breath before looking at his mother again.

"Thank you, Mother." He took her hand and kissed it. "Take care of her for me."

"Anything for you, my son. Anything."

———— ◆ ————

Armistead awoke just after dawn to Joe's gentle rap on his door informing him that the doctor had finally arrived. Armistead could smell fresh whiskey on the doctor's breath as he debriefed Armistead and Polly on his examination of Charlotte. He told them that he had medicated her with an opium tincture to relieve her hysteria and her pain. He instructed Polly to continue to administer the drug until Charlotte was free from physical distress. Cautioning Armistead, he explained that expanding Charlotte's mind with politics was diverting energy from her reproductive system and, thus, was most likely the cause of her miscarriage. His prescription was bed rest, opium, and the elimination of worry. Armistead was to do nothing that would upset her fragile condition. And most important, there were to be no conjugal visits to her chamber. Armistead, though infuriated, held his tongue at his mother's stern look of warning at the doctor's last instruction, and smiled politely at the inebriated doctor before sending him on his way with fee in hand.

It was four days before Armistead was permitted to see his wife. When he entered her room, he was overwhelmed by a stale smell of sickness. She was sitting up in bed with her eyes closed and her head turned toward the window. Her face was so pale, her skin so thin, that he could see the blue of her blood through its translucency. With his whisper of her name, she opened her eyes and slowly turned her head. There was a lethargy in her affect that unnerved him. She smiled at him, but not with the warmth and adoration to which he was accustomed.

She seemed distant, distracted. This was not his Charlotte, but some vacant soul inhabiting her body. He took her hand and kissed her forehead as he sat next to her. "How are you, my darling?"

Charlotte seemed disoriented. "I do not know. How am I?"

"You are going to be just fine, love. Just fine."

Charlotte smiled at his encouraging words and, much to Armistead's relief, began to find clarity. She apologized that she had worried him so much. She was sorry that she had lost their child. Sorry for so many things.

Armistead lifted her chin with his forefinger and softly hushed her. "It is not your fault, my darling, and there is nothing for you to be sorry for. The doctor says you mustn't worry."

She tried to smile again, but the smile quickly faded to tears. Armistead impulsively took her into his arms. He was surprised by how frail she felt and how thin her shoulders had become. And, for the first time since the days following the funeral of his first wife, he wept.

CHAPTER 29

NOVEMBER 10, 1817, CEDAR GROVE, FAIRFAX, VIRGINIA

Summer had faded to autumn at Cedar Grove, with the leaves of the silver maple, box elder, and sycamore melting to gold, auburn, and crimson against the bay's glittering reflection of the blue morning sky. The pages of newsprint on Jack's lap rustled in a breeze as the red-winged blackbirds clattered in the reeds behind him. His peace on the south porch was interrupted as two bald eagles clashed overhead in a talon-grappling midair battle. Jack glanced up at the raptors' skirmish before repositioning his chair in the sunshine to warm himself from the chill of the western wind. Settling back into the chair, he pulled another newspaper from the stack that his mother had stockpiled for his return. On the front page was an advertisement for a slave auction at the quay in Alexandria. He grew nauseated and closed his eyes.

Natchez. How old could the enslaved boy have been? Twelve? Thirteen? In all his life, Jack would never forget those eyes filled with anger and fear and pain. Jack choked back bile at the memory—the driver dismounting from his horse, lash raised, repeatedly striking the boy stumbling through the thick black mud.

Yes, he had witnessed overseers disciplining the enslaved at Cedar Grove and Mount Air, but this he could not stomach.

"Get up, nigger!" The driver commanded, bringing the whip down in a whistle across the boy's head. The child fell to his knees, causing the man chained to him to stumble as well. "Get up, you stinkin' nigger!"

It was the next crack of the whip that brought Jack to his senses.

"That's enough!" he roared as he spurred his horse past the manacled, enslaved men toward the brute with the lash.

"I decide what's enough," snarled the man, raising the whip above his head. When he hit the boy again, Jack saw red blood seeping through what was left of the child's shirt. Had Townsend not been close on Jack's heels that hot, muggy afternoon just east of the Forks of the Road markets, he was certain he'd have killed the bully with the whip.

Try as he might, Jack could not force the images of that July day from his mind. Enslaved men—barefoot, shackled, and chained together in double files under the close supervision of mounted drivers armed with guns and whips. Women walking in bare feet with tattered skirts caked in mud. Children and the infirm riding alongside in overloaded wagons. Their silence in the face of such inhumane treatment screamed at him; their suffering obvious as they shuffled and clanked down the road from Virginia through Tennessee and the Natchez Trace. For days he couldn't sleep, and still visions of their anguish haunted him.

Jack lifted his gaze from the slave auction advertisement across the bay to Gunston Hall. *What do I do now?* More than anything, he needed his grandfather's counsel. The questions he had. About birthright. About his own purpose and place in the world. Taking one last look at his late grandfather's plantation, he returned his attention to the newspaper on his lap, turning the page. *TO THE PEOPLE OF LOUDOUN.* It was a notice published by Charles Fenton Mercer challenging Armistead's contest of the last election.

Reading Fenton's demands, Jack felt his pulse quicken. *Proof of land and slave ownership, property deeds, leases on indentured servants, proof of citizenship, proof of allegiance oath*—Fenton was insisting that everyone who voted in the election provide documentation to validate their right of suffrage or their vote be removed from Armistead's poll. His demands seemed absurd and would surely alienate the freeholders. *Why would he do that?* Jack cast his eyes again at his late grandfather's home across the bay.

"You seem awfully preoccupied with my father's place there across the water, Jack," said a raspy voice from behind him.

Jack turned his head to find his mother crossing the porch with a cup of coffee in one hand and a rolled newspaper in the other.

Her smiling eyes brought him comfort. "Not preoccupied, but occupied with thought."

"Indeed, I can see that." She handed him the mug. "You know, you remind me of him sometimes."

"You've told me a thousand times that I share his image."

"Your father's image, yes. But I meant *my* father. You have his mind."

"You've never shared that."

"I've been holding out on you." With longing in her eyes, Sally moved her gaze to the opposite shore. "Just as he was, you're outspoken, principled, bright, ambitious, and oh, that cutting wit. Sally looked back to Jack with a smile. "The two of you certainly have that in common!" She laughed. "You should run for office, Jack. Your grandfather would have liked that. Why don't you campaign for Fenton's seat in the legislature?"

"I hadn't considered it."

"Well, you should. You've got big dreams of what the world ought to be like. And you'd make your old mother prouder than she already is!"

"Not sure what I've done to make you proud—"

"Now, Jack. Just because you didn't find your dreams on this trip doesn't mean you won't find them on the next. You must always keep looking, son. You can never stop dreaming. The day you stop dreaming, is ... well ... you know." She laughed again as she tightened the roll of paper in her hand. "It's the day you stop living."

Jack wanted neither to discuss his trip nor share his uncertainties with her. He noticed the paper in her hand. "What's that you've got? Did you find another one?"

Her eyes strayed to the stack by his chair. "Have you gotten through them all?"

"Not all of them. I tackled the liberal Tom Ritchie and his *Richmond Enquirer* first, while I still had patience."

"That's my boy! You know, I've come to the decision to stop reading the papers—'slander sheets,' as I call them, filled with little more than the gossip of men. Good for nothing but use in the privy!"

Jack laughed at her words. "True indeed!"

"That said, here's the most scandalous one of all."

"You holding out on me again, Sally?"

Sally's expression turned serious. "I just didn't want you to find this one randomly." She narrowed her eyes and waved her index finger at him. "Now, Jack, I don't want you to get in the middle of this thing with Fenton and Armistead. Even if others try to push you into it. Do you hear me?" She tightened her mouth and handed the paper to him.

"While I think the world of Fenton, I have no intention of fighting his or any man's battles when he brings them upon himself. And from my reading, Fenton is bringing the full wrath of the freeholders onto his head with his outlandish demands."

"It is not the wrath of the freeholders that concerns me, Jack. It is the wrath of Armistead Mason that I wish you to avoid. Fenton had no business calling Armistead a blackguard."

Jack rested the cup on the arm of the chair and looked at his mother with wide eyes. "What? Fenton is a devout Christian and would never say such a thing."

"He didn't say it. He published it."

"When did he do this?"

"A couple of weeks ago in M'Intyre's paper." Sally shook her head. "I'm not sure what's gotten into Fenton. His dear father is surely rolling in his grave at his son's conduct. But Fenton Mercer is none of my concern. Turn to the second page."

Jack unrolled the latest edition of the *Leesburg Washingtonian* and folded it open. On the second page was a reprint of an article from the Winchester paper, an article by the editor slandering the character of General Armistead T. Mason. It cited Armistead's exchange with Jack at the hustings, reporting that Armistead had cowered and was openly fearful of Jack. Among other things, the article accused the general of cowardice.

Reading the words, Jack whistled and shook his head. "I had nothing to do with this, Sally, as I have been gone for the better part of half a year. And further, it isn't true."

"I know that, Jackie, and you know that. But Armistead doesn't. Knowing that boy and his temper, it'd be smart for you to address this with him straightaway and let him know the truth. Not to be in the middle of your business or anything, as I certainly don't want to meddle."

Ha! Jack was going to rib his mother about her getting in the middle of everything, but he noticed the worry on her brow. Tapping a finger on the armrest, he considered what to do.

"Tell you what, Sally. I'll ride out to Leesburg tomorrow to visit William, and we'll map out a plan to see Armistead together. How's that sound?"

"That would be a great plan, Jack, but William is gone for a few weeks."

"Gone where?"

"To Philadelphia to bring Emily home. Just left last Tuesday, and I don't expect him back for at least another ten days or so, maybe longer."

"Philadelphia?"

"Seems Emily got it into her head to take the stage up there to stay with Lucinda Lee. She wrote to William once she arrived. Said that the stage was just dreadful and she refused to return in the same manner, so William would have to send for her. William decided to make a bit of a holiday of the situation, so off he went."

At the mention of Lucinda Lee's name, Jack felt familiar feelings that he had purposely been trying to avoid.

"What is Lucinda Lee doing in Philadelphia?"

"She's staying with some distant relations up there. A second cousin or long-lost aunt or some such relative. Singing or something, she's doing."

Jack's mind was racing. "She's joining the theater?"

"Well, I don't know if it is theater or what, but nothing scandalous, if that's what you are thinking. Singing is all I heard. Old Fannie was being vague when I caught up with her at a dining a few weeks back. You know how mothers can be when they suspect they're being prodded for information about their daughters on behalf of an admirer."

"I wouldn't know anything about that, Sally."

"Why, of course you wouldn't." There was enough exaggeration in her tone that Jack felt sure of her intention. "Just remember what I said about Armistead and Fenton. Stay clear of the two of them in this thing. I have an ominous feeling that this is not going to end well between them, and I don't want any of my boys caught up in it." There was sincerity in her voice and worry still on her brow. Jack nodded and reached over to take her hand.

"Not to worry, Sally. I'll do what's right."

CHAPTER 30

NOVEMBER 12, 1817,
MRS. PEYTON'S BOARDINGHOUSE,
ALEXANDRIA, VIRGINIA

Upon Jack's return to his boardinghouse, Mrs. Peyton, the round, matronly proprietor with salted hair and a tattered face, handed Jack a week-old letter addressed from Selma. With trepidation, he broke the seal.

Sir,

You will no doubt be surprised at this address; I will briefly explain the cause of it. The altercation that occurred between us at the hustings in Loudoun last spring has been basely misrepresented by John Heiskell, the editor of the Winchester Gazette, a fellow who is like a certain animal that wallows in his own filth! The publisher of the Washingtonian, Patrick M'Intyre, with whose name I would not soil this sheet but that it already contains Heiskell's, joins in the cry, throwing his own filth around with Heiskell's. As your name has been used to sanction their lies, I am appealing to you because your character is as much involved as mine. Notwithstanding the harsh and injurious language that we directed against each other at the hustings, I cannot believe that a gentleman such as yourself will permit your name to be employed for the purposes of such defamation. The swine, Heiskell and M'Intyre, have attempted to produce the impression that I shrank from contest with you, and they are using your good name to strengthen their statement. You know that any such statement is utterly false. I never shrank from a contest with any man unless he was such a despicable wretch as the editor of the Winchester Gazette, with whom any contact would result in certain contamination. I have greatly mistaken your character if you do not contradict the impression which that slanderous villain has attempted to create or enable me to do it on your authority.

Your obedient servant, Armistead T. Mason

Jack breathed a sigh of relief and drafted a response for immediate delivery to Leesburg.

Sir,

Your correspondence has just reached me. A duty to myself urges my declaration that I did not enlist any printer or printer's devil to defame and make false statements against General Mason, or any other man.

Your obedient servant, J. M. McCarty ·

P.S. If you feel disposed to publish the above, you have my approbation.

CHAPTER 31

DECEMBER 12, 1817, UNION TAVERN, GEORGE TOWN

Friday night was card night at Union Tavern, and the gentlemen at Fenton Mercer's table included Jack, James Dulaney, John Randolph, Benjamin Leigh, another congressman and friend of Fenton's, and Sam Snowden, the publisher of the *Alexandria Gazette*. Despite the jovial atmosphere, Fenton seemed more miserable than ever, his morose mood responsible for not only his heavy drinking but the loss of each hand he played. Every man in Washington City and throughout the District of Columbia had heard that General Mason had given Fenton Mercer an ultimatum: either retract his insults or fight the general. Fenton Mercer had no mind to do either.

"I sat down before breakfast just a few days ago and wrote him my reply," Fenton told the group. "I told him that I could not violate my solemn vows to God for the applause of the world."

"Are you saying you declined the general's challenge?" Jack asked, having been under the impression that Fenton was in negotiations over the terms of a duel.

"As a man of the law and as a Virginian—a state that specifically made the act of dueling a crime punishable by hanging—I ought not accept his challenge. And as a Christian, I could not," Fenton said, no doubt trying to convince himself more than the gentlemen at the table.

"And I, for one, my friend, applaud you!" said Leigh. "You should take pride in your refusal. To act according to your own ideas of duty in defiance of the opinion of the world ought to give you no pain. It is your duty to our Father in heaven. That, my friend, is the duty that you must put before everything else."

"While I appreciate your vote of confidence, defending my conduct has given me nothing but pain. It has been the most trying event in all my life," Fenton said, casting his gaze to the floor.

In Jack's mind, Fenton's predicament was of his own making, and it took every ounce of restraint for Jack not to say so. James discreetly shook his head, affirming what Jack knew already—for once, Jack needed to keep his opinions to himself.

"I'd be more concerned about defending my person than defending my conduct, if I were you, my friend," said Randolph, in a chartreuse jacket as loud as the room.

"What are you suggesting?" Fenton asked, lifting his moping eyes to Randolph.

"I'm saying that I wouldn't put it past the bastard to shoot you outright," Randolph said in a loud voice, seemingly unconcerned about being overheard. "Mason's got himself an out-of-control temper and a scheming mind. He might take to shooting you in broad daylight and then convince the authorities—including that local sheriff friend of his—that you had it coming or that it was in self-defense or some such justification."

"There were rumors that, during the last war, General Mason labeled any man who disagreed with him a deserter and shot him. Thus, his loyal following, I suppose. Go along or get shot," Snowden said.

"Are you suggesting that I should arm myself?" Fenton asked.

"If it were me, I would carry a pistol under my cloak just in case," Snowden said. Fenton gulped down the remaining whiskey in his glass.

"Well, I am sorry that I put you in this position, my friend." Randolph shook his head sympathetically at Mercer. All eyes at the table turned to Randolph.

"How could you have possibly put me in this situation, John? It is Mason's temper and my poor judgment that has landed me in this quagmire and nothing you have done."

"Not entirely true, my friend, not entirely true. While I cannot take responsibility for your poor choice of words to Mason, I must confess that I had a hidden hand in the present circumstances." Randolph paused and stroked his chin. "I convinced my Republican colleagues to force the general's resignation from the Senate because I wanted his seat." Confusion spread across Fenton's face, while Jack, like everyone else at the table, was shocked by Randolph's admission. "And I am sorry, my friend. Had I not done that, you would not have had to run against him. Mason would still be the conspicuously dumb senator from Virginia, your election to the House uncontested, your character unchallenged, and your well-nourished body safe and sound from any balls of lead propelled by Mason's pistols."

Jack wondered what role he himself had unwittingly played in Randolph's scheme to oust Armistead from the Senate. Hadn't he disclosed Armistead's age to Randolph at the party at Aldie? His stomach felt as if it had flipped over in his abdomen.

"Fenton's run for the House seat wasn't the only thing that set Mason off," Leigh said. He turned to Fenton. "He was itching to call you out for your objection to his election to the Senate in the first place. As a Christian, you are compelled to do what's right. And your duty to God compels you to abstain from un-Christian acts, as you are doing now."

James slammed his shoulders against the back of his chair, foregoing his own cautionary advice to Jack. "That may be true, and I mean this with no disrespect, but how can one claim God as a reason not to partake in an un-Christian act and then, in the same breath, partake in an un-Christian act?"

"To what acts are you referring?" Randolph said, straightening in his seat.

Exactly where are you going with this, James? thought Jack, aware of rumors that John Randolph and Fenton Mercer were sodomites.

"What I mean, sir, and again with no disrespect intended, is that on the one hand, Fenton has stated he cannot duel the general based on his allegiance to God. Yet on the other hand, Fenton branded the general a blackguard and a bully—hardly the Christian thing to do. Fenton also opposed the amendment to the militia bill, denying religious objectors a paid substitute to fight on their behalf, yet himself refuses to fight the general based on religious convictions. What are we to say to members of the party—gentlemen who are staunch Federalists—when they question Fenton's actions and accuse him of hypocrisy?"

Silence fell awkwardly around the table. After a long moment of nervous glances, Fenton broke the tension. "All I can offer, son, is that I have strayed from the true source of Christian consolation. I do not know how I will ever overcome these moral prejudices against my conduct."

Jack rolled his eyes. He glanced at James, who was reacting similarly.

"Aye, don't be so hard on yourself, Fenton," Randolph said. "Maybe this will all work out like your poker game has tonight. Sometimes when you lose the hand, it's best to simply walk away from the table. Maybe your safest option is for the Committee on Elections to rule in Mason's favor. I know the chair quite well, and perhaps he can be persuaded to make this whole thing go away. We can fix it so that Mason wins his petition and gets your seat in the House. Maybe then he'll forget all about wanting to shoot you."

Jack couldn't tell if Randolph was serious about his ability to influence the Committee on Elections or not. And judging by the fear spreading over Fenton's face, Jack wouldn't be surprised if Fenton started carrying a pistol tonight.

"Well, it doesn't appear to me that Mason really wants to shoot you, Fenton," Snowden said. "I think he's just as worried about getting shot as you are. If you read the notice he published last month, he made all sorts of lame excuses for why he hadn't challenged you immediately following your insult the month before. Claiming his wife was ill! That the governor needed to accept his resignation! On top of that, he had every reason to call out Jack for his conduct at the hustings last April, but clearly was afraid to do so. My opinion is that Mason is nothing more than a bullying coward."

Jack could hold his tongue no longer. "I served under him for a few weeks early in the war, and while I found his methods merciless and belittling, I believe it is a step too far to accuse him of cowardice. My brother served under his command in Baltimore and has often spoken of his heroism. And his wife is indeed in poor health and has been bedridden for months. I think you have it wrong, Sam. As long as I've known him, Armistead Mason has never backed away from a fight."

"He backed down from you, Jack," James said. "At the hustings."

"What are you talking about, James? He threw every insult imaginable at me."

"But he never threw a fist, did he?"

"Why do you go to such lengths to defend him, Mr. McCarty?" Randolph said. "The man is a poltroon!"

"I am not defending him," said Jack. "I am simply stating facts as I know them."

"The facts as I see them, Jack, are that it is unclear whose side you are on," Snowden said. "Just two weeks ago, you publicly supported Mason's blasphemy of two of our colleagues, Heiskell and M'Intyre. And now you object to Mason's slandering a Federalist in private? Heiskell, by the way, is so insulted that he is considering a suit of defamation against Mason and may include you as codefendant."

"Defamation? For what? Simply clarifying the truth? I had nothing to do with the publishing of that article in the *Winchester Gazette*. Nor M'Intyre's reprint of it in the *Washingtonian*. Further, I have published nothing about Heiskell, M'Intyre, or anyone else for that matter!"

"Mason published a joint statement by you and him declaring Heiskell a villainous scoundrel."

"What joint statement? The general wrote me and asked if I had slandered his character. I told him that I never encouraged nor enlisted any printer to defame him, and I gave him permission to say so on my behalf. That's the extent of it."

"It seems General Mason has skewed your meaning, then. Have you not seen his latest notice?" Snowden asked. Jack shook his head.

"Barkeep!" Snowden shouted to the man with bushy sideburns behind the bar. "Bring here that newspaper." Snowden was pointing at a stack sitting on the edge of the counter. The man held up the newspaper from the top of the pile. "No, no. Not that one. The *Genius of Liberty*. The one with the eagle on the masthead." The bartender riffled through several papers before lifting one and turning its front page to Snowden. "Yes, yes. That's the one." The bartender walked over, handing the newspaper to Snowden. "Give it to him." Snowden pointed to Jack.

Taking the paper, Jack thumbed through and found what he was looking for on page three.

TO THE PUBLIC

I publish the letter of Mr. John Mason McCarty along with this brief joint statement. Every man who insinuates (as some scoundrels in the press already have) that I shrunk from the contest with John McCarty at the last Loudoun election, is a blatant liar and vile calumniator.

ARMISTEAD T. MASON

"I never endorsed this!" Jack said, his annoyance and voice rising above the clamor of murmured voices and clanking coins, glass, and ice.

"See what happens when you defend that man? He turns it right around on you," Randolph said, smirking while he rearranged the cards in his hand.

Jack was in no mood for Randolph's sermon and had half a mind to say so, but he was cautious not to offend yet another gentleman. Armistead had already done enough. Reading Armistead's words once again, he shook his head.

"I just can't believe he did this."

"Well, he has, Jack," Snowden said. "I tell you what. Come by my offices tomorrow and bring the letter that Mason sent you. If I publish his letter to you, you can attest which parts you endorsed and which you didn't. You can clarify your intent and clear your name in association with any slander."

Publishing Armistead's letter was risky, and Jack knew it. Armistead would no doubt be infuriated and publicly exposed, but Armistead had implicated Jack in his defamation, and now Jack was liable. "All right, then," said Jack. "I will seek you out tomorrow in Alexandria. The last thing I want is a dispute with Heiskell and M'Intyre."

"Be careful, Jack. Nor do you want to pick a fight with Mason," Fenton said, his face still void of color.

"Not to worry," Snowden said. "Jack here has a right to give his valedictory. Mason certainly cannot fault him for simply clarifying what he meant."

Jack folded the paper and pushed it aside. *Nothing is simple when it comes to Armistead Mason.*

Although the games went on until midnight, it wasn't much past nine before Jack and James had had enough of Mercer's self-pity and Randolph's bluster. After a few more hands, they excused themselves from the table and left Union Tavern. While Jack was keen for billiards on the tables at City Tavern, James was interested in visiting the girls at the House of Rose. On his return from Natchez, Jack had made a conscious decision to stay away from such establishments. But it didn't take much arm-twisting from his friend to break his vow.

CHAPTER 32

PAST MIDNIGHT, GEORGE TOWN

Jack lifted his half-clothed body from the soiled mattress. In the same corset she had worn when he saw her last, Lillie was lying on her back beneath him. Her face was pasty white with cheeks stained the same color that Rose wore and the red waxy paint on her lips was smeared over her mouth. She looked older, and the luster in her eyes that had once beguiled him was gone. Had she always looked this way? Or had the last eight months hardened her? There was a familiarity in the look of Lillie's face. *New Orleans.* The brothel on Gallatin Street. Those three prostitutes and that never-ending night. A flood of regret washed over him. "What was I thinking coming here?" he said under his breath, closing his eyes to block Lillie's image and the memory.

"Not to worry, *mo ghrá*," Lillie said, moving her hands to his groin. "These things happen from time to time."

His eyes flew open at her touch. "Please. It's not that," he said, pushing her hand from him and rolling onto his back. He pulled up his trousers and fumbled with the buttons. "I cannot do this."

Lillie sat up on the bed beside him. "No, no, *mo ghrá*. 'Tis too soon to end our homecoming." She leaned onto his chest and bent to his ear. "Let me remind you how much you missed me," she whispered, flicking her tongue against his neck. Tresses of her hair fell onto Jack's face, and

182

he nearly gagged from the mix of perfume, liquor, and sweat. As Jack held his breath, Lillie thrust a hand under the waistband of his trousers, grabbing at him again.

"Stop, Lillie." Jack shoved her away. He sat up and moved to the edge of the bed. "This is not what I had in mind."

Lillie stared at him. "Then why did you come here and buy me for the night?"

Slowly he shook his head and lowered his gaze to the floor. "I don't know."

"I know why," she said, nestling close to him. "It's because you missed me while you were on your holiday, for sure you did."

Jack's brow furrowed, not knowing quite what to say and not wanting to lie. "It is true that I longed for home while I was gone, but it would be a falsehood to say that I missed coming here. I am through with brothels." Jack turned to her. "It's no life, Lillie. It hardens you. And ultimately harms you."

Lillie nuzzled closer to him. "Then get me out of here, Jack."

"Let me talk with Rose. Maybe I can negotiate an agreement with her." He hesitated as his mind worked through the details. "I have a friend in New York, John Keith. Before the war, we were at the college in Princeton together. He can make arrangements for you—a place to live and legitimate employment. You can tell Rose that I am moving you to a private apartment. Once you're good and gone to New York, I will complain to Rose that you have abandoned me. I'll insist my fee be returned, a demand to which Rose will never agree. In a years' time, she'll have forgotten all about you."

She nodded and smiled, lifting a hand to touch his face. Jack moved his head from her reach. "I will become your mistress then."

His brow furrowed in confusion. "What?"

"You are taking me as your mistress."

Jack leaned back and looked at her. "Lillie, I don't want a mistress." His voice was steady and stern. "Nor do I need the publicity of such an arrangement."

A flash of anger ignited Lillie's eyes. "So, I am good enough for you in private but not in public, eh?"

Jack released a frustrated sigh. "I will help you leave the brothel. But I have dreams and ambitions, and those do not include brothels, prostitutes, a concubine, or a paid mistress."

"My becoming your mistress has nothing to do with your dreams or ambitions."

"Surely you know that a paid mistress will tarnish the reputation of a gentleman."

"After all that I have done for you!" She pulled away from him. "Now you say that I bring you shame?"

"That's not what I meant, Lillie. But you know the rules."

Lillie's eyes narrowed. "For years now, I have met all of your desires. I have given you strength when you were weak and brought you pleasure in times of pain. Those are the only rules I know, Jack McCarty."

Jack was of no mind to argue and in no mood to stay. He stood from the bed and buttoned his shirt. Grabbing his jacket from the floor, he reached into the breast pocket and pulled out several bills before putting it on. "This should be enough for the stage to New York and any expenses you might have until you reach Mr. Keith." He walked over to the writing table in the corner and found a quill in the drawer. "Here," he said, inking the pen, "is Mr. Keith's place of residence." Jack wrote out the address and handed it to Lillie along with the money. "It's a chance to start over, Lillie. A chance for a new life."

CHAPTER 33

DECEMBER 21, 1817, SELMA

The winter solstice was the shortest day of the year, but already it felt like the longest. Armistead sent the cue ball flying, breaking the neatly racked balls across the green felt of the table. He had hoped that billiards would distract him. He was wrong.

Armistead could hear Sarah bellow from the top of the landing. "Nelly, please. Go on! Do as I say and pack her things."

"I will not permit you to take her from here!" Polly shouted with feet pounding across the floor above his head.

"If she stays here, she'll see an early grave!" Sarah said.

"We will see what the general has to say about this!" Polly said, her feet thundering above as she walked toward the stairs.

Armistead drew a long breath to prepare himself for this latest spat between his mother and Charlotte's sister. His objective in inviting Sarah to Selma had been to assist in the care of his wife, who remained bedridden and listless, barely eating, and seemingly wasting away. Since Sarah's arrival the week before, tension between his mother and sister-in-law had escalated with each passing day.

"Armistead, I need a word with you," Polly said, barging into the billiard room. He sent a yellow ball into the corner pocket before moving his gaze to her.

"Yes, Mother?"

"She wants to take Charlotte away. To Esmont. She has accused me of terrible things. Awful things. Says I'm trying to kill her! Armistead, we cannot allow them to take her. She is your everything, darling, and you need her here. With you. I am certain she will get better. We just need to give the medicine time to work. And give her body the care and sustenance it needs. Here. At home." Her sentences burst like gunfire as she spoke.

"Slow down, Mother. Of course you are not trying to harm her." Armistead laid the cue aside and put an arm around her. "She is just trying to help."

"The insolence of that woman! Just because her husband is a physician, she thinks she knows more than I do about these matters."

"What does Dr. Cocke say?" Sarah's husband, Dr. Charles Cocke, had arrived the day before and had served as a welcome relief.

"Considering the influence that shrew has over him, he agrees with her!" Polly spoke through her teeth, her neck reddening, her jawbone ready to explode from her face.

"Please, Mother, calm yourself before you, too, end up on a sickbed. I'll have Joe put on a kettle for some tea, and you can rest while I talk to Dr. Cocke. All right?" He took her hand.

"I don't need a rest, Armistead. But I'll do as you wish. You talk to Charles and you explain that I know exactly what I'm doing and that I am following Dr. Edwards's instructions to the letter."

Despite her insistence to the contrary, the fatigue on Polly's face told Armistead that tea with brandy and a little luck would soon have her napping. After escorting her to the quiet of the guest room on the north end of the house, he asked Charles to meet him downstairs. The two sat by the fire in the billiard room with the doors closed.

"I'm very concerned, Armistead," Charles said, as the lamps of the chandelier reflected on the shine of his forehead. "Her womb seems to have recovered, but she lost an incredible amount of blood, which has weakened her physically. And mentally, I don't know. She's absent from this world." Charles hesitated and drew a long breath. "Armistead, I'll be frank with you. I believe it's the opium tincture that is ravaging her. According to my research, when it is administered to extremes, the drug creates a dreamy euphoria that makes one silent, reticent, and withdrawn, while it slowly deteriorates the body. She is already frail from the miscarriage, and I believe the drug's grip will most certainly send her to the grave."

Armistead had seen the euphoria Charles had mentioned on the faces of the wounded and dying after they'd been administered generous quantities of the drug. It wasn't until now that he correlated it with his wife's condition, and it horrified him. "Stop giving it to her."

"According to my study of cases like hers, it isn't that simple. Once the tincture has tightened its hold on a patient, an abrupt cessation of the drug may cause more irreparable harm than the drug itself, especially in someone as fragile as Charlotte. We need to slowly wean her from the habit, while at the same time providing her round-the-clock care to restore her health."

"And you want to remove her to Esmont for this care?"

"If you want your wife to have any chance of recovery, she needs to come home with us."

Armistead furrowed his brow. "I'm not certain I understand your logic, Charles."

Charles leaned forward in his chair and lowered his voice. "I realize that Mrs. Mason is your mother, and let's not forget she's my aunt. She certainly means only to help, but she is partially responsible for Charlotte's condition. She administers entirely too much of the tincture and too frequently. Sarah has watched her. There is not a doctor that I know who would recommend the dosages Mrs. Mason delivers, and I cannot in good conscience trust that she will follow my instructions."

Armistead stared into the flames of the crackling fire. How often his mother had administered the drug to his siblings and himself to treat any and every ailment when they were growing up. And was she now killing Charlotte with it?

Charles reached over and gently grasped Armistead's forearm. "Your mother means no harm, Armistead. We must not blame her."

Armistead returned his gaze to the burning embers, struggling to control his conflicting emotions. Drawing a long, silent sigh, he brought his eyes to Charles's. "Take her to Esmont, Charles. And promise to bring her back to me."

The argument with his mother had been as ugly as Armistead anticipated. Polly packed her things into the carriage to return to Raspberry Plain, leaving behind a prophesy of Charlotte's most certain death at Sarah's hands, along with a reminder of the suffering Armistead would endure for his actions. When the front door slammed behind her, his house was, at long last, quiet. Armistead poured himself another drink and resumed his game of billiards to clear his head. He had just sunk the first shot when he was interrupted by a messenger at his door. The correspondence delivered was from Sam Caldwell, a close friend and the publisher of the *Genius of Liberty* newspaper.

Wanted you to have this right away. Let's meet at my office in the morning to discuss—S. B. Caldwell.

Enclosed with the note was a clipping from the *Alexandria Gazette*.

TO THE PUBLIC

Seeing that General Mason has published my letter unaccompanied by his own, I wish to explain why I wrote to General Mason and to clarify what part of his letter I endorsed and what part I did not endorse.

JOHN M. McCARTY

Printed below the notice was a complete transcript of his private letter to Jack McCarty. Armistead's heart pounded in his chest. Not only did the letter expose that Heiskill's editorial had bothered him, but it publicly revealed his slander of the editors of two newspapers. *Why, Jack?*

Armistead knew exactly who was responsible. *Mercer and his Federalist friends!* He crumpled the paper in his hand as his discomfiture turned to anger.

They impugn my character, soil my public image, and now they have written my own brother-in-law into their plans!

"That stupid, stupid boy!" He moved his gaze to the moonlit field beyond the window as the pieces of their conspiracy fell together in his mind. Armistead shook his head. *If you are fool enough to become Mercer's shake-bag, Jack McCarty, then it's a fool I'll show you to be!*

CHAPTER 34

DECEMBER 24, 1817, BELMONT

"Merry Christmas!" A jolly-faced, crimson-clad Colonel Ludwell Lee flung open the ornate door of the Belmont manor house. "Come in out of the cold, boys, and warm yourselves with some wassail before your mother empties the bowl!"

"Merry Christmas to you as well, Colonel," Thomson said, shaking off the chill with the frigid northwest wind following them into the house. "It's brutal out there!"

"We brought you a little something." Jack handed the colonel a bottle of French cognac that he had purchased in New Orleans.

Holding the bottle at arm's length to read the label, Colonel Lee gave an appreciative whistle. "Now that's a bottle I'll tuck away," he said as the butler took their hats and coats. "There's a heated debate ongoing in the library, and your mother is holding court in the drawing room, discussing whatever it is that ladies discuss. There is dancing in the conservatory and gambling in the billiard room. It's Christmas at Belmont, boys! Oh, and don't forget the wassail. The bowl is right there." He pointed to a table in the corner over Jack's shoulder. "And you'll find the supper and spirits back there." He waved his hand in the direction of the dining room behind the archway at the end of the hall.

"We know the way, Colonel," Jack said. The two brothers walked to a silver bowl filled with steaming spiced wine and poured themselves each a cup before heading toward the billiard room. Their challenge was to make it past their mother without being waylaid.

Sally was standing beside an enormous Christmas tree in the center of the drawing room. It was a cedar, beautifully decorated with paper mâché ornaments and beaded strands of gold and silver. Sally, too, was beautifully adorned in a crimson taffeta gown with elegant long sleeves, cuffed in white satin with pearl buttons. Her neck and ears were bejeweled with pieces from her vast collection of rubies and diamonds. On her gloved left hand, she wore the engagement ring given to her by Jack's father, a pear-shaped diamond set on a ruby-encrusted band. She had powdered her hair for tonight's party and, with every strand perfectly coifed, her cheeks flushed and lips stained, she looked like Mother Christmas herself. She held a silver cup, laughing and gossiping with other matrons of the aristocracy. A veiled Fannie Carter Lee was seated in a chair to Sally's left. Jack quickly deduced that there was no way to avoid either woman.

"There are my handsome boys!" Sally said upon seeing her sons enter the room.

"Good evening, Sally," they said with a quick embrace and kiss on the cheek.

"Are you just arrived?" Sally asked, steadying the cup of wassail in her hand.

She's been here a while, Jack thought as the wine sloshed over the rim. "We have and are anxious to join our friends for a game in the back," Jack said. "Mrs. Lee." Jack acknowledged Lucinda's mother and quickly moved toward the door.

"Why don't you amuse your old mother and her friends for a spell?"

"We would love to, but, unfortunately, Sally, those tables will not sit idle for long." Thomson bowed and turned to join his brother.

From the expression on her face, Sally was not pleased.

"Don't worry, Jack. She'll make us pay for it later," Thomson told Jack as the pair made their way to the conservatory.

The conservatory at Belmont rivaled the dance halls of Alexandria and George Town, with its high arched windows, luscious draperies, and opulent furnishings. The colonel's wife, who had a keen eye for fashion, coordinated the embellishments on the ropes of holly and pine with the color palette of the room, using dried roses, rose hips, and satin ribbons of gold and green to accentuate the fabrics on the chairs and walls. The lamps of the crystal chandelier seemed to gild the air, their glow pouring like honey over the warm, rosy walls. The room was teeming with couples dancing to the music of a Viennese piano, making passage nearly impossible. Jack and Thomson lingered in the doorway, waiting for the floor to clear at the change in music selections. Looking over the room, Jack spotted Lucinda sitting alone on an oversized settee near the French doors. In front of her was a small stool upon which her shoeless left foot, splinted and wrapped, rested on a silk pillow. A set of crutches leaned beside her against the settee. In an ivory chiffon gown with her fair hair pulled up in a braided chignon, she looked demure and helpless. Every emotion Jack had deliberately stuffed away came rushing forward at the sight of her.

"Hold here a moment. There's someone I need to say hello to," Jack said, handing his cup to Thomson.

"I'll hold here until the dancing clears. Then I'll meet you in the billiard room. If you make it there." Thomson chuckled under his breath.

Unfazed by his brother's comment, Jack waded through the dancers to Lucinda. As he approached, she smiled warmly at him. "Why, is this an apparition I am seeing, or is it Jack McCarty in the flesh before my very eyes?"

"I am no ghost yet, Miss Lucinda." It felt good to hear her sweet Southern drawl again.

"I would stand to greet you, Mr. McCarty, but as you can see, I am presently indisposed," Lucinda waved a hand at her foot.

"Then I will come to you."

Jack dropped to one knee and took her hand in his customary manner.

"Up to your usual antics, I see."

"How have you been, Lucy?"

"I suppose one could say I have been better."

"What happened?"

"I was dancing and slipped, twisting my ankle in such a contorted and painful manner that the doctor does not know what use it might be to me. He said that most certainly I will be lame, but, then again, I do not put much merit in what doctors say. They are more often wrong than right."

Jack brought her hand to his lips once more. "I am so sorry, Lucinda. It will get better. You are too young to be lame."

"Let's hope you are right," she said, pulling her hand from him and tucking it into her lap. "I have heard from your sister-in-law that you had quite a journey."

"Yes, we managed a stay in New Orleans as well as Natchez. It took us nearly five months to travel through Kentucky, down the Ohio and Mississippi Rivers, and back again. And although I found adventure, I didn't find my dream."

"No? And why is that?"

"Because it's here, Lucy. While I love the adventure of travel, my dream, whatever it might be, is where my home is, here in Virginia."

"I, too, feel that way. I spent three months in Philadelphia, singing and dancing, and I loved every minute of it except when I laid my head on my pillow at night. All I could do was miss Virginia. But I will do it again if my ankle heals enough to allow me."

"So that's why you were in Philadelphia?"

She nodded in response. "To sing and be in the theater. I stayed with a cousin who arranged for me to audition with a troupe, and I was invited to join. Then I fell, and my dreams of performing on the stages of London shattered with my ankle. *C'est la vie!*"

"You will not be lame. I promise you will dance again!" Jack glanced over to where his brother had been waiting. He was gone.

"What better time to start than now? Would you have this dance with me, Miss Lucinda?" Jack stood from the settee, squaring his shoulders as the pianist started a new tune.

"And how might I do that?"

"If there is a will, my darling, then there is a way. But you must first say yes."

Lucinda thought for a moment before nodding her head. "Fine, Mr. McCarty. As you wish. I shall accept this dance from you, although I will be quite the scene hobbling about out there on walking sticks!"

As she reached for the crutches, Jack moved them against the wall behind the settee. "How exactly do you expect me to dance without assistance, Mr. McCarty?"

Jack bent to her, scooped her into his arms, and lifted her from the settee. "Put your arms around my neck, Lucy, and I will show you how."

"Jack. Put me down. People are going to talk."

"Let them talk. You accepted my offer to dance, and I am entitled to a dance." He flashed a heartwarming grin. "Now put your arms around my shoulders like a good girl and let me give you the dance of your life."

Lucinda returned his smile with a mischievous grin of her own. "My mother is going to have my head on a plate."

"Not before she has mine! Now come on, let's have that dance."

The room all but stopped as Jack carried Lucinda onto the dance floor. Moving his feet methodically to the music, he twirled with her in his arms. A few couples joined them while others stood against the walls and watched in bewilderment. Her sisters, Winnie and Fanny, were standing on the far side of the room with the Carter twins, aghast. But Jack was oblivious to their stares, unable to hear the whispers, unable to feel their judgment, as all of his attention was focused on the beautiful fair-haired maiden in his arms. The two of them were lost in a world of their own, his eyes fixed on hers as they glided across the floor. Waltzing with her in his arms stirred a comforting, unfamiliar passion—an all-consuming desire. A yearning to care for her, to serve her, to love her. His heart was on the verge of exploding with affection when the music ended, and the room erupted in applause.

"Lucy, honor me with another." Jack's face beamed with a smile that dimpled his cheeks.

"Mr. McCarty, I am not sure your arms can carry me about that long."

"My arms can carry you all night. Come on, Lucy. Another dance?"

Lucinda's eyes darted to where her sisters were standing. "I'm not sure the other guests could countenance another."

"It is not the other guests I wish to dance with, Lucinda Lee. It is only you," Jack said, pleading to those sparkling eyes that had mesmerized him. Lucinda readjusted her arms around his neck to hold on to him tighter.

"On that thought, I would love another dance, Mr. McCarty."

CHAPTER 35

JANUARY 6, 1818, MORNING, MOUNT AIR, FAIRFAX, VIRGINIA

"You survived the blizzard, William! I hear you were up to your waist in snow out there," Jack said upon entering the billiard room. Despite the pungent smoke from Edgar's pipe, Mount Air still smelled of Christmas, the scent of pine boughs and the aroma of baking puddings wafting through the house.

"You don't know the half of it!" William moaned with a wide grin as he and his brother embraced. "I had to take the gelding over to Raspberry Plain to get Polly's men to open the road or we might still be snowed in. Poor horse had snow up to his barrel!" Shortly after their wedding, William and Emily had moved to Strawberry Plain, a smaller farm adjacent to the Mason family estate in Leesburg.

"How was the ride from Leesburg?" Jack asked.

"The road to Alexandria was icy but passable yesterday. Though the road to Cedar Grove is quite another story." William pointed at the side pocket with his cue before launching the red ball across the table.

"The mud and frozen ruts at the Dogue Creek were treacherous when I came through this morning." Jack drew a quick breath. "Were you able to stop by Coton Farm on your way down?"

William grinned. "We did. And last I checked, your guest and my wife were still sleeping upstairs."

"As I am not surprised!" Edgar said, removing the pipe from his mouth. "The ladies were up later than William and I last night, nattering on until the wee hours."

"Did Peggy and Nancy stay up that late with them, too?" Jack asked, surprised as Edgar's wife Peggy and Jack's sister were usually in their chambers by sunset.

"And Sally," William said. "She came over to join us for supper last night."

Jack shook his head at the thought of what his mother might have said to Lucinda. He poured a little brandy into his coffee and watched William take another shot. Unable to sink the ball, William stood from the table and glanced at Edgar. Edgar silently nodded and rested on his cue stick, not taking his turn. Jack noticed. The two of them had something on their minds.

"Jack, have you read the Loudoun papers since Christmas?" William asked.

Jack shook his head and took a drink of his brandied coffee. "I haven't seen a newspaper since the storm. James and I had been playing cards most of the time, using the opportunity to empty the pockets of those unfortunates stuck in Alexandria by the blizzard." Jack searched their faces. "I can tell that there is something I've missed. What is it? Something more with Fenton? Or is it Armistead?"

"Armistead," William said. "He's responded to that notice you had Sam Snowden print in the *Alexandria Gazette*. His reaction was … inflamed."

"Inflamed?" Jack said, raising his brows.

"More like infantile, if you ask me," Edgar said.

"To be fair, Edgar," William said, "Jack brought most of this on himself."

"What do you mean?" Jack asked. "Brought on what?"

"Your publication of his private letter. He thinks it's part of some conspiracy against him."

Jack's head was spinning. "A conspiracy among whom?"

"Among you, Mercer, Heiskell, M'Intyre, the Federalist Party, the proverbial 'them,' whoever 'they' may be in his fevered mind," Edgar said.

"He is still furious at Mercer and outraged that the Committee on Elections summarily dismissed his petition without so much as looking at his evidence," William said.

"They dismissed his petition contesting the election?" Jack asked.

"Yes," Edgar said. "Right after the new year. No reason given. They simply dismissed it."

"Be that as it may, it doesn't excuse you, Jack," William said. "What on earth were you thinking publishing his correspondence like that?"

"What choice did I have? Armistead publicly called Heiskell and M'Intyre vile scoundrels and implied that I endorsed his defamation when, in fact, I had no part in it. All I did was clarify that I did not authorize any slander against the general or anyone else. What on earth did he say?"

William nodded his head toward the buffet. "The paper is over there. Third page."

Jack opened the paper and scanned to the notice. As he read Armistead's words, he could feel his blood rushing through his chest, up his neck, and into his face.

"Easy there, Jackie," Edgar said, placing a furry hand on Jack's shoulder. "These are only words—not swords. Do not let them prick you, my brother."

"Prick me! He is calling me a 'vile instrument' on behalf of—I cannot tell whom, other than perhaps Fenton. What does he think? That Fenton, who is too afraid to fight him, has somehow gathered the courage to puppet me as a surrogate? Only words, Edgar? His words prick with his intent to pick a fight!"

"I agree with you," Edgar said. "Armistead is frustrated like a stag in musth, looking to fight anything in his way. I say walk away and don't publish any more notices or you'll risk a public mauling or worse, being gored by the frenzy of his delirium."

"So you are saying I should do nothing? Let him get away with calling me 'depraved,' 'the willing instrument of their hellish purpose' ... 'a man with the *reputation* of a gentleman.' He just stated, in print, that I only have a *reputation* as a gentleman, implying that I don't possess the qualities of a gentleman at all! He is insinuating that I am some sort of dupe. A marionette whose strings are controlled by others."

"We all know he feels aggrieved by the election, and, frankly, his outrage regarding its outcome is somewhat justified," William said. "However, to direct all of that outrage toward you is clearly unreasonable. But he's not been himself. Em and I spent Christmas with him at Raspberry Plain. His wife was not with him. Her sister has taken her to Albemarle to convalesce. And he appears inebriated more often than not. Although I'm not making excuses for him—"

"Indeed, you are! Why is it you are always defending him? Why? Because of what the two of you suffered at Baltimore? Because he is your wife's brother? I am your flesh and blood!"

Edgar, putting both hands on Jack's shoulders, turned him away from William, forcing Jack's face to his. "William would never turn his back on you, John Mason! He is simply pointing out that the man is under duress."

"Duress or not, that doesn't excuse him. If he wants a war of words, then I will give him one!"

"Be careful what you start with him, Jack," William said. "Armistead Mason doesn't like to lose, and he doesn't quit. I saw it in '14 with my own eyes during the Baltimore campaign when he got sick. So sick that we thought he might die. The officers of the Fifth Maryland were running their mouths about the cowardice of our commanding officer lying in his tent all day while the British continued their assault on Fort McHenry, inching their way upriver to our position. All that did was make Armistead more insolent and stubborn. He should have gone home to convalesce, but he refused. And when our regiment was ordered to engage, Armistead managed—by God somehow—to pull himself off that cot and onto his horse to lead us through the hell that was Godley Wood as we chased the British to the sea." William paused with a seriousness in his face. "If you start this thing with him, it will be Armistead who finishes it."

"So how do we get Jack the redress he desires without stoking Armistead's fire further?" Edgar asked.

"We'll talk with Colonel Lee," William suggested, "and enlist his support. Perhaps he can negotiate a truce and bring this thing to an amicable conclusion before it grows into something far more dangerous"

"Armistead won't agree to it," Jack said. "Compromise is the same as losing."

"No, Jack, compromise results in peace," William said. "It's the need to win that results in war."

"If we nip this before it buds, I think we can avoid a war," Edgar said. Jack couldn't ignore the seriousness on his brothers' faces.

"All right, William. If Colonel Lee can convince Armistead to rescind his insults, then I will remain silent."

"You are doing the right thing, Jack," Edgar said. "None of us wants this thing to escalate any further, for your sake and for the sake of the family."

Edgar picked up his cue to resume the game. Jack poured himself another brandy as he watched his brothers clear the table without a word between them.

"So Sally told us that you are planning to run for the Virginia legislature this spring," William said, returning the cue stick to the rack and pouring himself a brandy.

"Is there nothing secret with that woman?" Jack said, welcoming the change in subject.

"Or sacred either!" Edgar said, and the brothers laughed.

"Yes, I'm considering it. You know, William, since you always disagree with our elected representatives, it might as well be me you disagree with going forward!" Jack said.

"As I'm sure I will when you win that seat! I'm proud of you, you know. You'll make a good legislator, just as long as you can keep that temper of yours in check," William said with a laugh.

"Marster Edgar, sir," said a voice from the hall just outside the doorway. "Your mother has requested you gentlemen join the ladies in the drawing room for coffee."

"Already? Thomson has yet to arrive," Edgar said.

"Sir, when he arrived a few minutes ago, Marster Thomson was … ahem …" The butler hesitated, searching for the appropriate word. "*Detained* by your mother."

Edgar rolled his eyes and shook his head. "Gentlemen, as much as I'd like to continue this discussion, we know what happens if we deny Sally what she wants."

"Indeed. We get detained!" William said.

"Thomson had penance due for snubbing her at the Belmont party. I suppose I'll have mine to pay shortly," Jack said, moving toward the door. With Edgar and William behind him, Jack stopped in the doorway and faced them. "And let me assure you both of this. I will heed your advice not to further incite Armistead. I will not, however, cower to him or any man. Not now. Not ever."

CHAPTER 36

JANUARY 6, 1818, AFTERNOON, MOUNT AIR

"Did you boys know that Lucinda's mother had nearly as many children as I did?" asked Sally as the servants removed the last of the ironstone dishes and what little was left of the Christmas pie and gravy from the table. "And nearly all girls! At Cedar Grove there were so many babies crawling around on the floor that I had to stand on a stool to dress my hair!" Sally laughed loudly as Edgar poured her another glass of Madeira.

"Mother says that if she didn't have a nurse for each one of us, she might have lost her mind," Lucinda said, smiling at the image of Sally McCarty on a stool with eleven babies crawling beneath her.

"I am about to lose my mind with the two I have, and here I am about to have a third!" said Jack's sister Nancy as she rubbed her hands over her swollen abdomen. This was the first time Lucinda had met Jack's sister and her husband, and the first time she had spent any significant time with Jack's family. Laughing with the women at the table, Lucinda envied the frank familiarity between the McCartys. Dining at Coton Farm was far more formal and not nearly as much fun.

"I had no challenges with my boys until I lost my Daniel," Sally said. "And then, in addition to being mother to you monkeys, I had the responsibility of both father and teacher!" She cast a knowing glance to Jack and Thomson.

Lucinda smiled at Sally's teasing, admiring her optimism and cheerfulness despite the loss of so many of her sons. Lucinda's mother had also lost children, but she was not at all like Sally McCarty, who seemed to Lucinda more of a force of nature than a matron in her fifties.

"Speaking of teachers, do you remember Mr. Boler, Sally?" William asked.

"Do I ever," Sally said with sudden seriousness.

"And I bet he will never forget the McCarty boys!" Edgar said. The brothers nodded in agreement.

"Who was Mr. Boler?" Emily asked.

"A cruel teacher that our father hired to instruct us as children," Jack said, all lightheartedness gone from his tone. Lucinda narrowed her eyes as she looked across the table at him.

"Cruel is too mild a descriptor for that man!" Sally said. "Had I known just how horrific he was to you boys after your father's death, I would have beat him myself had you not gotten to him first."

"A teacher?" Lucinda said, her eyes wide.

"A private tutor from somewhere up north. Father hadn't been dead a month before he started on us. And Jack here was his favorite," William said.

"I was hardly a favorite," Jack said, shifting uncomfortably in his chair. Lucinda noticed.

"His favorite to abuse!" Edgar said.

"Abuse?" Emily asked, looking horrified. "What on earth … ?"

Edgar leaned forward in his chair, his eyes scanning their faces. "Jackie here wasn't but six or so. Father wasn't in his grave, what, couldn't have been more than a couple of weeks, right, William? This Boler fella beat Jack on his palm with a ferule until he fainted, he did."

Lucinda watched as Jack lowered his gaze to the table. She felt a sudden worry.

"Right you are," William said. "And it didn't stop there. Maybe a week or so later, Jack had gotten himself into some sort of mischief—nothing more than childish silliness—and Mr. Boler pulled his shirt from his shoulders. Then the tyrant flogged him with a strap until his back bled. And you know what? Jack uttered not a sound. Your man here, even at six, had too much honor to cry."

Lucinda was appalled.

"If I had cried, I'd be letting him win," Jack said. He pasted a smile on his face, but his eyes were awash in pain. Lucinda could feel his hurt. She desperately wanted to change the subject.

"Tell them what you did, Will. Tell them," Thomson said before she could think of something to divert their attention.

"The bunch of us," William said, "there were seven of us still in school then, I guess, as Edgar and Daniel were in Williamsburg and Thomson here was too young yet for schooling—we were goaded to fury by the injustice and cruelty this Mr. Boler had inflicted on our little brother. The only plan that satisfied our sense of justice and, at the same time, avenged Jack's wrongs was to give the tyrant a taste of his own medicine. So we cut a number of stout hickory switches and concealed them in the schoolroom. These switches, mind you, would tear the bark off a tree, so imagine what they might do to the skin of a man. Then we had Demas, one of our trusted slave boys, lock Mr. Boler in the room with us while we set upon him." William's eyes were gleaming.

"And had Demas not unlocked the door and allowed his escape, I believe the lot of you might have killed Mr. Boler," Edgar said.

"What happened to him? Mr. Boler, I mean," Lucinda said, caught between wanting to change the subject and wanting to know what happened to the pedagogue.

"Sally took care of him," Jack said, exchanging glances with his mother over the dwindling candles.

"When Demas alerted me as to what you boys were doing," Sally said, "we rushed to the schoolhouse and unlocked the door. When the coward came running out, I marched his bloodied body down to the garden with a loaded musket pointed squarely between his shoulders and put him on a little boat that we kept along the water. I told him that if he ever set foot on McCarty ground again, I'd bury him in it! Demas rowed him down the Accotink Creek to the Potomac, where he boarded a fishing smack heading back up north. And that would be the last time I ever saw him, and the last time we employed a Northerner at Cedar Grove!"

"Did he die?" Emily asked, confusion stitched on her brow.

"Not at our hands," William said. "But hopefully someone else has put an end to him by now."

"William!" Emily said. "You're a man of the law!"

"And I'd be sure to prosecute him to the fullest extent of the law should he ever cross my path again," William said.

Lucinda looked across the table at Jack, who was sitting preternaturally still, staring into nowhere beyond his mother's shoulder. Lucinda narrowed her eyes, not quite sure what she saw on Jack's face. Maybe it was pride that his brothers and mother had defended him. Or maybe it was pain from being unable to defend himself. Or maybe it was something else.

A painting on the wall behind Jack caught her eye—masked revelers in a gilded ballroom, ladies in extravagant gowns and round black masks, men in capes and tricorne chapeaux wearing half masks of white porcelain. What she saw in Jack's expression suddenly was clear. Jack was protecting himself, hiding his vulnerability behind a veneer of stoicism.

Lucinda smiled at Jack with empathetic eyes. Reaching for her crutches, she stood from the table. "Mr. McCarty, might you accompany me into the conservatory for a little music?"

Jack at first looked surprised, but his expression relaxed as his eyes met hers. He pushed his chair back from the table and stood with her. "I would be delighted, Miss Lucinda."

The McCarty brothers and Nancy's husband sang the lyrics of their mother's favorite Thomas Moore tune with Lucinda, Nancy, and Sally harmonizing, while Emily accompanied them on the fortepiano.

Believe me, if all those endearing young charms

Which I gaze on so fondly today

Were to change by tomorrow and fleet in my arms

Like the fairy gifts, fading away.

Jack was singing, too, but his mind was on the conversation from the dining room. For so long he had buried the memory of Mr. Boler and the day his shirt was ripped from his back. The day he was beaten until the world went white. *Why me and not the others?*

"Come on, Jackie! Sing third major with me!" Sally said. Jack changed his key and harmonized with his mother. Until that moment at the table, he had not remembered his mother parading the abuser at gunpoint to the creek's shore.

Jack could see the pedagogue's face so clearly—his sandy beard, cold eyes, and rotting teeth. He remembered holding on to the post so that he wouldn't fall, the crack of the strap, the searing heat on his skin. Jack winced and drew a quick breath. *He singled me out because I was weak.* Jack's thoughts moved from the classroom whipping to visions of Natchez to the lashing Armistead had given Shane McNally at Orchard Camp. Jack looked at his mother, who was tilting her head, struggling to hit the lower register of the harmony. *I am no one's fool, and I'll be damned before I let anyone beat me again!*

CHAPTER 37

JANUARY 21, 1818,
STRAWBERRY PLAIN

"To what do I owe the pleasure this morning, Colonel?" William said, looking up from his plate of griddle cakes at the dark figure entering his dining room.

"Where's the missus?" asked Colonel George Rust, crossing the floor in heavy boots that caused the dishes in the china press to rattle.

"Mrs. McCarty is at Cedar Grove for a few days helping my sister with the new baby."

"Hopefully the child is in good health," George said, pulling a chair from the table.

William narrowed his eyes as George sat. "As far as I know, yes. And I know you didn't ride over here to inquire as to my wife's whereabouts or to ask about my sister's baby."

George drew a long sigh. He glanced toward the window before returning his eyes to William. "We have a problem."

William motioned to his butler standing at the doorway. "Jedediah, would you bring a coffee and some breakfast for Colonel Rust, please?"

"Certainly, sir," Jedediah said, disappearing into the hallway toward the kitchen.

William raised his brow. "What is it, George?"

"Armistead is breaking the terms of the truce we negotiated with Colonel Lee regarding your brother."

"What? Why? Has Jack done something to provoke him?"

"Not that I can tell. You saw your brother's notice in the paper. It was contrite enough, although I suppose his remark about Armistead not challenging him at the hustings left the matter of the general's courage somewhat unanswered. But it complied with the agreement made to end the controversy. No, it's Mercer's pamphlet that has enraged Armistead."

"Mercer's pamphlet? What pamphlet?"

George pulled a booklet with a pale-blue cover from his pocket and slid it across the table.

"What is this?" William asked as he picked it up.

"Mercer's version of the dispute between himself and the general, and it makes Armistead look irrational and like the aggressor."

"Jesus." William shook his head as he thumbed through the pamphlet. "Why in the world would Fenton publish this now?"

"Who knows why Fenton Mercer does the things he does. He's your friend. You tell me."

William furrowed his brow. "While we share the same political beliefs, Fenton and I are hardly friends. But he is close to Jack—at least he was before all of this." William closed the pamphlet and pushed it back across the table to George. "But I don't understand why this would inflame Armistead to break the truce with Jack."

"You know how suspicious Armistead has become these days—obsessing over this 'great conspiracy' he thinks is going on."

"Conspiracy? The man is coming unhinged!"

"And Sam Caldwell isn't helping any. That vermin will print anything to sell a newspaper! I ran into him last night at Osbourne's tavern. Caldwell, Handy, Alexander—Armistead's posse—scheming with Armistead on the response to Mercer. And they were reviewing a proof of Armistead's rebuttal to what they call 'McCarty's veiled apology.'"

"Christ! Don't tell me Armistead is publishing another notice slandering Jack."

"Looked to me like he is. I tried talking some sense into Armistead, but he wasn't listening. He was drunk and looked as if he hadn't slept in a week. He was unshaved, his clothes were wrinkled, his whole appearance disheveled. And you know him, William. The man was born creased and pressed! I've seen him like this a few times before. After his brother died in '15 was the last time."

"It's because Charlotte is gone."

"Is she still recuperating over in Albemarle?"

"Yes. According to my wife, she's expected home any day now."

"Thank God for that."

William moved his eyes to the window and shook his head. "For the fear of God, he must let this go."

"Armistead does not fear God." William turned to George. "He fears what other men think of him."

William knew the truth of George's words. "Then what do you suggest?"

"My plan was to talk with Armistead directly this morning, see if I can convince him that taking his anger toward Mercer out on Jack is misguided at best. Maybe I can convince him to pull this notice back. I think you should speak to your brother. If this notice gets published, perhaps warning him will temper his reaction. And you know your brother. He's a spring buck with a hot head, much like Armistead when Armistead was young."

"Unfortunately, I know my brother's temper all too well. And I know that if another assault against his character is published, I may not be able to intervene. I mean, look at it from Jack's point of view. He had an agreement with Armistead. And if Armistead doesn't honor his word—"

"I know, William. Trust me, I know."

CHAPTER 38

JANUARY 29, 1818, MRS. PEYTON'S BOARDINGHOUSE

"Let's not overreact, Jack," William said as Jack threw the *Genius of Liberty* newspaper across the table in front of him.

"Overreact? Exactly how would you expect me to react to this latest, unprovoked attack on my character?" Jack said, pacing about the room as William, James Dulaney, and his brother Thomson sat watching him.

"I suggest we let Colonel Lee and Dr. Heaton remind Armistead of the agreement he made," William said.

"Remind him of his agreement?" Jack almost yelled. "You mean call him out for disgracing himself and breaking his word!"

"Sorry. Poor choice of words on my part. Armistead breached the agreement and, yes, to restore his honor, he will be compelled to retract his statements."

"Armistead hasn't got it in him," Thomson said. "He's too proud."

"How about a good old-fashioned apology?" James suggested. "No pride needed for that."

"Just humility—the one thing God forgot to bake into him!" Thomson said.

"I am certain we can work out a compromise where he publicly retracts his statements," William said.

Jack stared at his brother in disbelief. "Are you that naïve? Armistead doesn't want a *compromise*. He wants to *win*. And the only way to win is to fight. If he wants a fight, then I'll force him to it."

"I think you should be the bigger man and bring the temperature down on this," William said, a line of worry marking his brow.

"Bring the temperature down? Have you read any of this?" Jack grabbed the paper from the table and held it at arm's length as his eyes scanned the print. "Let's see ... ahh ... here the general calls me 'a coward scoundrel.' And two paragraphs down I'm a 'blackguard and scoundrel,' and then near the end, he calls me 'an infamous rascal.' Oh, and let's not forget this proclamation." Jack cleared his throat as he read aloud. "'Half-witted as he is, John Mason McCarty is always ready to box, bite, and gouge with any blackguard in the street, but he shrinks from honorable combat. He is a despicable wretch of the most abandoned depravity and most shameless disregard of character. To his nocturnal orgies in the alleys of Alexandria, let him return.'" Jack looked at William with wide eyes and indignation on his face. "Thank Christ, Sally has stopped reading the newspapers!" Jack shook his head. "And then, after all his blasphemy against my character, he professes warm feelings for my family." Jack turned his focus back to the paper. "'I deeply regret being *compelled* to publish my opinion of Mr. John McCarty, as I hold such cherished feelings for his mother and his brothers, and it is my sincerest hope that amicable relations will continue between our families.'" Jack threw the paper back onto the table. "Now how exactly would you like me to bring the temperature down on this inferno, William? Hmmm?"

"It's not you he wants to fight, Jack. It's Fenton Mercer."

"That's not how I read his slanderous rant!"

"And what about your promise to Colonel Lee?"

"Null and void!" Jack's voice boomed across the room. "I did exactly as prescribed by the truce. Exactly what he agreed to. And now he does this? No, I am going to show the public his true colors."

"And what colors might they be, Jack?" William said, unable to temper his frustration.

"The color of cowardice."

"Words like that will get you killed," William said, his face reddening.

"It will take a fight to get me killed, and it takes two to fight. And my bet is General Mason will not fight. He had ample opportunity and good reason to challenge me after the incident at the hustings last year. But he didn't. And you know why? Because I'm not Fenton Mercer! Armistead knew that Fenton didn't have the guts to fight him. So there was no risk to Armistead in challenging him publicly. But me? He knows damned well I will never back down. And I'm betting he's lost his nerve, and I intend to let him walk right into the box he built for himself!"

"You underestimate him, Jack," William said, with a warning in his glare and a grimness in his jaw. "Such action is a sentence to the grave."

"Trust me, William, he will not challenge me. Whatever courage he had in the war has long left him. And now he is nothing more than a blustering bully. I saw it at the hustings, but I didn't recognize it at first. I came at him swinging. He spewed every epithet his adolescent mind could conjure, but he never physically responded to my aggression. James saw it, too. He never raised a hand to me, only his words."

James nodded in agreement. "Jack's right. Armistead didn't so much as clench a fist."

William shook his head. "You don't know him."

"I know fear, Will. He's not the brave officer you think he is. Not anymore."

"Jack, you are being too cavalier with your life."

"There's no need to worry about my life, William, because Armistead Mason is too worried about his own."

———————————

Laying the quill on the desk, Jack picked up the parchment to read his words one last time before sending the notice off with the messenger who was waiting impatiently at his door.

TO THE PUBLIC

I cannot condescend to reply *to every detail* of the publication of a man whose latest conduct has sunk him beneath the scorn and pity of mankind. Instead, I refer the public to the publications that have passed between General Mason and myself and let the public decide whether he has the principles of an honorable gentleman. If he was so offended by my conduct last year at the hustings, as he now claims, then why did he not challenge me to fight him then? And why, after giving his word as a gentleman to accept my apology for any misunderstanding between us, does he continue in his last publication to insult my character so vulgarly? General Mason's continued attempt to draw me into a fight with him, when, in fact, all he wishes is to wage a war of words, leads to no other conclusion than GENERAL ARMISTEAD T. MASON IS A DISGRACED COWARD.

John Mason McCarty

Jack closed his eyes as he lifted his chin toward the ceiling. *Choose your weapon, Armistead. The pistol or the pen!*

CHAPTER 39

FEBRUARY 4, 1818, SELMA

"How delightful to have you join us this afternoon, Jonathan! Let me guess what brought the good doctor across the ridge from Woodgrove on such a glum day," Armistead said as Dr. Jonathan Heaton walked into the study. In his usual spot behind his desk, Armistead had that cold-fire look on his face, icy as a loaded barrel ready to explode at any moment.

"Dr. Heaton," George said from the chair across from Armistead, his face ruddier than usual and his tension as high as that in the room.

"Or perhaps you haven't come from Woodgrove at all, but from Belmont Plantation instead," Armistead said, his every mannerism exuding sarcasm.

"As a matter of fact, I was at Belmont earlier this morning," Jonathan said as he took the chair next to George.

"And it wouldn't happen to be that you were discussing with Colonel Lee this blasphemy published in the last *Washingtonian*, would it?" Armistead said.

"For God's sake, Armistead! You know damned well why he's here!"

"Goddamn it, George! I have argued with you half the morning on this and now I have to argue with the good doctor as well?

How can I allow this scoundrel to get away with such slander? I simply cannot!"

"I have advised you how," George shouted. "You simply refuse to acknowledge him suitable to meet you in honorable reparation. And that is the end of it!"

"Gentlemen," Jonathan said. "Please. Let's lower our voices before we unnecessarily arouse the lady of the house, yes?" Armistead shifted uncomfortably in his chair at the suggestion that his wife, who had just arrived home only two days before, might overhear their conversation. "You are correct, Armistead. I've spent the morning with Colonel Lee discussing ways for you to peacefully receive the redress you deserve. He agrees that you have the right to defend your character against McCarty's proclamation. However, he cannot condemn McCarty's action entirely, as it was you who first breached the agreement. That said, the colonel is convinced he can persuade McCarty to stand down and let you have the last word without violence."

"Violence is the only language that brute understands!" Armistead said.

George drew a long breath to quell his own flaring temper. "I have tried to point out, Jonathan, that continuing in this controversy is hurting Armistead's business and may have long-term impact on his political aspirations. If McCarty were a gentleman, he should be called out for his latest blasphemy. But the bloke is no gentleman, thus relieving the general of any such obligation."

Armistead nearly jumped from his chair in anger. "And how do I achieve redress in that scenario, George? Hmmm? How is my honor restored?"

"General," Jonathan said. "I think George's point is that a rogue is incapable of dishonoring a gentleman, just as you have reminded us all countless times about stallions lying with swine—the mud of the pig's sty cannot reach the stall of the horse."

"And what happens when the swine gets into the stall of that horse? The horse tramples him to death!" Armistead barked, nearly coming out of the chair again.

"Then trample him, Armistead!" George said, shouting with equal volume. "Step on him. Beat him back into the mud where he belongs, but do not look him in the eye and challenge him as a stallion would another stallion. Trample him for the swine that he is!"

"Gentlemen, please," Jonathan implored. "We must mind our voices." Jonathan glanced at the doorway and shifted in his chair. "As a Christian, I cannot condone the trampling of another human. I suggest rising above him. Walking proudly beyond his filth will speak volumes."

"Volumes to whom? God? You're telling me that God thinks I should hold my head high while McCarty walks all over my reputation?"

"Walk like Jesus would and turn the other cheek," Jonathan suggested.

"While I turn a dagger in his chest!"

"It's not worth dying over, Armistead," George reminded him.

"I thought you were a better soldier than that, George. For every soldier, it's kill or be killed!"

"What, like on Craney Island? Yes, kill or be killed, but when the opponent is defenseless or unworthy? And at what consequence, General? What about the collateral damage? Or have you forgotten?" George's voice was rising to a fever pitch.

"Don't you dare!" Armistead seethed as he glowered across the desk.

George looked directly into Armistead's eyes. "You had no way to predict the British would take their revenge on the citizens of Hampton. But you can predict the outcome if you fight McCarty. Spare your family—your wife—should the worst happen. Jack McCarty isn't worth leaving Charlotte a widow, Arm."

A heavy silence fell among them. Armistead seemed lost in thought even though his eyes remained fixed on his friends. After a long moment, he stood and turned his back to face the window. He stared out over the winter lawn, saying nothing as George and Jonathan remained silent in their seats.

"Do you believe Colonel Lee can hold McCarty to a truce?"

"I do," Jonathan said.

"And that I will have the last word?"

"Yes."

Armistead's gaze remained steadfast out the window as they waited in silence. At long last, he spoke.

"Tell Colonel Lee that if he will guarantee I have the last word, then he has mine."

CHAPTER 40

FEBRUARY 14, 1818, STRAWBERRY PLAIN

"Lucy, you take my breath away," Jack said half under his breath, holding her hand as he helped her from the coach. Lucinda stepped onto the cobblestoned drive, her pink, fur-lined pelisse casting a rosy glow across her face. Although most of her flaxen hair was tucked under a beaver cap, strands that had escaped glistened like gold in the midday sun.

"Perhaps you can borrow mine then, Mr. McCarty," Lucinda said with a flirty toss of her head.

"Is that an offer, Miss Lee?"

"It depends, Mr. McCarty. It all depends on how many dances I might receive from you this evening."

"Will I be required to carry you around the dance floor again, or is that foot of yours strong enough to keep up with me?"

"Should it tire, it will most certainly rely upon the services of your arms again."

"Ahem, Mr. McCarty," called a voice from the carriage. "Perhaps you could redirect your attention from my sister for just a moment and assist me? It is so icy out there, I don't want to chance two of us having broken legs."

Jack turned his attention from Lucinda and extended his hand to her sister Fanny, who was struggling to get her head, with its ornate golden dressing, through the carriage door.

"Why, of course, Miss Fanny," Jack said. "How thoughtless of me! Here, let me assist you."

Fanny was as bright as a daffodil, dressed in yellow literally from head to toe, with a large satin headpiece adorned with gold ribbons and feathers dyed to match her yellow satin dress. She, too, looked radiant in the frigid sunshine.

Most of Virginia's aristocracy, already weary of the snow and cold weather, did little more than attend dances, dinners, and levees—those most extravagant receptions—to melt the time away until spring arrived. William had invited a number of his friends from town for an afternoon of billiards, cards, and conversation. Emily, hearing that her husband had invited half the county's eligible bachelors to her home, could not resist the opportunity to play matchmaker before the Valentine's dance that evening and had invited every unmarried friend she had.

Jack escorted the Lee sisters up the steps and into the old stone manor house. When the sisters started toward the parlor where other ladies were having tea, Jack held fast to Lucinda's elbow. "I'd like to show you something, should you have a moment, Lucinda."

"I always have a moment for you, Mr. McCarty."

Jack offered her his arm. "Come this way."

"Very well, then." Lucinda took his arm and walked with him gingerly down the hall, the limp in her left ankle still prevalent. When they reached the music room, Jack swung its double doors open as a butler might open the doors to a great dining hall. On the bench of the fortepiano at the center of the room was a long, narrow box tied with an enormous pink ribbon.

"For my valentine." With a broad grin, Jack lifted the box from the bench and, with outstretched arms, presented his gift. "It's both beautiful and practical, and most definitely temporary."

Lucinda untied the ribbon and lifted the lid. Creamy silk lined the interior of the box. Within the folds of the fabric lay an ivory cane with a prismed crystal at the end of its handle. "A cane?"

"Indeed, a cane, my love. A beautiful cane that will allow you to walk a bit better and give the ankle more time to convalesce. I know how important it is for you to dance again, and I thought this might help."

Taking the cane from its wrapping, Lucinda examined it closely. It was indeed a beautiful cane, the rock-crystal facets on the handle casting small rainbows across the room in the early afternoon sunlight. By the expression on Lucinda's face, Jack could see that she didn't know how to react. At first, he saw appreciation, but he also sensed despair. He wanted to take her in his arms to reassure her that, with the right regimen, her ankle would heal, and she would once again dance on the stage. He lifted her chin with an index finger. There were tears welling in her eyes.

"This is the most thoughtful gift any gentleman has ever given me. And it's beautiful." She reached up and kissed him on the cheek. Wanting more than her platonic offering, Jack looped his arm around her waist and pulled her closer, attempting to kiss her. Lucinda gently pushed him back.

She scolded him as the emotional moment turned playful. "Now, Jack McCarty, are you again attempting to take liberties to which you are not entitled?"

"Did you not promise your breath to me out on the carriageway?" Jack held on to her, pulling her toward him again.

"I stipulated, sir, that my offer was conditional." With a hand on his chest, she halfheartedly resisted his embrace.

"Ah! I don't recall any specific conditions other than a dance or two that I will gladly deliver." Jack pulled her closer again and made another unsuccessful attempt to kiss her.

Laughing, she pushed free from his grasp and waved the cane playfully at his head. "Mr. McCarty, it appears this cane has several practical applications, including striking you should you not behave!"

Jack sighed. "It's the story of my life, Miss Lucinda. My good intentions turned against me to do me harm."

"I shall not assault you unnecessarily, Jack. Only when you deserve it!" Lucinda hesitated, bringing her eyes to the cane she held in her hand. "Seriously, though, Jack, this was a very thoughtful gift. Thank you."

"You are welcome, my love. And my offer to help you strengthen that foot still stands. I can show you some things to do, should you allow me. Perhaps this week, weather permitting, I might come by Coton Farm? With Mr. Deese or your mammy in view the entire time as to not bring the wrath of your mother upon my head. Would you allow me?"

Lucinda nodded. "I'd like that."

"It's a date, then!" Jack offered her his arm. "Allow me to escort you to the parlor with your friends until we dine."

"That would be nice, Mr. McCarty, but completely unnecessary. You see, I have a new friend that will assist me in getting there."

"I see that you do." With a sweeping arm gesture, Jack ushered her in front of him into the hallway, she along with her cane.

Jack stood aside, flooded with the warmth of adoration as he watched her delicately walk down the hall with the assistance of his gift. As she disappeared through the parlor doors, he turned to make his way to William's study at the back of the house. Behind him stood his sister-in-law, with her auburn hair pulled in a tight knot and a similar look on her face.

"Good afternoon to you, Mrs. McCarty," he said, crossing his hand over his waist with a bow.

"Mr. McCarty." There was a curtness in her tone.

"Have you been deployed by Lucinda's mother to keep an eye on the two of us?"

"You and Lucy aren't my concern at the moment. Might we have a word?" *What have I done now?* he thought as he followed her into the music room. Emily shut the doors behind them.

"Now, Jack McCarty, I am only having this conversation with you directly as I know that to have it with William will not guarantee that you will heed my words."

"What on earth are you talking about, Emily?"

She put her hands on her hips. "This business between Armie and you, that's what I'm talking about! This fighting between you in those dreadful scandal rags, and the threats to shoot each other! You two need to stop acting like children and behave like grown men and just shake hands and be gentlemanly!"

Jack smiled a reassuring grin. "There is no reason to fret so, Em. It's already resolved."

"Well, that is not at all what I have heard."

Jack placed his hands on her shoulders. "Colonel Lee and Dr. Heaton negotiated a truce between me and your brother. I can assure you that it is all over."

She fixed her eyes on his, scrutinizing them. "A truce?"

"Yes, a truce."

Emily held her stare. "So you and Armistead are friends again."

"Well, that may be going too far."

"Give me your word, Jack!"

"Look, Em. I cannot go so far as to say we have resumed friendly relations, or ever will, but I can assure you that I have no intention of fighting him and have committed to let the matter rest."

"You must promise." She was demanding now.

Jack placed his hand over his heart. "I promise."

"On your word as a gentleman."

"On my word as a gentleman."

Emily drew a long sigh and straightened her dress, seemingly satisfied. "Very well, Mr. McCarty. I will hold you to your word. And I intend to have this exact conversation with my brother, whether he wants to have it or not. I love you both too much for the two of you to go off and kill each other!" She turned and proceeded down the corridor.

Jack shook his head as he followed her into the hall. How Emily had become aware of his controversy with Armistead was beyond him. He felt a fondness for Emily. Like Sally, she frustrated him with her persistence until she got her way. And like his mother, Emily had an ability to see the world, and him, without judgment. He trusted her. And he had given her his word.

CHAPTER 41

MARCH 19, 1818, OSBOURNE'S TAVERN, LEESBURG, VIRGINIA

With tankards of beer on the table, Gerard Alexander and William Handy were sitting at their usual spot, exactly where Armistead had expected to find them. "Have you gentlemen seen this?" Armistead asked as he tossed a copy of the *Leesburg Washingtonian* newspaper on the table. In the center column of the front page was a notice announcing John Mason McCarty as the Federalist candidate for election to the Virginia legislature.

"Yep. Saw it yesterday. Seems you were right all along, General," Handy said.

"A damned conspiracy, just like you said," Gerard agreed, balancing his chair on its two hind legs.

Armistead was fuming. "This entire assault on my character was a scheme for McCarty to use my reputation to gain visibility among the voters so he could win a seat in the legislature!"

"What do you want to do?" Handy asked.

"What I'd like to do I cannot, as I have given my word that I would not challenge the scoundrel. But it doesn't mean I cannot sabotage him indirectly."

"What do you mean, General?" Gerard asked.

"What I mean is that I need information on him to ruin his life for his assault on mine. We need to ensure he does not win this election. And, Gerard, you are the man for the job."

"Whatever you need, sir. What are my orders?" Gerard asked, bringing the chair back onto all four legs and straightening his shoulders as if he were receiving directives from his commanding officer.

"Travel to the District—Washington City, George Town, and Alexandria—to find out everything you can about McCarty's derelict conduct." Armistead turned his attention to Handy. "And, Will, to undermine him politically, I need to understand his position on issues. We need to stir the freeholders' passion over his youth and inexperience."

"I can do that sir," Handy said.

"McCarty cannot be permitted to win this election at my expense."

"An ingenious plan, General," Gerard said with a sly grin.

"And let's ensure my imprint is not on your activities. Otherwise, I'll have Lee and Heaton all over me for antagonizing the scoundrel and breaching the agreement."

A whistle and sudden loud crack from the fire interrupted the murmur of conversation in the room. Gerard and Armistead jumped in their chairs at the disturbance.

"That sounded like one of those damned hellfire rockets!" Gerard said, his shoulders shaking.

Armistead closed his eyes momentarily. The hissing, whistling, and red glare of the rockets across the nighttime sky; the sound of cannons, gunfire, and canisters exploding; the wails and screams of the injured and dying; the smell of gunpowder and smoke and burning flesh. Armistead shuddered and pushed the memories away. "You men have your orders."

CHAPTER 42

APRIL 3, 1818, OSBOURNE'S TAVERN

"So, Gerard, what have you uncovered?" inquired Armistead in the dim light of the tavern. Two weeks had passed since Armistead met with William Handy and Gerard Alexander. Tonight the conspirators were joined by Sam Caldwell.

"As for McCarty, it seems he has quite the reputation for bedding whores and barmaids," Gerard said, pulling folded parchment from his waistcoat.

Armistead interrupted. "Hell, Gerard, even my mother knows that!"

"That may be, General," Gerard said as he opened the paper. "But it seems that this past winter, McCarty swindled hundreds of dollars from at least a half dozen gentlemen stranded in Alexandria during the snowstorm. He and his friend James Dulaney were running some sort of scheme—extremely dishonorable conduct from what I hear. One of their victims complained to the sheriff, asking for their arrest."

"Do you have the name of the man?" Armistead asked.

Gerard shook his head.

"Without his testimony, Gerard, the information is useless. What else do you have?"

"I have confirmed that he has a concubine," Gerard said.

"A concubine?" Armistead was intrigued. Although McCarty was a bachelor, living in sin with a woman would surely be a mark against his character to the Quakers living in the valley and the more conservative members of the aristocracy.

"Yes, a concubine of sorts. He is a frequent patron at an establishment on Water Street in George Town. More of an upscale house than some of the others down there that serve the sailors. This one is an Irish brothel—quite extravagant, I might add—catering to the most distinguished gentlemen."

"McCarty is anything but a distinguished gentleman, Gerard," said Armistead.

"A gentleman of four outs," Caldwell said. "Except for money. He has enough of that to pretend to be distinguished."

"That would make him a gentleman of three outs, Sam," Handy said. "Without wit, credit, or manners!" The men laughed in agreement.

"There is a specific whore to whom McCarty has taken a fancy," Gerard said. "Had bought most of her time and now has paid a year in advance for her company. Irish blonde with quite the set of kettledrums. Goes by the name Lillie." Gerard looked at his notes. "MacKall is the surname. Lillie MacKall. Because she was already bought and paid for, I had to pay the old madam double to have a go with her."

"And how was she?" Handy smirked with a wink.

"Quite accomplished in the straw, that's for sure. And I gave it to her pretty good, I did!" Gerard boasted as Handy and Caldwell laughed.

"While I am happy that you enjoyed the wench, Gerard, I need more than a whore's name to indict McCarty. Anything else?"

Gerard looked at his notes again. "Nothing much else. Most of his time is spent in Alexandria with his friend James Dulaney, at Cedar Grove with his family, or at Coton."

"Coton Farm?" Armistead asked, his interest piqued.

"He's in courtship with Miss Lucinda Lee of Thomas Ludwell Lee."

"We all know who she is, Gerard!" Armistead's patience was wearing thin.

"Lucinda Lee," Handy said with a whistle. "Now that's a bit of crumpet."

Armistead shot Handy a disapproving look. "Let's not be crass. The Lee family is a respected family. Anything else?"

"That's all I have, sir."

Armistead moved his gaze to Caldwell. "The election for the legislature is in a few short weeks. What can we do to unwind McCarty's campaign?"

"I suggest we use our pseudonyms and ghost writers to sabotage his reputation publicly," Caldwell said. "'Junius' is always ready and willing to launch measured attacks that appeal to the aristocracy and the educated."

"Yes," Armistead said, "but it is not the aristocracy that will be the deciding factor for McCarty in the election. It's the common man—the freeholders in Loudoun. We must expose the depravity of McCarty's moral principles to impugn his character among the God-fearing Quakers and Germans in the west. We must also draw attention to his inexperience. We need to provoke him, get him to show his temper publicly so that the freeholders will see firsthand his recklessness and foul temperament."

"I can bait him, if you'd like, General," Handy said. "We all know that the average fella likes a bit of controversy. I can revive my 'Juriscola' alias to antagonize him in the press, provoke him, and escalate the exchange to the point McCarty feels aggrieved."

"But what if he were to learn your identity?" Gerard asked.

A plan formed in Armistead's mind—a devious, wonderful plan. "Perhaps we should ensure that McCarty learns the identity of 'Juriscola' once he feels aggrieved."

"Why would we want to do that, General?" Handy asked. "McCarty would most certainly challenge me."

"McCarty will not seek honorable reparation, Will. I promise you, he will not issue a challenge," Armistead said.

Handy was not satisfied. "McCarty has a temper. Remember last year at the hustings? He came at you with his fists. He may assault me, given the opportunity."

"That is why you will be armed! Should he approach you in the street, you will shoot him dead in self-defense and no one will be the wiser," Armistead said, a slow grin growing on his face. "It's a marvelous plan. Antagonize him, stir his Irish ire, and kill him when his temper flares."

Handy shifted uncomfortably in his chair.

"Brilliant, General, if I do say so," Gerard said, his eyes wild with excitement. "Feels like we're picking off the Brits on the shoals of Craney Island again!" Armistead glanced at the embers glowing in the fireplace across the room. *Kill or be killed.*

"Sir, with all due respect, the only gun I own is a musket for hunting. Surely you don't think I should carry a musket around with me over the next two months," Handy said.

"I shall loan you my pistols," Armistead said as he turned his attention to Handy. "Very smart pistols, they are. I will deliver them to you at once."

"General, how might we be assured that McCarty will not shoot Will first?" Caldwell asked. "I mean, if he's as ill-tempered as they say, doesn't it stand to reason that once he learns Juriscola is William Handy, he may attack Will before Will has an opportunity to defend himself?"

"Not to worry," Armistead said. "McCarty is not a marksman. As a matter of fact, I don't believe he even owns a pistol. When he approaches Will, his only weapon will be his fists. William will have ample opportunity to shoot him before he throws the first punch."

"If I shoot him, how can I be assured that the sheriff will not arrest me?" Handy asked as the color drained from his face. "And that I won't subsequently be hanged at the gallows?"

"When the time comes, I will have warned the sheriff that McCarty has made threats upon your life, so that when you shoot him, it will be of no surprise to the authorities. Trust me. Your only job is to be on your mark. Spend some time with the pistols to improve your accuracy." Armistead slapped Handy on the back, cutting off all avenues for Handy's escape. "You have nothing to fear, my friend!"

Handy slowly nodded his head, smiling weakly as Armistead took him by the shoulder. "Will, your bravery will not go unrecognized. I promise to do everything in my power to protect you, though I am certain that no harm will come to you. And should McCarty perish, your effort in his demise will not go unrewarded." Handy pressed his lips together and forced a wan smile. Armistead, flashing a convincing grin, had left him no way out.

CHAPTER 43

APRIL 16, 1818, THE RINGGOLD HOUSEHOLD, GEORGE TOWN, DISTRICT OF COLUMBIA

When Armistead arrived at the handsome brick house, Molly's attendant, Janny, met him at the door. Janny, who had moved from Coton Farm with Molly, was pure African. With a white kerchief around her head and another one in her hand to wipe perspiration from her brow, she took Armistead's hat and his calling card and directed him to wait for her mistress in the parlor.

Molly's engagement to widower Terence Ringgold had been announced shortly after Armistead's engagement party, and the two had been married a few months later. Armistead wondered if Molly had found happiness, or if she was as miserable as she had prophesized that night at Raspberry Plain. His thoughts were interrupted as Molly, dressed in her usual seductive attire and smelling of French lavender, glided across the floor in a waft of perfume with her hand extended to greet him.

"Armie!" Molly exclaimed, welcoming him with her sultry Southern charm.

Armistead took her hand with a gentlemanly kiss. Offering him an overstuffed armchair, Molly sat opposite on a dusty-blue sofa that straddled two windows facing the street as she served him tea.

"So, you have news regarding my sister? I have been so worried since receiving your message."

"I am concerned that your sister is in courtship with a dishonorable gentleman, could he even be called a gentleman at all."

"You are, no doubt, referring to Jack McCarty. And yes, he is presently her suitor. And yes, the entire family and the entirety of Virginia is aware of your dispute with him."

"It is no secret that I have had conflict with Mr. McCarty, but our controversy has been negotiated to a truce. My concerns are for your sister and your family, of course, and have nothing to do with my personal feelings toward the rogue." Peering at him from above the rim of her teacup, she could not mask her skepticism. "On my honor, Molly, what I am about to tell you has nothing to do with my rift with him."

Molly politely sipped tea from her dainty cup. "I'm listening."

"Now, I am not one to engage in idle gossip. That said, I have it on good authority that Mr. McCarty, your sister's suitor, is a frequent visitor to the brothels here in George Town."

Molly laughed at his seriousness. "Oh, Armistead, we've all heard the rumors. And Lucinda knows that Mr. McCarty has had that reputation."

"Remember, his brother William is husband to my sister, and I approached him on the subject. And when pressed, William confirmed the rumors as truth."

Molly straightened her posture, lifting the small of her back off the sofa. Sitting pertly, she cradled her cup in her hand, waiting for him to continue. Armistead now had her attention.

"So, given that Mr. McCarty is in courtship with your sister, I took it upon myself to look into the matter further. And while I cannot give specific details of who told me, I have irrefutable evidence that Mr. McCarty is a frequent patron of the House of Rose on Water Street—a well-known house of ill repute. My source informs me that there is a particular fancy named Lillie MacKall in whom Mr. McCarty has keen interest. This Lillie has become Mr. McCarty's concubine, of sorts. Seems he has paid for a full year of her service, keeping her for himself on those nights when he tells your sister that he is in Alexandria. And worse, Molly, is the likeness of the whore. Word is she looks similar to your sister, although not nearly as delicate and refined. Which leads the mind to wonder, of course, whether the resemblance is the reason for his fascination with your sister."

Molly's face turned ashen.

"Further, I have it on good authority that Mr. McCarty copulates with this harlot in the most perverted orgies that one can imagine. The sheriff has been made aware, as the two often disrupt the peace of the neighborhood. Apparently, bystanders on the street heard the two of them carrying on with their aberrant screams and lustful squeals just last week! Yet all the while Mr. McCarty remains in courtship with your sister, pretending to be a gentleman of honorable reputation."

Molly put a trembling hand to her mouth.

Armistead rushed to sit beside her on the sofa. "Molly, I am sorry you had to hear of such debauchery, but I fear that I had no choice but to tell you."

"Oh, Armie! What do we do?"

"The remedy is quite simple. You must tell your sister all that you have heard here today. No one will ever fault her for engaging in courtship with a man who had deceived her."

"Oh, Armie! The thought of her being courted by someone so depraved—"

Molly fell against him, sobbing. After a moment, she lifted her face to his, her blue eyes dewy with tears, her lips pouty and full. The vulnerability in her face, the sweetness of her breath, the feel of her so close to him overpowered him. Bringing his face to hers, he kissed her, slowly at first with his lips barely upon hers. Wanting more, she opened her mouth, stirring his desire for her that he had fought so very long to repress. As their kissing intensified, he shifted his hand to the nape of her neck and moved his mouth to her jawline and along her throat. Moaning unintelligibly, Molly pushed her bosom toward him. *Step away!* cautioned a voice in Armistead's head.

Suddenly self-aware, Armistead pulled away from her and rose from the sofa. He ran his hand through his hair and straightened his shoulders to regain his composure. "I apologize for my action, Mrs. Ringgold. I did not mean any disrespect."

Molly stood with him. "You didn't disrespect me, Armie. I wanted you to kiss me. And I would permit you to kiss me again." Her cheeks were flushed with passion. Reaching for his hands, she interlocked her fingers with his and stepped closer to him.

"Come with me upstairs, Armie," Molly pleaded. "Mr. Ringgold has left for Boston on business and will be gone for much of the summer. Come to my chamber." Her musky scent under the perfume and its hint of what lay beneath the dress aroused him further.

The voice in Armistead's head was screaming *Step away! Step away!* Molly moved even closer, her crystal blue eyes beseeching. Unable to control himself, he wrapped his arms around her and kissed her again, this time without restraint. *Step away!* Molly's hands slid down his back to his hips, and she pushed provocatively against his growing hardness. *Step away before you do something you'll regret!* When her hand moved to the front of his trousers, he could no longer resist her. He shut out the nagging voice of better judgment and took her hand, allowing her to lead him upstairs.

As the sun broke over the horizon, Armistead awoke with Molly in his arms. Her face was turned from him and her dark hair lay over his chest and arm. For a moment he thought he was next to Charlotte. Then he remembered. Without waking Molly, he dressed and slipped out the side door to the alley, praying to God that no one was witness to his departure. But it was a risk he would take, over and over, as their affair intensified with the heat of summer.

CHAPTER 44

MAY 9, 1818, BELMONT

"Congratulations, Jack! I hear you are headed to the legislature!"
Colonel Lee said, waving from the back porch as the men returned
from a morning of foxhunting.

"We missed you this morning, Colonel," Jack said, extending his
arm as he stepped onto the porch.

"Aye, my hip has been giving me fits. Maybe next week!" The colonel took Jack's hand and the two embraced. "I read that Juriscola
article in the paper after your win. Completely inappropriate!" Colonel
Lee shook his head. "It is one thing to lob insults during the campaign,
but entirely another to insult you now that you are an elected official."

Jack grabbed a tankard of beer from a servant's tray. "Agreed,
Colonel, and I spoke to Sam Caldwell about it. Believe it or not,
he gave up Juriscola's identity." Jack scanned the wide-eyed looks on
the faces of the men surrounding him. "Juriscola is none other than
William Handy!"

"Are you serious, Jack?" James said. "Caldwell just gave him up?"

"Indeed, he did. And I intend to pay Mr. Handy a visit at Osbourne's
Tavern on Monday to demand an apology and his word that all such
slander will cease!"

As they drank from their tankards of beer, the men nodded in agreement—all but Dr. Thomas Tebbs, a friend of the colonel's who also had been on the hunt.

Tebbs cleared his throat loudly, drawing the attention of the group. "Might I suggest, Jack, that you carry a sidearm when you visit Handy?"

"Why on earth would I arm myself to walk into a pub in downtown Leesburg?" Jack asked.

"Because I have heard rumors that Handy may shoot you," Tebbs said.

"Shoot me! Why would William Handy shoot me? I can understand him attacking me in the press, but shoot me?"

"I'm not sure, exactly. But I think he's being goaded into killing you and then claiming self-defense," Tebbs said. Jack set the tankard of beer on a table.

"How in God's name did you learn of this, Tom?" Cary Selden asked.

"By complete happenstance, I can assure you. Last week, I stopped at Osbourne's for supper on my way back to Middleburg. Gerard Alexander was at a table with another fellow. The two were highly intoxicated, talking loudly and being generally obnoxious as they exchanged stories and gossip. I caught only snippets of their rantings—something about shooting a rogue from Alexandria."

"A rogue from Alexandria?" Jack asked.

"Yes. I just now put it together when you said Handy was Juriscola."

Jack felt the heat rise on his chest and neck. "What exactly did you hear, Tom?"

"The gist of their conversation was that Handy had done something designed to draw this fellow into a confrontation. Alexander was laughing heartily as he told his friend that Handy was loaned a set of pistols with strict instructions to shoot the man should he come within thirty feet of Handy. Then Handy was to claim self-defense to avoid prosecution. Apparently, Handy was not keen on the plan, but he was operating under the instruction of someone else, an instigator of sorts. The two drunks were quite amused at Handy's sheepishness over the entire affair, and they wagered whether Handy would go through with it or not."

"William Handy was instructed to assassinate me?"

"Well, I'm not positively sure that they were referring to you, but in hindsight it seems logical."

"By whom, Tom? Who instructed him?"

"Presumably by whomever gave him the pistols," Tebbs said.

"Then I will go find Handy right now and insist he tell me who wants me killed!"

"That's a bad idea, Jack," Cary said. "If you come near him, Handy will most likely shoot you."

"Son of a bitch!" Jack swore under his breath.

"Let me talk to Handy," Tebbs said. "Since I'm the one who overheard the conversation, I would have good reason to make the inquiry."

"I want to know who put him up to this. And I swear on my father's grave that I am challenging the bastard who is behind this. And fight him I will!"

CHAPTER 45

MAY 13, 1818, CEDAR GROVE

The tension on the back porch was as thick as the humidity in the air. Jack pulled the watch from his pocket and checked the time. *He's a half hour late!* Upon closing the case, his grandmother's eyes smiled at him. Jack shoved the watch back into his waistcoat and scanned the porch. William was sitting in a rocker pretending to read, and James Dulaney was leaning against the corner post in the sunshine with his eyes closed, chewing on a piece of straw. Thomson and Edgar were somewhere inside as the four brothers and James waited for Dr. Thomas Tebbs to arrive.

Jack heard the dogs barking long before he heard the iron wheels of the coach grinding against the stone on the carriageway. William looked up from his newspaper, and James opened his eyes.

"Looks like our guest has arrived," William said, laying the paper in his lap.

"It's about Goddamned time," Jack said, leaning over the railing to catch a glimpse of Tebbs's coach.

A few moments passed before the screen door opened, and Edgar, Thomson, and Dr. Thomas Tebbs came out onto the porch. Jack's pulse raced.

"What news have you for us today, Thomas?" William asked, as the men exchanged greetings and handshakes.

"I wish the news were better," Tebbs said. The McCarty brothers exchanged anxious glances. "I have spoken at length with Handy. He confirmed that you, Jack, were indeed the target and claims that he was told you were intent on beating him to death."

"That is complete nonsense," Jack said. "I never spoke to anyone about approaching Handy except you men on the hunt. You and James were there and can bear witness to exactly what I said."

"And that is what I told Handy," Tebbs said. "But here's what's disturbing. Handy was as jumpy as a cat on hot bricks. Clearly, there was more to it."

"Who put him up to it, Tom?" Edgar asked.

Tebbs looked uneasily around the porch at the faces.

"The pistols were given to Handy by Armistead Mason."

Jack felt his blood in his veins. "I shall cast him into the fires of hell, I shall!"

"Jack, you are understandably angry, but let's not rush to judgment," William said. "Just because he lent his pistols to Handy doesn't mean he intended to have you assassinated."

"What in heaven's name is wrong with you, William? Has living out there on that Mason plantation completely divorced your mind from all logic and reason? Handy is a known operative for Armistead and his knot of Republicans. How can it not be he who is responsible for placing a mark on my life?" Jack shouted. He kicked a chair with his boot, his anger raging.

"I do not disagree with your conclusion, as it is all very damning," William said. "I am simply suggesting that there might be another explanation."

"Why in hell, William, are you always rushing to the bastard's defense? Why?"

William glared at his brother.

"Jack, your hot head is going to get you killed."

"It is your wife's brother who is going to get me killed! Not my temper!"

"Talk some sense into him, Edgar!" William threw up his hands and went back into the house, the screen door slamming behind him.

"William isn't defending him," said Thomson. "He's just suggesting that we not overreact."

"That's right," said Edgar. "William's torn, Jack."

Jack drew a long breath to clear his head and temper his rage. "James, what do you think?"

James, who had been silent, was leaning against the porch's column. He took the straw from his mouth and looked down at his feet before bringing his gaze to Jack's. "Beneath all his good breeding, Armistead Mason has the blackest heart of any man I know. There is no doubt in my mind that this is his doing. That said, William is married to Armistead's sister, who loves her merciless brother as any innocent would love a sibling.

"William must respect that bond. For William's sake, I think you must give the bastard the benefit of the doubt. Give Mason the opportunity to explain his role. And if he denies it, we let it go. If he admits to it, well, we have no choice other than to ask for reparations."

The three brothers and Tebbs stood in silence, weighing James's words. Although he didn't like what he was hearing, Jack knew that James was right. After a long moment, he turned to Tebbs. "Tom, would you agree to approach Armistead on my behalf as to his intentions?"

"I would be most agreeable to that, Jack," Tebbs said.

James caught Jack's gaze and nodded before turning to Tebbs. "I'll go with you, Tom. There's safety in numbers."

CHAPTER 46

MAY 19, 1818, MRS. PEYTON'S BOARDINGHOUSE

The door to Jack's apartment flew open, and Thomas Tebbs and James Dulaney burst into the room.

"We came straight from Leesburg, Jack, as we knew you would want to see it right away," James said, his hair disheveled from the long ride.

"What is it?" Jack asked.

"You're gonna want to read it for yourself," Tebbs said, handing Jack a correspondence pulled from his pocket. Jack unfolded the letter and read the words that he had hoped would prove his brother William right.

May 18, 1818

Dr. Tebbs:

I will inform you that I had no agency in the business, except I confirm that the pistols are mine. While I did not know or even suspect Mr. Handy's purpose, that is of no consequence, for had I known all of the circumstances, I would have gladly lent them to

Mr. Handy anyway.

To repeat, I am responsible for the loan of the pistols to Mr. Handy and would have been happy had Mr. Handy used them for their express purpose.

I am your obedient servant, Armistead T. Mason

Jack clenched a fist. "That bastard! You know damn well that he had every intention of having me killed in cold blood. I should like to ride out there tonight and shoot him dead on the spot before he has one of his hired guns shoot me down in the street! Of course I'd be dragged to the gallows and strung up by the neck, but not the glorious General Mason. No! He can get away with saying and doing whatever he wants without consequence."

"There's more, Jack." James wiped sweat and dust from his brow with a handkerchief.

Jack raised an eyebrow.

"He wanted you to know that he, unlike Fenton, did not wish any of his friends to fight his battles for him. He called you a scoundrel who, in his words, 'has come from Alexandria on a bullying expedition.'"

"Is that what he thinks? That I have somehow taken on Fenton's fight?"

"Oh, Armistead wants a fight, all right. He stated that he would not receive any communication from you unless it was a direct challenge and that he promised to accept your challenge after he made proper preparation," James explained.

"He said that he would gladly descend to your level and fight you for encouraging Handy to assassinate you."

"So he admitted it! It was an assassination plot!" The blood pulsed in Jack's temple.

"Not an admission," Tebbs said. "Just that he would have been enthusiastic had you been assassinated. He seems to relish the idea of your being killed by pistols belonging to him."

Jack's face reddened, and his fury burned hot.

"He seemed a madman, pacing and spewing commands at us like we were his soldiers. You remember how he was at Orchard Camp when they caught those deserters." James hesitated. "I think you should walk away from this. The general has said nothing in public to impugn your character. And Handy wouldn't dare shoot you now that the scheme has been exposed. Walk away, Jack."

"Are you kidding me, James? Has William been feeding you the same 'compromise' nonsense that they serve out there in Masonland? I will not turn my back, gentlemen. I have had enough. No one levies an assassination plot on my head and gets away with it. And let me tell you this." Jack narrowed his eyes and pointed at them with his finger. "The next time I lay eyes on Armistead Mason, he will be at the end of a barrel on the field of honor!"

CHAPTER 47

JUNE 8, 1818, STRAWBERRY PLAIN

It was a perfect June day, the sun high in the clear blue of the Virginia sky. Emily was tending her roses, trimming the leaves on the bushes and collecting the blooms in a basket. Her hair, now cut short in the latest Parisian fashion, was completely covered by a large hat to shield her face from the early summer sun. Humming while fast at work, she startled at a voice behind her.

"Miss Emily?" Emily jumped and spun around, nearly dropping her clippers. It was her Irish cook, Connie, holding a glass of lemonade.

"Why, Connie! You frightened me out of my wits!"

"I be sorry, ma'am. I didn't mean to startle ya. But I thought that ya might like a tall drink, ma'am, to cool ya a bit," Connie said in a heavy brogue.

"Oh, how kind," Emily smiled, putting the clippers in the basket. She accepted the sweating crystal and took a long drink.

"Ma'am, might I have a word with ya? In private, betweens just us?"

"Why, of course, Connie. Is everything all right?"

"No, ma'am. Everything is not all right. Not all right t'all," she said, rubbing her hands nervously on her apron.

Emily lowered the glass from her mouth and narrowed her eyes. "Come over here, my dear. Let's move to the shade and chat for a spell." Emily led her to the marble bench William's mother had given Emily as a wedding gift. She set the lemonade on the bench and took Connie's hand into both of hers. "Now what is it, Connie? Tell me what is troubling you."

"Miss Emily, I don't mean to upset ya, nor do I mean to put me nose in situations that are none of me business, but I think too much of ya not to tell ya what I've heard."

"What in heaven's name, Connie? What is it you've heard that might upset me?" This was the exact way one of her friends from the academy was told of her husband's infidelity. Emily braced herself for the worst.

"It's your brother, the general over at Selma. And Mr. William's brother from Alexandria, Mr. Jack. They're about to fight each other, they are. With guns, ma'am. My husband, Johnny, says that it's all over the papers. And the boys down at the pub are a-wagerin' on who lives and who dies. Johnny says that it will be Mr. Jack who takes the fall. And he put near an entire month's wages on the bet. But the general could die, too. And me knows how ya love him so."

Emily was dumbstruck. Although she was relieved that William was not unfaithful to her, she could not believe that Armistead and Jack had gone back on their words—on their honors—to end the feud.

"Miss Emily? Are ya all rights? Miss Emily?"

"Are you certain, Connie?"

"As sure as I am sitting here with ya, ma'am. Johnny would ne'er place a wager he didn't intend on winning. And it's in the papers, too, ma'am. Johnny says."

Emily bit her bottom lip. She wanted to be alone to think.

"Thank you, Connie. For coming to me. But let's not tell Johnny that you told me. I wouldn't want him to become cross with you."

"Oh no, ma'am. I would never tell Johnny that I told ya his business. Never."

As songbirds chirped happily in the tree above her, Emily remained on the bench, wrestling with her doubts. *These are simply rumors. That is all.* She watched as a robin hopped across the garden path. *Connie was so insistent.* The bird bobbed its head and tugged at something in the grass. She moved her gaze from the bird to the far side of the house. *There is only one way to find out.* Emily stood from the bench, startling the robin into abandoning its prey and flying into the thicket. Lifting the hem of her dress above the grass, Emily marched across the lawn to the side door of William's office. Opening the door with a sudden jerk, she slipped inside. On a shelf behind William's desk were newspapers stacked in a neat pile. Emily crinkled her nose. *Dirty, disgusting scandal sheets!*

Careful not to touch the ink with her fingers, she started opening the papers. It wasn't long before she found it. Her brow furrowed and her temper flared as she read the notice. *How dare they!* With a pair of shears, she cut the column from the paper. *William will be livid with me for spoiling his newspaper.* She folded the evidence into her handkerchief. *He'll just have to get over it!* Restacking the newspapers, she moved the one she had cut to the bottom of the pile.

Emily looked out the window. *How to stop all this?* Staring into the rose garden, she searched for answers. Her freshly cut flowers were sitting in a basket by the marble bench, wilting in the hot sun. *The bench!*

She raced from William's office, down the hall. "Jedediah! Jedediah!"

"Missus Emily! Are you all right?" the butler asked, emerging from the dining room with a cloth in his hand.

"I'm fine, Jed. Just fine, but we must make haste. Go at once and prepare the carriage. I need to go immediately to Cedar Grove!"

CHAPTER 48

JUNE 10, 1818, MRS. PEYTON'S
BOARDINGHOUSE

"Mr. McCarty?" Mrs. Peyton called as she entered his room. Engrossed in drafting a brief for a property dispute, Jack hadn't heard her rapping on his door. Glancing out the window, he hadn't noticed that it was raining either. "I am sorry to disturb you, sir, but there is a visitor here to see you in the parlor." Mrs. Peyton smiled as she handed him a calling card.

Mrs. Sarah Eilbeck Mason McCarty. He moved his eyes to the window and saw the muddied cobblestones in the street below. *Sally never travels in the rain.* Jack bolted from the chair and raced down the stairs in front of Mrs. Peyton.

Standing at the far window of the formal room stood his mother. She was dressed handsomely in a deep-gray linen skirt. Her matching jacket, with tiny black buttons from the waist to the collar, was tailored to fit her perfectly. She left the collar open to show off the multiple strands of pearls wrapped around her neck. Her hair was tucked up under a great gray hat adorned with a black cockade from the era of George Washington's presidency. She carried an overly large black tapestry bag with black leather handles and a black umbrella. Everything about her demeanor told Jack that something dire had happened.

"Sally," Jack said, greeting his mother with a worried look and a kiss. "Is everything all right?"

"Mrs. Peyton, might we close those doors for a few moments to afford me and my son a bit of privacy? If you don't mind, dear?"

Jack felt his stomach sink as Mrs. Peyton fumbled about with the parlor doors.

"What is it, Sally? What is wrong?" Jack asked once the doors had closed. "Has something happened to one of my brothers? To Nancy? Or one of the children?"

"Nothing of the sort, Jack. All of your siblings are of sound body and sound mind—which is more than can be said for you."

Jack shot her an indignant look. "What have I done now?"

Without a word, Sally pulled a half dozen or more folded newspapers from her gigantic bag and tossed them on the small serving table that separated the sofa from the parlor chairs. Jack knew exactly why she had come to call.

"I thought you said you were finished reading the news, Sally. 'Slander sheets,' I believe you called them. Good for nothing more than use in the privy? Isn't that what you said?"

"Don't you mock me, boy!" Sally seethed in a voice so dark and a tone so low that Jack could barely hear her.

"Mother, I'm sorry. I should not have said that to you. I'm just so fed up with the whole of the affair with Armistead. I've had to listen to William's constant criticism. And Edgar's advice as well. And now you." Sally glared at him in silence until he could no longer stand it. "What do you want me to say, Sally?"

She kept her eyes on him for a moment more, uttering nothing. Drawing a long sigh, she moved her attention to the window and the rain gently falling in the street beyond.

"It is not what I want you to say. It is what I want you to do."

Another long pause passed before she spoke again. "You will withdraw this challenge, John Mason McCarty."

"It's moot to withdraw, Sally, as Armistead has already rejected my challenge because I—"

"Just stop, Jack!" Not looking at him, Sally held her hand up with her palm facing him to hush him. "Stop defending this nonsense and listen to what you are going to do. I have spoken to William and to Edgar, and they agree. You will withdraw this challenge, regardless of your opinion of the validity of Armistead's rejection, of his counter, of his terms, of whatever it is that he believes is proper etiquette. I care not. Further, you will not disappoint me again by challenging your cousin, or any other gentleman, to the most barbaric and idiotic practice I have ever heard of—standing at the end of a loaded barrel because you feel insulted!" Sally shook her head in disgust.

She turned to face him, her visage red with anger. But as he caught her eyes, he realized it wasn't anger he saw, but pain. And worry. And love. Suddenly, he felt as if he would cry.

He hung his head, his eyes welling with tears. Sally dropped her carpeted bag on the floor and, with outstretched arms, took him into her embrace.

"I'm sorry, Mother," Jack said, burying his face in her shoulder.

"It's all right, Jackie. It's all right," Sally whispered as she held him.

"I have been so afraid," he said, struggling to hold back the tears and the fear that, until now, he had managed to keep at bay.

"I know, my son. I know your heart. And I know your temper. We must learn to keep it in check."

Jack pulled away from her and wiped his eyes with his palm. With both hands on his shoulders, Sally forced him to look at her.

"My boy, Jackie. What to do with you?" Sally shook her head, smiling. "You will do these things I ask. And Ludwell has assured me that he will have a word with Armistead once Mrs. Mason has had her discussion with her son." Jack's brow knitted in confusion. "Yes, Jack, I was at Raspberry Plain just yesterday with Colonel Lee. Mrs. Mason has agreed to confront Armistead, much as I have confronted you."

Jack was stunned and it showed on his face.

"Do not underestimate a mother's persuasive powers, Jack. She has assured us that Armistead will see things her way. And if there is one thing I know about Polly Mason, it is that she would never make a claim that she cannot guarantee. Have faith, Jackie boy. Have faith."

"You realize that he won't stop, don't you? He may agree for the moment, but he will never stop until he kills me or I kill him."

A somber expression fell over Sally's face and she looked him in the eye. "It takes two to fight. You must have the courage to walk away should he provoke you again."

"He was to have me assassinated!"

"So you say. But it was your temper that would have lured you into the trap. When your enemies know your weakness, they exploit it."

"It was not my temper, Sally. It was the insult to my honor."

"My dear Jackie boy. Don't you know this by now? Your honor is how you hold yourself, not what others think or say. Hold yourself high above the fray, high above the reach of others. There, on that high ground, they can never harm you." Smiling with warmth and kindness in her eyes, she hugged him once more before picking up her bag and umbrella to leave.

"We have monopolized Mrs. Peyton's parlor long enough," Sally said, straightening the collar of her jacket. "I must head back to Cedar Grove before this rain makes the streets so thick with mud that the entire carriage is swallowed by the road. William will work with you and Ludwell on what to do next. In the interim, do nothing. No more notices, no more letters, no more ... ," her voice trailed off. "Are we good, then? Yes, of course we are!"

Jack nodded his head in agreement and walked with her to the parlor door. As he placed his hand on the knob to turn it, he looked at Sally once more. "I love you, Mother." He couldn't remember the last time he had told her that.

"I love you, too, John McCarty." Sally put her hand on the side of his face and smiled at him warmly. With a toss of her head, she patted his cheek. "And don't 'Mother' me, please!"

CHAPTER 49

JUNE 10, 1818, RASPBERRY PLAIN

"Mother! I received your note and came at once," Armistead said as he hurried into his father's study.

Polly Mason was sitting stoically in Armistead's father's chair like a queen, her folded hands on the desk.

Polly nodded toward one of the chairs in front of her. "Sit."

"Mother?"

"Sit, Armistead."

Polly glared across the shiny buff of the oak that reflected the morning light from the window behind her. Reluctantly, Armistead pulled up a chair and sat.

"I had visitors yesterday." Again, there was a long pause. Armistead weighed his options, whether to take the bait or simply outwait her. After a suspenseful minute, he decided to acquiesce.

"Anyone I might know?" He assumed a bemused look. He didn't know yet the setup, but he was most familiar with the game.

"Your father's cousin, Sally McCarty."

"Good God, that awful woman! I can understand why, having had to entertain her, you are in such a foul mood this morning."

"And Colonel Ludwell Lee."

At the mention of the colonel, Armistead knew the reason for his mother's ill humor.

"Now, Mother, before you let some old relic and that drunken woman fill your head—"

"Don't start with me, Armistead! I will not sit here and listen to your manipulation of the facts nor your twisted version of the truth. Not this time. You cannot deceive or charm your way out of this. I know exactly what you've been agitating for, and it must stop!"

Armistead was outraged by her disrespectful tone, yet dared not show it. Not yet, anyway. He knew how to temper her. He flashed his boyish grin. "Now, Mother, you have no idea how aggrieved—"

"Armistead, don't. I had two respected members of the community come to my door yesterday informing me of my son's foolery—including public diatribes, name-calling, backroom schemes to assassinate a brother-in-law, and challenges to shoot the boy directly in the name of honor. And it is going to stop. Right now. Today."

Her words cut him to the quick. Not removing his eyes from hers, he sat silent. Minutes passed before Polly, her hands still folded, pursed her lips and lifted her chin.

"Are you finished, Mother?"

"No, actually. I am not. Because I have yet to tell you why you will stop."

Armistead waited for her until his patience gave way. "All right, Mother, I'll ask. Why will I stop?"

"Because I will not forgive you should you leave your child an orphan."

Armistead's eyes narrowed. "What are you saying?"

"I'm saying your wife is pregnant."

"Charlotte is with child?"

"I advised her to wait to tell you. I didn't want you to get your hopes up, only to be disappointed should she lose the baby again. But yes, she is with child. Your child, Armistead."

His buried outrage instantly ignited. "My wife is with child and you told her to keep it from me?!" He stood from the chair. "I must get home and speak to her at once."

For the first time since his arrival, Polly raised her voice. "You'll do no such thing! She must not think that I betrayed her trust. If she knows that I told you, she will want to know why. And we certainly cannot tell her why, now, can we?"

"You don't tell me what to do!"

"Do you want to lose another wife? Charlotte does not need the stress of learning about your abhorrent behavior, especially in her condition! And we all remember last time what happened when she was overwhelmed with your political controversies. So, you will agree. No dueling, no more newspaper controversies, no more assassination plots, and no talking with Charlotte about any part of our conversation today. Unless you feel so inclined to risk her life by informing her of your detestable behavior."

Armistead fumed at her accusation and the unreasonableness of her demands.

Polly's lips thinned as she spoke. "Are we in agreement?"

Armistead could barely control his anger. How dare she manipulate him like this? How dare she blame the miscarriage on him? With every resolve, he clamped his jaw to keep the words he was thinking from exploding from his mouth. She had him beat.

Armistead repeated words that had so often burned his tongue. "Yes, Mother."

Polly relaxed her pinched expression and curled her lips into a smile. She sat back in the chair contentedly.

"Good, then. I was confident we would come to an agreeable conclusion. I took the liberty of having tea set for us. Come, darling. Let us retire to the parlor and celebrate the joyous occasion. You are finally going to be a father! Such grand news!"

Armistead seethed under his pasted-on smile. He would just as soon scald her with hot water than drink tea with her.

Polly rose from behind the desk, extended her arm, and invited Armistead to escort her to the parlor where tea was waiting.

CHAPTER 50

JUNE 27, 1818, COTON FARM

Blackbirds, with their high-pitched alerts and rattling calls, fussed as Jack waited on the porch facing the pond. He watched the crimson blaze on the birds' wings flicker amid the reeds like flames along the water's edge. The skies were cloudless and a warm breeze rustled the leaves of the maples and oaks that surrounded the Coton manor house. At the slam of the screen door, Jack turned his attention from the clattering of the birds to the pretty blonde in a floral-embroidered dress behind him. She was without a sunbonnet and her hair was tied back with a lilac ribbon.

"Lucy!" he said, taking her hand and giving her a gentlemanly kiss. "Let's sit for a moment. There is something I'd like to ask you."

"I see no reason you cannot ask me while standing, Mr. McCarty."

Jack cocked his head to one side, searching her face. There was a foreboding about her eyes. He drew a quick breath, pressing forward with his intent.

"Very well then, I'd like you to attend the Independence celebrations next weekend with me. Would you honor me by allowing me to escort you?"

Lucinda crossed her arms over her chest. "I'm not quite sure, Mr. McCarty. It depends on whether what I hear is true."

"What, Lucy? What have you heard?"

"I am in receipt of a letter from my sister, Mrs. Ringgold in George Town. She has come into information that you are a frequent patron of a brothel, the House of Rose, down along the water."

Jack drew a slow breath. William had warned him that he would regret such behavior. "'Tis true, I had in the past visited that establishment. And I admit to you now that it is something that I am not proud of. But these are things that most gentlemen do in their youth, Lucy. Not once a man becomes of age."

"I don't believe you."

"On my word as a gentleman, I am telling you the truth."

"That is not what I have heard, Mr. McCarty."

"Tell me what it is you've heard, Lucy. Tell me so that I can assure you of the truth." Lucinda knitted her brows together and scrutinized his face. Jack knew this look.

"I have been told that there is a particular woman who lives at that house. And that you see her all the time. That on the nights you tell me that you are in Alexandria, you are with her. In her bed. And that you are in love with her. Or in lust with her, as I am not sure which it is. Is this true?"

Jack felt a blow to his stomach as panic tore through his veins. *Who told your sister about Lillie?* James Dulaney called on Fanny from time to time. Had James betrayed him? But if that were the case, Fanny would have spoken to Lucinda directly.

"Is it true, Jack?" Her eyes narrowed further, searching his.

Jack redirected his thinking from who said what to what to say. *She will never forgive me if I tell her the truth.* Jack rushed to kneel at her feet and took her hand. "No, Lucy. It is not true."

"What about this woman? Do you have feelings for her?"

"There is no woman that I have feelings for other than you. Only you, Lucinda. No one else." Caressing her hand, he found the words that he had longed to say.

"I am in love with you, Lucinda Lee. And what a fool I have been. I have professed my feelings for you to all of my friends. I have told my brothers how much I care for you. Even my mother knows my heart.

Yet I have neglected to tell the one person to whom it matters most." Jack smiled at her, sharing the words that had frightened him for so long. "When you look at me, it's as if you see through to the very core of me. My wealth, my family name—none of it seems to matter to you. You see me for me. And I love you for it. When I'm with you, I feel as if I can do anything—soar high in the sky, dive to the depths of the ocean. I only pray that I give to you the same joy you give to me. You mesmerize me, Lucy. And I am in awe of you." Jack fought the tears welling in his eyes and brought her hand to his lips. "You have pierced my heart and captured it for your very own. Please, I beg you, treat it gently, for it is all that I have to give you."

"I care for you as well, Jack." Lucinda moved her eyes to the floorboards of the porch before lifting her head to look at him again. "But I cannot give my heart to a man who is so reckless with his life."

"Whatever do you mean?"

"I know that you have challenged General Mason to a duel. A duel, Jack!"

"This is true, Lucinda. But—"

"How can I give my heart to a man who will only shatter it when he falls dead from the ball of a pistol? Why would I invite such pain and sorrow into my life, Jack?"

"Let me explain."

"What explanation can there be? You admit to challenging a known duelist to a shooting match in which you are the target! A man who most certainly would kill you dead! How can I allow my heart to be broken into a thousand pieces at the same moment yours is shattered by a ball of lead!" Lucinda turned her face toward the reeds.

Jack took her chin in his fingers, redirecting her attention. "There is nothing to worry over, Lucy. Your uncle has negotiated a truce between the general and myself. The matter is resolved."

"Are you certain?"

"As certain as I am of my love for you." Jack smiled reassuringly at her.

"Do you promise?"

"Cross my heart, hope to die," he said, crisscrossing his heart with two fingers.

"Oh, stop it, Jack! Don't say a thing like that when we are talking about you getting shot!"

"I promise, Lucy. Ask your uncle if you don't believe me."

"I most certainly will!" Lucinda crossed her arms.

"Now is there anything else that is troubling you?" Jack asked, pulling her folded arms to take her hands in his.

"Not that I can think of at the moment, but I'm sure that there will be something in the future."

There's my sassy girl! Jack smiled. "Very well then, what about my offer?"

"Offer?"

"Will you be my guest at the celebrations on July Fourth?"

"Perhaps. On one condition."

"Another one?"

"At least for now, only one."

"And what condition would that be, Miss Lee?" He delighted in the way she toyed with him.

Lucinda brought her eyes to his. "That you promise, on your word, that you will never challenge Armistead Mason—or anyone—to a duel again."

Jack placed his right hand over his heart. "I promise. On my honor, I will not challenge Armistead again. Ever. Now, about my request?"

Lucinda looked at the sky, pretending serious thought. "Hmmm," she said before returning her eyes to his. "I will be delighted to accompany you to the celebrations."

Jack squeezed her hands, pulled her toward him, and kissed her on the cheek.

"Oh, what fun we shall have!" he said gleefully, moving his feet in an Irish jig. "My carriage will come for you around ten that morning. It will be warm for certain that day, so be sure to wear as little clothing as possible."

"You are indeed a scoundrel, Jack McCarty. I will wear what I like, including a chastity girdle for good measure." She pushed him away.

"What kind of gent do you take me for, Miss Lucinda? Why, I would never consider doing anything that might stain your chastity."

"I'm going to call my mother out here, Mr. McCarty, should you not make haste. I will see you next Saturday." She laughed as he bowed to her in farewell.

"Next Saturday, my darling. And ten o'clock sharp," Jack reminded her, skipping down the steps toward the front drive.

"I shall be ready, chastity belt and all!"

CHAPTER 51

AUGUST 28, 1818, LEESBURG

The Leesburg courthouse and adjoining streets were bustling on August Court Day. In addition to the judge and the attorneys, defendants and plaintiffs were all in the county seat for the month's business of jurisprudence. Merchants had moved their wares outside their shops as prospective customers eyed the goods on display. It was hot, the air thick with powdery dust and the humidity of the dog days of summer.

Jack and William had appeared before the court early in the day, arguing a case involving a land dispute. After their court appearance, the plan was to rendezvous with Lucinda and Emily for lunch at the inn next door. Having finished earlier than expected, they made their way toward Leesburg Tavern for a quick beer. To the south of the courtyard, a group of men crowded around a small table stacked with portfolio-style booklets.

"Why, there he is right there," said one of the men.

Jack turned his head to see a man pointing at him. "Pardon?"

"Aren't you John McCarty?" the gentleman asked.

"I am."

"Well, I'll be," the nameless man said, turning back to the table. "Yes, sir. I'll buy me one of them there books, sir."

Jack looked at William, who appeared just as confused.

"What book?" William asked as the two walked toward the crowd around the table.

Behind a stack of booklets sat Sam Caldwell, counting coinage as he handed a copy to one of the patrons. William leaned over the table and cocked his head sideways to get a better look at what Caldwell was selling and read the imprinted gold lettering on the cover.

"What is it, William?" Jack asked, unable to get a good look himself.

William picked up one of the booklets from the table and held it up.

Armistead T. Mason – John McCarty Duel, Selma 1818

Jack's mouth went dry, and his pulse raced. "Are you kidding me?" he said and took a step toward Caldwell.

William grabbed his brother's arm and leaned toward Jack's ear. "Not here, Jack. Not now."

"I asked you a question, Mr. Caldwell. What the hell is this?" Jack said, ignoring William's advice.

"It's the truth and nothing but the truth, Mr. McCarty. Something you would know little about," Caldwell said, his thick spectacles enlarging his eyes as the corners of his little mouth turned up in a twisted smile.

Jack felt William's grasp tighten on his arm. "The last thing we want is to create a scene here on the street on Court Day. Seriously, Jack, calm down."

"I am calm, Will," Jack said through clenched teeth.

"The hell you are. We don't know what this is yet. Go on to the pub. I'll be up in a minute with one of these things, and then we'll see what we're dealing with."

Jack glared at Caldwell.

"Go on, Jack."

Fighting the urge to grab Caldwell by the collar and pull his bony body over the table, Jack drew a long breath. William was right. The last thing he needed was a confrontation with the likes of Sam Caldwell, a newspaperman who looked for any excuse to make a profit and wouldn't hesitate to provoke Jack to generate a story. Relaxing his arm, Jack nodded to William. "I'll see you up there." He turned toward the tavern at the end of the street and walked away.

By the time Jack arrived at the pub, his anger had cooled. But when he entered, he could feel the eyes of the men in the tavern on him. Jack guessed that whatever the details of Caldwell's booklet, it was the gossip de jour. *You know the truth, Jack,* he said to himself and held his head high as he walked past them.

He took a booth in the far corner of the room out of earshot of the other patrons. A buxom barmaid took his order. Within a matter of minutes, William's broad shoulders darkened the door. Jack beckoned him over to where he was sitting as the barmaid brought two tankards of beer. With the booklet in his hand, William slid onto the bench beside Jack. The folder was large—the size of a newspaper, bound in a dark-gray cloth with gold engraved letters in the title.

"What does he think he's publishing?" Jack said. "The Treaty of Ghent?"

"I'm betting it's anything but a treaty," William said, and opened the cover. Inside the folder was a full-page spread of select correspondence from Armistead to Jack. Jack shook his head in disbelief. Armistead's commentary skewed even a note by Dr. Thomas Tebbs as a maligning of Jack's character. Jack clenched a fist under the table. He took a breath. *Don't let him goad you, Jack. You don't need his respect.*

"I can't believe he is stirring this again," William said as he lifted his eyes from the publication. "He has not included a word of your correspondence to him, nor has he included any of the newspaper notices that you published. It's misleading."

"Not to mention that he publishes this now, two months after he agreed to a truce," Jack said as William moved to the opposite bench.

"You haven't said or done anything to incite him, have you?"

"Of course not! I gave Colonel Lee my word, our mother my word, and Lucinda my word. I have walked a wide circle around Armistead. I don't attend any of the parties or levees where there is even the remote possibility that he or his wife might appear. I even declined Colonel

Monroe's summer barbeque at Oak Hill last month because I knew he would be there."

"Hell, I forgot about that! Emily couldn't believe that you declined the invitation for the president's summer party. She was so upset that day because our family was so divided over all of this."

"Emily blames me?"

"She was actually blaming me at the time. But frankly, she doesn't know who to blame. Plus, she's emotional now that she's with child."

"I tell you, William, Armistead will not stop. I don't care how many truces are negotiated. Or how much pressure his family puts on him. He will not stop until he goads me to fight him and kills me dead!"

"He can't kill you unless you oblige him."

"You're right. It's not like any of this is new. The public must see this for what it is—the one-sided ramblings of a madman!"

William sat back on the seat with surprise on his face.

Jack forced a small smile. "Walk away—isn't that what you keep telling me, brother?"

"I do, but you never seem to listen!"

"I guess this is another one of those 'first times,'" Jack said with a laugh.

William smiled. "I know it's hard to swallow, but for the family … for the sake of your courtship with Lucinda, you're doing the right thing by letting it lie. Anyone with any intelligence who reads this will see it for what it is."

"I hope you are right, William." Jack lifted the pewter mug and pulled a long drink from the top of the tankard.

William was turning his tankard back and forth in the ring of water that had sweated from its sides. "Tell you what, Jack. Let's get out of here."

"Sure, I'll sign for the beers." Jack waved to attract the attention of the barmaid.

"No. I mean, yes. Let's settle the account, but let's get out of town. We'll meet the ladies on the road and turn back to Strawberry Plain to enjoy the day. There's nothing but trouble here."

CHAPTER 52

"William, what on earth is going on?" asked Emily, her bonneted head halfway through the open carriage window as William and Jack approached on horseback from the other direction on the Carolina Road.

"The dust in town is strangling. Jack could barely breathe! Best if we dine at the farm," William said as he slowed his horse at the carriage door. Jack shot William a scowling glance from the other side of the road. William winked back, riding his mount past the coach and allowing room for it to turn around.

"When I said you had to make an excuse for why we didn't want to stay in town for Court Day, I didn't agree that you should blame it on me!" Jack said, spurring his mare to take the lead.

"It was the most believable excuse I could come up with. Besides, how can she argue with me if staying in town might cause you to choke to death?" William said.

"Next time, consult me first," Jack said, shooting his brother another scowl.

Upon arrival at the farm, William headed inside to direct the servants to accommodate their change in plans, while Jack helped the women from the carriage. In a big white bonnet shading most of her face, Emily stepped from the coach first, wearing a white gossamer dress trimmed in green ruched ribbons. Lucinda emerged next in a similar dress cut from a pale-blue fabric, and trimmed at the neckline, waist, and hemline in ribbons of the same color as her eyes. She had pinned her hair under a broad-brimmed blue hat, and a few strands of her blond locks were falling loosely around her face. Jack couldn't keep his eyes from her as she stepped onto the ground.

"Are you all right, Jack?" Emily asked, her eyes narrow with concern.

"I'm fine, Mrs. McCarty. Your husband is simply being overly cautious," Jack said.

"Well, better to be overly cautious than to be sorry later, for certain. Let me go see what Connie can put together for us on such short notice," Emily said and headed into the house to find her husband.

"Seriously, Jack, is there something wrong with your lungs?" Lucinda asked, looking up at him with genuine concern.

"Not at all. Occasionally, things like smoke or dust will cause a cough. That's why I don't smoke a pipe."

"Well, let's pray that there is nothing abnormal. Lungs can be fickle."

"I apologize should you be disappointed about missing the Court Day." Jack took her hand and tucked it through his arm.

"There is no reason to apologize at all. Although, I suppose that if you had lost your breath, I would have had to lend you mine," Lucinda said with that mischievousness in her voice that he so loved.

"Perhaps then we should go back to town so that I can take you up on your offer."

"But if my breath isn't enough to revive you, the coachman will need to lend his as well."

"In that case, Miss Lucinda, I think it best that we stay here."

"As you wish." Lucinda smiled at Jack, hugging his arm and strolling with him toward the porch. "Jack, what is that over there?"

"Over where?" Jack said, following her gaze across the front lawn toward the north edge of the yard.

"There. Those rows? What are they?" She pointed to several long, low trellises covered in green leaves.

"That is the vineyard."

"I hadn't noticed it before. The arbor is awfully low. Has it always been there?"

"Actually, it has. Emily's brother planted it a decade or so ago. When he died a couple of years back, the Masons let it go. William has taken it over and made wine from the harvest last year. He hasn't shared any of it yet, of course, but he's hopeful it will be as good as the French."

"Wine? It's a wine vineyard?"

"What other kind would it be?"

Lucinda threw her head back and laughed. "Jack McCarty, are you sure that you grew up on a plantation?"

"You're mocking me, aren't you, Miss Lee?"

"Perhaps. Certainly there were other kinds of grapes growing at Cedar Grove."

"I suppose, but wine grapes interest me more."

"Then perhaps you should show me."

"All right, Miss Lucinda. Come with me!" Jack grinned, redirecting her toward the vineyard.

Simply being with Lucinda brought Jack a peaceful contentment. The ease of her laugh and the warmth of her smile melted away his troubles with Armistead. When they reached the vineyard, Jack led her into the rows, explaining how William had trellised and trimmed the vines. He pointed to a cluster of small, dark berries. "Now these here, Lucy, are called fox grapes."

"A fox grape? Why on earth is it named after a fox?"

"Apparently, the wine tastes a bit like a wet fox, or at least that is William's explanation."

Lucinda crinkled her nose. "That is disgusting! Who in the world would want to drink something that tastes like a wet, mangy fox?"

Jack had never quite thought of it in that manner. "Probably someone who has never smelled a wet, mangy fox!"

"Sounds like a wine that only a hound would enjoy!" Jack watched her intently while she closely inspected the tiny berries on the vine. Lucinda picked one from a cluster and brought it to her nose, sniffing the berry's skin. "It doesn't smell like a fox."

Jack bent to smell the tiny grape she held in her fingers. "Doesn't resemble the scent of any fox I have smelled." He moved closer to her, inhaling the aroma of her neck and shoulder instead of the grape. "The smell of this fox is much more pleasing."

Lucinda brought her eyes to his. He brushed an errant strand of blond hair from her brow for an unobstructed view of the fair face under the hat. At his touch, she closed her eyes. Unable to contain his desire any longer, he took her into his arms and kissed her. She brought her arms to his waist, holding him close as the passion of their kiss intensified. After a long moment, he removed his lips from hers.

"And now you have tasted the fox, Mr. McCarty."

"I should like to taste her once more." Jack kissed her again. When he pulled back from her, he was searching her face, desperation in his eyes. "Tell me, Lucy. Tell me that you love me."

"You know that I do, Jack."

"Then say it, Lucy. Say it." The rawness of Jack's emotions poured from his soul. "Today of all days, I need to hear the words. Please tell me, Lucy."

Lucinda grew quiet as if to collect her thoughts or her nerves or both. "All right, then. I shall make my confession." She drew a long breath. "Hardly a day goes by that my mind doesn't think of you or that my heart doesn't feel you. The sound of your voice, even the mention of your name, stirs such conflicting feelings within me. When I am with you, sometimes I can barely breathe for your intoxicating presence. There are times I want to run from the allure of you, to hide from your charms. And there are other times when I want nothing more than to fall into your arms. You have melted my heart. And I have tried desperately to stop you from doing so. I have been afraid to fall for you, so afraid of what I thought would be most certainly heartbreak." Lucinda paused, biting at her lip, glancing momentarily at the vines. "Yet, despite all my resistance, my heart refuses to listen to my head. For every moment that I am with you, my affection grows stronger and my feelings deeper, to where I am helpless." Lucinda's voice faltered. She shifted her eyes to the ground to find her words. Her eyes were moist with tears when they returned to his.

"I feel helpless, Jack, for I have fallen hopelessly in love with you. I have shared so much of myself with you—my hopes, my dreams, my passions—yet I have been too afraid to share my heart. Afraid that once you knew my true feelings, having achieved your conquest, the love you profess for me would leave you, and you would be gone. And the only thing left would be the thousand shards of my heart." Lucinda pursed her lips to keep them from quivering. Despite her efforts not to cry, a tear escaped her eye and rolled down her face.

"I would never do that, never hurt you like that." He cradled her face in his strong hands. "My God, Lucy, is this how I have made you feel? So afraid? I would never leave you—forsake you for another. I would never, could never ..." He, too, struggled to find the right words. "I, too, have a confession. When I left for Natchez, I admit that I tried to forget you. I tried to distract my mind and purge you from my heart. Then one June evening, when the full moon was rising over the grasslands of Kentucky, everything changed. I was desperately struggling to find my purpose—the reason for my life—when I found your beautiful blue eyes in the face of that moon staring back at me. I know that you were watching it rise that night and that you were dreaming of us. I could feel you, Lucy. I could feel your heart in the silver dust of the moonlight streaming over that field. I felt us. And from that moment I have trusted in nothing else."

As Jack spoke, the flood of tears Lucinda had held at bay streamed down her face. "Shhh, my darling," Jack whispered, taking Lucinda into his arms. "Please don't cry."

"I remember the night. My God, Jack. I remember." Lucinda lifted her face to his and the hat fell from her head to the ground. "Promise me, Jack. Promise that you will never shatter it. Never shatter the dream. That you will never break my heart."

"To break your heart would be to break my own. I will never hurt you, my darling. Never."

Lucinda searched for reassurance in his eyes. "How do I know, Jack? How can I know for certain?"

With the back of his fingers, he caressed the side of her face and wiped her tears away. "You must trust, Lucinda. Trust in our love. Trust in us."

"Oh, Jack," Lucinda cried, burying her face in his chest, holding him. "I have loved you for so very long. I should have told you before."

Smelling the sweetness of her hair, Jack closed his eyes, engulfed in warmth and consumed by the love he felt. "It's all right, my beautiful Lucy. You told me now, and that's enough." Jack kissed her hair as he fought back his own tears—tears of joy at the realization of what she meant to him. Somehow she had become everything to him.

The two were embracing in the early-afternoon sun when William and Emily emerged onto the north porch where the four of them were to dine.

"Look, William, over there," Emily said, pointing to the vineyard. William followed her finger to the partially obscured form of the embracing couple among the vines.

"That rascal," William said under his breath at the sight of Lucinda in his brother's arms.

"Well, it's about time. He has taken just about forever to get to it."

"Whatever are you talking about, Em?"

"Do you know that Jack has yet to kiss her? In all these months, he has never laid a hand on her. Not a one. Nothing more than a friendly peck on the cheek."

"Don't tell me you are actually complaining because my rogue of a brother has been a proper gentleman."

"I am indeed! There are times for gentlemanly conduct, William McCarty. And there are times when a lady likes a little mischief. Not too much naughtiness, mind you, but just enough to keep a girl's interest warm. For the life of me, I simply cannot understand the daftness of you McCarty men sometimes!" Emily shook her head.

"McCarty men? How did I get roped into this?"

"You're all the same, you and your brothers. When it comes to courting, you're as slow as the Second Coming of Jesus Christ Himself! All talk, no action," Emily said, adjusting the silver on the table.

"No action, eh? And how did you get yourself with child, Mrs. McCarty, if your husband is all talk and no action?" William grabbed Emily from behind and wrapped his arms around her waist while kissing her cheek.

Emily turned in his grasp. "Oh, I'll show you how. I'll show you exactly how." Roping her arms around his neck, Emily kissed him.

William pulled back from her momentarily, taking an obvious look down the neckline of her dress. "You realize, Mrs. McCarty, that since you've been with child, your bosom has become quite a distraction."

"Is that so?"

William took another appreciative look at her chest. "More like a call to action."

"Well, then perhaps you should answer that call."

William glanced out toward the vineyard. "I don't know if it is safe to leave my scandalous brother out here alone with your best friend."

"Perhaps you need more of a distraction?" Emily moved her hands under her bosom to push her breasts high in the dress. "Is this distraction enough, Mr. McCarty, to trust that your brother is indeed a gentleman?"

A sly grin twisted over William's face. "Who cares what indiscretions may be underway in the vineyard?" He lifted his pregnant wife off her feet. "Distract away, Mrs. McCarty. Distract away!" William carried Emily through the doors and to his chamber, leaving Jack and Lucinda alone in the vineyard to, at long last, affirm their love.

PART THREE

The Year 1819

"FOR EVERY GUILTY DEED HOLDS IN

ITSELF THE SEED OF RETRIBUTION

AND UNDYING PAIN."

—*Henry Wadsworth Longfellow, "The Masque of Pandora"*

CHAPTER 53

JANUARY 5, 1819, CEDAR GROVE

Steam obscured Sally's face as she poured hot brew from the pot into the silver strainer that balanced on the rim of the teacup. "It is so nice that you came out for afternoon tea today, Jack. Most days I have only my thoughts and the birds outside the window to keep me company." Finishing Jack's pour, she moved the neck of the pot to the china cup with pink and yellow roses that sat in front of her. Tea service for two was always served in the parlor at Cedar Grove, rain or shine, every afternoon at four o'clock, whether Sally had guests or not. And every afternoon, the tray held not only the silver service belonging to her husband's mother, but also a crystal decanter filled with brandy, for Sally McCarty always fortified her tea with something stronger.

"I have good news, bad news, and a request. Which would you like first?" Jack asked, watching as his mother poured brandy into his cup.

"Well, I say we get to the bad news first so that we end on a high note." Sally moved the decanter of brandy from Jack's cup to hers and administered a long pour.

"All right then, Sally." He watched the brandy swirl through the tea before looking back at her. "As you know, I was to assume my seat in the legislature last month."

"Indeed, and very proud of you I am, for your ambition and your win." Sally lifted her cup to salute his accomplishment.

"Yes, I know. And that is why I am here—so you hear the disappointment from me first." Sally raised her brow. "Before the legislature convened, I was required to swear under oath that I have abided by all the laws of Virginia. Knowing that I haven't, my conscience would not allow me to make such a declaration. As a result, I did not assume my seat and have resigned from the legislature."

Sally stared at Jack in disbelief. "What law have you violated, son? What have you done that would warrant you to take such action?"

"I violated the Anti-Dueling Act when I challenged Armistead last May."

"But there was no duel. You never fought him."

"The act of issuing a challenge in itself is a violation of the law. And I did so after I was elected, which makes my conduct even more questionable. But it's all right, Sally. There will be other opportunities for me in politics in the future, should I decide to pursue them. At the moment, William and I are doing well in our law practice. Plus, I have other ambitions in land speculation. The travel required for those pursuits would keep me from Virginia for long periods of time."

Sally looked into her cup, disappointment heavy on her brow.

Jack offered a reassuring smile. "I know it's upsetting, but I had to do what's right."

Sally lifted her eyes to Jack. "I understand. And I am proud of you. Proud that you made the tough choice. We all are accountable for our actions—if not in this life, then in the next. This was a costly punishment, but one you willingly accepted. And you have paid a considerable price." She smiled. "So what's the good news?"

"The good news is that I am here to ask your blessing."

"My blessing? You always have my blessing, Jack, without ever having to ask for it."

"Well, it's the sort of blessing one must actively give."

Sally set the cup and saucer on the table and folded her hands in her lap, waiting silently. Jack drew another long breath.

"Tomorrow night, I intend to propose to Lucinda—to ask for her hand in marriage at the Twelfth Night party in Washington City."

Sally brought both her hands to her face. "This is wonderful news! She's a beautiful girl, and I know how much you care about her. I couldn't be happier. However, it is not my blessing you need. Have you spoken to her mother?"

"Indeed, I have."

Sally's raised eyebrows bore a look of mischief. "And what did the ol' widow have to say?"

"Well, she said that I wasn't her first choice in a husband for her daughter."

Sally laughed as she lifted the pot and served more tea. "At least you weren't her last choice! What else did she say?"

"She said that although I wasn't her first choice, I had sufficient means and that Lucinda would never want for anything, and she would somehow learn to find comfort in that."

"Sufficient means? The old hen! You have sufficient means, all right! The nerve of her!"

"Now don't get your skirts all in a bundle, Sally. She was polite. Just a little direct in her honesty, but polite none the same. She gave me her blessing, and that's all I wanted, whether I'm her first choice or her last. All I care about is that I have her permission to marry her daughter."

"Not that she could have stopped you!" Sally scoffed before settling back in her chair. "I'm very happy for you, Jack, truly I am. I always knew this day would come. Now, Jack, you need to listen to me, as I know better than anyone what constitutes happiness in a union." She lifted the decanter and poured more brandy in their teacups. "It's all about intimacy, Jack. There must be intimacy in a marriage no matter the age of the bond." Jack shifted uncomfortably on the seat. "As I say this, you will find it hard to believe that intimacy will become an issue. You are both young and handsome and, I am certain, can hardly wait to get into bed with each other, if you haven't already—"

"Sally!"

Sally tossed her head and laughed. "I was just testing you. Of course, no son of mine would compromise a virgin's purity. But I am serious about this, because after you are married and the newness wears away, intimacy can wane. Especially after childbirth. She may reject your visits to her chamber or you may not find her as attractive as you once did. Your visits to her bed might become less frequent. And there are other pitfalls. Now, please don't mistake my intention here, but Lucinda may not find your lovemaking all that exciting. Should her needs go unmet, her eye may wander to someone who might appreciate her a little more. These are things that you must be prepared for and work to ensure don't occur, Jack. Make certain that you visit her chamber often. Hell, why the need for separate chambers in the first place? Share the same bed, I say. And make certain you satisfy her needs. It is most important for a woman to be fulfilled, especially in the chamber. Your father always made certain that his lovemaking was as pleasurable for me as it was for him. And he made certain to visit my chamber frequently—sometimes every night for weeks on end."

Jack was mortified and blushing. "For God's sake, I do not want to even think about you and my father in this manner!"

"Well, how do you think we made eleven children? And I am certain there would have been more had the Lord not taken him from me. My point, son, is that you need to take care of business in the bedroom. That is how you keep the passions that you have for each other now alive forever. And love, of course. I know that you have that. I just hope that she will continue to love you when your hair turns silver and all that Bushmills and beer bloat your belly. Because it will happen, of course. And I worry that, with that wandering eye of yours, you may stray."

"Sally, you worry too much. I love Lucinda with every ounce of my being—more than I love my own life. My eye would wander from her only should I gouge it out."

Sally smiled. "That may be, my son, but there are many trials before you both. Many trials indeed." She picked up the pot and poured more tea into their cups, followed by a longer pour of brandy. "Now, there was a third matter you wanted to discuss. I am all ears."

"It is actually a request," Jack said, turning his eyes to the crystal decanter. "Would you consider parting with the ring my father gave you so that I might present it to Lucinda as affirmation of my love?"

Sally smiled and lifted her hand to her chest. "Oh, Jack! There is nothing more I would love to do, but that is the one thing that I cannot give to you. I'm certain you know that this is not the first time I have been asked. I cannot choose one son over another to bequeath the ring."

Jack, of course, knew this but felt compelled to ask, more for Sally's benefit than his own. "I understand completely, Sally. I was simply hopeful."

"You are welcome to choose a diamond from the necklace that was my mother's and have a ring made. All of your brothers have done this. If you prefer rubies, there is the necklace my father gave me. You are welcome to choose a stone from that. Or any stone from my jewelry that you wish to have. Just not the ring. I hope you understand."

"I will choose a diamond from your mother's necklace. But I will wait until after Lucinda accepts so that she can design whatever ring she likes with the goldsmith. If that is all right with you."

"I think that is a grand idea." Sally took a long drink from her cup and finished it. She picked up the teapot for another pour and found it empty. "Humph!" Sally frowned. "Would you like another cup? I can send for more."

"That's all right. I should be getting back to Alexandria before nightfall. Once the sun sets, it's a frigid ride."

"You might stay the night and join me for supper."

On any other occasion, Jack would have begged off and made an excuse to leave. But this afternoon, he made an exception. Although Thomson and he still had their childhood chambers filled with their clothing and belongings, they rarely stayed at the plantation with their mother anymore, and Jack knew she was lonely.

"I'd be delighted to stay." Jack finished the last of the diluted brandy in his teacup. "Let's have another pot."

CHAPTER 54

JANUARY 5, 1819,
THE RINGGOLD HOUSEHOLD

"Good afternoon, Janny," Armistead said to Molly's servant as she peered out the crack between the front door and its frame.

"Afternoon, General." Recognizing him, Janny opened the heavy oak door. "Come on in and get yourself out of the cold, sir."

"Why, thank you." Armistead gave a gentlemanly smile as he stepped through the doorway and presented his card. "I am here to call on Miss Lee. Is she in?"

"Sure 'nough, she's here. I'll go and get her for you." Taking his card, she turned and lumbered down the hallway. As the shadows engulfed her large frame, her white mobcap appeared to float magically through the air, bobbing to and fro until it, too, vanished in the blackness of the hall.

Armistead invited himself into the dusty-blue parlor to wait. A recent portrait of Molly hung on the narrow wall between the faded velvet draperies of the windows fronting the street. Drawn in colored chalk, it was a lovely depiction of Molly's profile, with her voluptuous bosom accentuated. His attention was interrupted by the sound of rustling skirts behind him. Flaunting a mesmerizing grin, Armistead turned to see Molly's bosom exploding from a form-fitting dress, except it wasn't

Molly. It was her sister Lucinda in a wintry-blue frock that looked as icy as her eyes.

"Good afternoon, General Mason," Lucinda said coolly. "What a surprise to see you here so far from home. Janny said that you wanted to see me. Is everything all right? Is it news from Coton of my mother?"

Armistead's grin melted from his face. He forced a polite smile. "Why no, Miss Lucinda, not as far as I know. Frankly, I am surprised to see you. Are you visiting?"

"Actually, yes. For a few days. So how can I help you?"

"I was here to see your sister, Mrs. Ringgold. Perhaps Janny was confused by my asking for Miss Lee. My apologies. I shall take my leave and allow you and your sister uninterrupted time to visit."

"Nonsense, General. I am heading out shortly anyway. Let me run upstairs and let her know you are here." Lucinda turned back to the front hall and Armistead followed. As Lucinda started up the stairs, she stopped on the landing. "Why don't you go back into the parlor, General, and make yourself comfortable there on the settee. I am certain that my sister will be down shortly and most pleased to join your company."

Armistead returned to the parlor, angry with himself. Although he had ended the affair with Molly last summer, he couldn't resist the temptation to see her when he'd heard from a colleague that her husband was out of town. Staring blindly at the portrait on the wall, he was regretting his lapse in judgment.

"Armie, darling."

The smoothness of Molly's voice was like silk caressing his ears and wiping away his earlier misgivings. He turned his attention from the portrait to feast his eyes on Molly in the flesh. Armistead startled. Molly's appearance was not at all what he'd expected. Her face was bloated, and her eyes tired. As she approached with her outstretched hand to greet him, her breasts looked uncomfortably constrained by the neckline of the dress she wore. And there was a puffiness in her arms and a large swell in her abdomen. Molly was pregnant—very pregnant.

"What brings you here, General Mason?" Molly said as he took her hand.

"It looks as if you are with child. Mr. Ringgold must be very happy."

"He pretends to be."

Armistead tasted lightning on his tongue. "I am sure he will be once the baby comes. My Stevens is just a few days old and already he is the light of my world."

"My apologies for not asking about Charlotte and the baby. A boy, even! You must be very proud."

"I am indeed. Very proud. He's a strong boy, which was to be expected, of course."

Reaching her hand to his sleeve, Molly glanced toward the open door and lowered her voice. "Armie, I had wanted to tell you about this, truly I did, but I thought it best not to cause you any undue stress. Mr. Ringgold surely knows that this child cannot be his. He has never asked me about it, yet I dare not give him cause to suspect it to be yours."

Armistead's jaw clenched as he forced a smile. "Molly, of course your husband is the father of your child."

"Armistead! You and I both know—"

"I know nothing, Molly!" Armistead grasped her arm and pulled her close, snarling as he spoke. "What I do know is that on one of the visits to your chamber, your swine of a husband impregnated you. You told me so yourself. And you will remind him of the occasion and insist it was just before he left for his extended business trip."

"That is not true, Armie! It had been weeks since he had visited my chamber before he left on that trip. It was those nights I was with you—"

Armistead tightened his grip on her arm. "There is no such truth! You will get that little sister of yours to attest that she was here with you those nights. And should anyone bear witness that a man was seen leaving your house in the darkness of night, you will tell them it was Jack McCarty who had spent the night with her. No one will have trouble believing that as truth."

"Armie, no one has said or seen anything." The force of Armistead's fingers was pressing white into Molly's flesh, bringing tears to her eyes. "It is true that Mr. Ringgold is not enthusiastic about the pregnancy, yes, but he has not openly questioned my fidelity. And I would never do what you suggest and have my sister lie. Armie, what has come over you?"

Molly yanked her arm from his grasp and stepped back from him, rubbing the marks, now blistering red, that his fingers had made.

Armistead drew a sharp breath to collect himself and plastered a weak smile on his face. The last thing he needed was to create a scene with her sister in the house. "Nothing has come over me. I simply do not appreciate my integrity being questioned."

"My intent was not to question your integrity. But to compromise my sister—"

"My apologies if I impugned your sister's character. But I am astounded that, knowing all she knows about Jack McCarty, she continues in courtship with him."

Molly, still rubbing her arm, gave a long sigh. "I don't like the charades of Mr. McCarty any more than you do, Armistead, but there is little the family can do. Uncle Ludwell thinks the world of him, and Lucinda, I'm afraid, is in love with him. We try not to speak of it, she and I."

"Again, Molly, my intention was not to upset you, especially while you are in a delicate condition." An awkward silence fell between them as Armistead stared out the window.

"Armie?"

He turned his attention to her. Tears were streaming down her cheeks and onto the fabric of her dress, leaving dark stains on the silk at its neckline. Reaching for him, Molly lifted her face to his and kissed him. Armistead stepped back. The thought of intimacy with her now disgusted him.

"I shall leave so that you may rest." Armistead turned toward the parlor door.

"You're going? I thought we might have tea." Molly grabbed at his elbow and hastened alongside him to the front hall. "Lucinda is heading out in a few minutes. And tomorrow night she is attending a party with my sisters. Perhaps I will suggest that she stay at the McKeown Hotel with them for the evening. You and I could have supper and, well ..."

Armistead took his woolen overcoat from the hook on the foyer wall and without a word opened the front door, hurrying to his carriage on the street.

"And why was Armistead Mason here?" Lucinda asked with an intonation that sliced the silence like a razor.

"He is such a considerate man, that Armistead. He had heard that Mr. Ringgold was out of town and stopped over to check on me to see if I needed anything," Molly said, turning from her stance at the window by the door, from where she had watched Armistead's coach disappear down the street.

"Come on, Molly. Certainly he didn't travel all the way from Selma to see if you needed anything. And while he was most likely in George Town for other reasons, a man like Armistead Mason doesn't just stop by a lady's house when her husband is out of town unless he's looking for something."

"What are you implying, Lucy?"

Lucinda raised an eyebrow at her sister, while brushing lint from her coat. "I saw his reaction when I came to greet him instead of you. And I saw the way he looked at you before he realized you were with child, at which point he looked as if he might faint. I don't need to say any more than to advise you to steer clear of him, Molly. Armistead Mason is not what he seems."

"What do you know about Armistead other than lies spewed by that rogue, Jack McCarty?"

Lucinda lifted her head to look directly at her sister. "What did you call him?"

"I know what I've heard."

Lucinda was in no mood to argue. "Just stay away from Armistead. You will only get hurt."

"Armistead would never do anything to hurt me. He and I are close, and he cares about me!"

"Who are you kidding, Molly? Armistead doesn't care about you anymore. And the two of you haven't been close since he broke off his courtship with you years ago. You lost your opportunity to marry him because you played too many games with him. And then, when you could not win him back, you married the first suitor to come along simply to spite him. And who is being spiteful now? You are in a miserable marriage, pregnant with a baby you don't want."

"That is completely untrue!"

"Come on, sister! We both know you are not enthusiastic about this baby. And God knows what indiscretion might have occurred this afternoon with Armistead had I not been here or if you weren't with child—"

The color drained from Molly's face and she dropped her gaze to the floor.

Lucinda stared at her sister, her eyes widening. "Oh my God, Molly! You're carrying Armistead's child!"

"It's not the way you think, Lucinda. Armie loves me—he has always loved me."

Incredulous, Lucinda scoffed. "Armistead Mason doesn't love anyone but himself."

Molly crossed her arms, glaring at her sister with angry eyes. "You must have Armistead confused with Jack McCarty."

"How dare you!" Lucinda's eyes flashed, her own temper flaring. "After carrying on with Armistead, you have the audacity to incriminate my Jack?"

"I have done no such thing! It is Mr. McCarty who has incriminated himself."

Lucinda shook her head. "For months now you have done everything in your power to undermine my relationship with Jack. You've said the most cruel and insulting things about his character to cast doubt in my mind about his intentions."

"I have only stated truths that you have been too blind to see."

"Did the thought ever cross your mind that Armistead was using you? That he was bedding you not only for his own selfish pleasure, but to lure you into his conspiracy against Jack?" Lucinda shouted as the picture became clear. Armistead Mason was behind the rumors about Jack.

Molly's composure snapped and tears welled in her eyes and streamed down her face. "He would never do such a thing. He loves me!"

"I'll spare us both and say nothing more about it. But let's be clear, you keep your opinions of Jack to yourself, and I'll keep quiet about your affair." Lucinda straightened her shoulders and stuffed her hands into her muff. Holding her head high, she, too, pushed past Molly and out the door.

CHAPTER 55

As the door of the town house slammed shut, the coachman rushed to help Lucinda into the carriage.

"Where are we off to, Miss?"

"Bridge Street," Lucinda said. "The gentlemen's clothier shop we saw on the drive into town yesterday."

"Yes, Miss."

With the latch-click of the door, Lucinda settled back on the seat. *How could Molly have room in her heart for someone so hateful and evil?* Lucinda shook her head.

The carriage turned the corner onto Bridge Street, and the gentlemen's shop came into view. Pushing thoughts of Armistead Mason aside, she focused on the purpose of her outing. Jack was always showering her with the most unusual gifts—from the walking stick with a crystal handle, to special riding goggles to shield her eyes from sunlight, to a lovely pair of gloves lined with swan's down that he had presented in a tortoiseshell box at the Belmont party on Christmas Eve. To date, she had yet to give him anything.

The establishment was small. It sold a variety of hats, gloves, scarves, cravats, and other accessories for distinguished gentlemen. When she entered the store, an elderly man with spectacles and a receding hairline greeted her. The shop's walls were lined with shelves filled with the finest of accessories imported from Europe and the British Isles. During a brief tour of the shopkeeper's inventory, a display of calfskin riding gloves caught her eye. As she asked the merchant to show them to her, a woman entered the store. She was not pretty, nor was she unattractive. Her lips were stained red, and her reddish-blond hair was pulled high on her crown, curls formed around her face. She wore a red cape and cap with black gloves, and entirely too much perfume, which overwhelmed the store in moments. The shopkeeper greeted the woman, promising to assist her once he finished his transaction with Lucinda. Lucinda turned her attention from the woman in red back to the riding gloves.

"I can't decide between the black ones and the brown ones. Which do you think?" Lucinda asked.

"Well, it all depends on his wardrobe, Miss," the shopkeeper said with a helpful smile. "Do you know which he wears most often? Most gentlemen prefer black to compliment the color of their boots and hat. But the brown is also nice, especially if the gentleman is a sportsman. Do you know what color gloves he currently wears? You could get the opposite color to provide some variety to his wardrobe."

For the life of her, Lucinda could not recall what color gloves Jack wore. She remembered that he often wore tall black boots, but then again she had seen him wearing brown ones on the foxhunts at Belmont. Her brows knitted together as she tried to recall the color of the gloves he had worn on Christmas Eve. The exercise was futile.

She released a frustrated sigh. "If I were to purchase the black ones, and he prefers brown instead, could he bring them to you and change them?"

"Why, certainly! I am more than happy to make an exchange as long as he hasn't worn them beforehand. Just give me the gentleman's name so that, should he come in, I will know who he is and can easily take care of it for him." Walking to the counter, he opened the ledger and took a quill and an inkwell from the drawer.

"Wonderful! That's perfect, just in case I get it wrong or Jack doesn't like them."

"Jack is his name?" the merchant asked, inking the quill.

"His given name is actually John. John Mason McCarty." Lucinda peered across the counter as the merchant wrote the name in the book.

The woman in red, now standing by the case that held cravats, turned her head abruptly. "You must be Lucinda! My, my, you are a beauty, just as I was told!" the woman said.

"Excuse me, ma'am, do I know you?"

"No, not directly, Miss, but aye, I know you through Jack, I do. He has mentioned you on a number of occasions, he has."

"You know Jack?"

"I do indeed know your man. I have known him for quite a while now. He sure is smitten with you, he is. Talks about you during the day and at night, he does. Why, just last week he mentioned you! You are a lucky woman indeed."

"Why, thank you." Lucinda's brows knitted together, and her pulse quickened.

"And I suspect Jack would like those black ones that you've chosen, for sure he will."

Lucinda looked at the gloves and then again at the woman in red. "I didn't catch your name, Miss. And you are?"

"Me name is Lillie, Miss. Miss Lillie MacKall."

Lucinda swallowed hard, trying her best to conceal her emotion as the pieces were falling together and her world was falling apart. "And how might you know my Jack?"

"Like I mentioned, I've known your man for a while, Miss. We see each other frequently. Jack and I are intimate friends. If you catch my meaning."

Lucinda put her hand on the counter to steady herself.

"Miss, are you all right?" the shopkeeper asked, noticing the color drain from Lucinda's face.

"I feel faint. I need a bit of air." Lucinda leaned farther onto the counter, panting.

Both the shopkeeper and Lillie rushed to Lucinda, each taking an elbow to steady her. Lucinda shrugged Lillie's hand away. "Don't touch me!" She leaned into the shopkeeper as her vision blurred. "Please. I just need to step outside for a moment. Would you help me?"

Lucinda held tight to the merchant's arm. With his assistance, she stepped through the door onto the street. The rush of cold air refreshed her, clearing her vision. Her knees, however, felt weak. She lost her balance and stumbled over the cobblestones. Her coachman hurried to steady her, assisting the shopkeeper to walk her to the carriage.

"Thank you, sir, for your assistance," Lucinda said to the shopkeeper, who was holding her elbow. "Matthew here will get me home."

"What about the gloves, Miss?" the shopkeeper asked.

"Just hold them, sir. Perhaps I will be back another time." Lucinda had no intention of returning to his shop again.

Her legs felt were jelly as she lifted her foot onto the step. Matthew hoisted her into the carriage and shut the door behind her. Sitting back on the bench, Lucinda felt as if her chest were being compressed by an enormous weight. She laid her head against the cold window, staring blankly out its frosty pane, lost in a white abyss. She tried not to think, not to feel, focusing only on steadying her breathing, moving air in and out of her lungs. She wanted to cry, to scream. The pain was overwhelming, the blow all-consuming. *Breathe.*

Unable to face her sister, Lucinda said she wasn't feeling well and retired to the guest chamber. Janny brought her supper, where it sat on the chest of drawers untouched. It was a long night of revisiting the scene at the gentlemen's shop in her mind—the slatternly look of the woman in red, her tawdry smell. With each replay, Lucinda felt more hurt and more humiliated. *I have been sharing his affections with a prostitute!* The thought of him with Lillie—sharing her bed, his lips on hers, their naked bodies in a lover's knot—sickened her.

As the night wore on, so did Lucinda's pain. The longer she suffered, the more the hurt turned to hate. She hated the woman in red, hated her for taking the man she loved from her. She hated Jack for lying to her, for shattering her dreams, and for breaking her heart. Again. For her father had broken it first, leaving her alone in this world with nothing but false promises and memories of his love. As hate and hurt consumed her, the present and the past fused, Jack and her father. Finally, when there were no more tears to cry, she slept.

With the morning sun came anger. Lucinda was enraged not only at the prostitute in red, but at Jack, her father, Molly, Armistead, and anyone and everyone who would cross her path today. Last night, her inclination had been to leave for Coton at first light and never to speak to Jack McCarty again. This morning's anger brought an entirely different plan.

CHAPTER 56

JANUARY 6, 1819, DAVIS HOTEL, WASHINGTON CITY, DISTRICT OF COLUMBIA

"I'm asking her this evening in front of the entire world," Jack announced, holding his head high with his shoulders pinned behind him.

"You plan to ask her what? For the first dance?" William said with a smirk.

"For the first dance as my fiancée."

"Assuming she doesn't reject your proposal."

"Reject me? John Mason McCarty? The dandiest bachelor in all of Virginia, Maryland, and the District of Columbia?"

"Spare us, Jack!" William laughed and grabbed a drink from the tray as the four of them—William, Emily, Thomson, and Jack—walked into the grand ballroom of the Davis Hotel. The ballroom was teeming with young couples dressed in finery for a masquerade celebration of the Twelfth Night of Christmas. The music was loud and the voices louder as the revelers talked over lutes and guitars to hear one another.

The arrival of the four did not go unnoticed. Perhaps it was because Washington society was unaccustomed to witnessing three dapper gentlemen escorting a woman heavy with child. Or perhaps it was the opulence of their attire. Emily and William were in matching masks of feathers and crystal the same bright yellow as his cravat and her dress. Thomson wore the green and blue hat of a court jester, complete with ringing bells at each of its points. Jack had donned a purple velvet cape trimmed in white fur, looking like a noble Irish lord. Jack didn't care why they were looking at him. His objective was to be crowned the King of Misrule and have Lucinda appointed his queen.

On the foyer table next to a silver bowl filled with fruited mulled wine stood two elegant fondant-covered cakes—a king's cake and a queen's cake. Within the king's cake a dried bean was hidden; somewhere within the queen's cake was a dried pea. The gentleman who received the slice with the bean would be crowned the King of Misrule, and she who found the pea would become his queen. Leaving nothing to chance, Jack paid the host handsomely to ensure that the bean would be in his slice and that Lucinda would receive the slice containing the pea. At the moment she was crowned his queen, he planned to ask for her hand in marriage.

"I see no reason that you should worry at all, Jack," Emily said as Thomson handed her a cup of the mulled wine. "Although I would never confess to you any of her secrets, I certainly know her heart and how fond it is of you. I am certain that she will be over the moon when you ask her."

"I, too, will be jumping over the moon—in leaps of joy when she accepts," Jack said, his face beaming with the passion of his heart.

The four maneuvered through the ballroom to a pair of upholstered chairs near the windows on the east side of the room. William and Thomson helped Emily into the gilded chair to rest, while Jack scanned the room looking for Lucinda. The coach from Coton was parked at the side of the building when they had arrived; however, with so many ladies wearing masks, finding Lucinda in the crowd was seemingly impossible.

"Em, do you see Lucinda?" Jack asked.

"The room is so crowded, I can't tell who's who. If I knew what gown she was wearing ..." Emily's voice trailed off as her eyes darted around the room from behind her mask.

From the balcony overlooking the massive hall, trumpeters sounded as the celebration officially began. Standing at the center table, the master of ceremonies bellowed across the room to announce the cutting of the cakes. As revelers gathered around the center table awaiting the cakes to be sliced and served, Jack's eyes searched for Lucinda among them. He saw no sign of her.

With much pomp and ceremony, the king's cake was sliced, plated onto small silver dishes, and served to gentlemen throughout the hall. The waiter served portions to William and Thomson, skipping Jack. William shot his brother a curious look. Moments later, a young woman brought Jack his slice of cake. Jack bit into the cake and found the dried bean.

"Well, how about that," he said, holding the bean high in the air.

William grinned and shook his head. "Fancy that. Now I know why the king's robe!"

"You are such a dog, Jack McCarty! You set this up, didn't you?" Emily said, swatting Jack on the arm.

"Woof! Woof!" Jack barked at her before leaving them to claim his crown.

"Ladies and gentlemen, we have a king!" announced the master of ceremonies as the trumpeters hailed from their perch on the balcony above. The master of ceremonies, looking like a grand wizard with his sorcerer's staff, pointed hat, and long silk robes, beckoned Jack to the center of the room.

"His Majesty, our Lord of Misrule!" the wizard said, placing a golden crown upon Jack's head and bowing. "Now let us find your queen!"

At the pronouncement of the king, the queen's cake was sliced into small pieces and served on delicate china to the ladies in the ballroom. After a few minutes, the master of ceremonies asked the crowd, "Do we have a queen?" He looked about the room for someone to step forward. The room became quiet with darting glances and anticipation.

A commotion stirred on the opposite side of the room. A rustling in the crowd rippled from the far corner toward the room's center. As the wave reached the crowd's edge, a diminutive blonde in a rosy-pink gown and a mask of blush-and-cream feathers emerged. In a gloved hand, she held a tiny pea. Jack's heart nearly leapt from his chest when he noticed a slight limp as she approached the table.

"We have a queen!" said the wizardly master. He took Lucinda's hand and presented her to Jack. "Your queen, Your Majesty!" Jack bowed as the master of ceremonies placed a crystal tiara on Lucinda's head.

"Might I address my lady?" Jack asked.

The master of ceremonies nodded his approval and stepped aside. The crowd hushed to silence. Clearing his throat, Jack glanced across the room at the many masked faces before turning his attention to Lucinda. Knowing her fondness for Chaucer and Shakespeare, he had prepared an ensemble of quotes to recite before proposing.

"'If music be the food of love, play on; Give me excess of it! … O spirit of love! How quick and fresh art thou,' and as fair as the rose of May are you. You are my queen, the only one for me, my lovely Miss Lucinda Lee!" Jack took her hand and knelt before her. "My queen, my dear Lucinda. Might you bestow on me the honor of sharing your life with me?" Placing his hand on his heart, he brought his eyes to hers. "Make my dreams come true, my love, and become my wife. Will you marry me, Lucy?"

The crowd stirred, murmuring with excitement at Jack's proposal, then quickly hushed to hear Lucinda's response. Lucinda remained silent, her eyes behind her mask fixed upon Jack's. His apprehension climbed as the seconds ticked by. There was something unfamiliar in her gaze, something about the way she held her head …

"Mr. McCarty, I would not marry you if you were the last man on earth!" Fire flew from her eyes and ire propelled her words.

Jack froze on his knees, unable to comprehend. A wild deluge of panic rushed forward like a violent river after torrential rain, uncontrolled and unstoppable, as he began to understand her meaning. He found his feet and stood, searching her face. The venom in her glare intensified.

"Lucy, what's wrong?"

"You have my answer, Mr. McCarty. Now let go of me!" Lucinda pulled her hand from his. She turned to walk away. Jack grabbed her arm to keep her from leaving.

"Lucinda, please, wait. I don't understand. Darling, I love you."

Lucinda jerked her arm from his grasp and backed away, glaring at him. "Well, Mr. McCarty, I don't love you. Not now and not ever again!" She spit the words.

"You don't mean that."

"I mean every word." She turned and headed for the exit.

Jack started after her when William put a hand on his chest to stop him. "Let her go, Jack." Emily rushed past the two of them and into the crowd.

"But I need—"

"Let Emily go to her."

Jack watched helplessly as Lucinda disappeared into the corridor with Emily not far behind. Her sisters Fanny and Winnie, too, were in pursuit, hurrying along the back wall toward the exit. As the women fled the ballroom, the eyes of the guests moved from the corridor to Jack. A silent embarrassment crawled over the room. For the first time in his life, Jack McCarty was without words.

"It seems the lady is a bit undecided," William said with a hand on Jack's shoulder. "Let's get back to celebrating the Twelfth Night, shall we?"

A fiddler took the cue and started a lively tune. With a few nods and gossiping murmurs, the guests turned their attention from the drama in the room's center to the celebration.

Jack removed the crown from his head and laid it on the table. He ran his hands through his hair, pushing his fingers into his scalp.

"She'll come around, Jack. Don't worry," William said.

Jack felt queasy. He moved his hands to the edge of the table, leaning against it to steady himself.

William wrapped an arm around Jack's shoulder. "Emily is back there with her and will sort through whatever is on her mind. You know how fickle women can be."

Jack swallowed hard to settle his stomach.

"I need to talk with her." Jack looked toward the corridor where Lucinda had sought refuge.

"I don't think that is a good idea, Jack."

"But I need to understand what has upset her."

"You've either done something or someone has told her something." Jack slowly shook his head. "I can't imagine what it could be."

"Well, whatever it is, Emily will sort it out. Let her take up your cause with a voice of reason." William offered Jack an encouraging smile. "Now come with me back to the chairs while we wait for her." He slapped him on the back. "Come on, Jack. It will be all right."

Jack drew a long sigh and raised his eyes to his brother. "I pray you are right."

"You and she are too much in love for me to be wrong."

Twenty minutes had passed before a maskless, somber-faced Emily appeared from the corridor to join the three McCarty brothers. "Lucinda has left the party and is on her way to the Ringgold house, where she is staying with her sister. She plans to return to Coton Farm in the morning."

"Why, Emily? Why is she so angry? Do you know?" Jack asked. Emily bit her lip and looked at William.

"It's all right, Emily. You can tell him, whatever it is," William said.

Emily shifted her eyes to the floor before looking at Jack. "This is very uncomfortable for me, Jack. Very uncomfortable. But as you wish, I will tell it." She drew a long breath. "Lucinda had a confrontation yesterday with a woman professing to be your lover, a woman by the name of Lillie MacKall. Apparently, this woman has a somewhat tarnished reputation. Lucinda is very hurt, Jack. And angry. Very angry. She asks that you not call upon her or write to her or have any contact. She just wants you to leave her alone." Without warning, Emily stomped her foot on the floor, causing the men to jump. "Jack, how dare you do this to her? You have broken her heart all to pieces!"

Jack's mind was spinning. "I must speak to her."

"She doesn't want to speak to you!" Emily's neck and cheeks reddened as her anger rose.

"I need to explain to her that there is nothing between me and Lillie. Nothing. Whatever Lillie told her is a lie."

"So, you do know this Lillie MacKall?" Emily said with disgust in her voice and on her face. Jack, realizing his error, felt even worse. Emily was the last person he needed to lose as an advocate. He pressed his lips together tightly and hung his head in shame.

"I do know Lillie. And I have made some very poor decisions in my past. But that was before. Long before I fell for Lucy. If Lillie told her otherwise, it is a falsehood."

Emily put her hands on her hips. "Swear it, Jack. On your honor as a gentleman, swear it."

"On my father's grave, Em, I swear. I would never dishonor Lucy like that," said Jack, his eyes pleading with her. "You must believe me, Em."

William and Thomson remained motionless while Emily interrogated Jack with her eyes. After a long minute, she submitted. "I believe you, Jack. I don't know exactly why, but I do."

"Thank you for accepting my word. I must see her and explain to her the truth. You said that Lucinda went to her sister's in George Town?"

"Yes, but you mustn't call on her now. She is too angry and too upset at the moment."

"Emily is right, Jack," William said. "Give her time to calm down. You can offer your explanation tomorrow when her emotions are not so raw."

"As you wish. But I shall not stay here with my heart torn from my chest. You gentlemen enjoy yourselves while I find a nice bottle of whiskey to drown myself in."

Collecting his coat and hat, the Lord of Misrule left the Davis Hotel to find Lucinda.

CHAPTER 57

JANUARY 6, 1819, GEORGE TOWN

"Is everything all right with my sister, Mr. McCarty?" Molly asked, winded from her race down the stairs. Standing in the foyer of the Ringgold house, Jack was pacing with impatience.

"No, it is not, Mrs. Ringgold. I'm trying to find her so I can set things right with the truth," Jack said, his tone curt.

"Whatever do you mean, sir? Isn't she at the party with my sisters?"

"She was earlier. But she left to come here—to your home," Jack said.

"Well, I can assure you that she is not here."

"I was told specifically that she was coming here. Are you sure she's not somewhere in this house?" Jack said. His eyes shifted to the parlor, looking for signs of her.

"I can assure you, Mr. McCarty, that she is not with me at present," Molly said.

"Are you certain?"

"How many times do you plan to ask me, Mr. McCarty? She is not here. And why, pray tell, did she leave the party so early?"

This was not a conversation Jack wanted to have, and to push Molly any further would be disrespectful. Jack relented. "Very well, then. Should she arrive this evening, please tell her that I came to call. And tell her that it is extremely important that I see her. Ask her to send me a message at the Fountain Inn should you see her this evening. And let her know I will be back in Alexandria tomorrow. Please tell her, will you?"

"I will when she arrives," Molly said without the customary politeness. "Now if you don't mind, Mr. McCarty, you've finished your business here."

Jack didn't care much for Molly Lee Ringgold, and tonight he cared for her even less. But he knew better than to let what was in his head out of his mouth.

"Thank you for your courtesy, ma'am. I'm sorry to have interrupted your evening." With all the gentility he could manage, he bowed and bade her good night. Molly had no sooner closed the door behind him than he fell apart again. He was desperate. Squinting to see more clearly in the dim light, he searched for Lucinda's coach on the street. He racked his brain for where she could be, frustrated and running out of possibilities. Not knowing her whereabouts fueled Jack's anxiety. His breath frosting in the frigid air, he mounted his horse and turned her toward Water Street.

The brothels along the river were lively with Twelfth Night celebrations in full swing. The rail outside Rose's was crammed with mounts whose riders were inside indulging their vices. Jack hitched Dove to a post on the west side of the building. Not the ideal spot to leave her, he thought, but his business wouldn't take long.

The House of Rose was packed with men and whores scattered throughout the lounge and at the bar. Jack didn't recognize many of the girls. They looked young and fresh—no doubt not long off the boat from Dublin. Jack barreled his way through the crowded, noisy parlor to the rear and made his way up the stairs to the hall outside room number five. He pounded on the door and heard the low voice of a man.

"Your time is up, fella. Time to rise and shine and get the hell out!" Jack shouted through the wooden door. There was a rustling of clothing, rumbling of voices, and the thud of boots on the floor before the lock was released and the latch lifted. A scrawny man in a rumpled coat with tussled hair emerged from the shadows and shuffled out of the room. Jack pushed through the door to find Lillie sitting in her chair, wearing her usual corset and smoking rolled tobacco. He locked the door behind him.

"Mr. McCarty! It looks like my Christmas wish has come true!" Lillie stood from the chair to greet him. "And my gift to you shall be a dozen erotic pleasures in celebration of the Twelfth Night!"

"Don't, Lillie," Jack said, extending an arm to keep her from him. "I'm not here for any gift from you."

"Why else would you be here then, *mo ghrá*, unless you've come to take me away?" she asked with a suggestive smile.

Jack exploded. "Is that why you did it? Is that why you sought her out and told her all your lies, under some delusion that if she rejected me, I would find it in my heart to rescue you?"

"*Cad é ainm Dé* … What in God's name are you talking about? Aye? What are you accusing me of?" Lillie said, her own Irish temper flaring.

"Don't lie to me, woman! I know that you confronted Lucinda!"

Lillie gave a complicated smile and stepped back from him. "Aye, so that is what this is about."

"So you admit it, that you sought her out to sabotage our courtship?"

"I did no such thing, Jack McCarty! No such thing! We were in the same shop and I recognized her. That's all!"

Jack shook his head in disgust. "And you spoke to her? Why would you do such a thing? What did you say, Lillie? What did you tell her?"

"I said that I knew you. I complimented her and told her that she was lucky to have the heart of a man like you!"

Adrenaline ran with abandon through Jack's veins. *For chrissake, you know the rules! Why would you acknowledge our relationship to a lady? Unless—*

"How did you recognize her? And how did you know she would be in that shop?" Jack asked, anger mounting. *Armistead most certainly had something to do with this.*

"I didn't know she would be there. I didn't even know for sure it was her until she said your name. But I thought it had to be her, based on how you portrayed her."

Jack felt his stomach drop, remembering the day he'd described Lucinda to her. "What did she say to you, Lillie?"

"She didn't say much of anything. She said she didn't feel well and left," Lillie said and shrugged her shoulders. "That's it, Jack. That's all I know. *Sin go léir.*"

Jack hung his head. The thought of Lillie and Lucinda together in the same room, with Lillie boasting to Lucinda, sharing tawdry de-tails—despicable details—of his lecherous behavior, made him retch. He gulped in air to keep from losing his stomach.

Lillie moved behind him and slipped her arms around his waist. "How about I take your mind off your troubles?" she said and thrust her hands under the waistline of his breeches and into his pants. Jack turned and grabbed her arms.

"How about you stay away from me and stay away from Lucy!" He shoved her and nearly knocked her onto the floor.

"Jack, why are you so angry with me?" she asked, catching her balance. She straightened her posture and walked to the bed, sitting on its edge.

"I'm not angry with you, Lillie. I'm through with you. I gave you an opportunity to get yourself out of here and the means to start a new life. Yet you stayed. No, Lillie, I am not angry with you. I'm angry with me. I'm angry with myself for my poor judgment, for my horrible decisions, for coming here in the first place."

"Gimme one last night." Lying back on the bed, she patted the mattress with her hand. "Only I know how pain pleasures you."

"I'm done with that, too, Lillie." The sight of her now sickened him. The thought of intimacy with her revolted him even more. He saw himself above her on the soiled mattress—his naked body between her parted legs. He shut his eyes to block out the sordid image. She simply was what she was—a whore. It was he who was revolting. He who was compromised. He, the pathetic one. He shook his head, disgusted.

Reaching into his coat, he took a note from his pocket to pay her the thirty-minute minimum. As he tossed the money onto the writing table in the corner, he saw a packet on the desk. The envelope bore her name with a return address of Abington Farm, Lexington, Kentucky. Jack read the words again. *Abington Farm, Lexington, Kentucky ... Abington Farm ...*

His body seemed to move in slow motion. The sounds around him—the ticking of the clock on the mantel, the piano's notes from the parlor below, the muffled murmur from the walls around him—blurred into a slow roaring in his head. He reached ever so slowly for the envelope and lifted it from the desk. An engraved invitation fell from the packet and drifted, leisurely wafting to and fro, onto the floor. As he reached to pick it up, Lillie came flying across the room, jolting him back into time.

"That is mine!" Lillie screamed and dove to retrieve the card. Jack beat her to it and picked it up from the floor. Reading the words, his nausea mixed with mind-numbing disbelief. *"Requesting the presence of Miss Lillie MacKall to the Twelfth Night Celebration at the Davis Hotel, January 6, 1819."*

"What is this?" Jack said hoarsely. Lillie ripped the invitation from his one hand and tried to tear the packet from the other. Jack raised the envelope high in the air above her reach.

"That is mine and none of your business!"

"I think it is every bit my business!"

It was all Jack could do to hold her at bay. She scratched and clawed to get the envelope from him. With his free hand, he pulled a banded wad of notes from the packet.

"Give it back to me!" she said, snarling and striking him with her fists.

He held the money high above his head and grabbed her arm, twisting it to contain her.

"You mongrel whore! You sold me out! You set this entire thing up, you and Ginny, didn't you?"

Lillie succumbed to the force of Jack's grip. "Give me my money, and I'll tell you whatever you want to know."

"You tell me first, whore! Then you get your money."

"On your word?"

"On my father's grave."

"All right then, if you want to know so badly." A cold smile suffused Lillie's face. "I don't know no Ginny. It was a gentleman. Came here to see me a few weeks back. Said he had a friend in Lexington. A General Henderson. Said the general had some business with you he needed to settle. Said that this general would pay me to tell Lucinda that I was your fancy. And I had to tell her to her face, and I had to make certain to upset her. To make her real mad. Paid me half that day. The other half would come after the deed was done. That there invitation came from Kentucky the next week. But I didn't need to go to no party. Lucky for me she was in that shop yesterday. Luck of the Irish, I say. Saved me from wasting the Twelfth Night at some toffee-nosed shindig. Now give me my fuckin' money!"

"You bitch!" he said in a whisper so low and so filled with blinding rage that he barely recognized the voice as his own. He clenched his fists, wanting to strike the sneer from her face. It took every ounce of self-control not to grab her by the throat and choke the lifeblood from her.

Jack threw the wad at her, the notes expelling from the band and scattering over the floor. He pushed by her, stepping on the money as he rushed through the door. Thundering down the stairs, he pushed through the men in the hall, unable to breathe and sick to his stomach. Emerging into the cold January air, he found his breath and pulled himself together enough to get into the saddle. Filled with anger and desperation, he cantered the mare onto Water Street and toward the bridge to Virginia, where, in the seclusion of his apartment, whiskey and self-loathing awaited him.

CHAPTER 58

JANUARY 18, 1819, ALEXANDRIA, VIRGINIA

James found Jack slumped over a half-empty bottle of Bushmills and a dirty glass in the same spot where he'd found him the last time. Like he was most days, Jack was drunk.

James pulled a chair to the table to join him. "When is the last time you saw your pillow?"

Jack lifted his head and his bloodshot eyes roamed over the floor and to the other tables. "My pillow? Is it missing?"

James laughed. "No, my friend. I mean when is the last time you slept?"

"I see no reason why I should sleep when there's more drinking to do."

As Jack picked up the bottle of Bushmills to refill his glass, James moved his hand to Jack's. "Come on, Jack, I think you've had enough for now. Let's get you on your feet and to bed." James stood and pulled Jack from the chair.

"But why do I have to get on my feet if I'm going to bed?"

"Because, my friend, I am not going to carry you to your room." James put his arm around Jack's shoulder to steady him.

"Fine, fine. But if you make me go to bed, then you owe me a bedtime story."

"You're the storyteller, Jack McCarty, not me." Jack staggered under James's arm as the two walked across the creaking wooden floor. It took nearly all of James's strength to keep Jack from falling as he stumbled out the tavern door.

"All right, I'll tell you a story, then."

"Whatever makes you happy, Jack." James kept his arm around Jack as the two weaved their way along the boardwalk toward the boardinghouse.

"It's a fairy tale of sorts. You'll like it!"

James laughed under his breath at Jack's foolishness. "I'm sure I will."

"There once was this beautiful girl, you see. Her name was Belle, and she lived with her ugly mother and her evil sisters."

"I can see where this might be going," James interrupted. "Are you sure you want to tell this particular story?"

"It's just a bedtime story. And it's the only one I know." Jack slurred his words as he spoke. "Now listen! You see, Belle was in her garden one day when she met this terrible beast. So brutal was this beast that he frightened her to her core." Jack paused, stopping on the walk to see if James was paying attention. "Are you with me, James?"

"Yes, Jack, I'm following you just fine. Just as long as you keep walking."

"All right, then," Jack said as he picked up his feet. "Now this beast, James, he kidnapped Belle and locked her up in his castle. He wanted her really, really bad, because she was so beautiful. But she wouldn't let him have her. So he showered her with gifts and everything she could possibly want. But she still wouldn't love him. So one day, he asked her—begged her, actually—to tell him why she wouldn't love him. And do you know what she said?"

"What did she say?" James played along as they walked through the front door of the boardinghouse.

"She said that she couldn't love him because he was a beast!" Jack teetered as they reached the stairs. "Because a beast does not know the difference between fornicating with someone and loving someone. And then he decided not to be a beast anymore! So she taught him what he needed to do to be a prince. And he practiced and practiced and practiced. And with all this practice, he didn't care about fornicating anymore. He learned how to love! But he still looked like a beast."

James opened the door to Jack's room. He was astounded at the mess. Jack's clothes and papers were strewn over the floor. Empty whiskey bottles sat on every surface.

"Are you sure you don't know this story, James?" Jack stumbled over the debris on the floor. James kicked a discarded Bushmills bottle out of their way. As they reached the bed, James tossed dirty laundry from the mattress so Jack could sit.

"It's vaguely familiar." As Jack sat on the bed's edge, James stood in front of him and picked up Jack's foot. "Now, let's get your boots off first, and then you can finish it for me."

Jack rolled his eyes toward the ceiling as James wrestled with his boot. "Now, where was I? Oh, yes! I remember! She was still afraid of the beast, but the beast had transformed. He had changed from wanting to have her and wanting, you know, the other thing."

"Wanting to fornicate?" James finished Jack's thought as the boot came free. He dropped it on the floor and lifted Jack's other booted foot.

"Yes, but he only thought about that. But not anymore. Well, maybe, but not like a beast would, you know. He was a gentleman now—on the inside anyway. He loved her more than his own life. She became everything to him."

The second boot slid from Jack's foot onto the floor. "All right, my friend, why don't you lie back on your pillow."

"My pillow! There's my pillow!" Jack furrowed his brow and scrunched the pillow under his head. "I thought you said it was lost."

"Well, it looks like you found it."

"Back to my story."

"Maybe we should forget the story."

"No, James! This is really important. You see, the beast loved Belle so much that he released her from his castle to let her go home

308

and visit her evil sisters. And on her way, this vile … nasty … putrid … vile …" Jack struggled to find adequate descriptors through the fog of his inebriation. "… woman-beast!—a nasty, wretched creature, she was—attacked Belle in the forest. Scared poor Belle half to death, this harlot did! But she didn't eat Belle. No, she did something far worse. She ate into her mind! She told Belle about the beast's past. Stories the beast was ashamed of. Then she did something even more detestable. She decimated Belle's heart! She LIED! She told her that the beast was secretly sneaking out of the castle at night and fornicating with the wretched creature herself. Belle was scared, so she ran from the vixen. When she got home, she told her evil sisters about the beast and how he had changed and how she loved him. But then she told them what the wretched creature said. And you know what, James?"

James could see wild pain filling Jack's eyes. "I think I know. Maybe you should save the story for later and try to get some rest. Why don't I pull your curtains—"

"No! I need to tell you. I need to finish the story!"

James shook his head, realizing that there was no use arguing with him. "Fine, then. Go on."

"Belle sent a message to the beast that she didn't love him and that she was never coming back. Then one day, she looked into the magic mirror." Jack lifted his head from the pillow. "Did I tell you about the magic mirror?"

"I don't think so."

"Well, before she left, the beast gave her a magic mirror so she could see him and be close to him while she was away. I guess I forgot that part, but it doesn't matter because we're getting near the end." Jack shut his eyes tightly several times before continuing. "So anyway, she became curious about how the beast was doing and looked in the mirror. And guess what she saw. Guess what she saw him doing!"

James sat on the side of the bed, hoping his best friend would fall asleep. "What, Jack, what was he doing?"

"He was dying! His heart was so sick and so twisted and torn and broken, the pain so excruciating and unbearable, that he lost the will to live! He was caught in the crucible between beast and prince. Without her love to complete him, he was destined to die."

James looked at his friend with pity, hoping against hope that Jack could find a happy ending for himself. "So what happens, Jack? How does your story end?"

Jack paused, his glassy and bloodshot eyes staring vacantly into a far corner of the room as water welled in their corners. Jack squeezed them shut before turning his head and looking at James again. "I don't know. He's still dying."

CHAPTER 59

JANUARY 19, 1819, THE STATEHOUSE, RICHMOND, VIRGINIA

Armistead had been pacing for nearly an hour in the anteroom before Andrew Stephenson, the Speaker of the House of Delegates of the Virginia legislature, invited him into his office. Making himself comfortable in the overstuffed leather chair in front of Stephenson's desk, Armistead presented his qualifications for nomination in the upcoming election for governor. Stephenson, with an expressionless long face that reminded Armistead of a Spanish pointer, sat in silence behind the inlaid desk with its high French polish. When Armistead finished his appeal, Stephenson remained emotionless and quiet. After a long pause, he looked over his muzzle of a nose and spoke.

"There's no doubt, General, that your qualifications are notable. And you certainly enjoy the most impeccable espousals from the party leadership. But even with the recommendation of Mr. Barbour and the endorsement from Monticello, I'm not sure that the legislature can consider your nomination. Your dispute with Mr. John McCarty has created an issue that, quite frankly, is problematic."

"While it is true that I had been involved in a controversy with Mr. McCarty, we settled our differences last year. I'm not sure why the legislature would have any concern about a matter that has terminated."

"You do realize that McCarty did not take his seat in the legislature."

"I had heard rumors to that effect."

"I'm taking it that you don't know why Mr. McCarty didn't assume his seat."

Armistead sat back in the chair and crossed a leg over the other. "Enlighten me, Andrew."

"He refused to swear the oath of office," Stephenson said, raising his brow like a hound on alert.

Armistead reclined farther in the chair. "Not surprising. Only men of honor can attest to the sacraments of such an oath."

"Well, that doesn't seem to be the issue, General. Mr. McCarty's honor is what kept him from taking the oath. He said that he, in good conscience, could not swear on his honor with God as his witness that he had, on every occasion, upheld the laws of the Commonwealth."

"I am not surprised at all. Andrew, the man is a rogue. A perjured scoundrel. He should have never been elected in the first place. And frankly, it is only because of his newspaper controversy with me that he gained the public's attention. That popularity is entirely the reason he received the votes that he did."

"There was a particular law that was of issue." Armistead raised his eyebrows inquisitively as Stephenson continued. "Mr. McCarty's conscience would not allow him to attest that he had not violated Virginia's Anti-Dueling Statute."

Stephenson's words exploded in Armistead's ears as if out of a cannon, striking every part of his body. He felt as if his face were on fire from the blast, hot and burning. His riddled gut felt a sharp, twisting ache, and his limbs were weighted with the heaviness of Stephenson's meaning.

Stephenson relaxed in his chair, surveying the carnage of his disclosure. "Perhaps you should electioneer to represent the eighth district and serve in the House of Representatives, General. The oath at the federal level doesn't require such affirmations. You see, General, our standards here in Virginia are higher for those who hold elected office or military commissions."

My military commission! A surge of adrenaline freed Armistead from his paralysis. He stared at Stephenson in cold silence, teeth clenched and temple throbbing. It took every ounce of composure not to reach across his shiny French desk and rip Andrew Stephenson's throat from his neck. His tightening fist in his lap, Armistead began to visualize it—Stephenson's choking, dying head on the desk, his blood pouring over its high polished glaze, his eyes popping from their sockets as Armistead crushed his bloodied throat in his hand.

As seconds ticked noisily on the clock behind the desk, Armistead's gaze remained fixed on Stephenson, who shifted uncomfortably in his chair, his self-satisfied smile fading.

Tapping his finger on the armrest, Stephenson moved his eyes to the door behind Armistead. "Surely you understand the situation, General. The legislature is simply in no position to make elections that contradict laws that we have enacted." Stephenson cleared his throat and shifted in the chair again. "I do believe a term in the House could remedy the issue. That and time, perhaps," Stephenson said.

Armistead finally broke his strangling silence, but not his icy stare. "Then a term in the House it will be, Mr. Speaker." He stood with his eyes still fixed on the dog sitting across from him. "It seems I have wasted enough of our time, sir."

Stephenson, too, stood from his chair, extending his arm to shake Armistead's hand. "Well, then, have a safe trip back to Leesburg. And give my regards to Mrs. Mason."

Armistead placed his right hand at the bottom of his rib cage and tipped his head in acknowledgment without taking Stephenson's hand. He straightened his shoulders and held his chin high. Flashing a final piercing look, he turned on his heels and marched across the floor and out the door.

The eastern sky beyond the hotel window blushed at the kiss of the setting sun. Armistead stared out over the lawn toward the statehouse. A maze of walkways meandered, carving diagonal and curved paths

between the magnolias, hollies, and oaks that had been recently planted. The path twisted, wending left then right, in senseless directions.
He turned his eyes from the window to the letter he had just written to
the governor resigning his military commission. A commission he had
suffered so much to achieve. His mind wandered to the day General
Parker had made Armistead the proposition, to his wedding day with
Eliza standing coldly next to him, and her bleeding to death in bed.
Then there was Craney Island—Hampton—Baltimore. Soldiers writhing, drowning, and dying in a red tide of blood. Wails of grieving wives
and mothers among the smoldering ruins. Bloated, mangled bodies
scattered over the battlefield. He could still smell gunpowder and rotting flesh. Armistead choked back emotion. He folded the resignation
letter and scrawled the governor's name across the wrapping before
applying his seal. Armistead laid the correspondence on the desk and
looked out the window once more. A dog ran across the brick path,
disappearing into a tangle of shadows. *Is that what I've become? A flash
across the path of greatness that disappears into obscurity and nothingness?*

He sighed and moved his eyes back to the letter. His hand was shaking as he put it in his pocket. *Who am I, if I am not General Armistead
T. Mason?*

CHAPTER 60

JANUARY 21, 1819, STAGE FROM RICHMOND
TO WASHINGTON CITY

General Andrew Jackson sat with military bearing in a fitted coat of midnight blue with its high collar drawn firmly under a resolute chin. His raw-boned shoulders were adorned with the golden epaulets of a general's rank, each emblazoned with three embossed stars. His hair was as stiff and as wiry as Armistead remembered, but now rusted by both weather and time. His eyes, piercing and blue, were fixed on Armistead sitting across from him on the leather bench of the stage from Richmond to Washington.

The two were alone in the coach sharing stories of the last war, from battles against the British to clashes with Congress and Henry Clay. But it was the mention of Charles Fenton Mercer that turned the conversation from simply lamenting their common enemies.

"Mercer! That whiny bastard!" Jackson said, his presence looming even larger when he swore. "Little Fenton with the big mouth! This morning I read his libelous commentary supporting Clay's censure of my actions in Florida. I have half a mind to call him out for his blasphemy or just shoot him outright on the House floor!"

"The man is a coward, General," Armistead said. "He won't fight you. When I challenged him last year for his slanderous statements against my character, he shrank from the contest."

"That's right, he did. And as I recall, Mercer's friend took up the cause against you in his place," Jackson said, watching Armistead intently.

"Are you referring to McCarty?"

"That's the one," Jackson said with an amused shrug of his shoulders. "And it seems to me that the boy got the better of you." The coach rocked over a rut, causing the braids of the general's epaulets to shake in what felt to Armistead like mocking laughter.

"I beg your pardon, sir?"

"As I recall, you allowed the man to label you a coward." Jackson scoffed without moving his eyes from Armistead's. "You sit here and brag about calling Mercer out, yet you let some scoundrel call you a coward and do nothing? Where's your honor, son?" Heat rose from Armistead's chest to his neck as his heartbeat pounded in his eardrums.

"Sir, I—"

"Listen, I was young like you once. And I know you have a wife and baby now, and people are telling you that you shouldn't fight with a family and all. Well, that's nonsense! Look, I hear what's going on. I know you're pushing for the Virginia governor's election. But you are never going to find yourself in that office—or any other high post—unless you address this thing head on, son. You gotta call this McCarty out. Either he chickens out or you kill him. Unless you're scared."

Armistead felt the hair rise on the back of his neck. "I am no coward, sir."

"Of course you're not, son. That's why you have to challenge him." Jackson leaned forward, his eyes knifing like a dirk. "And let me tell you this. If you don't call the bastard out, he won't be the last one to disrespect you. Trust me. If you don't show them what you're made of now, they'll just keep coming. You'll never have credibility. You'll never have honor. You'll be nothing more than a planter living in shame." The general sat back on the bench.

"But I gave my word to let the matter rest," Armistead said, trying to conceal the mix of anger and fear that he felt.

"To whom? A bunch of old men who don't understand the first thing about honor? Hogwash! What do they matter? I let a bunch of old men convince me not to fight once, and I regret it to this day. It wasn't until I killed that scoundrel Dickinson that I got the respect I deserved. And since that day, a wise man will think twice before insulting my character. You want the respect you're entitled to? The honor of your father? Then defend your honor, Armistead. It's the only way to get what you want. To get what is rightfully yours. To get what you deserve."

Armistead wordlessly shifted his eyes to the window, a fire igniting within him—a clear, blue, burning flame from his core. With it came clarity. After a long moment, he drew a sigh of relief and turned his attention back to the legend sitting across from him.

"Thank you, sir." Armistead fixed his dark eyes upon the general's. Jackson nodded. They both knew what had to be done.

CHAPTER 61

JANUARY 21, 1819, RASPBERRY PLAIN

Somewhere between the rest of sleep and the respite of a dream, Charlotte was awakened by voices in the hallway beyond the guest chamber's door. *Why does Armistead insist I stay in this noisy house when he is away!* She closed her eyes to drift back to her dream when she heard the low murmur of whispers again. Frustrated by the nattering of whomever was in the hallway, she kicked the blanket aside. Slipping her feet into embroidered slippers and wrapping a woolen shawl around her shoulders, she had given up on her afternoon nap. Nearing the door, she identified the voices as those of Nelly and Nelly's mother, Hester, talking while the two folded linen in the hall. With the door's knob in her hand and ready to scold them, she heard Armistead's name.

"Marster Armie? Are you sure?" Nelly asked.

"Phillis says Janny told her that he has to be," Hester said.

"How does she know that for sure?"

"Janny told her that whenever the marster goes up north on business, he spends the night with her."

"Well, that don't mean that he's the daddy."

Charlotte's eyes grew wide. Uncertain she'd heard their words correctly, she leaned closer to the door and listened.

"Janny said that her husband was gone the whole month that she got knocked up. That only Marster Armie was in her bed. All sorts of bumpin' an' a-humpin' an' a-thumpin' going on in that bed. About to keep Janny from gittin' any sleep at all!" The two giggled.

My God! Charlotte brought a hand to her lips and swallowed hard.

"Well, thank the Lord that Marster Armie don't do all that to Miss Charlotte. I needs my sleep!" Nelly said.

"Oh, don't you worry about that. Marster Armie loves Miss Charlotte too much to do all that to her."

Charlotte was caught between the urge to turn the knob to admonish them for their disrespect of her husband and wanting to go back to bed and cry. Her instinct to defend her husband's honor outweighed her desire to flee, but as she started to turn the knob, Nelly spoke again.

"Is Miss Molly mad with Marster Armie for giving her a baby she don't want?"

Molly! Charlotte's world imploded. She was paralyzed, her hand frozen on the knob.

"Janny says that for sure she don't want the child, but I don't think she is mad at the marster," Hester said. "Phillis said that Janny told her that Marster Armie was just there two weeks ago, and Miss Molly would've gone to the bed with him then, heavy with child, but Marster Armie got Miss Lucy all upset instead."

"Miss Lucy? Marster Armie was in the bed with Miss Lucy, too?" Charlotte's knees weakened.

"Heavens no! Miss Lucy caught Miss Molly kissing Marster Armie and got all mad at her sister. A big fight they had. Miss Lucy left and then came back and was a-crying all night. She just left and went home to Coton without saying nothin'. Then Miss Molly and Janny came to Coton with Miss Molly all sorry for fightin' with her sister. That's when Phillis saw Miss Molly with her own eyes. Phillis says that Miss Molly's belly is real big with the child."

"Do you think Miss Charlotte knows?"

"Lordy, no! Marster Armie wouldn't tell her something like that. And she can't never know. Poor thing nearly died last year from all the stress that man gives her!"

"Marster Armie don't mean to give her the stress, Mammy. It's just the way he is."

Charlotte's knees weakened again. The room started to spin around her. Her vision grew fuzzy, then green and warm. She saw the angels of God dancing before her with their halos glowing brightly as she fell unconscious to the floor.

CHAPTER 62

JANUARY 23, 1819, SELMA

The still morning air was biting cold, waiting for the warming breath of the eastern sun to thaw its chill. Escaping the restlessness of sleep, Armistead scratched out his last words to his uncle, his mother, and his wife. As he melted the wax and embossed his seal, the cries of his young son interrupted the quiet. The chandelier's lamps flickered, stirred by the movement of pattering feet above Armistead's head. How long he had waited for those sounds! At long last he had a son—that was *his*—and a wife who loved him.

But Charlotte had not been herself of late. When Phillip brought her home from Raspberry Plain the evening before, she had gone straight to bed with hardly a word to him. His mother had told him that she had had a fainting spell and seemed depressed but was recovering well from delivering the baby. She assured him that these emotions were normal after having a child and would pass. Armistead furrowed his brow at the thought of Charlotte's illness after her miscarriage and her continued struggle with anxiety. He had hoped a baby would relieve her of the worry that plagued her.

Taking another sheet of parchment from the desk drawer, he dipped a quill into a well of ink. He provided no explanation, only a simple request.

Mr. John M. McCarty,

It is time to end the controversy between us once and forever. I challenge you to meet me upon the field of honor. My friend Colonel George Rust will deliver this to you on my behalf and shall receive your response.

Armistead T. Mason

As the early-morning darkness beyond the window's pane softened to hues of blue and gray, Armistead pushed his frame from the desk, satisfied. He knew that George and Jonathan would attempt to talk him out of the fight, but there were no words or arguments they could offer that would change his mind. At long last, his honor would be restored and he would be redeemed.

CHAPTER 63

JANUARY 25, 1819, ALEXANDRIA, VIRGINIA

"My God, James! Either I am hallucinating, or I am delirious and have lost all perspective as to where I am!" Jack said, his eyes wide and fixed beyond James on the doorway of the tavern. "Tell me, my man, are we in Leesburg?"

"Of course not, Jack," James said. "We're at Gadsby's in Alexandria, where you've been for weeks now. Have you gone mad?"

Jack picked up the near-empty bottle of Bushmills in front of him and smelled its contents. "Perhaps it is a bad batch—toxic, you know—for surely my mind has been compromised."

"Your mind was compromised long before you opened that bottle," James said, paying little attention to Jack's ranting. "I call. What are you holding?"

Jack had not left Alexandria in weeks. His brothers, too, had tried to intervene, but to no avail. William was particularly agitated by Jack. Despite their partnership, Jack had ignored his casework, leaving William with the responsibilities. But Jack couldn't have cared less. His only interests were drinking, gambling, and self-loathing.

"Seriously, James. Either you are correct, and I have gone totally mad, or Colonel George Rust is walking toward us." James followed Jack's eyes and turned to see what his friend was rambling on about. Sure enough, George Rust was walking toward them.

James stared at the backlit figure. "Why on earth would Colonel Rust be in Alexandria?"

"I have a message from General Mason for you, Jack." George handed him a letter under Armistead's seal.

"Why, isn't this a pleasant surprise!" Jack said, waving to an empty chair nearby. "Pull up a chair, Colonel, and join us for a hand or two. Barmaid! Bring our friend here a glass so I can pour him a horn. You do drink whiskey, don't you, George?"

"That's quite all right, sir. I haven't time for cards or for whiskey. I am here to deliver this to you and receive your answer."

"Aw, come on, Colonel. One hand and one whiskey?" Jack said, lifting the Bushmills bottle from the table and waving it at George.

"Seriously, I cannot," said George. "I am here only to deliver the general's correspondence."

"Well, that's just too bad, George. I was hoping to give James here a break from my taking all his money by taking a little of yours," Jack said, laying his cards on the table. Seeing Jack's winning hand, James threw his cards down in disgust.

"Sir, General Mason's correspondence?" George said.

"Oh yes, a message from my dear friend General Mason," Jack said. "What words of wisdom does he have to impart to me today?" Jack broke the seal on the envelope. He read the message without emotion. "Tell General Mason that I accept." Jack folded the paper and set it aside.

James knitted his brows together. "You accept what, Jack?"

"It seems that General Mason wants to fight. He has challenged me to meet him on the field of honor," Jack said as he poured more whiskey in his glass.

"And you are going to accept his challenge just like that?!" James asked.

"Finally, an honorable way to end my suffering!" Jack said, lifting his glass to drink.

"Jack, you don't really want to do this." James turned to George. "And why now after all this time? What happened to cause the general to challenge Jack now? Colonel Rust? Can you elaborate?"

"Sir, I have no insight into the general's mind," George said.

"Oh, James, it matters not, because I shall accept regardless of the reason," Jack said, finishing the whiskey in his glass. "You tell General Mason that I accept. And as I recall from my last challenge to him, the challenged party—which would be me in this instance—gets to select the terms. And since I promised at the hustings I would damn him to hell, I want to make sure that I keep him company in that eternal inferno. So, I propose that we set ourselves upon a keg of gunpowder and light it. Together we shall explode our flesh into Dante's fiery pit."

"That is ludicrous!" James said. "General Mason will not accept those terms. Tell him, George, that Armistead would never accept such absurdity."

"And why the hell not? I think it is the perfect end to our explosive relationship!" Jack said.

"Sir, you are drunk," George said.

"And what has that to do with it?" Jack asked with amusement.

"Jack, the general has a wife. Such a death would not allow her the opportunity to say goodbye to her husband, nor would it afford your mother the opportunity to say goodbye to you." James was trying to talk sense into him.

"Good point, James. Such a wretched scene might prove too much for my sweet mother. Hmm ... I have a better idea! Colonel Rust, tell the general that we can link arms—or better yet, bind ourselves together with rope—and jump from the dome of the Capitol in one great, giant leap. We both shall perish on the ground below, but we would not be so disfigured that we would offend our mothers or, heaven forbid, Mrs. General Mason!"

"But, sir—" George said, red rising to his face.

"But, sir nothing! Write it up, James, and then our friend here can take it back to Selma. And make haste so as not to keep the general awaiting my answer."

Despite the best efforts of their friends, both Armistead and Jack were resolved. They agreed to fight at the dueling grounds in Bladensburg,

Maryland. The weapons chosen were muskets loaded with a single ball, and the agreed distance was three paces. The pair was to meet at dawn on Saturday, February 6, to terminate their dispute.

CHAPTER 64

FEBRUARY 5, 1819, ALEXANDRIA

The forest burned as Jack followed a blistering path through the hellfire. In one hand he carried a staff and in the other a long dirk, its carved obsidian blade reflecting crimson from the flames. Trees exploded into blazing bursts, as wild creatures ran between the burning bushes along the path. Jack longed for the beasts to kill him and save him from a fiery death. *Perhaps the staff and dirk are keeping them at bay,* he thought. Jack lifted his arms to cast them aside when the roar of the fire was pierced by the shrill screams of a woman. Holding tight to his staff and knife, he sprinted toward the cries, faster and faster, the heat of the flames and his desperation intensifying. Ahead, a monstrous creature was mauling something on the ground. The pale arm of a woman flailed under the creature's shadow—fighting, scratching, clawing. Jack jumped on the back of the fiend, plunging his obsidian blade between its shoulders. The creature screeched, reared its head, and thrashed to pitch him off. It writhed and twisted, flailing its head to bite. Jack held tight to its mangy hide and stabbed again. The beast bucked, flinging Jack into the fiery coals of charred bushes at the path's edge. Jack cried out from the singeing pain and, with a rush of adrenaline, found his feet and charged the beast, plunging the knife deep into its chest. The beast shrieked and staggered toward him before collapsing onto the ground. Jack raced to the motionless body of the young woman lying facedown on the path. Reaching for her shoulder, he gently turned her onto her back. Her white dress was stained with blood and her face charred by smoke and ash. Jack wiped the black away from the lifeless face. *Lucinda!* "My God, no!" He took her into his arms, weeping and rocking her. First came the awful helplessness of gut-wrenching grief. Then came the agonizing feelings of guilt and shame.

From somewhere deep in the forest he heard a man's voice—low and faint at first, then deeper and louder. He stopped his sobbing, sniffing back his sorrow so that he might make out the words. "Jack," said the voice. "You are not to blame." The voice and its comforting warmth were familiar. *"Father!"*

Jolted from his nightmare, Jack sprang from the mattress. He was sweating profusely, his breathing uneasy. He looked around his apartment to gain a bearing on his whereabouts. *It was a dream. Only a dream.* He ran his hands through his hair.

Jack looked out the window. It was already daylight. *What day is it?* He thought for a moment. *Friday.* He was to be in Bladensburg tonight. The realization of what he was about to do came crashing upon him. Tomorrow he would die.

He pressed his fingertips into his forehead and hairline to think. He needed a drink but needed to be sober more. Sober was his only option. Lightheaded from the hangover of last night's whiskey, he staggered across the cold floor to the basin to wash up. As he poured water from the pitcher into the bowl, he caught his reflection in the looking glass. He pressed his chin toward the mirror, barely recognizing the man staring back at him. *Dear God!! What has happened to you, Jack?*

CHAPTER 65

FEBRUARY 5, 1819, SELMA

"Armistead, I simply do not understand," Charlotte said, her whole body tense while Armistead packed his case with papers from his desk. "You just returned from Richmond after being in Washington City and George Town the week before, and now you must go again? And on the weekend? What business is to be attended to on Saturday and the Sabbath?"

"I have discussed this with you already, Charlotte. I told you that both the governor's office and the Senate are unattainable unless I serve in the House of Representatives. Without this meeting tomorrow, I will be unable to defeat Mercer in the election for the next Congress this April."

"I'm sorry, Armistead, but this makes no sense to me. How on earth can one meeting determine whether you will win an election?"

"It won't determine a win, Charlotte. But it sure as hell will guarantee a loss if I do not show," he said, searching his desk drawer.

Charlotte paced in front of the desk, clenching her shawl tightly around her shoulders. "There's something you're not telling me, Armistead. I don't know what it is, but you're hiding something from me."

Armistead looked up from his search and stared at her with impatience in his eyes. "And what on earth would that possibly be, Charlotte?"

She stopped in her tracks, looking at him, and said nothing. After a long minute, Armistead returned his attention to the desk drawer and found what he was looking for. The accounting ledger for Raspberry Plain that he had kept for his mother. He needed to give it to George. Just in case. He shoved the brown leather book into his bag with the ledger from Selma that was already packed. Picking up the case from his desk, he walked past Charlotte into the hall. Charlotte followed behind, pulling her shawl even tighter. A great garment box sat on the hall rack by the door. Armistead set his case on the floor and opened the box. Inside was the new overcoat from London that he had commissioned last summer when she had given him the news of her pregnancy. Armistead could no longer wear his officer's uniform, and he grimaced at the thought. He removed the overcoat from the box. It was exquisite, woven from the finest cashmere with long skirts trimmed in leather. As he put his arms through its sleeves, he felt Charlotte's eyes burning into his back.

"What, Charlotte?" he asked and turned to face her. Not only did he feel her anger, it flashed from her eyes like the glinting blades of two swords.

"I know, Armistead. I know all about it. You are going to see her, aren't you? That's what you are hiding!" Charlotte's arms were folded under her taut shawl.

"Going to see who, Charlotte?"

"Do not make me say her name, Armistead Mason. I will not blaspheme this house by uttering that harlot's name."

"What on earth are you talking about?"

"Your affair with Molly Lee!"

"I have no time for this today. None."

"That coat has sat there in that box for over a week now, and you have yet to wear it. Not with me to church. Not with me to your mother's. Not anywhere! But now, on a Friday morning before you've even had breakfast, you announce suddenly that you must leave at once for

George Town and that you have business on Saturday. And that you may not be back on Sunday either. And that there is a meeting regarding the election. Oh, you are having a meeting, all right. A meeting in that vixen's bed!"

Heat rose to Armistead's face and his anger surged. "You're right, Charlotte. That's exactly my plan. I have concocted an elaborate scheme that involves wearing a new overcoat so that I might entice a married woman to bed, because, after all, nothing gets me aroused more than copulating with another man's pregnant wife!"

"So, she *is* with child," Charlotte said, with tears adding to her storm of anger and distrust.

"And that is exactly why your accusations are so preposterous. Why on earth would I care to fornicate with a woman heavy with child? What is wrong with your head, woman? Where has my Charlotte gone? Who, in God's name, is this woman standing before me, eaten to the core with jealousy?"

"I am not eaten to the core with jealousy, Armistead. If there is nothing going on as you say, then why would you think me jealous? I simply don't believe you. I want to know where you are going, and I want you to tell me the truth. What are you hiding from me?"

"Mrs. Mason, I am hiding nothing from you. There are no secrets between us. I am going to George Town and staying at Uncle John's. I have a meeting early tomorrow morning. Should all go well, I might be home by tomorrow evening. At the very latest, I will be home on Sunday after services."

Charlotte shook her head. "Do you understand what will happen if this affair is exposed? Do you? Your dreams are over, Armistead. Over! And what about us? Our dreams—all that we have worked for—gone. Up in smoke! And all that will be left is ruin. Please, I beg you. Do not go to her bed tonight. Do not go to her bed ever again. If not for me, then for you."

Armistead drew a quick breath to control his temper. "How many times must I tell you? There is no affair. And I am not going to her bed—not tonight, not ever. I have asked you to believe me, Charlotte.

Believe only me and not all of this nonsense from my enemies. Today of all days, I ask that you trust me."

Charlotte shook her head and stared at him, her arms crossed and her mouth tight. She said nothing. Armistead could see it in her eyes. She didn't believe him. And he didn't care. He pulled the belt of his new coat around his waist and tied it. Picking up his satchel and setting his hat on his head, he opened the mahogany door and let it slam behind him as he walked out of the house.

The ordinary in Bladensburg was nearly empty. Armistead had selected a table in the alcove by the window, sitting alone as the skies thickened and darkness fell early. The air outside was raw and damp with winds kicking up from the west. *Seems a storm is in the making.* He glanced out at the deepening shadows, preparing himself for the moment that was long overdue.

With his nose at the rim of the hock, he inhaled the musty bouquet of the Haut-Brion, savoring the aroma of the wine. He had saved this gift from Mr. Jefferson for a special occasion, hoping it would be the day of his inauguration as governor. But without tomorrow, there would be no inauguration. He inhaled the bouquet in the glass again, closing his eyes at its ethereal scent. *There is no other way. Whether I live or die, I will be victorious.*

CHAPTER 66

FEBRUARY 6, 1819, DAWN, BLADENSBURG, MARYLAND

"Here comes McCarty now," Jack heard as he and his seconds crossed the bridge and rode along the narrow path adjoining the creek. Jack looked over to where Armistead and his seconds were standing.

"I'm surprised he showed up. Let's see if he actually has the nerve to walk out onto the field." Armistead's words drifted to Jack as wind gusted through the reeds, slicing the snow into sheets across the stony bank.

"We'll see if you still have that smirk on your face when you're looking down the barrel of my musket," Jack whispered under his breath as he, James Dulaney, and Dr. Cary Selden rode past them through snow to the other side of the field.

The three dismounted at the tree line along the base of the hill and hitched their horses to a scraggly branch of a sycamore. The site selected for this morning's contest was not the primary field near the road, but a path just around the corner between two hills that provided some shelter from the relentless northwest winds. It was bitterly cold, with the wind howling through the trees like hounds on a hunt.

The field marshal, who had been huddled along the creek near Armistead, started toward the center of the field with Colonel George

Rust and Dr. Jonathan Heaton in tow. Cary headed to meet them as James held back. "Jack, are you sure this is what you want? You can walk out of here right now. All you need to do is to tell me, and I'll negotiate a peace."

"There will never be peace with Armistead. You know it, and I know it. I will always be looking over my shoulder for him to come at me, and I would rather die than live like that. His erratic attacks on my character and sabotage of my life—they won't end until I face him out there. All I can do is pray that I take him with me to the hell that surely awaits us both."

"Jack, you don't—"

"I do, James, I do. It is the only way out. The only way."

James grimaced and nodded. Pulling his hat down farther onto his head, James turned to join the others in the middle of the field for one last attempt to settle the dispute. A few minutes later, James and Cary were walking back toward Jack, shaking their heads.

"The general is resolved to fight you, Jack," Cary said, the weight of his words showing on his face. "There's nothing he will agree to other than your public profession of cowardice and dishonorable conduct toward him and the issue of an apology."

"I told them that while you would be willing to offer him an apology in return for an apology for his slander against you, you would never proclaim yourself as dishonorable or a coward. They informed us that Armistead is unwavering on his conditions," James said, repeating George's words verbatim. "Either you admit to disgrace and cowardice, or you fight. I told him if that was the general's position, then you were left with no alternative than to fight him."

"As I reminded you both last night," Jack said, "even if Armistead agrees to a peace, he would not uphold it. He's proven that how many times now? Let's just get it over with. Because sooner or later, this is where we are destined to end." Jack reached into his coat, pulling out four folded letters affixed with his seal and an envelope tied with a leather cord.

"James, should the inevitable happen and I be shot to death, take my body to my brother Edgar's at Mount Air. My mother does not need to be surprised by such a gruesome sight. Edgar will know what to do with me, and instructions on how to handle my affairs are here." Jack handed James the letters and the envelope containing the will he had drafted the day before. "Please make sure these get delivered to William, Thomson, and my mother. And make sure to tell Sally that I'm sorry to have disappointed her so."

"I will, Jack. You have my word," James said.

"That last letter is for Lucinda. And give her this," he said, pulling his father's watch from his pocket. He handed James the jewel-encrusted casing with his grandmother's portrait in its center. "Tell her that every tick is the love in my heart that will forever beat for her—in death as in life. And tell her that I am sorry for the pain I have caused her."

James's eyes welled with emotion. Cary, too, had to look away to keep Jack from seeing the water in his eyes.

"It's all right, James, it is," Jack said. "This is what I must do." He slapped Cary on the back and removed his hat, throwing it into the wagon that waited to haul his body from the field. Jack took off his coat and gloves and tossed them in the wagon with the hat.

"What are you doing, Jack?" James asked.

"I'm getting ready for the fight of my life—or death, as the case may be," Jack said.

"You'll catch pneumonia out in this weather without a coat," Cary said, furrowing his brow.

"Not before I catch a ball of lead." Jack gave a somber laugh.

Both James and Cary grimly smiled. Jack removed his jacket and rolled up his sleeves to his elbows. "I need my hands to be free. Armistead is an old soldier and an expert marksman. I need every advantage."

As Jack stripped himself down to shirt, trousers, and boots, from across the field through the haze of blowing snow, he discerned Armistead's bemused reaction. Armistead himself was impeccably dressed in a fancy overcoat with heavy skirts over a high-collared blue coat. His shirt beneath the coat was as white as the blowing snow and his boots, gloves, and hat as black as coal. "I guess he's dressed for the victory parade," Jack said.

"Or to meet his maker," said James with a wry smile.

The field marshal, after completing his inspection of the weapons, nodded his head. He motioned for the antagonists to come forward for positioning on the field. The court of last resort had just been called to order.

Three paces and a foot of snow were all that lay between Jack and his enemy. Jack threw his head back to toss the hair from his forehead as he stared at the man he had come to hate—the beast of his dream. The bully from Peach Orchard Camp.

Through the blizzarding snow, he fixed his eyes on Armistead's. Memories of the war and the dream swirled in a blur through his mind—Shane McNally's cries, deserters pleading for mercy before the firing squad, and the thud of their bodies falling into their graves intermixed with Lucinda's screams, her dying face, and his own fierce will to live in order to save her from burning hell. Adrenaline released into his veins. He tightened his grasp on the musket's stock. There was no turning back.

The marshal approached the center of the field where Armistead and Jack were positioned. His movement aroused the crowd of townspeople who had gathered on the hill above and on the bridge. The marshal explained the rules of engagement, and both men affirmed their understanding. As he stepped to the north side of the field to avoid their line of fire, Armistead and Jack readied their stances and awaited the signal to fire. Armistead, pinching his shoulders back, stood even taller. Jack, with his frozen hands on the musket's stock, tightened his grip and tossed his hair from his eyes. Armistead's eyes fixed on Jack's. Jack stared back. The air, though bitter cold, was acrid with adrenaline and resolve. Any remaining fear had been replaced by the consuming fire of determination.

Within an instant, word was given, and a red handkerchief dropped to the snowy ground. In the same moment, Jack and Armistead rushed to fire, raising their muskets to their shoulders, the barrels' ends nearly touching. As Armistead lifted his gun, the muzzle caught on the skirt of his coat, causing his aim to waiver. In the next instant, both men fired. The silence on the field shattered as the guns' hammers sparked the flint, igniting the black powder in a crack that ripped through the stillness of the snow-filled sky. In a fiery burst, the load in Jack's musket propelled down the barrel and out the muzzle's end, through the frigid wind, through Armistead's elbow, and into his chest. Armistead's barrel, though not as steady, was effective none the same, delivering its load into Jack's flesh. The crowd screamed as both men fell to the ground. The two lay motionless, their blood quickly engulfing the whiteness of the surrounding snow. Besides the howling wind, the only other sounds were the cries of the crowd and the echo of gunfire ringing through the hills.

CHAPTER 67

FEBRUARY 6, 1819, RASPBERRY PLAIN

It was a frightfully cold morning, and a tempest was raging. On clear days Charlotte could see Selma on the crest of the hill about a quarter mile to the northwest. This morning's fierce winds and blowing snow had obscured the hillside, making it impossible to see much of anything from the north windows of Raspberry Plain. Charlotte moved her attention from the howling blizzard outside the parlor's French doors to the swaddled infant in her arms. An adoring smile spread across her face as she watched him sleep. *How he looks like his father—that wisp of auburn hair, refined nose, broad eyes, and strong brow. What a handsome man he will become.* As she studied the innocence of his face, her eye caught something stirring outside the doors. She glanced up. Out on the north lawn, Armistead was standing in the driving snow. Her heart leapt. *Why is he back so soon?* Oddly, he was wearing his old woolen overcoat, not the new one that had catalyzed their fight. She shook her head and cast away the thought of their ugly exchange. *He must have returned to Selma and changed. What's that in his hand? A musket?* She squinted through the

338

swirling white of the storm. *Why would he be hunting on a morning like this?*

Charlotte rose from her chair with the baby in her arms and waved to Armistead from the door. He didn't acknowledge her. He stood there staring on the lawn, strands of his hair blowing from under his hat. Charlotte tried the door to let him in, but it had been latched above her reach. She waved for him to come around to the front. He was motionless, his hair and overcoat blowing wildly in the wind. She called for Jakes, Raspberry Plain's butler. "Armistead is home. Can you come to the parlor and open the door to let him in?"

"Marster Armie is home already?" Jakes asked as he came from the back corridor to the front hall.

"He is."

"That's a long way for him to travel in this weather, Miss Charlotte." Jakes looked out the window of the Great Hall. "I don't see his horse out there. Are you sure he's here?"

"Why, yes. He's over on this side of the house—out on the north lawn. He must have walked over from Selma. Please, can you open these doors and call him in?"

Jakes came into the parlor, stepping past her, and unlatched the locks at the top of the door. Pushing aside the door's curtain, he peered out the glass onto the lawn before opening the doors. "I don't see him out there, ma'am."

"Why, he's standing not ten yards from the porch, Jakes." Charlotte laid the baby in the cradle and joined Jakes at the door. Armistead was no longer standing where she had seen him. "Hmm. He must have walked to the front door. Go let him in, Jakes."

"Yes, ma'am."

Jakes left the parlor to greet Armistead. A blast of wind and snow blew into the hallway when he opened the front door. "Marster Armie? Marster Armie?" Charlotte heard him call her husband's name through the howls of the wind before slamming the door shut and returning to the parlor. "He isn't here, ma'am. And I don't see any sign of him."

"Can you check the study entrance? Or back at the kitchen door?"

Jakes nodded and headed down the back corridor in the direction of the study. Charlotte waited in the parlor by the doors, searching the lawn for her husband.

After a few minutes Jakes returned, shaking his head. "Ma'am, Marster Armie isn't at the other doors either. He must have gone back to Selma."

"You must be right, Jakes. I'm certain he will send Phillip over with the landau once the storm passes."

Charlotte felt a sudden chill and shuddered. *Not to worry. He will send for us soon enough.* As Charlotte warmed herself by the fire, she stared out the panes of glass into the white blindness in the direction of their home on the hill. Although she was unable to see the mansion, obscured as it was by the storm, knowing that he was there was enough to ease her anxiety. She turned her attention to their son sleeping peacefully in the cradle and smiled. All her previous anger melted away. Armistead had come home.

CHAPTER 68

FEBRUARY 6, 1819, BLADENSBURG

Bits of flesh, clothing, and blood were splattered over the white ground and surrounding snow-covered bushes along the Blood Run. The wind whipped and whistled while a dark, thick pool grew between the two bodies lying still on the frozen earth. With medical bags in hand, Dr. Jonathan Heaton and Dr. Cary Selden raced across the snowy field toward the carnage. James and George ran behind them in a desperate effort to help.

Cary reached the scene first and fell to his knees beside Jack's body, which lay facedown in the snow. The back of Jack's shirt was mangled and bloodied on the left side. Reaching for his shoulder to turn him over, Cary hesitated and held his breath, afraid to confirm what he surely knew. Then Jack moved. Exhaling with urgency, Cary grabbed Jack's shoulder and heaved him onto his side. Jack was covered in blood, the flesh of his left arm was ripped apart, and a gaping wound ran from wrist to shoulder. "My God!" Cary said.

"Jesus Christ!" Jack said, wincing and grasping his arm.

James caught up to Cary and fell to his knees on the opposite side. "Jack! By God's grace, Jack, you're alive!"

"Christ Almighty, it hurts like hell!" Jack said, holding the arm and writhing on the ground. "How bad is it?"

"Looks like the ball tore through your arm and out your shoulder," Cary said, pulling at remnants of Jack's shirt for a closer look.

"Ouch! Goddamn it, Cary!" Jack said, moving his shoulder away from Cary's prodding.

"Are you hurt anywhere else?" Cary asked, ignoring Jack's complaints as he continued to pick bits of fabric from Jack's wound.

"I don't know. Jesus, do you have to do that? It hurts!" Jack said.

"Yes, now let me see what's underneath," Cary said and pulled Jack's shirt open from his chest. Despite the blood covering him, the arm seemed to be Jack's only injury.

"You're alive, man! You're alive. I cannot believe that you are alive!" James said as another strong gust howled through the branches and whipped snow around them.

"Armistead. Is he ... Is he ... ," Jack said, moving his eyes to where Armistead lay only a few feet away.

"Heaton is with him now. Let's worry about you, Jack," Cary said, looking over to Jonathan for the answer to Jack's question.

Jonathan was kneeling next to Armistead, who had fallen facing the creek. Jonathan turned his eyes to Cary's and shook his head.

The pain in Jack's arm was excruciating. Moving hurt, but he was freezing and knew well enough that he had to get off the ground. "Help me up, James."

"Not too fast, Jack. Just sit first," Cary said.

"I've got to get up, Cary."

With James's help, Jack raised his upper body to sit. The pain made him sick to his stomach. To steady himself, he moved the hand of his uninjured arm behind him. A warm stickiness between his fingers startled him. He brought his hand to his face. His palm and fingers were covered in thick, dark blood. He took in the gore on the ground and the surrounding brambles. The horror of the scene sickened him more.

"My God," he said and started to heave. He turned his head away from the creek and lost his stomach.

"Easy, Jack," James said, holding on to Jack until he had finished purging.

"You'll be all right," Cary said. "Let's get you up easy."

James and Cary, each taking an arm, brought Jack to his feet. Light-headed and dizzy, Jack's knees weakened. "I don't think I can do this," Jack said.

"You need to get to the wagon so I can tend to that arm. I need to stop the bleeding and apply the salts. Come now," Cary said.

Jack stepped forward and stumbled, nearly falling back to the ground. As James put his arm around Jack's waist to steady him, James's hand brushed against Jack's wound.

"Jesus!" Jack said under his breath. As he winced, his eye caught Dr. Heaton on his knees examining Armistead's body. George Rust was standing over them. Armistead had fallen nearer the creek, and the amalgamated black pool that had gathered was now spilling over the bank and dripping onto the ice and water below. Armistead's chest was a splayed mess of flesh, blood, and bone that no man could have survived. His eyes were open and lifeless, staring into angry gray skies overhead. Jack looked away, trying to focus instead on the wagon at the far side of the path, but the gory sight had seared into him and was replaying like the images of his dream.

Trembling with shock and shaking in the freezing temperatures, he was barely able to walk without tripping. James removed his coat and threw it around Jack's shoulders as Cary pulled Jack's uninjured arm over his shoulder to provide him more support. With Jack between them, the three crossed the field to the wagon and their horses that were hitched to the sycamore. Jack turned his head back toward the creek where Armistead lay in blood and snow. He lowered his head as his nausea returned. *The beast is ME!*

CHAPTER 69

FEBRUARY 6, 1819, EVENING, STRAWBERRY PLAIN

The wind screamed around the house and down through the chimney, its gusts fanning the flames into an erratic winter dance. Sitting by the crackling fire with his favorite hound at his feet, William had settled into a new book, while Emily knitted in the chair next to him. It had been a quiet day until Jedediah announced that William's mother-in-law and his neighbor, Colonel George Rust, were at the door.

"Why on earth is she here this late?" William said to Emily. "And why is George Rust with her?"

When William and Emily greeted them in the foyer, Polly was standing at the front window and George was pacing.

"Colonel," William said, offering George his hand. "I'd say it's a pleasure to see you, but considering the hour, I have a sense that there is something urgent. Is everything all right?"

"I need to speak to my daughter, William," Polly said as she started toward them. Her eyes were red and the skin underneath them swollen. "Alone."

"Mother, what is it?" Emily rushed past William to her mother.

Polly reached for Emily's hand, taking it into hers. "Come here, my child. Let's step into the parlor."

Emily turned to William hesitantly. William shot Polly a questioning look. His gut told him that he should accompany them. Emotionless, Polly stared at him, her eyes daring him to defy her request. "I'll entertain George, then."

As the doors into the parlor closed behind the two women, William turned to George. "What's going on? What's happened that you brought Mrs. Mason over here after nightfall and couldn't wait until morning?"

George's face was haggard, his eyes vacant and tired. "Might we have a word?"

William gestured toward the dining room. "In here." As they sat at the table, William observed exhaustion and something else in his neighbor's face. "What is it, Colonel?"

George leaned onto the table, cradling his head in his hands before drawing an uneven sigh. After a long minute, he lifted his head to look at William. "It's your brother-in-law, my best friend." George brought a hand to his face and wiped it over his mouth and chin. "He's dead, sir. Armistead's been killed." Water welled in George's eyes at the articulation of the words.

William stared at him in disbelief. "What! Armistead?" George nodded. "How?"

George glanced nervously into the hallway toward the closed parlor doors. "I don't know how to tell you." George sighed again. "Your brother, sir. It was your brother Jack who killed the general."

William's eyes darted wildly, struggling to understand his meaning. "Jack? How?"

"In a duel, sir. With muskets. This morning at Bladensburg."

Fear roared through William like the wind outside. "And Jack?" William's mouth was dry and his tongue thick. "Dear God, is he dead, too?"

"No, sir. Injured, but alive last I saw."

A long, shrill wail erupted from beyond the foyer and behind the doors of the parlor. William exploded from his chair, knocking it over as he bolted to the parlor and threw open the doors. He didn't give a fig about Polly's request for privacy. Emily was crying hysterically as Polly held her. William rushed to Emily's side, removing her from her mother's embrace, and took her into his arms. "I'm here now, sweet Em. I've got you now." William felt the burn of Polly's eyes.

"Oh God! Oh my God!" Emily cried, clinging to him.

"It's all right, my darling. It's going to be all right."

"It is not going to be all right! It will never be all right!" Emily was screaming and crying all at once. "Armie is dead! And Jack KILLED HIM! How can it ever be all right?"

"I know, my darling. I know, I know. Shhh. Shhhh. I'm here. We're here together. We'll get through this," said William, rocking her in his arms to console her.

"I brought some laudanum to calm her," Polly said, pulling her bag from the floor. "That and some hot tea with a little brandy will help ease her mind and cause sleep to come more easily."

"I don't want that poison, Mother," Emily said. "I just want it not to be true!"

"But it is true, my dear. So horribly true," Polly said with tears of her own welling in her eyes.

William pulled a handkerchief from his pocket for Emily as she sobbed. George had now also found his way to the parlor and was standing awkwardly in the doorway.

"George, what the hell happened?" asked William.

George cleared his throat. Emily, regaining some of her composure, raised her face from William's shoulder. She sniffed back tears and listened as George recited the events that had transpired over the last week.

"So it was Armie who started all of this?" Emily said.

"Yes, ma'am. It was your brother who issued the challenge," said George.

"But why? Why, George?" Emily asked between sobs. "Everything had been settled between them."

"After his last trip to Richmond, your brother felt he had no recourse other than to right the wrongs that had previously been made against him. And your brother, sir," George said, redirecting his attention to William, "he was in a depressed state when he accepted the terms. So depressed that I was surprised he fought back at all. But he did, sir."

"And he's survived, yes?" William said. "But he is injured, you said." George nodded. "How badly injured, George? And where is he?"

"I don't know where he is. Armistead's ball tore into his arm quite extensively. But he was able to ride. That's all I know. James Dulaney was with him. He will know more."

James Dulaney. Jack would have instructed James to go to Cedar Grove. Sally! William's heart ached at the thought of Sally. Thomson and Jack were her babies. If anything happened to either one of them, it would devastate her.

Emily clutched William's hand and squeezed it tightly. "I want to see him. My brother. Take us to him, George. I want to see him now."

"Ma'am, he was at your Uncle John's and then on to Osbourne's in Leesburg," George told her. "I am not certain that the hackney has left George Town. With this weather, I'm not sure where he might be at present."

"Take me, William," Emily pleaded, her eyes glistening with tears.

"Em, it's pitch black out now. As George said, we don't know exactly where he is. I think we should wait until we know that he is in Leesburg." Emily burst into sobs.

"Emily, my child. I must agree with William," Polly said, fighting through her own emotion. "We need to wait until your uncle has had time to prepare him properly. And we need to tell Charlotte."

Emily sniffed back her tears. "Charlotte doesn't know?"

"No, child. I thought it was important to let you know first, since you and your brother were so close," Polly said.

William looked at Polly in bewilderment until it occurred to him why Polly hadn't told Charlotte. *You needed to get to Emily before James Dulaney made it out from Alexandria to tell me.*

"But, Mother! She's his wife!" Emily said.

"I plan to tell her first thing in the morning. I think it's best to allow her to rest this evening since she will have little peace in the coming days. Perhaps you will join me when I tell her. The two of you are close, and I think your presence will bring her comfort."

Emily looked to William, her eyes pleading. "Please, William," Emily implored. "I want to be there when Charlotte is told."

"Emily, it is your decision. But I think that Charlotte needs to be told tonight."

Emily turned to her mother. "William is right. I would be quite cross with you if something like this had happened to William, and everyone knew and I didn't. We need to tell her now, and I will come with you to do so." She turned back to William before allowing her mother an opportunity to answer. "William, are you all right if I overnight at Raspberry Plain? For Charlotte?"

"If that's what you want to do, then it is all right with me," William said. "I will collect you in the morning."

"Very well, then," Polly said. "George, you will help us inform her. And William, I do think it best that you stay here."

"Of course I will stay here." William caught Polly's glare. *What kind of a boor do you take me for? My brother killed her husband.* "Just make sure you rest, Em."

Emily nodded as she dried her eyes and stood from the settee. "Let me get my wrap, Mother, and we'll go."

Standing with Emily and putting an arm around her shoulders, William led his wife from the room. "Emily, darling, I am so terribly sorry. I can only imagine your pain," he said as he helped her with her coat.

Emily bit her lip and tried not to cry. "It's not your fault, William. It's Jack's fault! And Armie's fault! I hate them both for what they have done to us!"

"Sweetheart, you don't mean that. You don't hate either one of them. You're just filled with grief and anger and hurt, as am I." He lifted her chin for her to look at him. "I'm so sorry, darling. Sorry I couldn't have done more to stop it." William's eyes, too, were welling with water at his own helplessness.

"Please don't blame yourself, William. We both know whose fault it is. It's just so awful." Emily sniffled as the tears came again. William pulled her close.

"I know, darling. I know." He held her and whispered in her ear, "Promise me you'll rest and not let any stress come to the baby. Promise?"

Emily nodded. "Charlotte needs to know. I need to help Mother tell her and be there for her, just like she would be there for me. I'll be strong, William." As Emily pulled back from him, he noticed the deep sadness on her face. He regretted allowing her to go. "As broken as my heart is, I need to do this." Emily offered him a weak smile. "I need to do this for Charlotte. With her sister so far away, she has no one here but us. And I promise to stay strong. For our baby."

"That's my girl," William said, hugging her again. He took her hand and walked her to the foyer where her mother and George were waiting. William looked at his wife again, watching as she fussed with her scarf. He prayed that she would be all right. As Emily was leaving, she stopped in the doorway and turned to face him.

"Find out why, William. I need to know why."

"So do I, Em. So do I."

CHAPTER 70

FEBRUARY 6, 1819, EVENING, RASPBERRY PLAIN

In an oversized armchair in the upstairs sitting room, Charlotte was enjoying the latest book that Dr. Cocke had sent her. Even with its twisted plot, the book was not enough to distract Charlotte's mind from her husband. She glanced at the clock. *Why hasn't Armistead sent the coach for us?* Drawing a long sigh to quell her anxiety, Charlotte turned her attention back to the mad creation of Victor Frankenstein. She had yet to turn another page before she was interrupted by a rap on the doorframe. Polly was standing in the doorway with Emily and George Rust.

"Charlotte, my dear. Might we have a word?"

"Mrs. Mason?" Charlotte said, placing the book facedown on the side table. "What is it?"

Polly pulled up an ottoman next to Charlotte. Emily took the chair on the other side of her. Charlotte had an awful, sick feeling in her stomach.

"Charlotte, darling. It's Armistead." Polly's eyes welled with tears.

Charlotte was suddenly filled with fear. "Has there been an accident?"

"Of sorts, yes." Polly took Charlotte's hand. Emily reached out and took the other.

"What sort of accident? Tell me he's all right!" Polly closed her eyes and shook her head. "Oh God! Please tell me he's all right!"

Polly bit her lip and opened her eyes. "Armistead was killed early this morning. In Maryland. It was in defense of the family's honor."

"What?" Charlotte said, whispering and wailing all at once. "That can't be! I saw him this morning. He was here—out on the lawn—hunting."

"Charlotte, darling," Polly told her, "you must be mistaken."

"No, I wasn't mistaken," Charlotte insisted, her voice firm in her conviction. "I saw him. He was here. You are wrong, Mrs. Mason. He can't be dead. He's over at Selma. I saw him!"

"Charlotte, George was there," Polly said. "George. Tell her."

"I wish I could say different, Charlotte. Truly I do. But Mrs. Mason is telling you the truth. Your husband was shot this morning in a fight defending his family's good name and his character. He was brave, ma'am. I have never known a man braver than your husband."

"I don't believe it. You are wrong," Charlotte said. "He would never fight a duel. Never, not now that he has a son. You are wrong, Colonel! He promised Emily, and he would never break a promise to her. Tell him, Emily. Armistead would never break a promise. And I saw him this morning with my own eyes!"

"Charlotte. Sweetie," Emily said gently. "I understand, but you have to—"

"I have to understand nothing! Take me to him! Take me to Selma now! I am certain he is there."

"Charlotte, I wish you were correct, but he's not there," Polly said.

"Take me there now!" Charlotte cried, shouting out the doorway. "Jakes! Jakes! Please prepare the carriage." Charlotte stood from the chair and hurried into the hallway.

"Charlotte, it's too late to go out now," Polly said as the women followed behind her.

Charlotte raced down the staircase to the first floor, barking orders to the servants as she went. "Hester, bring me my wrap and bonnet.

Tell Nelly to stay here with Stevens until I send Phillip over to retrieve them. I'm going home to my husband."

"Charlotte, I'm coming with you," Emily said. "Mother. George. You're coming, too. We're all going to see if Armie is at Selma."

"But, Emily," Polly said.

"But nothing, Mother. There is only one way to know for certain if Charlotte is right. We need to give her that." Emily turned to George. "Come with us, George. I am certain Armie will want you to know that he's all right, should we find him there."

"Yes, ma'am," George agreed, shaking his head and following the women to the front door.

The four crowded into the coach, bundled for the cold. Their breath frosted the carriage windows as the iron wheels, muted by the blanket of fresh snow, rolled silently over the icy road.

"He's fine, Emily. I'm certain of it. Why, I saw him this morning. He had changed his coat, you know, wearing his old one as to not ruin the one from London that just arrived. And he had his musket. Most likely a bear or mountain cat got too close to the house, you know. He most certainly wounded it. That's why he didn't come inside this morning. He had to track it down, for they are most dangerous when they are wounded. He must have tracked it into the woods and then went back to Selma. I am certain he was planning to join us for supper this evening after the storm broke. I would be surprised if we don't pass him on his way over to Raspberry Plain now." Charlotte looked through the frosted window for any sign of his stallion or the carriage on the road.

When the coach pulled up to the front of the mansion, the house was relatively dark. The porch lamps were lit, as were the lanterns inside the Great Hall. Those were the only lamps she could see. There was no smoke from the chimneys that flanked the house and no light emanating from the upper floors. The stable boy came rushing around the corner to help with the horses. Joe emerged from the front door as the coach halted. When George opened the carriage door, Charlotte nearly jumped across his lap to exit.

"Miss Charlotte, I wasn't expectin' you tonight," Joe said, helping her to the ground.

Picking up her skirts, Charlotte waded across the snow-covered cobblestones to the front steps. "Where is he, Joe? Where's my husband?"

"Well, I don't know, ma'am," Joe said as he hurried alongside Charlotte to assist her on the slippery steps.

"What do you mean, you don't know?" Charlotte asked as a horrific, sinking hole opened in her chest. "Isn't he here?"

"Why no, ma'am."

"Of course he is, Joe. You must be mistaken." Charlotte rushed across the front porch and into the house. The house was cold and the only heat was emanating from a basket of coal burning in the fireplace on the far side of the Great Hall. Charlotte hurried to the back of the house to her husband's library, calling his name. "Armistead! Armistead, darling. I am home, darling. I am here. Armistead?"

As she rounded the corner, the library was dark, the lamps of the chandelier cold, and there was no fire in the fireplace. The sinking hole in her chest grew into a mighty cavern. "Armistead?" She waited for his smoky voice to emerge from the darkness. There was only silence. She ran into the hall and shouted his name up the stairs. "Armistead?"

"Miss Charlotte. The Marster isn't here," Joe said.

Charlotte's eyes darted about the hall as the others joined her. "But he was here, yes?" Charlotte said, desperate for an explanation of his whereabouts. "He came back this morning. And changed his coat. Perhaps he went out again?"

"No, ma'am," Joe said. "He's not been here since he left yesterday morning."

"That can't be right," Charlotte insisted, her eyes darting wildly around the hall for any sign of him.

"Charlotte, honey," Emily said sympathetically, reaching a hand to her.

And then Charlotte saw it. Hanging on the rack by the door. His old woolen coat. Exactly as he had left it the morning before. And that was all. Not the hat that he always wore—the hat she saw him wearing this morning. Not the new coat he left in. The hole in her chest grew to an all-consuming abyss. The horrendous sound of an injured animal erupted from her as she fell to the floor. George rushed to steady her, but his efforts were pointless. She lay on the floor, half on her knees, half melted into the rug, sobbing hysterically, decimated.

"No! No! No! My God in heaven, no!" Emily and Polly tried to comfort her—to console her. But there was nothing they could do. Her Armistead—her savior, her alpha, her omega, her everything— was gone.

CHAPTER 71

FEBRUARY 7, 1819, COTON FARM

"Miss Lucinda," Mr. Deese said from the doorway of the upstairs sitting room. "There's a gentleman at the door here to see you. A Mr. Dulaney. He did not have a card, but he says it's urgent."

"James Dulaney is here? Is Mr. McCarty with him?"

"No, Miss."

Lucinda knitted her brows together. "Not hiding out on the lawn somewhere?"

Mr. Deese cleared his throat. "No, ma'am. Mr. Dulaney mentioned something about the newspapers and it being a matter of life and death. He was quite persistent."

Lucinda put down her reading. "Thank you, Mr. Deese. I will be down to receive him at once." As Mr. Deese left the doorway, she bit her lip and stood up from the chair. *Life and death?* Smoothing the folds of her skirts, she drew a long breath before heading down the stairs.

From the top stair, she spotted James Dulaney pacing in the front hall with his hat in hand, looking worried and cold. Lucinda held her breath as she descended the staircase. "Mr. Dulaney, I hear you have news. Life-and-death news. Is your friend Jack McCarty all right?"

"Miss Lucinda," James said with a bow. "Yes. Jack has been injured, but his prognosis is good."

Lucinda exhaled in relief, now convinced this was just another one of Jack's ruses to coerce her to see him again. "Injured? How? Was he drunk and fell off his horse?"

"No, Miss Lucinda. If only it were that. I'm not quite sure how to tell you. Jack was injured in a fight. A duel, actually. With General Mason. General Mason is dead, Miss Lucinda. And our friend Jack, too, has been shot."

Lucinda felt the air leave the room as his words roared in her head. "Shot! How shot? Is he going to be all right? A duel? Jack challenged Armistead to a duel?"

"No, ma'am—I mean yes. Yes, that he was shot, shot in the arm, and he's going to be all right, I think. And no, Jack did not challenge the general. General Mason challenged Jack. And I fear he had no choice but to fight him."

A volatile, confusing mix of panic, fear, anger, and concern churned inside Lucinda. "Of course he had a choice, Mr. Dulaney! He could have said no."

"Yes, I suppose he could have. But he has not been in his right mind recently, Miss Lucinda. And it is no use fretting over it. What's done is done."

"And you are sure he is going to be all right?" Lucinda asked again, worry rising above the clash of her emotions.

"Well, there's no guarantee—infection and all—but the doctor did his best."

Lucinda knew an emotional storm was brewing inside her. She needed James to leave before she lost her composure. "Well, if that is all, Mr. Dulaney—"

"Actually, Miss Lucinda, I am here to give you something."

"To give me something? I hope it is not another letter, because I will not receive it, and you'll just have to take it back to him in Alexandria."

"It's not a letter, Miss Lucinda. Although he did write one to you that I was to give to you at his death, which he was most certain would result from his fight with the general. But Jack was lucky, so lucky he was that he didn't die. And he's not in Alexandria. He's gone."

The rawness of James's words cut her to the quick. *"Give to you at his death."* This was not at all what she had planned—not at all what she wanted. "Gone? What do you mean gone?" Lucinda asked, struggling to maintain an even tone.

"He's gone north. He's fled, as he's fearful that he might be assassinated by Mason's men. Fearful, too, that, should he remain in Virginia, he will be arrested, prosecuted, and hung for killing the general."

Assassinated? Hung for killing the general? "North to where?" Lucinda managed to ask.

"He said either New Jersey or New York and will write to you when he arrives. He asks that you please accept his letter and read his words."

"I'll do no such thing! And, if that's all—"

"Actually, there is one more thing." James reached into his overcoat pocket. "He wants you to have this." James pulled out a watch on a chain and handed it to her.

Jack's grandmother smiled at her with warm, forgiving eyes as Lucinda turned the case over in her hand. "I cannot accept this."

"Miss Lucinda, you must. Before the duel he asked me to make sure that you received it. He told me to tell you that even in death, every tick of the watch's hand is the love in his heart beating for you. Then, after the fight, when I tried to give it back, he refused to take it. He insisted that you have it." James caught her glance before continuing. "He loves you so much."

Lucinda bit her lip and moved her eyes back to the face smiling from the watch's case. "Miss Lucinda, Jack would never want me to tell you this, but I feel that I must. Since the general challenged him, Jack, as the challenged party, had the right to select the terms. He proposed preposterous terms at first, all in an attempt to end his life quickly. Perhaps he thought such fatal terms would dissuade the general from fighting. Perhaps not. In the end, he chose muskets ... at three paces. A certain death sentence. I believe he did so because when he lost your love, he lost his will to live. On the field I saw his will return. I think it was because he wanted to see you once more before he met his Almighty God. I'd like to think that, anyway—that it was his love for

357

you that saved him. He told us as he was riding off that all he could think about out there on that field was you."

Holding her tears at bay, Lucinda managed to steady her voice. "I'm certain, Mr. Dulaney, that I had nothing to do with anything that went on out there on a dueling field. Now, mustn't you be getting on your way?"

"Yes, Miss." James lowered his head and was turning toward the door when he stopped abruptly. "Oh, I almost forgot. Jack told me to tell you something specific. He said to tell Lucinda that 'I found my trust in us.' That you would know what he meant."

Lucinda remembered that day in the vineyard. The tenderness that she felt for him that day ripped through her again, melting her defenses and tearing apart what little of her heart she had pieced back together. She managed to usher James to the door without breaking down. "Now if that is all."

"Yes, Miss Lucinda, that is all." As she opened the door, he turned toward her. "I can only pray that I will find someone in my life to love as much as Jack loves you. Although his heart is in so much pain, I envy him in a way. You both are so very lucky."

"I don't think you appreciate how lucky you are, Mr. Dulaney."

As the door shut, Lucinda braced herself against it to keep from collapsing, her emotions exploding from the dam that had retained them. A hysterical sob erupted from deep within. *Oh, God! Jack, what have you done?*

CHAPTER 72

FEBRUARY 10, 1819, LEESBURG

Charlotte held it together until the moment the coffin was lowered into the ground. That was the hardest part—handfuls of dirt cast by loved ones into the abyss of the final resting place.

Through it all Charlotte had remained stoic. She had consoled his family, informed the enslaved, written the letters, and received the guests. She had walked with her head high into the church, sitting in the front pew with Emily on one side and Polly on the other, holding their hands with her composure intact as their tears flowed throughout the service of Masonic rites. There were at least a dozen speakers paying tribute to the character and integrity of her husband. James Barbour had been particularly moving as he recounted Armistead's bravery during the war. She hadn't noticed how packed the church was, and that those who gathered to pay their respects had overflowed into the churchyard. It wasn't until the service concluded and his coffin was carried to the graveyard that she understood just how many had trekked through the snow and the cold to attend his funeral. Hundreds. More than she could count. From across the region they had traversed to say their goodbyes. And through the tributes and tears, Charlotte had held it together.

Until now. As the coffin was lowered inch by painful inch into the damp, cold, rooted darkness, unrelenting agony overpowered her determination to remain strong. She nearly crumbled under its weight as Dr. Charles Cocke and Colonel George Rust held her elbows to keep her from falling. When she fell apart, so did Emily and Polly, each sobbing more hysterically as the coffin inched its way to the bottom of the earthen pit, where Charlotte's beautiful Armistead would remain for all eternity, his golden shining light extinguished forever under the cold, damp mantle of Virginia clay.

CHAPTER 73

APRIL 20, 1819, NEW YORK CITY

It was stifling in his room with the morning sun burning through the window like the flame of a furnace. Jack lifted the sash to release the suffocating heat and capture the freshness of the spring breezes blowing across the Sound from the south up the East River. He grabbed his coat and hat to take a walk and enjoy the morning, when the butler rapped on his door with a letter for him. The letter was addressed to John Keith from a gentleman in Philadelphia whom Jack did not know. The seal had been broken, revealing another letter inside. That correspondence was addressed to him. It was from Cedar Grove and was affixed with his brother's seal. He broke the wax and opened the folded paper.

April 13, 1819

My dear Brother,

I wish I were writing to you with better news. Our beloved brother Edgar has left this earth to join our father and brothers in the arms of our Savior in heaven above. His heart gave way in his sleep. Peggy and Sally are in mourning, as is our sister and the rest of the family at the loss of one who was loved by so many. We buried him in the family plot at Mount Air alongside his twin Daniel. He was memorialized by many friends and shall be truly missed by all who knew him.

Edgar's passing is followed by happier tidings. My beautiful wife has given birth to a healthy son. We have named him William Thornton, as Emily has insisted he carry his father's name; however, we shall call him "Thornton" after his beloved Uncle Edgar Thornton McCarty. Emily and little Thornton are staying with Sally at Cedar Grove for now, away from Leesburg and the stress of the Masons until a bit more time passes to heal the wounds of their loss. I have been traveling between Strawberry Plain and Cedar Grove and the courthouses of Fairfax, Prince William, and Loudoun, as my caseload has doubled with spring's arrival. In times like these, I miss my law partner! And I miss my brother more.

Colonel George Rust has been elected to fill your seat in the Virginia legislature, and Fenton ran unopposed in his reelection to the House. As to the latter, I have no comment or affection other than I am happy that our party is still represented by at least one of its members from the Commonwealth, although recently his allegiance seems more aligned to Clay and Monroe than to our cause.

In regard to you returning to Virginia, it is too precarious. Although I have personally heard no rumblings from the Masonites for your assassination, rumors are rampant. Publicly they state that they intend to find you and bring you to justice. From my last conversation with the sheriff, he stated that he will arrest you should you return. There are, however, Federalists and Republicans from throughout Loudoun and Fairfax, the District, and as far as Richmond who see your conduct as completely honorable. With time, I believe most will recognize that no other course of action was available to you, and Virginia will once again embrace you with open arms. I pray that day comes sooner than later, as you are missed by your friends and your family and, most of all, your brothers.

Take care of yourself, Jack. I don't need to caution you against direct correspondence with any of us here in Virginia, as there are spies all around, especially with Republicans in control of the post offices. Nothing would delight them more than to inform your enemies of your whereabouts. Watch your back and be careful in using our intermediaries to keep in touch. As soon as it is safe for you to return, I will send for you. And remember that, though we may be silent, you are loved by many.

Your obedient servant,

William

Jack tossed William's letter onto the desk and sank into the chair. He fought back sobs of grief, unsure that his heart could take any more. *Poor Edgar! Poor Sally! Peggy and the children!* Despite his resistance, tears flooded his eyes and grief consumed him. How he loved Edgar. How they all did. And how he longed to saddle his mare and ride hard to Cedar Grove to be with his family at a time when they needed him most. He lifted his gaze to the window, searching for answers as to why so many of his brothers had died so young in life. Why was God punishing him by taking nearly everyone he cared about? *Why?*

Wiping the water from his eyes with the heel of his palm, he stood from the chair. *To hell with a morning stroll.*

Jack knew exactly how to distract himself from his grief and his all-too-familiar self-loathing. And O'Malley's on Broad Street wasn't far.

"Mr. McCarty. Kinda early for you, isn't it?" asked the ruddy-faced proprietor as he looked up from cleaning behind the counter. "I thought you would be hard at work with Mr. Keith this morning."

"Good morning to you, Sean. Indeed on most days, but Mr. Keith is north in Albany and has closed his law office for the week, so I am left to my own devices."

"Or vices. What can I get you this morning?"

"A bottle of Bushmills."

"A full bottle? Or a tall glass?"

"An entire bottle." Jack pulled up a stool to the counter. The gentlemen to his right and his left made room and looked at Jack curiously as Sean pulled a bottle of whiskey from under the shelf. Sean uncorked the bottle and poured Jack a drink. Jack glanced around the pub at the other men. "Sean, grab a few glasses for my friends here. No point in drinking alone." Sean nodded and brought out more glasses, pouring whiskey from the bottle for the four patrons at the counter. The men nodded appreciatively. "Gentlemen, this morning I learned that I lost my brother. A good man he was, and taken from us all too soon. I'd like to propose a toast to my brother Edgar!"

"To your brother Edgar," the man to Jack's right offered with a raised glass.

"To Edgar," said another.

Even Sean poured himself a bit of the Bushmills to join in the tribute.

"To Edgar!" Jack toasted.

"To Edgar!" the patrons said and raised their glasses. Jack clinked his glass to the gentleman's sitting next to him and downed the amber liquid in one gulp. Sean poured more of the whiskey into Jack's glass.

"How about a toast to the luck of the Irish for those of us living?" Sean said and raised his glass again.

"To the luck of the Irish," Jack said and lifted the glass.

"To cheating, stealing, fighting, and drinking," Sean said. With the whiskey at his lips, Jack hesitated.

"Hear! Hear!" said the gentleman to Jack's right. "Here's to us lucky ones who have cheated death." Jack placed the glass down on the counter.

"And to stealing the heart of a beautiful woman," said the man at the end of the counter.

"And to fightin'," Sean said with a grin. "And having a brother's back."

"And don't forget the drinking," said the man to Jack's left.

"Drinking with friends," Jack whispered. He stared at the whiskey in his glass. When he had given that same toast three years before, Edgar, Thomson, William, and Armistead were all together. And now only Thomson and William remained. Since that party at Raspberry Plain, Jack had fallen madly in love with a beautiful woman, yet he had broken his promises and lost her. Against the better judgment of his brothers, he had fought his brother-in-law and killed him. Jack had indeed cheated death. And here, now, he was drinking once again to drown his pain and mask his sorrow, but with strangers, for other than John Keith, Jack had no friends here.

"Tell you what, gentlemen," Jack said, "enjoy the Bushmills on me. Sean, add it to my account. I forgot that I have casework today and must bid you gentlemen adieu." Jack pushed himself back from the counter. Putting his hat on his head, he left the bar and returned to John Keith's.

When Jack walked into his room, the window was still open and the breezes stirred the lace curtains that hung above the desk. He stood at the window, looking—thinking. Across the street in front of the Battery, orphaned children were pitching a ball as the wind tossed the branches of the elms to and fro against the spring sky. Passersby cast disapproving glances as the children laughed and played. They were dirty and disheveled in their appearance and dress. Yet there was joy in their voices and on their faces. They were happy—in spite of their lot in life. *Was I ever like them?* Jack knew the answer. It was the answer to his next question—*Why not?*—that changed everything.

Jack pulled the chair from the writing table and set to work. He first wrote to William, then to his brother Thomson, and then to his mother. He wrote to James Dulaney and to Cary Selden. He told them how much he loved them and shared his feelings of regret and sorrow. Next, he wrote a letter to Emily—he was heartbroken for her more than anyone else.

As the morning turned to afternoon and then to early evening, Jack was exhausted, but he knew he had one more letter to compose. If he could only find the courage.

He stood and paced the room before sitting down once more. Pulling a final sheet of paper from the drawer, he dipped the tip of his quill in the ink. *"My dearest Lucy …"*

CHAPTER 74

APRIL 29, 1819, COTON FARM

The messenger was still pacing when Lucinda reached the bottom of the stairs. She crossed the foyer and handed him a correspondence, instructing him to return it to the sender.

"But, ma'am, it's addressed to Coton Farm. Ain't this Coton Farm?" the messenger asked.

"Yes, it is addressed to Coton Farm; however, I want you to return the correspondence to Cedar Grove, please," Lucinda said.

"Well, aren't you going to open it first, ma'am?"

"Actually, no, as that is the entire point. Now please, sir, if you would take this and be on your way."

"All right, ma'am. Just seems kind of silly to me." The messenger scratched his head, looking at the envelope.

"I can assure you, sir, the matter is anything but silly. Now good day to you," Lucinda said and showed the messenger the door.

CHAPTER 75

JUNE 7, 1819, CEDAR GROVE

Sally's hands were shaking. In them was a correspondence that had arrived moments before by express messenger. The return scrawl said John Keith, New York. No address. No way for a spying eye to deduce where exactly her son might be. But Jack's friend would not be writing to her unless something was dreadfully wrong. Sally McCarty had, unfortunately, become too accustomed to bad news. She braced herself and broke the seal. Reading the words, she put her hand to her mouth. With the letter from John Keith in hand, she raced down the hall to the study. "William! Oh my God, William! You must get to New York! You must bring Jack back to us!"

William looked up from the papers on the desk. "It is not safe for him here, Sally. You know that. Perhaps in a few months, things might—"

"We do not have a few months! Look here." She handed William the letter. "I cannot bear to lose another son, and I will not allow Jackie to die alone. Please, William, go to New York and bring him home."

As he read the letter, William's face grew grim. Jack was suffering from a brain fever, possibly typhoid. For John Keith to have written and to have sent the correspondence by express, the situation must be severe.

"Perhaps we should go to him, Sally. But to bring him back ... I don't know how without the risk of him being arrested, tried, and hung."

"I have every intention of going to him. Every intention. But you need to find a way to get him back here. You're a lawyer. Figure out a way around the law."

"It's not that simple!" William's exasperation was showing. "I only defend clients in accordance with the law, Sally. I don't make the laws."

"Then find someone who makes the laws, William! And convince them that my Jackie is no criminal and their damn law needs to be changed!" Sally had lost her patience and was shouting.

"That would be someone in the Virginia legislature. And I don't know anyone in the legislature who would be willing to put their neck out for this."

"Yes you do," said a voice from just outside the room. Sally turned on her heels toward the hallway. Emily, still wearing the black gossamer netting of mourning, stood in the doorway.

"I didn't mean to interrupt," Emily said, "but I heard shouting, so I came to make sure everything was all right."

"What do you mean, Em?" William asked. "Who do I know who would take up such a cause?"

"Colonel Rust," Emily said.

"Colonel Rust? As in Colonel George Rust?" William asked with a bewildered look on his face.

"Yes. Colonel George Rust," Emily repeated. "He just took his oath of office and assumed his seat in the legislature, according to his wife, Maria."

"Why in the world would Colonel Rust help Jack?" Sally asked. "I mean, he was your brother's best friend."

"Exactly, Em," William said. "I'm certain the colonel would be just as happy to see Jack swinging at the end of a rope as any of the others who hold Jack responsible for Armistead's death."

"I don't believe that George holds Jack responsible any more than I do," Emily said. "And there are many in the family and many of Armie's friends who share my sentiment. Certainly not his mother nor his wife, of course, but I'm fairly certain that George feels that Jack did the honorable thing and respects him for it."

"Even so," William said, "George's personal feelings are one thing. Going before the legislature is something completely different. Why would George stick his neck out?"

"Because he's neck deep in it," Emily said.

William put down the letter that he had been holding and smiled. "Mrs. McCarty, what would I do without you?"

"I don't understand," Sally said, giving them both a puzzled look.

"Colonel Rust was Armistead's second, Sally. And Jonathan Heaton, the new leader of the Democratic Republican Party in Loudoun, was his other second. In the eyes of the law, the two of them are just as culpable as Armistead and Jack. And further, if my brilliant wife is correct, Colonel Rust just took his oath of office and attested that he has upheld the anti-dueling law, which may not be entirely accurate. Which gives me leverage."

"Seconds?" Sally asked. "What in heaven's name—?" William's meaning suddenly dawned on her. "So you are going to blackmail him!" There was excitement in her voice.

"Of course not, Sally. I am a man of the law. And that's all I shall do—remind Colonel Rust of the law and how it should be changed or at least encouraged to be set aside in this case, since to prosecute Jack would lead to prosecution of all those involved. Something I am sure the Virginia legislature and the sheriff would just as soon avoid, considering all who may suffer the consequences." William got up from his desk and walked over to his wife, who was standing in the doorway. Wrapping his arms around her, he kissed Emily on the top of her head. "You are indeed brilliant, Em. And you've a heart of gold."

"There's been enough dying and heartbreak in this family already," Emily said. "We don't need any more. Convince them to let Jack come home."

CHAPTER 76

JUNE 24, 1819, COTON FARM

**"I am amazed how much little Thornton looks like his father,"
Lucinda said as she glanced at the baby sleeping in the cradle.** "All
that ebony hair!"

"And that dimple right in the middle of his chin. All the McCarty
boys have it, you know," Emily said, sipping the tea in her cup. "He's
on his way home, Lucinda."

"William?"

"Yes, William, too. But it was Jack to whom I was referring."
Lucinda tightened her mouth and said nothing. "William went to New
York to get him, you know. Jack was very ill. Near death, I was told. But
he is recovered now and on his way home with William. They should
return any day now."

"I could not care less."

"I do not believe that for a minute. And neither do you." Lucinda
glared out the window. "I know how it hurts, Lucy."

Lucinda looked back at Emily. "You can't possibly know, Em. You
just can't."

Emily's eyes ignited. "Are you kidding? I have lost my brother!"

"I'm sorry, Em. I didn't mean to be insensitive to your loss. But I
don't understand how you can talk about Jack like this, considering
what he's done."

Emily narrowed her eyes. "We must forgive him, Lucinda."

"Forgive him? Are you mad?"

"It's the only way, Lucy. It's the only way for healing."

"But you just said it, Emily. He killed your brother. He fought a duel after he promised us both that he would not. How can you expect me to forgive him?"

"Because I have," said Emily. Lucinda stared at her in disbelief. "While I do not understand this foolishness that compelled Armistead and Jack to lay down their lives in the name of honor, it was their decision. I cannot blame Jack any more than I blame Armistead. For me to hate Jack would mean that I must also hate my brother. How can I hate someone whom I loved so much?" Emily gave a heavy sigh. "We must forgive and accept the choices they made so that we can live on in peace and find happiness again." Emily reached across the table and took Lucinda's hand in both of hers. "Lucinda, you are my best friend. I cannot watch you carry the anger around anymore."

"But he lied to me, Em. How can I ever trust him? How can I not feel the fool?"

"Oh, sweet Lucinda. We have talked about this before. At the academy, remember? You cannot be shamed for something over which you had no control."

"But this is different, Em."

"Is it? I believe it is exactly as when your father died."

Lucinda's eyes sparked in a mix of anger and fear as she pulled her hands away. "It is not the same at all."

"Oh, but it is, Lucy. Before our fathers died, they assured us that they would always support us. 'Papa loves you and will take care of everything, my little sparrow.' And then they died. They broke their promises and left us, shattering our young hearts to pieces. How old were we? Ten?" Lucinda nodded. "When I lost my father, it hurt so badly that I promised I would never love anyone again. But when I stopped blaming my father and let go of the anger, I was able to find happiness again." Lucinda lowered her head as her tears welled. "Lucy, you must let it go." Emily reached again and squeezed Lucinda's hand, her eyes pleading as she spoke. "You must forgive both your father and Jack before this anger devours you."

Lucinda wiped the corners of her eyes. "I know that my father's death was not his fault. And, yes, I do blame him for leaving us without economic security. But that has nothing to do with Jack. Look at what Jack did—I mean, how can you just accept him like that?"

"I received a letter from him. In his apology he made no excuses. He accepted responsibility for his actions and wrote that he understands completely if I hate him. But he never asked for my forgiveness. In fact, he asked nothing from me. His only concern was for me and my loss." Emily moved her gaze to the tea in her cup. "As I read his letter, I could feel his heart. It was as if his regret poured from his hand into the ink and onto the paper. He was humble, Lucinda. His words touched me." Emily looked up from the table. "He wrote to you, too."

"And I returned his letter unopened to Cedar Grove so William could send it back to wherever he is."

"I know." Reaching into the folds of her skirt, Emily pulled Jack's letter from her pocket. As she placed it on the table, she watched Lucinda's eyes drift to the handwriting on the envelope. "Perhaps if you read his words, they might bring you peace."

"I cannot."

"Why not, Lucy?"

"Because if I read his words, I risk opening my heart to him. And I can never allow him to hurt me again and to play me for a fool."

Emily fixed her eyes on Lucinda's. "So which way would you rather be wrong?"

Lucinda looked confused. "Whatever do you mean?"

"It seems to me that you have two options. The first is that you read his words, forgive him, and allow him back into your life. If you are right, he will betray you and, once again, you will be made the fool. But if you are *wrong*, and he has truly changed, you will be in a love so deep with the man of your dreams. Your life will be more wonderful than you could ever imagine."

Emily paused, glancing out the window at the stone springhouse across the green lawn before bringing her attention back to Lucinda. "Your second option is to close your heart and never forgive him. If you are right, he is the scoundrel you suspected and he will go back to his lascivious ways. And you will take comfort in watching him self-destruct, which surely he will. You will hold on to your anger and never be made to feel a fool. But if you're *wrong*, and he truly loves you, he will never find anyone who can fill his heart as you did. And you, my friend, will never have room in your heart for true happiness, because your heart will be too full of rage."

"My God, Em. You make the second option sound awful."

"The challenge with the first option is that even if you are wrong—and he truly loves you and never betrays you—you will still suffer pain. Because you cannot have one without the other."

"So, what are you saying, Emily? That no matter what I decide, I could be wrong? I will be hurt no matter what?"

"Unfortunately, yes, I think so. If you allow him back into your heart, Jack will no doubt hurt you again. And you will hurt him. It's just the way it is, Lucy. He won't mean it any more than you will. I think it's all part of being in love."

Lucinda leaned back in her chair, glancing out the window. A silence fell between them. After a moment, Lucinda looked back at Emily.

"Forgiveness, Lucy," Emily said. "It's the only way to be wrong."

———

After Emily had gone, her words lingered in Lucinda's mind, weighing heavily on her heart as she stared at Jack's letter. His penmanship had the distinctive double scrolls on the *L*s in her name. She drew a long breath as she picked it up. She ran a finger over the handwriting before turning the envelope over in her hand. The seal on the back was embossed with the initials *JMM*. She sighed again and broke the wax with her fingernail, watching as bits of red fell onto the table. Pulling the interior parchment from the envelope wrap, she unfolded the letter.

April 20, 1819

My dearest Lucy,

By now you know what happened and have heard the varied versions of the affair between myself and Armistead Mason. I have broken promises I made to you. I have misled you. And I have brought you shame. I cannot find the words to express my sincere regret for my actions and the pain I have caused our families. And the pain that I have caused you.

Until recently, I have spent my life hiding from my fears. I have built façades around my image and walls around my heart, thinking they would protect me. That because I was a McCarty, I was entitled to do and have whatever I wanted. And then I met you. You saw through me and for some reason loved me anyway. Had I known that you would be in my life, I would have lived my life differently. But I didn't. I made mistakes and did things that I am not proud of. And I have let you down. For that I am most regretful.

Lucinda Lee, I have been in love with you all my life, even before I knew you, for God made you for me and me for you. It was the love that we shared that sustained me on that dueling field. It was my trust in us. And now, without you, I have learned to trust in myself, a man with fear and doubt and shortcomings. But he is all I have and all that I am.

When it is safe, I will return to Virginia and I ask—I pray—that you will allow me to call upon you once again. I hope that your answer will be yes. And I will understand and accept if your answer is in the negative, for certainly I do not deserve you. But no matter what your answer, know that I will always love you, Lucy, and will always be waiting for you to change your mind. For it is only your mind that stands in the way of what both our hearts know as truth.

I love you, Lucinda Lee. For now and for all eternity.

Your obedient and loving servant,

Jack

Lucinda dropped the hand that held the letter into her lap. She closed her eyes tightly as the dike that had held her emotions began to falter. She needed to talk to someone, and it dawned on her who. She sprang from the chair and, with the letter in her hand, she rushed into the hallway toward the stairs. There was one person to whom she could talk who had yet to weigh in. The one person who could help her decide what to do. *Mother!*

CHAPTER 77

JULY 1, 1819, CEDAR GROVE

"Sally. Do you hear something?" Emily asked, rising from the settee where the two were sewing.

Sally, with a threaded needle in one hand and fabric in the other, dropped both hands to her lap and tilted her head. Thunder rumbled overhead. "I do believe I hear a storm brewing."

"No, Sally. On the drive. Horses. It's horses on the drive!" Emily dashed to the window. Sally jumped from her chair, tossing her needlework onto the seat, and hurried to join her.

"Oh my God! They're home! They're home!" Sally said at the sight of two men galloping on horseback toward the front of the house. The two women raced to the front hall, flung open the front door, and rushed onto the porch. It was William and Jack, riding side by side.

William leapt from his steed, dropping the reins as Emily ran into his arms. "William, how I've missed you!" Emily exclaimed as William lifted her off her feet.

"And I you, my darling Em," William said, kissing her.

Jack, riding his old gray mare, dismounted from the horse. He was thinner than the last time Sally had seen him. There were shadows around his eyes and small lines in their corners. A new gauntness filled the hollows under the bones of his cheeks, and there was melancholy about his brow. The dimple in his chin was still there. But he looked older, tired, worn. Sally rushed onto the drive and hugged him.

"Jackie! Oh, my beautiful boy! You are home! Home at long last!" Sally kissed his cheek. Jack wrapped his arms around his mother in a hug so tight she could barely breathe.

"I've missed you, Sally," Jack said. They embraced, mother and son, laughing and crying as lightning flashed across the sky. Wind gusted, tossing the branches of trees as Emily and William walked toward them, hand in hand and smiling.

"Jack," Emily said, interrupting the homecoming.

"Em," Jack said. Sally saw remorse in his eyes as he looked at his brother's wife.

"Thank you for your letter," Emily said and stretched out her arms to him.

Jack rushed to her, embracing her. "I am so very sorry, Emily. So very sorry. I don't deserve your forgiveness. I don't. But it means the world to me. And I thank you. Thank you, Em."

"I forgave you the day I forgave my brother. As you bear the same responsibility, you deserve the same forgiveness," she said with kindness and love. "For you are both my brothers."

Her words brought Jack to tears.

"Come on, Jack. Emily," said Sally, as thunder clashed overhead. "Let's get inside and out of this storm before we all get struck by lightning." She laughed as she ushered them toward the door.

Her boy—her Jackie—was finally home.

CHAPTER 78

JULY 3, 1819, STRAWBERRY PLAIN

"Jack McCarty, certainly you are not wearing *that* to Belmont, are you?" Emily asked as she glided into the study in the tightest-fitting gown Jack had ever seen her wear. It was made of deep-purple bombazine and laced so tight that Jack wondered how she could breathe. A matching purple headband wound through her cropped auburn hair, and a velvet choker with a cameo in its center was tied high on her neck.

"First, Mrs. McCarty, what is wrong with what I'm wearing?" Jack asked as he sank a billiard ball into the leather side pocket of the emerald felt-covered table. "And, second, what on earth makes you think I am going to that party?" William leaned on the cue stick, watching his brother slowly clear the table of the balls.

"That's William's old jacket, and it is older than he is," Emily said. "And I believe it's been eaten by moths. You can't wear that to the party."

"He says he's not going," William said as Emily slid her arm around his waist.

"Not going?" she asked, her brows knitted crossly. "But he has to go!"

"Why do I *have* to go, Emily?" Jack asked. "I am perfectly happy to work on my game. I'm out of practice and rusty."

"Rusty? I'd hate to see how you shoot when you're polished," William said, yet to have a turn.

"You have to go, Jack," Emily said. "And you know why." She glared at him with a hand on her hip. Jack continued to shoot the balls across the table without responding.

"Mr. McCarty, are you listening to me?" Emily asked, tapping her foot, her annoyance with him growing.

"I'm listening," Jack said, not taking his attention off the billiards table.

"No, he isn't," William said. "He's not listening, and I think he might be cheating."

"Yes, I am listening," Jack said and shot another ball into the pocket. "And there is no possible way I could be cheating. You simply made the mistake of allowing me to break."

"Oh, you two stop it! Stop it, I say," Emily said, scolding them. "And yes, Jack, you are going because you were specifically invited. I saw Colonel Lee's note."

"Have you been reading my mail again, Mrs. McCarty?" Jack asked, finally looking up at her.

"She does that, you know," William said.

Emily shot her husband a wistful glance and pushed away from him. "Well, it was in plain sight, so I could not help but see it."

"I really don't feel up to a party tonight," Jack said, sinking another ball into the leather pocket at the far end of the table.

Emily fixed her eyes on him, scrutinizing his face. Suddenly, she threw her hands in the air as if she had received a revelation from above her head. "You're afraid!"

Jack stood from the table and looked at her. "I am not afraid."

"Oh, yes you are, Jack! I can see it in your face." Emily waved her index finger in his direction. "And there is no reason for it, Jack. None at all. You will be with friends. And family. Your mother and Thomson are coming up. And you know how Colonel Lee and Miss Flora love you. And all your friends will be there—James and Cary and Tom and all the boys from the hunt. I think even Fenton is coming. I know for a fact that the Rusts were invited and plan to attend. I spoke with Maria just this morning, and she says that Colonel Rust plans to reestablish friendly relations with you. Like all of us, he feels terrible about the senselessness of what happened and knows that it wasn't your fault." She paused the lecture and brought her eyes to his. "Please, Jack, you must forgive yourself. All of us who care about you have already done so."

Jack smiled at her as he leaned on the cue stick. "I have, Emily, for the most part. I've realized that I can't change the past. My only option is to accept it for what it is and move forward. And I'm doing just that." Jack could tell from the look on Emily's face that she still wasn't satisfied. When she began to tap her foot, Jack sighed. "I promise I will attend the July Fourth celebrations in Leesburg tomorrow with you and William. I'm just not up for Belmont yet. All right?"

Emily shook her head. "But Colonel Lee is expecting you. And Lucinda will be there."

"Lucinda?"

"She loves you, you know."

At Emily's words, a glimmer of hope flickered in Jack's chest. "How can you possibly know that?"

"Because I know her. She's just too afraid to admit it."

"Afraid?"

"You know how she is. Just like you, always protecting her heart."

"She will never forgive me, Emily. I hurt her too badly." Jack glanced away to avoid Emily seeing tears welling in his eyes.

Emily went to him, placing one hand on his shoulder and the other on his sleeve. "She will, Jack." She smiled at him, her voice filled with compassion. "Just as I have, she will, too."

A flood of emotion rushed over him. Emily reached out her arms and hugged him. Embracing her, Jack buried his head in her shoulder. "I know I've said it before, but I am so, so sorry."

Emily whispered in his ear, "I know, Jack. And we've all had enough hate and fear and pain for a lifetime. It is time for love and happiness again."

"All right, all right, John McCarty. Get your hands off my wife," William said, bringing levity to the room, "and get to working on finding one of your own." Jack released Emily and took a deep breath, inconspicuously drying his eyes. "Why don't you go get dressed, Jack. There's that blue jacket in my armoire you can borrow for the evening. You know, the one with the crest. We'll need to get you to the tailor soon for some proper garments so that you are not compelled to wear my old stuff that Em has squirreled away in the guest chamber."

"I've squirreled nothing, William. I'm just holding on to those jackets and trousers in hopes that one day you'll be able to fit into them again."

"Ouch!" Jack winced as William raised a brow at his wife's barb.

"And perhaps on that day, my love, that dress won't fit so tight," said William, jabbing back.

"Well, at least I can still wear it, Mr. McCarty!" Emily spoke with a teasing smile and a twinkle in her eye.

"And you wear it well, Mrs. McCarty. Well indeed!" William laughed and reached for Emily's hand. Scooping her into his arms, William took an appreciative look at her bosom protruding over the taut neckline.

"All right," Jack said as he put the cue away. "I'll leave you two lovebirds alone and find myself another rag in the guest chamber for this evening."

"Try that blue jacket in my chamber. It should fit you fine," William said again, kissing his wife's neck.

"Will you come with us in the coach, Jack?" Emily asked, without diverting her attention from her husband's affection.

"I don't think so. I'll ride Dove over. It's not that far," he said and left the room.

Jack made his way down the corridor toward the stairs. Reaching the bottom step, he hesitated. He hadn't felt this nervous since the Twelfth Night party. He closed his eyes at the painful memory. With a deep breath to calm his anxiety, he opened his eyes and took the first step.

CHAPTER 79

JULY 3, 1819, BELMONT

The distance between Strawberry Plain and Belmont was only a few miles, but the ride seemed to take forever, and Jack's apprehension grew with each step of the mare's hooves. It was a clear night with the moon nearly full and rising behind jagged tops of loblolly pines that carved a serrated edge in the summer sky. The dusty path was illuminated in silver and gray as rider and horse made their way across the field to the road leading to Belmont. Reaching the gates of the plantation, lamplight from the manor house radiated from below the horizon like the expiring sun in the night sky. The warm air became increasingly thick to breathe as Jack's chest tightened with anxiety.

Rounding the corner beyond the reeds and cattails that grew along the pond's shore, the manor house came into view. Guests could be seen in the glow of lantern light through open windows, their voices squawking like starlings over a wheat field. Dove, too, could feel Jack's apprehension and hesitated at the pond's edge. Jack urged the mare forward to the circular path of the carriageway. As he halted the mare at the front of the house, a river of anxiety rushed from his toes to the top of his head. He wanted to turn back and ride to the safety of Strawberry Plain but managed to push through its current. *If you can stand in front of Armistead Mason with a loaded musket, Jack, you can attend an*

Independence Day party. He grimaced at the memory and dismounted, handing the reins to the stable boy. Jack tried again to breathe through the stabbing ache below his ribs. He walked across the limestone tiles of the porch and placed his hand on the knob. Drawing another breath of thick air, he turned the knob and opened the door. As Jack crossed the threshold, a hush fell over the room. All eyes were upon him—shocked, judging, afraid. This time he couldn't find his breath at all.

Like Moses parting the Red Sea, Colonel Lee in a crimson coat cut through the crowd with outstretched arms. "Jack McCarty! I have missed you, lad. I have missed you, indeed." The colonel wrapped Jack in his giant arms. "It is good to see you, boy!" The colonel's welcome seemed to break the tension, and guests moved their eyes from Jack back to their conversations.

"It is good to be home, Colonel," Jack said, forcing air into his chest.

"Let's get you a drink, my boy," Colonel Lee said as he put his arm around Jack's shoulder and escorted him to the drawing room and a glass bowl filled with ice, fruit, and wine. Jack was not surprised to find his mother standing at the bowl looking radiant in a red silk gown and wearing a ruby necklace and matching earrings. The pear-shaped diamond ring sparkled on her finger as she steadied a glass of punch in her hand. She was laughing with another guest when Jack and the colonel approached. At the sight of her son, she rushed to hug and kiss him, nearly spilling the wine over the three of them.

"There you are, my Jackie boy!" Sally said as the punch splashed over the rim of the goblet. "I am so happy that you decided to come after all. Emily mentioned that you had reservations, and you had me worried, being late and all."

"I'm late by my own design, Sally. Isn't that what you taught me?" Jack asked with a chiding grin.

"Indeed, Jackie! Indeed," she said with another laugh. Jack knew how hard the past few months had been on her, but tonight she looked happy.

Thomson was standing nearby and greeted him with a slap on the back and a huge hug. Since Jack's absence, his younger brother had spent most of his time at Cedar Grove with Sally. Jack noticed that the family had become closer since the duel with Armistead.

With the news of his arrival, his friends gathered around him in the drawing room. James Dulaney and Cary Selden, the two men who had been with him on the fateful day, were the first to approach. Embracing him, the men fought back tears, and James, in particular, was overcome with emotion. "I thought I might never see you again, my friend. It's good to have you back, Jack. So good!"

Jack could not get away from the bowl of iced wine as the gathering grew. Those around him offered hugs, tears, and words of encouragement. But there were others at the party who were not as enthusiastic. "Masonites," as Cary referred to them, were the many friends and fellow officers of the late Armistead Mason who still grieved the loss. Jack felt the burn of their eyes judging him and knew that they wished it had been Jack who had fallen instead of their beloved General Mason.

It wasn't until the announcement of the performance that Jack felt the stares and judgment subside as the guests moved to the conservatory.

"This way, Jack," Sally said with a twinkle in her eye. "We don't want to miss the performance, now do we?"

Jack gave her a puzzled look. His mother rarely cared about musical performances unless she was singing.

Sally took Jack's hand and led him to the other room. When they entered the conservatory, Emily beckoned them to where she and William were standing by the piano. Jack and his mother crossed the floor and joined them.

"Now that coat looks much nicer than that old rag," Emily said, admiring her husband's blue jacket with the McCarty crest that Jack was wearing.

"Why thank you, Mrs. McCarty," Jack said. "I took your husband's advice."

"There's a first time for everything!" William said with a laugh as Miss Ann Mercer emerged from behind the folding panel. Miss Mercer, a cousin of Fenton's, was renowned as an accomplished musician.

It was a pleasant surprise, Jack thought. Sally had most likely conspired with Fenton to make the arrangements for his homecoming. Jack looked around the room for Fenton but didn't see him. Miss Mercer moved her fingers across the keys to quiet the crowd. As conversation fell to a hush, a commotion stirred near the folding panel that fronted the French doors leading to the west lawn.

"Here comes the singer now," Jack overheard a guest whisper.

Miss Mercer cleared her throat and addressed the audience. "Ahem. Ladies and gentlemen, before I begin my recital, I am honored to accompany a very talented vocalist in a special rendition of Thomas Moore."

Jack's heart stopped as the singer emerged from behind the folded panel. "Ladies and gentlemen, may I present the lovely Miss Lucinda Lee."

The crowd applauded, and Lucinda stepped forward to face the audience. She was dressed in a pastel gown with the scoop of the neckline and wrists trimmed in creamy lace. She wore multiple strands of pearls around her neck, which seemed to glow against the luster of her skin. Her blond hair was partially tucked under a pale pink and green cap adorned with lace and pearls, while the rest of her golden locks streamed across her shoulders like moonbeams. To Jack she looked like a fairy princess from a midsummer's dream. As Miss Mercer began to play, Lucinda smiled at Jack. Jack smiled back, trying to swallow the lump that was rising in his throat. When Lucinda parted her lips to sing, his knees weakened. Her voice, sweeter than he remembered, cut to the core of him, filling him with an all too familiar warmth that quickly flared to a raging fire. The words of her song ravished his ears, and his heart pounded as if it might explode.

Come rest in this bosom, My own stricken deer,
Though the herd have all left thee, Thy home is still here!

Lucinda's eyes glistened with emotion as she sang. By the end of the verse, emotion overwhelmed her voice. Unable to sing, she lowered her eyes to the floor. Miss Mercer stopped playing to allow time for Lucinda to regain her composure. Silence fell over the room. Jack didn't know what to do. He stood with his mother, paralyzed, caught between wanting to rescue Lucinda and knowing that it wasn't his place. Lucinda had told him that she no longer wanted him in her life. And no matter what Emily said, Lucinda had given him no indication that she had changed her mind. Jack had learned to accept her heart, in spite of how he felt and what he wanted.

After a long moment, Lucinda lifted her face. Tears were streaming down her cheeks. As her eyes found Jack's, Lucinda rushed toward him, calling his name. Jack's heart exploded from his chest as she ran to him. He scooped her into his embrace, spinning with her in his arms until her feet lifted from the floor. Locks of her hair fell about his face, overpowering him with their angelic scent. When Jack lowered her back to the floor, he cupped her face in his hands and wiped tears from her cheeks with his thumbs. He brought his eyes to hers and whispered, "I am so sorry, Lucinda. So sorry for breaking my promise. For breaking your heart. For everything."

She took his hands in hers and squeezed them. "I know, Jack." His eyes followed hers to the terrible scar on his wrist that ran under his sleeve. A sadness fell across her face as she caressed the reddened edge. "And I am sorry, too."

Jack knitted his brow in confusion. "For what?"

She looked up at him. "For losing my trust in us." She smiled. "I love you, Jack McCarty."

At her words, a torrent of emotion rushed through Jack. Instinctively and without hesitation or thought, he fell to his knees in front of her, his eyes pleading. "Then marry me, Lucy. Marry me. For us."

The tears Lucinda had tried to blink away rolled down her cheeks. There was not a sound in the room. Slowly, Lucinda nodded her head, mouthing the word—"Yes."

Jack leapt up from the floor. Taking Lucinda in his arms, he moved his mouth to hers in a long, tender kiss. The aristocracy of Virginia, who, on any other occasion, would have scorned such public displays of affection, applauded. Sally broke into tears. She looked down at her aged hands and the ruby-encrusted diamond ring that her beloved Daniel had given her when he had asked for her own hand in marriage. She smiled at the memory as the diamond captured the candlelight in its prisms.

"Jack," Sally called from behind him. As Jack and Lucinda turned to face her, she removed the ring from her finger. Fighting to keep the emotion from her voice, she extended her arm and offered Jack the ring. "Take this and put it on Lucinda's finger."

"Mother? Are you sure?"

"I have never been so sure of anything." Sally pushed the ring into Jack's palm and forced his hand closed around it. She placed her hand over his. "Please, son. Take it. For me."

Jack smiled at his mother and nodded. Without a word, he turned to Lucinda and placed the heirloom upon the third finger of her left hand. It fit perfectly.

Jack looked into Lucinda's eyes once more. "I have loved you all my life, Lucinda Lee."

"And I will love you for all of mine." Lucinda held her hand out to admire the ring. "But you must make me a promise."

"A promise?" Jack saw that familiar mischief return to her eyes. "Anything for you, my love."

"Anything?"

Jack gave a confident nod. "Anything."

"Promise me that the next time my heart is broken—because there will surely be a next time—that you will never again allow me to lose my trust in us."

Jack grinned, his cheeks dimpling. "Under one condition, Miss Lee."

Lucinda put her hand on her hip. "And that might be?"

"That you do the same for me."

Lucinda smiled at him, her eyes filled with adoration and affection. She reached for his hand, and he pulled her close. As she laid her head against his chest, he thought of the night at Raspberry Plain, the night she had mesmerized him. How close he had come to losing her, to losing everything—all that he held dear nearly ruined by his folly. Never again would he be so cavalier—so reckless—with his words or in his actions. Jack knew now that honor had nothing to do with what others said about a man, but rather came from within. And nothing but pain and ruin came to the fool who believed anything else.

EPILOGUE

MAY 1, 1820, SELMA

"**How handsome you are,**" Charlotte whispered as she gently brushed the auburn hair from the brow of her sleeping son.

"Shhh … you rest now, my love." She smiled as his long dark lashes fluttered at her touch.

Charlotte lifted her gaze from the baby in the crib to the leaves of the oak tree outside the window, watching as they danced in the spring breezes. The sunshine poured from the sky like streams of gold from a milk-blue bowl, the fresh lawn dappled in patches of green and gold. *Today is Mrs. Mason's birthday*, she thought as she moved her focus across the field to the rooftop of the Raspberry Plain manor house. After Stevens's nap, she would pack him into the black landau and join the family for the celebration. As the lace curtains billowed in the spring winds, she was reminded that today marked another anniversary—her wedding three long years ago. How happy she had been that day. How much she had loved him.

Charlotte closed her eyes, thinking back to his funeral and that morning after. She had been sitting behind his desk in his study when she found the pistols he kept there. How carefully she had loaded them. How ready she had been to join him wherever he might be. And then the cries of her infant son and the shuffle of the nursemaid's feet across the floor in the room above her head had stopped her. What would become of her baby without his mother?

Young Stevens had saved her that day.

Charlotte opened her eyes and glanced at her little boy in the crib. He had no idea how important he was to her.

She turned her attention again to the window and the view of Leesburg and George Town in the far distance. So weary she was of their constant reminders. The wedding of Lucinda Lee and Jack McCarty at the chapel in Leesburg. The christening of the dark-eyed, auburn-haired daughter of Molly Ringgold at the church in George Town. And then there was the news from Washington City and Richmond. The election of John Randolph to the Senate. Charles Fenton Mercer's unopposed reelection to the House. And the announcement of President Jefferson's own son-in-law as the newest governor of Virginia. Where was her God now? Then she remembered. God had left her when she put her belief in Armistead above her faith in Him.

Armistead! She was unable to bring herself to say his name aloud. So angry, she was. For believing in him. For trusting him. For leaving her with nothing but anxiety and loneliness. She hated him for what he had done, so much so that she had refused to mourn him, refused to wear the black in his honor.

Honor ... nothing more than a mask to hide lies and deceit!

The baby stirred, restless in his sleep.

"Shhh," she whispered. "Mother is here. I will protect you, my love."

AUTHOR'S NOTE

My inspiration to write this story began with the purchase of an abandoned, dilapidated plantation manor house north of Leesburg, Virginia, off the Old Carolina Road (now US Route 15), named Selma. Throughout the restoration of the house, I found myself intrigued by not only the history of the property, but also the stories of its previous residents and the man who built it, General Armistead Thomson Mason. Encouraged by both my husband, Scott Miller, and my screenwriter friend, Anthony McCarten, to write a historical fiction about the stories I uncovered, I delved into research for months to learn all I could about the man who first lived at Selma.

Many of the accounts published about the Mason-McCarty duel proclaim that Armistead was a shining hero felled by the rogue John Mason McCarty. So when I began this project, I was confident that Armistead was my protagonist and I was writing the tragic tale of *his* hero's journey. Yet as I researched the original source documents, a different story emerged. While both men escalated tensions between them, it was Armistead who was the aggressor and Armistead who, after truces had been negotiated, refused to let the matter go. This changed my approach to the story, and I redirected my efforts to learn as much as I could about Jack McCarty.

Regardless of which man is the protagonist of the story, when I first started this project, I could not fathom what had transpired to compel these men to stand with loaded muskets at a distance of only ten to twelve feet (the record is unclear if it was three paces or four), each facing the other (they were not standing back-to-back and turning to shoot, as in most duels), and to lift their muskets and fire at each other. But, after an exhaustive review of both eyewitness and hearsay accounts, and careful examination of each man and the family and friends around them, I found a narrative that explained it. It is my hope that my portrayal of Armistead Mason and Jack McCarty, while not intended to be a nonfictional account of their lives or the events surrounding the duel, captures the essence of who they were and how each struggled in a world where life was fragile and honor was everything.

In creating this novel, I researched not only Armistead and Jack, but the people close to them. I examined the writings of their friends and of their fathers and brothers. I researched the families of their mothers and the men their sisters married. I looked at birth order as well as Jack's and Armistead's ages when they lost their fathers and siblings. I discovered where they went to school and who their professors and mentors were. I read what they wrote and what was written about them: from letters and newspaper articles in the *Genius of Liberty*, the *Leesburg Washingtonian*, the *Winchester Gazette*, the *Richmond Enquirer*, and the *Alexandria Gazette* to pamphlets published by both Jack and Armistead in the summer of 1818 regarding their controversy, as well as the pamphlet published by Charles Fenton Mercer in the winter of 1818 about his conflict with Armistead. From all of this research, I not only built a timeline of events that formed the basis of my plot, but also developed psychological profiles of Jack and Armistead and of other characters, including Lucinda, Charlotte, Polly, Sally, and William. For Mercer, I relied on the published work of Professor Douglas Egerton at Le Moyne College. I consulted with psychologist Julie Fender, who reviewed these profiles and helped "diagnose" my characters and validate my assumptions. For example, upon close study of Armistead, many of his writings appear to be the product of a manic mind (see his *Genius of Liberty* notice published March 3, 1818). In his own writings, Armistead comes across as loyal to his friends and loving to his family (as demonstrated in an 1813 letter to his brother-in-law regarding the death of his sister Mary, which I did not include in the book). According to accounts of his service during the War of 1812, he was a decorated officer and an inspiration to the men who served under his command. Others who knew him paint a different story, portraying Armistead as quick-tempered, impulsive, and overly sensitive to criticism. In the bluster in his writings, I sense great insecurity. I feel empathy for him. In my eyes, Armistead Mason was a man torn between his desire for power—which he considered his birthright—his self-doubt, and his inability to control what others thought and said about him.

Much of what I learned about Jack McCarty came from his writings and the correspondences of his family. With Jack, I had the benefit of his having remained in the public spotlight for decades after the duel. As documents from the 1830s and 1840s are better preserved than those from 1816–1819, Jack's speeches and the press about his public life were more readily available. I relied heavily on the memoirs of his daughter, Sally McCarty Pleasants, and documents provided by Jared Banta, Jack's great-great-great-great-grandson, in developing his portrayal in the novel. Jack being the second youngest in a fatherless family of so many boys, his unrestrained behavior made sense to me. A careful read of his correspondence during the time of the duel illustrates that Jack, too, had a temper and difficulty with self-regulation. In 1816, Jack had just turned twenty-one, an age when most young men are trying to find their place in their world. I believe this was true of Jack McCarty. During his election to the legislature in 1818, a letter to the editor of the *Genius of Liberty* published on March 24, 1818, supports these theories. The author complained that Jack's "youth, inexperience and moral instability" should disqualify him from the election and demanded "better evidence of an entire reformation from his [Jack's] former improprieties" before Jack asked for the community's vote. As I pored over the dozens of letters exchanged between him and Armistead, Jack clearly had attempted to walk away from the dispute, yet he found himself continually embroiled in the controversy by either the coercion of others (as I dramatized in the fictional scene at Union Tavern) or his inability to control his own emotions.

Once I had created profiles of Armistead and Jack, I set the specific details of my research aside. Using the timeline of the historical records, I set out to tell their story in a manner that captured the essence of the events and the spirit of their characters and, at the same time, to create a story that would appeal to a wider audience than fans of historical fiction. Several events were altered, some were combined, others removed or, in a number of instances, fictionalized to achieve that result. For example, the historical record shows that Armistead was in George Town when he learned of Mercer's alleged maligning of Armistead's character before the legislature, not at a party at Raspberry Plain (a fictional scene). The record also indicates that Mercer was staying in George Town with John Randolph at Francis Scott Key's mansion, not at Aldie, when he received the first letter in early April 1816. There is no known record of who informed Armistead of Mercer's alleged insult. Further, there were three exchanges of letters between the two, whereas I depicted only a single exchange in the novel. This is one example of where I altered facts and consolidated activity to streamline the narrative without impacting the significance of the events. The results of the actual events and my fictional depiction are the same: Armistead was unable and/or unwilling to reveal the identity of his source, and Mercer had successfully boxed him in. Armistead begrudgingly let the matter go, and the incident set the stage for the ensuing rift between Mercer and Armistead during the election of 1817 that triggered Armistead's conflict with Jack.

I consolidated newspaper notices and letter exchanges between Jack and Armistead, particularly those in May and June 1818 regarding the loaning of Armistead's pistols to William Handy for the purpose of assassinating Jack. And while I do not know for certain that Polly and Sally intervened directly to stop the fight in 1818, in September of that year Jack wrote that a "white servant," most likely one of the indentured Irish employed in the Mason household, had learned of the impending duel and that the women of that house had intervened. I also excluded two pamphlets that were published, one in 1817 by Armistead attacking Mercer and another in 1818 by Jack attacking Armistead. Again, this was done to improve the pace of the plot and had no impact on the outcome of the story.

The most markedly fictionalized scene in the book is the affair between Molly Lee and Armistead. There is no evidence whatsoever that
these two had any relationship. What we do know is that one of Jack's
notices in the *Leesburg Washingtonian* accused Armistead of questionable judgment and promiscuous conduct. We also know that after the
funeral, Charlotte never uttered Armistead's name aloud again, not
even to her son. She carried her bitterness toward Armistead until the
day she died, never remarrying, and requesting that she not be buried
next to him. Having Charlotte discover that her husband was unfaithful to her was a logical explanation.

Other fictionalized areas of the book are scenes around the War of
1812. The opening chapter at Peach Orchard Camp and the flogging
of Shane McNally (a fictional character) are entirely from my imagina-
tion, as is my fabrication that Armistead ordered deserters shot. While
during the War of 1812, both General Andrew Jackson and General
Winfield Scott were known to order such executions, I have no evidence that Armistead did. I took license to shed light on such actions
during the War of 1812 and to further dramatize the plot.

It is true that Armistead was in command of the Fifty-Seventh
Regiment on Craney Island just before the British attack in June 1813. A
letter that Armistead wrote to his brother in Kentucky while encamped
on Craney Island days before the British assault describes his experience
there. Egerton's biography of Mercer indicates that Mercer also served at
Fort Norfolk and went home deathly ill from malaria. I relied on Mercer's
and Armistead's attacks of each other's war records in newspaper notices published in 1817 to articulate their opinions of one another. By
most accounts, the men under Armistead's command respected Colonel
Armistead Mason. As an aside, my great-great-great-great-grandfather,
Captain Michael Everhart, a "Dunkard" from the German settlement,
served under Armistead during the War of 1812 and was most likely a
supporter of Armistead's proposed amendments to the militia bill.

Since I was unable to determine the location of the Fifty-Sixth and
Fifty-Seventh regiments at certain points during the war, I extrapolated

from the data I had to create the war storyline. For example, it is unclear from my research if the Fifty-Sixth Regiment was at Peach Orchard Camp or at Fort Norfolk or somewhere else in August of 1813, and I could not confirm if Jack, James, and William were a part of that unit at that time. Further, I have no knowledge that Armistead briefly assumed command of the Fifty-Sixth Regiment. This part of the story, too, is fictionalized. The record shows that William McCarty served in Captain Ball's company under Armistead in Baltimore. It is true that Armistead was very sick during that campaign and was relieved of his command for a period of time by Colonel Minor, who led Virginia's Sixtieth Regiment in 1814. Jack McCarty served under Colonel Minor during the Battle of Bladensburg (it is not known whether the regiment saw action in that battle) before his regiment joined forces with those encamped on Hampstead Hill. Whether Jack was in Baltimore or not is uncertain.

Nearly all of the supporting characters in the book are based on real people who lived during the time and were aligned with either Jack, Armistead, or Mercer, as I depicted. In many cases, I created personalities for those individuals and often combined multiple real people into a single character to simplify the story. For example, George Rust is a combination of himself, Dr. Jonathan Heaton, Temple Mason (Armistead's half-uncle), and Archibald Mains (an officer who served with Armistead). All of these men were close friends and advisors to Armistead. In my depiction of George, I wanted to show that he was not only a loyal friend, but one who loved Armistead unconditionally, like a brother, standing by him without judgment. I believe that Armistead had this kind of relationship with Temple Mason and Dr. Heaton, as well as with George Rust.

Both Benjamin Leigh and John Randolph were close friends of Fenton Mercer in this time period. In the case of Mr. Leigh, where possible, I quoted him. I also attributed a number of statements to Mr. Leigh that were in actuality statements made by Francis Scott Key and James Hobart, other close friends of Mercer's at the time. According to

SHARON VIRTS

the Egerton biography, the four men were known to congregate at the Union Inn and Union Tavern in George Town; however, it should be noted that the friendship between Mr. Leigh and Mercer would sour in later years.

I took a few liberties in the depiction of the Lee family. While Fannie Carter Lee was indeed left in debt and her property in chancery court after the death of her husband, Thomas Ludwell Lee II, I made an assumption that the daughters had little to no inheritance. Flora Lee was the first wife of Ludwell Lee, but she had died by 1817. Ludwell Lee and Thomas Ludwell Lee II were not brothers but cousins. Because the relationship between the two families was so close, I took license to make him "Uncle Ludwell" and brother of Lucinda's deceased father for the purposes of the story.

Fictional characters include the Henderson sisters as well as Mr. Deese, Terence Ringgold, Gerard Alexander, Connie, Sean O'Malley, Paddy, Shane McNally, and the many enslaved people (Jakes, Hester, Nelly, Joe, Janny, Phillis, Phillip, Matthew). For those bonded in servitude at Raspberry Plain and Selma, I attempted to use the names of the enslaved that I found in the Raspberry Plain accounting ledger and in Selma property records from the Loudoun County courthouse. A note on dialect of the enslaved in the novel. According to my research, the term "marster" was used by the enslaved in Virginia for the word "master." As for Rose and Lillie, both were well-known prostitutes in George Town and Washington, but that was decades later. They are fictional characters in the context of this novel.

My purpose as an author is to write page-turning stories that my readers want never to end. My task in doing so is to find a blend of fact and fiction that entertains while at the same time stays true to the essence of the story. There is more truth in *Masque of Honor* than fiction. Yet it is a work of fiction. I believe that my portrayal of both Jack McCarty and Armistead Mason reflects the actuality of the lives they lived and engenders the respect that both men deserve. Regardless of our opinions of them, both men stood on that dueling field, facing their fears to defend what, at the time, was of utmost importance—their honor. To me, such action is not simply a testament to their courage but represents the constitution of their characters. My hope is that Jack and Armistead touch you as they have touched me and that their story, the meaning of honor, and the power of forgiveness resonate and remain with you a long, long time.

ACKNOWLEDGMENTS

Writing this book has been one of the greatest challenges I have undertaken and would have been impossible without the help and support of so many. To Anthony McCarten for encouraging me to write this story. To my early readers—Wylie Cooke, Peter Johnson, Jason Richards, Julie Fender, Susan Graham, Lucas Mason, Sylvie Laly, Tracy Fitzsimmons, Bonnie St. John, Allen Haines, Michael O'Connor, Steve Fredrickson, Keith Early, John Rust, Mary Rust Montgomery—who offered their advice, reactions, and wise counsel as the story unfolded. To Wylie Cooke for his help in describing early nineteenth century architecture. To Julie Fender for all of her "diagnoses" and helping me stay true to the nature of my characters' personalities. To Mary Frances Fortier for her guidance on the history of the period. To the staffs at the Library of Virginia and the Thomas Balch Library, especially the late Mary Fishback, for all of their assistance in my research. To my friend Bonnie St. John for her early advice on story structure and on the publishing business. To Pastor Michelle Thomas and Ron Campbell of the Loudoun NAACP and Freedom Center for their advice on presenting the enslaved in the story. To my artists, Maria Morga, Luke Greer, Hannah Blankenship, and Lucas Mason, for sharing their many talents. To my literary coach and my "secret" agent, Jenn Schober, for her patience, consult, and connections. To my editor, Debra Gitterman, who not only guided the development process but who also taught me how to "show" and not "tell." To Peter Behrens for his assistance in streamlining the story. To my publisher Arthur Klebanoff, Brian Skulnik, and all the folks at RosettaBooks for their tremendous support in publishing this novel. To my publicist, Sandi Mendelson for her tireless work and unfaltering belief in me and this project. To all my followers on social media for their support as I wrote this book and their patience in waiting for its release. To my four sons for providing me years of insight into the minds of handsome young men. And finally, to the person I need to thank most of all: my husband, Scott Miller, who encouraged me every step of the way, read chapters over and over again, listened to my many "what if," "what does this mean," "what do you think," and "how does this sound" requests. Scott not only put up with my distraction as I wrote, rewrote, and revised the manuscript, but tolerated sharing my attention with two other men—Armistead Mason and Jack McCarty. I cannot thank him enough for his love and support.